MW00653063

A. Sethumadhavan (born 5 June 1942), popularly known as Sethu, is a Malayalam fiction writer. He has published more than thirty-five books. He received the Kerala Sahitya Akademi Award in 1978 and 1982 for *Pandavapuram,* a novel and *Pediswapnangal,* a collection of short stories. His novel *Adayalangal* won the Vayalar Award in 2005 and the Kendra Sahitya Akademi award in 2007. *Marupiravi* won the Odakkuzhal Award. Sethu's other literary works include *Velutha Koodarangal, Thaliyola, Kiratham, Niyogam, Sethuvinte Kathakal* and *Kaimudrakal.* Sethu has served as the chairman and CEO of the South Indian Bank. He was also the chairman of National Book Trust, Delhi.

Catherine Thankamma is a retired associate professor in English. She worked in various colleges under the government of Kerala, including a brief stint in Jesus and Mary College, Delhi. She has a Ph.D in theatre studies from Jawaharlal Nehru University and has published short stories and articles. Her translation of Narayan's *Kocharethi* for Oxford University Press won the Crossword Book Award for 2011.

AlINAM

Aliyah

The Last Jew in the Village

SETHU

Translated from the Malayalam by
CATHERINE THANKAMMA

HARPER ● PERENNIAL

NEW YORK • LONDON • TORONTO • SYDNEY • NEW DELHI

HARPER PERENNIAL

First published in India in 2017 by Harper Perennial
An imprint of HarperCollins *Publishers*

Copyright © Sethu 2017
Translation copyright © Catherine Thankamma 2017
P.S. copyright © Catherine Thankamma 2017

P-ISBN: 978-93-5264-062-1
E-ISBN: 978-93-5264-063-8

2 4 6 8 10 9 7 5 3 1

Sethu asserts the moral right
to be identified as the author of this work.

This is a work of fiction and all characters and incidents described in this
book are the product of the author's imagination. Any resemblance to actual
persons, living or dead, is entirely coincidental.

All rights reserved. No part of this publication may be reproduced,
stored in a retrieval system, or transmitted, in any form or by any means,
electronic, mechanical, photocopying, recording or otherwise,
without the prior permission of the publishers.

HarperCollins *Publishers*
A-75, Sector 57, Noida, Uttar Pradesh 201301, India
1 London Bridge Street, London, SE1 9GF, United Kingdom
Hazelton Lanes, 55 Avenue Road, Suite 2900, Toronto, Ontario M5R 3L2
and 1995 Markham Road, Scarborough, Ontario M1B 5M8, Canada
25 Ryde Road, Pymble, Sydney, NSW 2073, Australia
195 Broadway, New York, NY 10007, USA

Typeset in 11/14 Cochin LT Std
by Jojy Philip, New Delhi

Printed and bound at
Thomson Press (India) Ltd.

Contents

The Scent of the Sea

One night, in his sleep, Salamon inhaled the scent of the sea. Inhaled the sea breeze. Amidst the scattered specks of light, a flock of sea crows landed on the ship. They perched everywhere – on the steps, on the loosely coiled bundles of rope, on the mast. Gasping for air they cawed loudly, almost tearing their throats, as though avenging themselves on someone. In the middle of that inauspicious cawing something rumbled up from the pit of Salamon's stomach and he retched into the unfamiliar darkness outside. Half-digested bits of meat from last night's meal stuck to the dirt- and rust-covered window bars.

'Entamme...' Salamon groaned. The crows echoed his cry and he took up theirs.

Eshimuthimma was the first to arrive. Evron, her son, followed.

'What happened, mone?' she asked, sitting on the edge of the cot, her heart pounding against her chest.

There was no answer. Salamon was seeing something, hearkening to something.

By this time Evron, whose eyes were prone to spotting failure, had noticed the wetness on the bed. Holding his nose he said, 'Look, the boy has peed in his sleep.' A note of disgust crept into his voice.

'Oh that…' Eshimuthimma said dismissively, 'something must have scared him.'

'Oh yes … yes … it is only an eighteen-year-old boy wetting his bed!' Evron's voice rose.

'Well, he's your son. He can even shit in bed if he wants.' Eshimuthimma bristled in defence of her precious grandson.

'Your tongue, Umma!' Evron muttered under his breath. But Eshimuthimma heard him clearly. Her ears were adept at picking up even a murmur of criticism. That was one benefit the Lord had conferred upon her to compensate for her age. Muthimma had seen the wetness on the sheet, on the checked mundu too. But she did not cover her nose. She acted as if she had not noticed it. As an infant he had urinated in her lap so many times, had wet so many expensive silk tunics. That was his privilege. Whether twenty or forty, muthis cannot accept that grandchildren grow… As they advance in age, the grandchildren seem to grow correspondingly younger.

'You go out.' Dismissing her son with that terse rebuke, Eshimuthimma began to stroke her grandson's head fondly.

'Did my mon dream? Did he see imbachi in his dream?' Eshimuthimma's voice dripped affection.

'Yes, yes, he's at an age when he should be frightened by imbachi!' Evron mocked.

Truth be told, Evron was furious. The woman was cosseting a boy who was almost twenty, the young buffalo. Yes, he was her grandson, but there should be a right and proper way for everything.

All the while, Salamon continued to murmur thickly, still half asleep.

'Sea … sea … crows…'

'Did the crow scare my mon?' Muthimma asked.

'Sea … water…' he repeated.

Words her ears had yearned to hear for so many years! Suddenly, as if from a strange revelation, Eshimuthimma's face brightened. Her body thrilled in the glow of an unseen world.

'Did you hear that? Did you hear what he said? He said "the sea". What do you think it means, Evrone?'

The meaning of sea? A crooked smile appeared on Evron's face. He couldn't believe the woman was asking him that. Of course he knew what 'sea' meant. There are two types of seas, the ones you have seen and the ones you have heard of. The ones you have heard of have a brighter hue than the ones you have seen. You can make them larger, smaller, deeper, shallower. In the mind's eye the sea becomes a vast expanse.

But which sea was this temperamental boy rambling about in his sleep? Evron wondered, perplexed.

'It is that one: the sea of Sinai, the river of Jordan.' Eshimuthimma had no doubt about it. And to think that he who could not even grasp the import of these words was dismissing his own son as good for nothing! 'It is about crossing over…'

Eshimuthimma felt her heart grow full. She had been longing to hear something like this from Salamon's mouth for so long. When everyone around them, relatives and kinsfolk, eagerly awaited their turn to go across, he alone remained unsure. Muthimma knew the reason. After all, his friendship was not with their own people. He became wayward when he made friends with the Ezhava lads from Vadakkumpuram and Karimpadam. Those who professed communism, respected nothing, denied God.

Finally the Lord had heard her cry. He had shown the path the new generation needed to follow. The reward for

going to the synagogue regularly and praying her heart out
before the ehal where the holy book, the Torah, was placed.

Eshimuthimma stood for a while, her eyes closed,
thanking those who were not visible. She then entered the
prayer room slowly, began the routine prayer she said at
dawn every day. Chants she had heard during her childhood,
in her own voice, her own style.

> *Praised are you, O Lord our God, King of the Universe.*
> *You fix the cycles of light and darkness.*
> *You ordain the order of all creation.*
> *You cause light to shine over the earth.*
> *Your radiant mercy is upon its inhabitants.*
> *In your goodness the work of creation*
> *Is continually renewed day by day.*

Along with her prayer, daylight spread all around her...

Well, at least for the time being Umma is at peace, Evron
thought, smiling wryly as he leaned against a pillar in the
veranda.

Umma pampered and spoilt her full-grown grandchild,
yet Evron could never say anything to her face for she had
borne the burden of that large family alone for so many
years. She had done it in memory of Isaac muthacha who,
with his boat, had been swept away near Palathuruthu by the
flood waters that came down from the hills a long time ago.
When those who searched the river and its banks for two
nights and three days came back with many a lamentation,
Eshumma did not waste time listening to them. She knew
well the path he had seen, the one who had taken her hand
when she was thirteen. It is a river in flood, don't go, don't
go, she had pleaded a hundred times. Yet if he still took
the boat into the water, paying no heed to her pleas, it was

not that he did not know; only the prompting of his heart mattered. The remains of the one carried away by the floods should have been washed ashore somewhere. But if the call he heard was the call he was fated to hear, the call of the sea...

When the water went down on the fifth day, the old boat was found near Thattukadavu. When someone brought home the spotted red cap with two mud-smeared gold-capped teeth sticking to it, Eshumma did not cry. She did not look at them either. She had a whole lot of work to do in the house and its surroundings – older ones, children, brooding chicken, ducks to be led to the water, the spotted cow mooing somewhere in the yard. She did not have time to waste.

It was a long struggle. In its throes she grew old without knowing it. She became muthimma to everyone. Even when the children she gave birth to called her by that name she did not protest.

Though the Jews in that land called their fathers 'vava', Salamon preferred to call Evron 'appa'. Gradually it became Evronappa, and the younger uncle, Elias, who should have been Evacha, became Eliacha.

Evron knew well the reason for Muthimma's affection for her grandson. The child had grown up without a mother. She, Rebecca, had died when he was barely five years old.

Moreover, Salamon was the bechor of the family – the oldest male offspring whose birth had fulfilled the yearnings of three fathers. The eldest was Menahem mutha, who lived in Thoppumpady. Then Evron. And Elias, or Eliacha. Evron was the first to get married. It was only after Rebecca died, after gifting Evron with a son, that Menahem got married, that too to an outsider. And what happened? She did not live with him for long, did she? Thus, Eshumma, who was over seventy, knew well the helplessness and the shame of being the only female in the family.

The gaze of the gods is always upon the eldest male of the family. After all, it is through him that generations lengthen. A long time ago the Lord had punished the sinful Egyptians by having their eldest born struck down by lightning ... The easiest means to scorch the roots of lineages.

As a result Eshimuthimma began to dread the monsoons, the lightning and the thunder clap. Evron later realized that it had been a mistake to tell Umma that story. Even after Salamon grew up the woman's deep fear persisted. In fact this irrational fear increased as she grew older. She never said anything openly but Evron could immediately recognize the pallor that appeared on her face, the weakness that seized her limbs...

It was the season of the south-west monsoon. The sky grew dark with rumbles. When daggers of lightning began to shoot through the dark clouds that had gathered in the heat of the day, muthimma trembled. She called upon the gods with all her heart to safeguard her grandchild.

'These are just exaggerated stories made up by our forefathers, Umma. How does the sky know the difference between male and female?'

The son tried to comfort her in vain, for she was one who saw layered meanings in the words of the elders.

'Lightning strikes the crown of the sterile coconut tree or the head of the sinful,' Evron reminded her once again.

But who is to listen? Evron heard his voice fall and shatter. Muthimma stood taut, wound up, holding the seven-year-old wrapped within her violet-coloured tunic.

Salamon on his part had no fear of thunder or lightning. If thunder was a cracker in the sky, lightning was just fireworks.

When sword-like flashes descended from the clouds, he saw firecrackers being readied to throw and smash against the cloud-walls of the sky.

The moment the smell that was the precursor of the monsoon hit his nose, thick walls of darkness appeared around Salamon, making him restive. Until the clouds and lightning moved away and the sky became clear, he was not allowed to leave the inner room. No one in the house dared to override Eshimuthimma's decree.

However, as the years went by and his eyes and ears gained experience, muthimma's fears became a matter of laughter for Salamon.

What bechor? What powers of discernment did the swords of heaven possess? He had seen the tops of the barren coconut trees on the hill catch fire during the monsoon. It was Ramanandan, who lived near the Konkani temple, who had explained why it was so. Among coconut trees too there were those that had been sinful and those that had been virtuous in their previous birth. Lightning struck the crowns of those trees that bore no fruit. The gods in the sky do not direct their gaze on trees that yield fruit.

Salamon laughed when he heard this. What previous birth for Jews? Moreover he was not that evil was he, that the lightning would strike the crown of his head?

But no one tried to argue with Eshimuthimma. Even the son she had delivered, after having borne him for eleven months in her belly, made himself scarce, for the moment such arguments began, the tumultuous river, flooded by water from the hills, and Isaac muthacha floated up as a painful memory. That was the prerogative of those who had undergone trials and suffering, who had weathered time. They were capable of showing things, of making things be heard at the right time.

Salamon's placidity as a child disturbed Evron but when he grew older it became a matter of anxiety. He lacked the vigour of youth and would sit idly, lost in dreams. Though he managed to scrape through the tenth standard examination, he hit pre-university, stumbled and acknowledged defeat. Evron offered to start a shop in Kizhakkumpuram but the boy did not want it. Most of those who lived along that street believed that anything and everything on earth could be bought and sold. Therefore, the moment their eyes and hands were ready, they were on the lookout to do some business and make money. The frog-like woman who sold vellappam since she was a child; David who went from house to house selling eggs; Ibrayi who bought cowhide from the neighbouring islands, mixed them with salt and dried them to take to Mala to sell; Aaron who bought bananas by the bunch from the Paravur market, ripened them and hung them for sale in the veranda of his house – of these Aaron was Salamon's classmate and Ibrayi two classes below him.

Most of the Jews in that land were ordinary folk. Though a few had studied well, gained a foothold on the ladder of employment and climbed to great heights, most of them were content to find some small employment or business that enabled them to scrape through life. For that very reason even their dreams had boundaries. The dream of David's vava – the same David who because of a corn on his heel limped from house to house selling eggs – was to own a big egg shop in Israel. It would save the boy the pain of limping around.

When Ibrayi, who traded in hide, told Salamon that he could join him, Salamon refused in disgust. I cannot go about carrying hide! The stink inside his house ... it's horrible!

There were many who traded in hide. In fact, when old cows were sold the saying was 'took to Mala'.

'What is bad about that work?' Evron asked, his face flushed with anger.

One thing led to another and father and son crossed swords.

'Apparently it stinks! How old do you think I was when I gathered the dung of Muthi's goats and chicken and took it to sell to the Christian traders of Gothuruthu? Seven, at most eight. Because of the stink from the sack I had to cross the river listening to ferryman Velu, the present ferryman's father, curse all the while. Velu was surlier than his son Ittaman.'

When he heard Evron hold forth, Salamon would suppress a smile. He had heard about Evron's failed business ventures many times, that too from his own mother, when she was angry. He knew that the enterprises that had done well during the time of Isaac muthacha had come to ruin because of Evron's lack of skill in managing them. When one thing led to another and his partner in the Ernakulam market quit, there was some loss of money on that account as well. Apparently that was how a fertile coconut grove in Kizhakkumpuram with its high yield slipped into the hands of the Konkanis. Anyway, it was after the failure of his business ventures that Evron's gaze turned towards public affairs. For the past so many years, he had spent all the daylight hours on the veranda of the Panchayat office. After drinking a cup of black tea at dawn, he would sit there long before the employees of the office and people with grievances arrived, waiting for the Panchayat peon's cycle bell to ring. He could hear the rotten doors of the tiled building open with a loud creak from the veranda of his house. By merely sitting in the veranda throughout the day, the title 'member' got stuck to him.

Evron thus became a member of the Panchayat without anyone voting for him. Since he was good-natured, the other members did not protest. Besides, the president, who was from Pallanthuruthu, suffered a certain degree of embarrassment in Evron's presence. The president had borrowed from Evron the ceremonial sword with its copper-covered hilt, which the Maharaja of Kochi had presented Isaac moopar's muthacha, on the pretext of showing it to the white men who came to see Mattancherry. Six winters had gone by since then. Lots of white men came to Kochi at the end of each winter but the sword was never returned. He once said that he had given the sword to a teacher to decipher the Vattezhuthu inscribed on the handle. That deciphering however went on for ever...

Did the president sell it to some Englishman, or did some Englishman cheat him of it? Whatever the reason, whenever Evron lamented the loss of the precious asset, Eshumma comforted him:

'Let it go, member, just assume that we were not fated to enjoy the wealth of our ancestors.'

As the term 'member' became reinforced through frequent usage, his real name was all but forgotten. It even became a term of affection for Eshumma to use. Member! Or, magistrate!

Among the members of the community Evron had the prestige of having passed the tenth standard examination in his first attempt, whereupon he received a certificate with the government seal on it. For that reason the responsibility of settling disputes between families and between neighbours often rested on him. As time went on when Christians from Kizhakkumpuram, and a few Muslims, began to seek him out to resolve disputes, the member really became a member, and in the eyes of the woman who gave birth to him, a magistrate. When she began to receive remuneration on that account, in cash and in kind, Eshumma's stooping shoulders straightened without her knowing it. 'Though he does not know how to do business, God has shown him the right path!'

Also, was it not Evron's initiative that prompted the Panchayat to pave the path to the top of the hill with laterite, a path that led through the thick forest where fox and mongoose wandered freely? And because of that a rickshaw can be brought to Jew Street sometimes, is that not so?

But his son was incapable of doing even that, Evron thought sorrowfully...

When as usual one thing led to another and father and son began to argue, Salamon got up. Without saying another word he left the house, piqued.

As he walked southwards he recalled that he had not seen his friends for several days, not since the falling out between contractor Paulose mapla and the labourers in Pallanthuruthu. The contractor tried to cheat the workers who pounded coconut husks but he had reckoned without comrade Pavithran. Salamon was sure that Pavithran would force the contractor to back down.

The Bechor is Born

On top of the hill stands the Vishnu temple. At the foot, within a radius of half a kilometre, are the church, the mosque and the synagogue. That is the layout of the Kottayil Kovilakam area.

This unique unity took shape at a time when, the world over, blood was being shed in the name of religion. Without any discord, on the land given by the king of Vilyarvattam, the different communities created a well-defined dwelling space, which became a model of living in harmony.

Around the temple were some Hindu homes. Down below on one side was the synagogue, with Jew Street on both sides, where some fifty Jewish families lived in houses that stood side by side but separated by walls and fences. Where these fences ended the homes of the Muslims began. The mosque had been built in such a way that it did not face the synagogue. The same harmony existed in the cemeteries as well. The cemetery of the Muslims was some hundred metres away from the mosque, and that of the Jews five hundred metres away. Similarly the houses of the Christians were about three hundred metres away from the synagogue. Next to their homes was the church, the police station, shops, the primary school, etc.

This was a time when the sound of the conch shell from

the temple, the muezzin's call from the mosque and the church bells were heard simultaneously, in harmony. As for the Jews, they blew the horn called shofar to celebrate the advent of the new year. When the festivals of these communities coincided, once in some eight or nine years, the sounding of the conch, the church bell, the muezzin's call and the blowing of the shofar became a rare symphony.

It was in these surroundings that Eshumma arrived from Mala, holding the hand of Isaac, called Isaac Sa'ib, when he married her so many years ago.

The huge, two-storeyed house, which stood near the synagogue just where the lane began, was built by Isaac's vava, Ephraim. Ephraim was the most eminent Jew the people of that village had ever seen. His reputation was such that he could request an audience with the king of Kochi whenever he wanted. Ephraim's only son, Isaac, too was able to maintain that relationship for some time. Perhaps it was because of this intimacy with the palace that father and son came to be known as Ephraim Sa'ib and Isaac Sa'ib.

Eshumma had three children.

To Salamon they were Menahem mutha, Evronappa and Eliacha.

The three brothers had three distinct personalities. While Menahem mutha lived in Thoppumpady, teaching Hebrew, interpreting the Torah and engaging in matters related to the synagogue, Evronappa and Eliacha continued to live with their mother in the village. It was understandable that Eshumma – rendered lonely after Isaac muthacha was swept away near Palathuruthu by the floods that descended from the hills – should long for a female companion. It was equally understandable that she made offerings for a grandson. Though there was not enough daylight in the two-storeyed house that the ancestor had built, there were many rooms. If Eshumma viewed the absence of tiny feet pattering around those rooms and in the yard as the greatest disgrace in her life, what was wrong in that?

But there was no way that the eldest son, Menahem, who was born to swim and row in the current of God's ways and the divine language, could climb on to the shore. When Menahem declared emphatically that he did not want a woman, Eshumma stubbornly opposed him at first. Later she pleaded, and finally she broke down. But the eldest was smart enough to evade such traps laid by the devil and retreat to his sanctuary at Thoppumpady. Should she not take pride in the fact that a great Jewish scholar had been born for the purification of the family from the stain of wealth amassed through various kinds of business? He was offended.

Eshumma just could not understand it. The desires that take shape in a mother's heart are always small and self-contained. She therefore did not hearken to the scholar's explanations and withdrew to bemoan her plight to the female heads that appeared on the other side of the fence.

'I delivered three male children, pennungale, that too in the bloodline of a great man. Yet I suffer all this in my old age,' she complained.

'Do not let go, Eshumma,' the female heads rose above the fence and prompted.

With that Eshimuthimma's prayers and offerings grew in number. It must have been those prayers and offerings that led the second son, Evron, to A.S. Bava's textile shop in Ernakulam Broadway one evening. It was there, after all, that he saw Rebecca for the first time. That day, Rebecca was wearing a blue blouse with polka dots and a long red skirt. A girl who gave forth the scent of a male, who had the high-spirited elegance of a mare…

At that age such blues and reds and dots were a great fascination. Particularly the way the two large dots appeared exactly where they should on the breasts.

What followed was a long period of exhausting wanderings for Evron – in front of Saint Teresa's, in front of convent schools, the Basilica, Kacheripady, Thevara, Shanmukham Road, Seventy Feet Road, Pullepady … The incessant walking made his feet swell. It was not easy to find out the name and whereabouts of a girl who had come to buy cloth in Broadway. It was a town that spread out wide, a town where men and women walked about freely in the streets. He could not tell her caste by her appearance or manner of dressing. She could well be a Latin Catholic. Jewish women were not so spectacular.

Evron was in a dilemma.

'What a mess it is, Manoolle!' Evron said mournfully to his friend Manuel. 'Just when you see a girl and feel she is the one…'

'Why, eda? Has she got into you that much?'

'What else?'

'Then blame your foolishness. You should have followed her scent right then.'

'But she came on a bicycle, didn't she?'

'You should have hired a cycle from a nearby shop.'

'But I don't know cycling.'

'Jews who do not know cycling should not go about eyeing girls.'

'But, eda…'

Seeing Evron crestfallen, Manuel softened. 'It is all right. We'll find a way,' he comforted Evron. 'After all, Ernakulam is not London, is it? It is our land. Tell me, will you recognize the bicycle if you see it?'

'Who knows! All I have is a faint memory of green creepers and red flowers on the cloth that covered the handlebars. There must be any number of such bicycles in town.'

The only relief was the conviction that when Manuel undertook to do something he got it done.

It was after much aimless wandering that they finally reached Panayappilly in Kochi. The first thing they saw as they looked through a black-painted gate at the end of the lane was a couple of crows tearing at a custard apple that had burst open in the middle. Then they saw the sand-spread yard, the tiled house, the well, and the custard-apple tree that grew near it. Leaning against the open veranda of the house was an old Hercules cycle with red flowers spreading around green creepers!

However, they were doubtful. It was not a street inhabited by Jews.

'If she is a Latin Catholic or something they will catch hold of you and baptize you, just you wait and see,' Manuel teased.

Evron trembled when he heard this.

In the past, the elders used to be wary of sending children to the church's schools. Someone had found that when children stood with their hands outstretched during drill it looked like a cross! When this was followed by the rumour that the guile of the parish priest – Cletus master's elder brother – lay behind it all, the Jews, who were few in number and suspected conversion, panicked.

Isaac muthacha alone remained unruffled. You need Christians to run a school or a hospital well, he stated categorically. He thus sent his three sons to the church's school.

For Evron the days that followed were filled with anxiety. In the meantime Manuel brought some good news. 'They are your people,' he announced. 'The father, Simon master, is a progressive man, and therefore decided to live away from Jew Street in Mattancherry, that is all.'

Thus, one day when the two friends ventured to go to Panayappilly, it was the girl's family that was surprised. The father, a teacher in a primary school, was in a quandary. He wanted his children to study as much as they could. The girl had studied till MA. The boy had not even got through the pre-degree course. When the members of the synagogue committee came to say that the children must join the Hebrew and Torah classes, Simon master told his daughters they could join if they wanted to. It was entirely their decision. When their mother insisted on it the two younger daughters joined the classes ... Rebecca alone stayed away. She declared that she would go only if Appa told her to. Appa did not insist.

While Simon master stood perplexed, unable to take a decision about the proposal, his wife – who had given birth to four daughters – had no doubts whatsoever. They came to ask for the girl, that too from a prominent family of Chendamangalam. They have not said anything about gold or money. They just want the girl. We need to give only what we can afford. What better way could there be to give away the eldest?

When the girl entered the room bearing a tray laden with achappam, poovan banana and flower-shaped biscuits, Manuel nudged Evron and murmured in his ear, 'Is this the treasure you mentioned?'

Evron, who had been staring at the girl, nodded, embarrassed.

'Do we need this, friend?'

'Of course.'

'She's big.'

'Oh shut up.'

'Hard to rein in.'

'Just keep quiet.'

With that, the questions that had sprouted in Manuel's mind dried up. Evron was truly enamoured by this Panayappilly girl. Therefore, with nothing left to say, Manuel fell silent diplomatically, and ate all the achappam, poovan banana and flower-shaped biscuits and drank tea.

Though Simon master approved of the boy, one doubt lingered heavily within him. Is it the boy who should come asking for the girl? Could he get only a Christian boy to accompany him?

Manuel could not say that Evron had seen the girl in A.S. Bava's shop and had become enamoured of her. So he said with commendable tact: 'They will come later. They are a prominent family. The elders will cross the threshold only after they know your response.'

In the meantime the prospective bride and her sisters had already started a conference inside. When Vava and Umma also appeared, everything was finalized. Appa had just one thing to tell his daughter. 'He is less educated than you. You should not regret it later, feel that we forced you into the marriage.'

'It is all right, Appa,' the daughter said. As the eldest of four sisters she knew how far her dreams could stretch. With that the green signal came on...

Eshumma was upset when she heard about it. An event for which she had been waiting so long! Is this how one goes about asking for a girl? Just the groom accompanied by a friend, without telling anyone at home? Was this an action befitting one from a respectable family? Their relatives in Mattancherry had not even heard of the girl's family. If Evron had said one word to Menahem in Thoppumpady, he would have gone and found out about the family.

'You at least could have said a word, Manoolle! You have had coffee and lunch in this house so many times,' Eshumma said, offended.

When he saw Eshumma's reddened eyes Manuel felt uncomfortable. 'That … When Evron said … But we have not given our word or anything,' he assured her. 'The relatives will come when everything is settled, that is what we said.'

'What sort of talk is that, Manoolle?'

'If the elders do not like the connection, you can send someone with that message, after all.'

'The one who wants to marry goes and sees the girl, now you say we send a message that we don't like the alliance … you want us to witness her tears as well?'

Manuel did not have a reply.

'You can test the quality of gold by rubbing it against stone. What do you do about a girl?' Eshumma's complaints did not end.

Manuel felt like laughing when he heard that. Which part of Rebecca would she rub to check her quality?

Though the saintly Menahem excused himself, two elderly relatives from Mala and the younger son, Elias, went to discuss the details of the wedding. During that visit the eyes of Rebecca's younger sisters lingered on Elias at least for a short while but later Evron himself squashed any idea of an alliance. He had not been able to understand Elias till now. How then could these girls? Moreover, Elias' world was different, it was a taller, larger one.

In spite of her initial qualms Eshumma was later relieved that Evron had at least chosen the right path. The eldest Menahem had said no straight to her face. As for the youngest Elias, who knew what went on inside his head? He himself probably didn't know which way he was going.

However, it was when Eshumma decided that henceforth everything would be according to her wishes that doubts began to arise regarding the ceremonies related to the wedding.

'Should not the elders from both sides sit together and fix a date?' Eshumma asked.

'They suggested a date. We said we would ask you and confirm,' Elias replied.

'Did you give the ketubah?'

'Huh?' Why, the expression on Elias' face seemed to say. 'They did not mention it.'

'You didn't ask?'

'Hmm no.'

Eshumma was stunned. The elders who got together to decide on the wedding would sign an agreement mentioning the date of the wedding and the amount of gold and money to be given. That was the custom. The deed that was handed over to the girl on the day of the wedding was her security against her husband's future behaviour. At one time there used to be young men in the land who would read the ketubah on the wedding day, loudly and melodiously, for everyone to hear.

'So you returned swinging your arms, without mentioning gold or money?' Eshumma's voice rose.

Elias left the room. Let his older brother deal with the rest.

Evron stood with his head bowed. After a while he said

hesitantly, 'They are good people, Umma. They will give what they can without our asking.'

'What they can! What custom is that? What will I say when the people around us ask?' Eshumma's eyes grew red. 'Once the sacred minnu is around the girl's neck, will they turn and look back? There are three girls below her to be married off.'

That is how it always is, Evron thought wryly. When it comes to the amount of gold and money received, other people are the ones who are more interested; the neighbours and the relatives.

He stood silent, unable to say anything. Eshumma was totally bewildered. Even Elias, who she believed was somewhat efficient, was being evasive.

'What if people ask, has Ephraim Sa'ib's family been reduced to such a state?'

The more Eshumma thought about it the more upset she became. What would she tell the people around to make them believe?

Later, as each son went his way without saying anything more, Eshumma became sure of one thing: those people at Panayappilly had entrapped her sons. From now on only what they said would happen.

As the discussions regarding the wedding ceremonies warmed up, her suspicions were confirmed.

A wedding that was about to take place after a very long wait. It was not just the family that had looked forward to it. The entire community in that street had been waiting for it. They knew that any event in the Isaac family would be impressive. Not just that, weddings were occasions for getting decked up and making friends. Umpteen times they had heard Eshumma wax eloquent about her own wedding, which had taken place in the synagogue at Mala years ago. Now that times had changed and conveniences increased, surely things would be on a grander scale!

'In the past the ceremonies lasted fifteen days. The entire street was decorated with banana trees and paper decorations. Then the excitement would be stirred up by the drummers and men with bugles. Sometimes the musicians would be divided into two groups and urged to compete with each other. The elders would then place wagers … There would be songs and games, eating and drinking. When it all ended, one would be totally exhausted,' Eshumma told her sons. 'Later when it was our time the celebrations were reduced to eight days. Even then it was such a festive affair, both in the house and in the grounds in front of the synagogue. All the people in the land came for the wedding feast. It was all so exciting.'

Eshumma was reliving those warm and thrilling memories. Things that the new generation could not understand.

Though the wedding took place on a Tuesday, festivities began with the girl's vava inviting the groom and his friends for a feast on the previous Sabbath day. It was called joyful feast. The boy was Aroos, the girl Aroosa. There was a ceremony every day. The giving of the ceremonial tunic and gown, the bangle ceremony on Sunday night, the exchange of gold and silver to make the taali and ring, the procession around the town, the tevilah ceremony of purifying the girl, and so many other rituals. And on all these days there would be sumptuous feasts, eating and drinking, songs and bustle.

Things have now come to such a state, everything has been reduced to one day; just a haphazard way of getting things done. No one has the time, either to plan a wedding or take part in it. Not just that, how many girls in the town do you think know how to sing the girls' songs?

On the wedding day the groom, who sits on a throne-like chair, represents the Jewish leader Joseph Rabban called Chiriyanandan. For that very reason the songs that the women sing as they sit around him are those that praise Chiriyanandan.

Eshumma sang:

> *... The land and the town, are all aglow*
> *Lamps are erected, Chiriyanandan son.*
> *A comely garland, ruby-like son*
> *A comely tunic, Chiriyanandan son...*

History had it that the Perumal who ruled the land in the tenth century presented a copper plate that included seventy-two rights to Joseph Rabban, who was the chief of the Anchuvannam traders, whereby Rabban became a regional lord and the king of the Jews. As he had come from Syria, Joseph Rabban came to be called Chiriyanandan.

But were they the descendants of Joseph Rabban from the mother's side?

Elias said no, at least that is what he had learnt from his reading. The Everayi ballad narrates how Everayi, who was called Arivalan, and his group travelled from Jerusalem across Egypt and Yemen and reached the coast of Kerala. Travelling through many lands they reached Chennoth.

Was it not possible that this Arivalan Everayi was their ancestor?

Elias was bewildered. He did not know how to enter Eshumma's labyrinthine memories. Finally he tried to intrude tactfully.

'Simon master said the wedding should be a simple affair in the synagogue in Ernakulam...'

'Which Simon master? What simple? It is the groom's

family that makes those decisions. You tell that master of yours to keep quiet,' Eshumma burst out in fury.

Dismayed, Evron directed a wary glance at Elias. Elias returned the look.

Though Eshumma had retorted angrily in the heat of the moment, she cooled down after two days. 'Let the wedding take place in the synagogue at Ernakulam,' she said. 'We will arrange for a special boat for those who are going from here to attend the ceremony.' But she would decide what the ceremonies would be. She had to ask the elders, she should ask the muliyar and the hazzan in the synagogue.

Elias nodded, relieved. Though there was Menahem in nearby Thoppumpady, all interaction with Panayappilly fell on his head.

Though things had calmed down for a while, Evron was worried about the problems Umma might raise in future.

'The strange practices that existed in the past!' Elias recalled. 'Do you know what they did to find out whether the girl was chaste before marriage? They made her lift her undergarment and sit on top of a pot full of arrack. She was supposed to sit in that manner for some time with her mouth shut. If after a while they smelt arrack when she opened her mouth it meant that she was not a virgin.'

'Of my God!' Evron panicked.

'Don't worry, these are all old stories, Evrones,' Elias consoled him. 'If we go demanding all that, today's girls will come after us with brooms.'

Evron's wedding took place without any hassles, just the way Eshumma wanted, with pomp and festivities. As soon as she returned from the ceremony Eshumma went and bowed before Isaac moopar's photograph that hung on the wall and told him, 'Though there weren't any relatives the ceremony took place without loss of face, I promise you…'

Thus, one evening – when with bag and baggage and the old cycle, with the scent of a male and the high-spirited elegance of a mare, the tall and straight-backed Rebecca climbed down from the boat – all of Jew Street woke up. As usual women's heads appeared in rows in the yard and behind the fence. A town girl wearing a fashionably cut dress with pleats and high-heeled shoes. Eshumma was not pleased with this kind of arrival. Neither were the women on the other side of the fence. Though Eshumma did not show it in her demeanour, the heads on the other side had a lot of things to whisper about. Has conversion begun among our people too?

When on the very next day after she arrived the new bride appeared on her bicycle at the ground on the slope of the hill where children played ball, it was a grand spectacle for the locals. A girl who rode a bicycle! Not even the men folk in Jew Street had cycles. When she saw that she had spectators, Rebecca was delighted. She began to show off the tricks she had practised in the ground in Panayappilly. She rode the cycle holding the handlebar with just one hand and then without holding the bar at all.

By the time she circled the ground once, the ball game had come to a standstill. Though a whistle heard from somewhere among the gathered onlookers turned into hooting after the second round, by the third round it changed into clapping and Rebecca got down from her cycle, panting.

In the meantime one of the bystanders came and looked at the cycle from all sides and said, 'This is a men's cycle.'

'Oh, don't be foolish! You don't have male and female among cycles!' His friend laughed.

'True, sometimes it is hard to distinguish whether it is male or female…'

'Let the dawn break, we'll know if it crows!'

Rebecca, who had begun to walk pushing her cycle, suddenly turned around.

'What is it?' she asked with a slight smile.

'Aye, nothing,' the youth said, shrugging his shoulders.

'Then you better go home, mone. Get into the coop before sundown. This is the time when evil spirits appear.'

With Rebecca's arrival the once silent house suddenly came alive. She hurried around, opening the shutters of windows and doors that had remained closed for so long and the others realized that light did enter the house.

When she dusted and tidied up the messy drawing room the faces of Ephraim Sa'ib and Isaac Sa'ib on the wall shone. Eshumma was satisfied.

'Seems to be a good sort! She has a neat and methodical manner of doing things,' she told the ancestors.

The ancestors on the wall looked down curiously.

But the women on the other side of the fence would not be impressed so easily.

'Oh yes!' The thorny fences laughed. 'Trying to impress! Do keep an eye on her when she climbs the roof to sweep it. Suppose she slips and falls…'

They had seen so many of this type, full of zest and fervour in the beginning.

In fact Rebecca's gaze had fallen on the messy state of that drawing room the moment she entered the house.

'When Menahem was here, everything looked very neat. How much can I, a lone woman, do on my own,' Eshumma said with a tinge of guilt.

Rebecca nodded as though she understood.

Heavy sofas made of rosewood. Seats and round cushions covered with elaborately worked silk fabric. In the middle of the room was a large teapoy with carved legs which did not suit the dimensions of the room. Huge corner stands made of rosewood. On one side stood a chest with four drawers. That too was made of heavy rosewood. Even when pulled with all one's strength it was not possible to open the drawers.

'No one ever opens those. After all, who has the time for all that?'

'Aa…'

'It is the best quality wood. Moopar himself made arrangements with the Muslim traders to bring it from the forests in Nilambur. Then for a long time carpenters from Puthenvelikkara worked on them.' Pride frothed on Eshumma's face.

It seemed as though Ephraim Sa'ib and Isaac Sa'ib nodded their heads from the wall.

Rebecca looked at them with curiosity. Painted in oil, Ephraim muthacha stood tall and erect in the portrait, which had a gold-coloured frame. Next to it was Isaac vava's picture in black and white. Ephraim wore the traditional formal attire of the Jews – a round cap and a long and shiny violet tunic. Elias told her later that the sword in his hand had been presented by the king of Kochi. Though Isaac wore more or less the same garments, he did not look as majestic as the former as his picture was in black and white.

'It was specially arranged for from Krishnan Nair's photo studio in Ernakulam,' Eshumma told her.

A Naik's clock from Mangalore hung between the two huge portraits, ill at ease, like a witness for the prosecution, as it had lost its ability to move its tongue.

As voice and as laughter, Rebecca's presence filled the

rooms, the yard, the lanes and the ground in front of the synagogue. In a short space of time she made a lot of friends of both sexes, who came climbing up the hill to see her. Most of them were from other communities. Most of them were educated, of her own age or younger. They had many things to discuss, many subjects to laugh about and argue about. Thus there was a lot of noise inside and outside the house.

As the number of people who came and went increased, those on the other side of the fence were filled with pity for Evron. A rackety girl. A Kochi girl whom no one wanted finally landed on that poor man's head.

In the meantime they discovered something else. The bride had hair on her upper lip.

'Does she, Evrone?' the mother asked her son anxiously.

'Oh let it go, Umma ... Those women have nothing better to do...'

Though Evron had dismissed the question in that manner, he too was seized by a slight doubt. Did she have a moustache?

Eshumma's suspicion was mounting by the day. How did the women in the neighbourhood discover a moustache that neither she nor her son had noticed?

So one day she held Rebecca close and looked at her carefully. Eshumma was shocked. It was true. Five or six blue hairs on her daughter-in-law's upper lip!

Rebecca alone did not know that she had acquired the nickname 'moustached girl'.

But by this time she had worked so hard, loved so steadfastly, that she had Eshumma in her grasp. Eshumma on her part did not realize that, unknown to her, the one who entered the house as a daughter-in-law had become a daughter to her.

As for Evrone, who was travelling around Kottapuram and Ernakulam with matters related to a business that was going down, he did not even make an attempt to know.

Eshumma was waiting for the bechor of the family.

Though summers and winters came and went in the valley below the Kottayil Kovilakam palace Rebecca had no news to give. As Umma's desire mounted Rebecca's belly continued to remain confrontationally flat.

When as usual the thorny fences began to chatter, Eshumma fell into despair.

'Why is it like this, Eshumma? Is the girl afraid to give birth?' the women asked.

'I don't know, pennungale...'

'Yet there is no look of regret to be seen on the girl's face. She goes about so lightheartedly!'

'That must be how they are in the town,' said another voice.

'Who knows!'

One day, as he was walking along the cut road, Evron met his old acquaintance Shambu Namboothiri. Shambu Namboothiri, the son-in-law of the Paliyam family, had gone to the Kunnathol temple to make an offering.

'Why, Evrone, why the delay? It must be two or three years now.'

Though it took some time for Evron to grasp the meaning, he hid it behind a weak smile.

'Is there a lack of interest?' The Namboothiri seemed unwilling to let it go.

'No, nothing like that, Thirumeni.'

'I felt curious when I saw her cycle along the embankment the other day. Strong tea and sprightly girls are equally exhilarating!'

Though over sixty, the Namboothiri's curiosity had not waned in the least, thought Evron.

That was how he came to know that Rebecca's cycling had gone beyond the foot of the hill and Kizhakkumpuram, and reached Paliyam nada.

When both Evron's enthusiasm and Eshumma's offerings failed to bear fruit, when Evron's body was beginning to acknowledge defeat...

It was at such a time that one day at dawn the inauspicious cry of the theendari bird was heard from the branch of a tamarind tree at the end of the street. With that Eshumma felt her heart sink. The counting that had begun when Rebecca did not have her period for two months had gone awry.

But defying all birds and the trees in which they nested, Rebecca did not have a period that month either. Then for a long time she did not have her period. Not just that, she began to retch and show other signs of discomfort that women display according to the time-honoured tradition. She also walked around with her protruding belly, swinging her arms, in the yard and the lane near the synagogue, where people could see. With that the fences fell silent but Eshumma was still anxious. If only the separation between mother and child takes place without any hitch and at the proper time!

As her belly increased in size Rebecca became increasingly peevish. When the vomiting stopped she complained of aches and pains in various parts of her body, developed certain unaccountable cravings and obstinacies. When Eshumma reacted with infinite tact, taking care not to show any displeasure, the girl's peevishness increased. As Rebecca's family from Panayappilly began to visit them periodically to enquire about their daughter's well-being, Eshumma's burden increased. As the workload increased

Kallu Moopathi, who came to help with the outside work, began to stay away frequently. What could she do, she said, if her husband Pangu Moopen who went to thatch a roof fell down and became bedridden? As for her oldest son, who wandered all over the land carrying his ashan's make-up box in the hope of getting a chance to enact Lavanasuravadham, what could she do if he lacked a sense of responsibility? The Kathakali ashan had him tagging along for so long now, enticing him with a vague promise of giving him the role!

Though Eshumma now bore double the load of work she was used to doing, she took care not to show it. Instead she prepared herself to go along with her fate. Though Evron too noticed some of it he was unwilling to utter any word of reproof to Rebecca. Her belly had come alive after a long wait. It was a time when the woman's mind became vulnerable. He should not say or do anything that caused her discomfort.

Finally, without any complication, completing the ten-month term, Rebecca gave birth to Salamon.

Eshumma looked at her darling grandson, looked again and again, then continued to look. Fairer than anyone born in the Isaac family. He must have inherited the colour from his mother's side. A well-formed infant. Everything in the right proportion. Laughter, crying, everything as it should be. So adorable that the women in the neighbourhood could well cast their jealous eyes upon him!

Achuthan vaidyar, who knew some astrology, calculated the day and time of birth and spoke to Evron, choosing his words carefully: 'The child will be more prone to illnesses than usual during infancy, but there is nothing to fear.'

Vaidyar stopped abruptly. Though Evron looked at him questioningly, the vaidyar refused to elaborate. Later when he saw an unusual crease appear on the latter's forehead and saw him pluck at his grizzled eyebrows one by one, as he became immersed in the intricacies of other worlds, Evron repeatedly tried to probe him with questions but the vaidyar continued to evade him.

Finally when Evron's anxiety escalated he said in a low voice, 'Wait till the fifth birthday, Evrone!'

Though the vaidyar refused to elaborate, Evron felt a flash of fear. Achuthan vaidyar was not the kind of person who spoke impulsively. If anything did fall from his tongue it had pointers in all four sides. However, Evron did not mention any of this to Umma, or to Rebecca, because the child was the much awaited bechor of the family. Umma would not be able to bear even the faintest hint of alarm.

Whatever it was, once the delivery was over Rebecca began to wither. As though the old scent of a male and the high-spirited elegance of a mare had disappeared somewhere. As she dragged herself from room to room plagued by a hundred maladies, Eshumma began to grow anxious. Rebecca was her only female companion among all these men. As part of the dietary nourishment the vaidyar prescribed to be given after delivery, she was given milk, ghee, and soup made of goat's legs ... but Rebecca seemed to grow feebler by the day.

'What punishment is this, Lord!' Eshumma looked skyward and lamented, her hand on her breast.

By then harassment from the other side of the fence began.

'Why is it like this, Eshumma? Usually women begin to bloom after delivery. Is it the lack of some nourishment?'

'She is all wasted after giving birth just once. She has to give birth to so many more. She looks like a snake touched by a snake charmer.'

'These are fashionable times, are they not? She must be thinking even one is too much.'

These days Eshumma did not give an ear to all that. She was even reluctant to look towards the fences.

Achuthan vaidyar, who said that the pale, anaemic eyes and physical exhaustion were due to lack of blood, prescribed the essence of iron. As Rebecca childishly avoided the medicine, which was difficult to ingest, Eshumma's worries multiplied.

'I alone have to carry both the child and the mother, Evrone,' she complained to her son. 'I can somehow comfort the one at my waist, but what about the older one?'

Evron had no reply to any of this. So every morning, making business an excuse, he got out of the house early to catch the boat. By the time he returned late at night, he would find supper laid out for him and everyone asleep. Though he said that he had certain business engagements near Kuzhoor and Madathumpady the youngest, Eliacha, did not really believe it.

It was not that Evron was unaware of his mother's tribulations. He just did not have the means to solve those problems.

Illness first manifested itself in the child when he was three years old, in the form of scurf that appeared all over his body. He was made to drink several ayurvedic concoctions. Oil was smeared all over his body; he was then bathed in nalpamaram water. As Eshumma smeared medicated oil on the oozing pustules, and walked about in the yard with the child against her shoulder, the words that came to her lips were old religious songs. Most of these were songs praising the Jewish chief Joseph Rabban, also called Chiriyanandan.

As for the three-year-old, he accepted the bitter medicine

and slimy oil smeared on his body with the maturity of a thirty-year-old.

However, due to the stinging pain, the child did not sleep much at night. So he had to be carried around. There was no one to hold him even for a little while. Rebecca, who confined her movement to the chair and the bed, did not even look towards that side. It was as though by giving birth she had fulfilled all her obligations to the family.

Eshumma had no complaints about that. It was her responsibility to take care of the bechor of the family. But a little bit of help perhaps…

To whom could she say all this?

Therefore, the length of her prayers increased, as did the weight of her sorrows.

Severing Ties

Evron went about feigning ignorance. His days and nights tumbled over each other in Parakadavu, the Kottapuram market and Tripunithura. The Ephraim family had had the contract to supply vegetables and provisions to the Tripunithura palace for a long time. In Isaac's time, the ties grew stronger, that was all. Muthacha's ties with the palace went back many years. The easygoing royals generally did not have any complaints. Therefore, Muthacha insisted that everything should be supplied as and according to need. To arrange for vegetables that retained their freshness from Parakadavu, Cheriyathekanam and Puthenchira, and high-quality grains and pulses, which reached the Kottapuram market from Pandinadu, and to load them into boats and see that they reached the palace at the right time was indeed a great responsibility. For that very reason he did not leave it to the labourers. His eyes were everywhere.

Muthacha often reminded Evron that this was a relationship that went beyond business. Now it had to continue through Evron. So it was essential that the son understood every aspect of the trade.

The Christian traders in the Ernakulam market tried hard to muscle their way in. They even had their bishop intervene on their behalf. And what happened? The royals did not allow them to come anywhere near them. 'Let Ephraim moopar say that he can no longer do it. Then we'll think about it,' they said and sent them away.

Ephraim muthacha did not say no, and took care of the business for as long as age permitted him. He stubbornly held on to the hope that the coming generations would carry on the business in the future.

But Ephraim's son Isaac did not hesitate to draw back from the many truths that the father had held sacred in his life and his dealings. For Isaac was in a hurry to advance in business, to make money. Times were changing. A struggle was going on in the land to force the white man to leave the country. Isaac had no doubt that if the English men left and some dark, worthless fellow came to power, the fate of the Jews in the land would be tricky. So what was wrong in looking for ways to make some money before that happened? Even otherwise, who would be there with the poor Jews when hard times descended upon them?

Whatever you say, the whites are whites, eda! How can our flag-bearing darkies acquire their firm and grand manner of doing things?

Not just that, a rumour had spread across the land that if the Congress came to power, the future of the kings was precarious. The Congressmen are not happy that many of the petty kings became close to the British. Their leaders have said as much.

Suppose the Kochi Thampuran too has to give up his power? Who would give the Jews the support the kings extended to them? Hadn't those kings invited the homeless people who had been wandering about the world to come and settle there? Then again, the many ties that they had with the palace...

It was when Evron went along with Vava a couple of times to understand the nature of business that he truly understood the exact manner of Vava's dealings. A Menon from the north who was in charge of the store took care of all the palace affairs. The moment Muthacha saw Menon, he would take the towel from his shoulder and tie it around his waist deferentially. That was how he invariably stood before him.

Then again, the way Muthacha addressed him – as 'Thampuran!' – when Evron heard it the first time he felt himself itch with irritation. Once he had muttered in Vava's ear, 'When did he become a thampuran?'

Vava winked as if to say: 'What do we lose?'

Muthacha almost always unloaded the wares in the afternoon. At that time the storekeeper, usually lethargic after a sumptuous lunch, would yawn prodigiously at regular intervals and ask, 'Everything is in order, isn't it, Isaac?' in a loud voice.

Menon considered it too much of a bother to open every corded bundle that was unloaded and check the contents himself.

'I think it is, but it would be better if Thampuran verified it,' Isaac would reply, lowering his voice.

'Hey, what is that for? You have checked, that is enough.'

'That's not it. Suppose the workers made some mistake? Just check them with this list. Then Isaac too would be happy.'

'Shhe, what are you saying?'

'Times are bad, Thampuran. Just one rotten fruit can ruin the good name of the bunch. Isaac has to climb these steps tomorrow as well, is that not so?'

'All that is not necessary. I have never examined your jottings till now, have I?' The rest of his words would drown in the yawn that followed … It was time for the customary afternoon nap.

Then Muthacha would mention an amount. Menon would nod his head sleepily. With that, the day's transactions were concluded.

It was much later that Evron realized that the roll of paper that Vava held out was not a list of the market prices of commodities. The jottings, made with a steel pen dipped in kaduka ink, could be anything. Muthacha was certain that the storekeeper, whose eyes were heavy with sleep, would not look at them. And even if he did, what would he make out from the sweat-smeared inky jottings? Therefore, when Muthacha spoke proudly about his long and enduring intimacy with the palace Evron smiled to himself.

Thus each time he went to deliver supplies, Muthacha would mention a random amount that came to his mind. To this storekeeper Menon added his own share and tallied the palace accounts. Muthacha never forgot to send a set of clothes and a large bunch of bananas to Menon's wife's house in Elamkunnapuzha every Onam.

Isn't all this wrong? When the son asked his vava this question, the vava had just one answer: 'They did not work hard and amass all this wealth, did they? So a part of it comes to us. Think of it like that.'

Apart from the dealings with the palace, Muthacha also had some trade partnerships in the Ernakulam market. It was through these that he bought several coconut groves and Eshumma's gold ornaments. Isaac undoubtedly had the ability to double the wealth that Ephraim moopar had made.

The one who opposed all this most vehemently was Menahem mutha, the preacher in Thoppumpady.

'Vava's tricks are not going to last, Evrone,' he would say to his younger brother. 'You at least try to find the straight path.'

Eshumma would lose her temper when she heard that. 'All he has to deal with is his synagogue and his speeches. What does a man without wife and family know about the expenses incurred in a house? Where is it said that business is all truth and politeness? If the seller and the buyer are not bothered, is it the one leaning against the wall who feels the itch?'

But Menahem, the preacher who had studied the Torah, felt the itch.

Evron, the member who had not studied the Torah, also felt the itch.

It was the same Isaac muthacha who was later swept away by the floods near Palathuruthu. The waters that descended from the northern hills that year were unusually turbulent, the elders said. There was also something ominous in the way they flowed, bringing down embankments…

Thus, with great reluctance did Evron take up the business that had gone on for two generations. He had no doubt that it was his vava who had destroyed the honest and straightforward dealings that had existed in Ephraim muthacha's time.

'Greed. He was not satisfied however much he got.'

Evron regretted the fact that the fame Muthacha had earned was destroyed during his time. 'Money and wealth are like our water from the hills. They come and go. What is the point of amassing wealth if the people around have nothing good to say?' he told himself.

Besides, as one involved in public affairs, Evron wanted to be known as Ephraim's grandson rather than Isaac's son.

'People quickly forget the great things that our elders do. Their foolish acts, on the other hand, remain – they cannot be scrubbed or wiped away.' When the elder brother said this, Elias just stood by, nodding his head. After all, a great many tales about Ephraim Sa'ib's nobility, acquired through hearsay, lay entrenched within him. There were no such glowing memories of Vava. When Evron stubbornly insisted that he would engage in business only if he could do it the straightforward way, Eshumma objected.

'Do not say ungodly things, mone,' she advised. 'In business you have to ignore certain things, dismiss them as unseen and unheard. All this did not begin today or yesterday. It is easy to waste what the elders amassed. It was because Valia Muthacha worked hard that a lot of worthless idlers could survive on rice gruel in this house. It was that difficult at one time. Do not forget that all that you see now was made with just one pair of hands.'

Evron too had heard something along those lines. Apparently, at one time, the two-storey house was filled with people. Relatives who had come to live off the generosity of Valia Muthacha, who was slightly better off than them. Men, women and children, who did nothing but sit and eat. Evron remembered some of them from his childhood days.

Finally, when this had gone on for a long time, Eshumma asked Isaac, her husband, 'Tell me truthfully, who are these people?'

'Who knows?' he replied evasively.

'So you too do not know?'

'They must be our people. That is why they are here, isn't it?'

'That may be true, but how long do you think we must bear this burden?'

'It is not something new. The elders started it…'

'Just because the elders started certain practices…?'

'I don't know.'

'Then whom should I ask?'

'Ask the Lord.'

Eshumma tried hard but the Lord too could give her no answer.

The feeble reply provided Isaac a temporary escape, but the unanswered question continued to whirr within him as well. Famine had ravaged the land. Income from business was decreasing but expenses were mounting. Though there was only one source of money the expenses were manifold.

By that time Ephraim moopar had stopped involving himself in such matters. It is the next generation's world, let them manage, he seemed to think. Besides, this was too trivial to gain entry into that scholar's mind. What was wrong if some relatives came along to share what he had made? Wasn't it desperation that made them leech off the family so shamelessly?

As time went by and the weight of the bunch of keys tucked into the folds of cloth at her waist increased, Eshumma's attitude changed. Why should I carry this load, she thought. I too entered this house from elsewhere as a bride. If the men in the family do not have the guts to put things in order, why should I bother? There are people older than me among the outsiders. Let them take charge of the keys. Then their true nature will be revealed.

Thus one evening, when the routine prayers were over, Eshumma held the keys out to her husband.

'Take these keys.'

'Why?' Isaac asked, bewildered.

'Just hold it. You will at least know their weight.'

'I know all that, Eshu … but why?'

'Give it to whoever you like.'

'Who's there who is suitable for that?'

'If there is a mouth to eat, there will be a hand to hold the keys as well.'

'Look, Eshu,' Isaac said placatingly, 'have I ever asked you for accounts?'

'That is because you know that I close my hold to keep tally of every anna-paisa spent.'

'Exactly.' As though relieved, he placed his hand on her shoulder and pressed it. He looked into her eyes searchingly and said, 'I can give these only to the one I trust, Eshu. That person must also have the strength to take on the responsibility. It is the ancestral home that the elder built, after all.'

At that moment Eshumma felt the sword in the glass case on the wall move, the sword that the king of Kochi had graciously presented. An unusually grave expression appeared on Ephraim moopar's face. Doubt and displeasure reflected in those eyes. Eshumma immediately retreated.

Things seemed to have settled down for a while, but Eshumma was not willing to give in. Minor squabbles among the children; taunts and gibes within the house; barbs that grew longer from across the fence; women taking each comment and blowing it out of proportion – it was becoming intolerable. Eshumma knew she had had enough. Someday, somewhere, the link had to be snapped. It should have been done long ago, she decided.

'He works hard so that my children get to eat; not to feed anyone and everyone around,' she began to murmur in the lonely corners of the house where light did not enter.

It was not as if her husband, Isaac, did not know any of this. But he did not have the courage to look at Vava's face and say something. The very sight of that face made Isaac's tongue go dry. The majesty of that expression – no way less than that of the king of Kochi. At one time Vava's prayer was that he should have enough to give one meal to all the people in Jew Street.

'He thinks he is the thampuran of the village,' Isaac murmured when no one was around. 'We will see what happens to these grand ways when the Englishman leaves.'

When Isaac could no longer bear Eshumma's complaints, he admitted that something like that could be considered only after Moopar's death.

'You can defer your honeyed words and cajolery till then.' Eshumma's voice rose.

After that she began to spend the night in the children's room.

'Though at times she stinks of the veluri fish, without her…'

Isaac quivered miserably. In the winter months of Vrichikam and Dhanu, when the mist descended upon the hill, he lay hugging his pillow, heat coursing through his body and soul. What could he do to make her a bit more understanding?

Eshumma knew well that Moopar could not sleep without her scent. Neither could she, without his hand on her breast. But she was also certain that she needed to make the cut; only then would things move forward. Thus, while they lay in adjacent rooms counting the hours of the night, snores in varied tones rose from the many rooms of that big house where their occupants slumbered peacefully.

But the discord did not last long.

During the scorching month of Medam, when all the wells and ponds dried up, when diarrhoea spread and Ephraim moopar became bedridden, there was only Eshumma to take care of him. Apart from standing at the threshold and peeping in, not one of the relatives took two steps inside the room.

'All they need to do is sit in the kitchen veranda and gorge. There is someone here to clean up the stool and urine of the elder, after all.'

This time Eshumma murmured in a place where there was a fair amount of light. Let them hear. Let all who need to, hear. But what could she do if they still lingered on shamelessly?

Ephraim Sa'ib died one evening, without suffering too much. With his death the majesty that adorned the forehead of that family also vanished.

In a way, it was a day Eshumma was looking forward to. After that, things began to happen. When murmurs from various corners grew in intensity Yose muliyar from the synagogue arrived to find an amicable solution. Though the conciliatory talks went on for the entire summer and half the rainy season, no one was willing to let go of what they had managed to get hold of.

'Avaricious lot! Give them whatever they want and send them off. At least there will be some peace in the family.' Eshumma had to concede in the end.

Thus, with great difficulty, each group was sent on its way. In order to make it happen they had to let go off a few paddy fields in Ezhikkara, coconut groves in Kanakkankadavu, some wooden furniture and even some copper vessels, but Eshumma's response was one of whole-hearted relief. On a day in Karkkidakam, when the last group walked out into the heavy rain and crossed the gateway – hesitant, looking back, hoping till the last moment to be called back by someone –

she let out a deep sigh, looked towards the sky and thanked the creator.

That day, for the first time, she placed her hand on her husband's bottle of wine. She who did not bother to touch it even on festive days thus came to know its taste.

'It is good, isn't it?' Isaac teased her.

'Of course.'

'Wasted your youth, didn't you?'

'Of course.'

That night as she entered her husband's bedroom, with her head bowed like a new bride, she told him coyly, 'I feel like having another child.'

'Did anyone say you shouldn't?'

When he embraced her with the frenzy of one who had waited too long, when his hairy hands groped for new boundaries, Eshumma quivered like a new bride. It was a new night for them.

Several years after Evron's birth, Eshumma felt her lower belly throb. That was how Elias was born...

Though they had their arguments and quarrels, Isaac was a treasure of rich memories for her.

'At one time all the ornaments that I brought from Mala as a bride were pawned at the cooperative society. Some of them were even sold in the auction at throwaway prices. When festive days and weddings arrived, there was not a bit of gold to wear. So what? Didn't he bring ten times more than what was lost and shower them at my feet? Forever trying, determined to prove himself. At times I asked him, towards whom is this vashi? He would say, "This land and these trees are not for Nairs and Namboothiris alone. Let the people know that if we, orphaned Jews, try we too can amass wealth.'" Whenever she recalled Isaac muthacha wetness spread in Eshumma's eyes.

'You, his sons, need to be reborn thrice to be as great as he was.'

Muthimma knew that Evron, who insisted on truth and straightforward dealings in business, would not be able to run it successfully for long. To some extent Evron knew it too.

By the time Salamon was nearing five the scurf had almost healed. But then he contracted chronic diarrhoea. He grew thin; his stomach protruded and he became a pitiable sight. Eshumma grew terribly anxious. The infantile diseases that Achuthan vaidyar had mentioned could take any form. If in olden times the weapon that the gods used against the bechor was lightning, now it took the form of contagious diseases.

Once again various concoctions, medicinal potions, dietary restrictions ... the child withered. The child wearied.

It was when he was almost five that a glow appeared on his face and his body filled out. But by that time Rebecca was utterly wasted. She sat listlessly, talking to no one.

Leaning back in bed she stared at the daylight streaming in from the square window. The synagogue stood close by. The church and the mosque were around her. On top of the hill was the Hindu temple.

To whom should she pray?

Everyday Rebecca recalled her school master appa who was adamant that at least his children should grow up without mentioning religion and caste. Thus, when he moved away from Jew Street and went in search of a place where people of all religions lived, her umma and relatives opposed him. After that, Umma began to go to the synagogue in Mattancherry every day to pray devoutly that Appa would

begin to think right. Even when the evachas attributed the
daughters' unmarried state to Appa's defiance of God, Appa
pretended not to hear it. He had become used to doing that.
'I am proud of my birth as a Jew,' Appa would say. 'But I
cannot live wholly as a Jew because my world is not made
up of Jews alone.'

Even as resistance fumed within the home, Rebecca was
always on her appa's side. It was he who told her not to call
him vava, to call him appa, as the Christians did. Moreover,
she had gone to the church more often than to the synagogue
as most of her friends were Christians. So many people
thought she was a Christian. Rebecca did not correct them.
Her friend Ambika knew that if she was permitted to enter
the temple, Rebecca would be willing to do that as well.

Rebecca was floundering amidst memories ... As her
school days in Panayappilly and college days in Saint
Teresa's flooded her mind, she trembled. Appa had cherished
the dream that after completing her BA in Saint Teresa's
College and MA in Maharaja's College she would become
a teacher in some college. It was natural that the zenith of
a primary school master's dream would be to teach in a
college.

But on the day before the MA final examination Rebecca
developed a slight fever. Ignoring it, she bathed in cold
water and went to write the exam, but on the day of the
third exam she fainted in the classroom. The fever that had
entered through her thumb had reached her brain. She was
unconscious for two days. When she opened her eyes she
found herself in the general hospital. It took another four
to five days for the fever and delirium to subside. As she lay
alternating between consciousness and delirium, the images
that flitted across her mind included those of students sitting

in rows in the examination hall. The teachers who moved between the rows holding question papers had horns and tusks. When amidst their ear-shattering grunts the answer sheets on the desks began to fly about, Emily, Ambika and she began to run after them, weeping loudly…

Though Appa tried to console her by saying that she could write the exam in September, she could never go back to those old books that she had once put down. Even touching their neatly covered jackets brought about a terrible sense of unfamiliarity … as though something was pulling her back. When the image of the teachers with horns and tusks moving about holding question papers appeared in her mind, the books slipped from her hand and fell. After that she was scared even to look in that direction.

'Why is it like this, Appa?' she had once asked, frightened.

'It is all your imagination, mole … My daughter was always good at studies. It will become all right in a day or two,' Simon master had replied, holding her close.

'I am scared, Appa,' she had repeated.

She still remembered vividly how she had held her father tight, fearing that she would lose him, how he had stroked her back, running his fingers through her hair, unable to speak because of the lump rising in his throat. Finally he had said, 'Then we'll wait till next March. There will be so many opportunities to write the exam. My mol should not worry.'

Several Marchs and Septembers went by in that manner. But no one noticed that the books, arranged in rows in the wall cupboard, had become damp and that termites had got at them. Some time later when she opened the cupboard Rebecca looked wistfully at the termite-ridden remains of three years of study. Finally she replaced them in the cupboard with a tinge of sadness and withdrew. At least the termites had profited from three good years of her life, she thought.

Eshumma was worried by the way Rebecca sat on her bed, not seeing or hearing anything around her. Achuthan vaidyar said that certain women became indisposed in this manner after delivery.

'The human body is full of different types of nerves, is it not so, Eshumma? Nerves that go to the head and the heart. When the life that takes root within the body tears itself free it is possible that some nerves may grow taut, some slacken. There is nothing to be frightened about. She will have to undergo treatment for a slightly long period of time and take rest. That is all.'

Somehow that day, for the first time, Muthimma did not really believe Achuthan vaidyar's words. These were things that were beyond Achuthan vaidyar's control, someone frightened her from within.

'Shall we take her to Paravur, Evrone?' she asked her son.

'But we just started vaidyar's mixture and pills,' the son replied. 'Moreover if we take her to the government hospital they'll give her allopathic medicine and injections. They might even use the knife.' When she heard the word knife Eshumma was frightened. Without saying anything further she retreated into the kitchen.

But when the fever started the next day she panicked. Rebecca's face looked pale and swollen.

'Evrone, this cannot...' Overwrought with sorrow Eshumma could not speak.

Evron, for whom it was unusual to be at home at that time, went out without saying anything. After a while compounder Velappan arrived on the ferry with a bottle of medicine and some white pills. However, Eliacha, unable to watch all this, ground his teeth. 'We'll take her to the hospital at Ernakulam, Umma,' he insisted. 'Cannot bear to see her lying like this.'

But how could they take her without telling Evron? She had seen him leave the house earlier. Who knew for where?

Eshumma was in a dilemma. Unable to control his anger, Eliacha raised his voice.

'If he does not come home by evening I myself will take her to Ernakulam. I do not have to ask anyone.'

He arranged a boat and helpers for that purpose.

But by late afternoon the fever shot up. Rebecca became delirious. When she began to talk incoherently Velappan said they should take her to the town and give her an injection.

On hearing the news Rebecca's parents rushed from Panayappilly. Seeing them Rebecca began to cry.

'I am scared, Appa.' She gripped her father tightly.

Simon master strove hard to control his tears when he saw her dark, parched lips murmur unintelligibly. As he sat close to her on the cot and stroked her head, he felt his palm burn.

'The teachers are coming with the paper. Do not let them go,' she rambled.

Simon master jumped up from where he sat. 'You let the fever persist for all these days and now at this stage…' He shook, unable to control the anger and sorrow that welled up within him.

'If you had said one word we would have taken her to the hospital in Ernakulam so much earlier.' Miriam could not control her sobs.

Eshumma stood stunned into silence.

As evening approached the sky grew dark. It started to drizzle. A turbulent wind raged.

'This is how the wind began last year too.' The neighbours,

who had heard the news and arrived, whispered amongst themselves.

It seemed like a bad omen.

The hurricane, which had struck the hills a couple of decades ago, remained a frightening memory for them.

The light breeze, which lay hidden among the coconut groves and clumps of banana trees in the valley during the day, had cast off its slumber towards evening. Oblivious of rhythm it had raged furiously across the land, making the soil and the trees tremble. Birds shaken off their perches flew away, in search of new shelter. Sensing the approaching danger, animals howled, their cry tearing through the wind. Like a witch whose very hair had given birth to a myriad evil spirits, the wind came down the hill.

As tiles flew off the roofs and the rain poured in, people huddled together, drenched and shivering, for a whole night, longing for daybreak.

Memories of that night still reverberated in their ears. So much so that every breeze that blew seemed the forerunner of another storm.

'It is somewhat like that…' someone said.

'Hmm,' another who heard it responded. 'How will they take out the boat in this wind?'

But they were mistaken. By evening the wind subsided. The boatmen arrived through the drizzle bearing a stretcher. Salamon still remembered how his mother was laid on the stretcher and was taken to the landing, and from there on to the boat. He remembered how two dark, thick-set ferrymen threw their oars into the water … He stood in knee-deep water, watching it all.

At that time Salamon did not realize that he was seeing his mother's pallid face and milk-froth-like smile for the last time. The sweetness of that froth still remained on his lips. The form that was brought back in another boat on the third day was covered with a white cloth. The strange look on the face as it was taken to the cemetery made him withdraw.

This is someone else. This is someone else.

The days went by. Evron was aware of a number of emotions churning within him. Oppressed by a terrible sense of guilt, unable to look anyone in the face, he avoided everyone. A number of questions were reflected on all the faces – Eshumma's, Elias', Rebecca's parents', the muliyar from the synagogue's...

That day, for the first time, he trembled as he thought of the worth of the precious life that was lost. The punishment for not supporting her, who had so trustingly taken his hand, in her hour of need. If he had taken her to the government hospital in the town in the beginning itself ... thoughts crowded within him.

Seeing Evron's anguish Achuthan vaidyar tried to comfort him. 'She was such a great woman. She chose to take a terrible fate upon herself, didn't she?'

Evron looked sharply at the vaidyar's face.

It was what the stars in the sky had told the vaidyar five years ago. Had the illnesses of infancy and the bodily ailments been directed at the child's life?

'And?' Evron asked, stunned.

'Confronted by a mother's heartrending cry even the propositions of the gods melt into nothingness.'

Evron continued to stare, not knowing what to make of the vaidyar's words. His words suggested devout prayer ... a mother paying the penalty so that the family should not be rendered heirless; sacrificed her own life for the sake of the child.

'You have to believe, Evrone. To be granted this life is itself a miracle, is it not? So we have to believe the miraculous things that happen in life.'

Evron unconsciously trembled. He had not been able to gauge the depth of that noisy girl's heart. He grieved.

With Rebecca gone, the rhythm of Evron's life was disrupted. A hitherto unseen cantankerousness appeared in his behaviour. With that, people close to him began to grow distant. His business partner in the Ernakulam market was alienated. In the meantime the ties with the royal family had slackened. When the earlier storekeeper – Menon from the north – became bedridden, a Pillai from the south was appointed in his place. Pillai was a capable man. He turned many of the old practices in the palace upside down. When he began to open the bundles and check the contents, and use a balance and weights, retreat became inevitable.

Evron knew that it was the mischievous hand of some Muslim traders in the Kottapuram market that was responsible for these changes. But he also knew he did not have the strength to confront them.

Evron went about as usual, pretending indifference, but Eshumma was unhappy. The ties with the palace were as precious as gold for Ephraim moopar. So many grand stories about those ties had been narrated to the locals.

'How could you, Evrone? The good name that the elders had made...'

What good name? Evron laughed to himself. A good name created by doing all kinds of wrong things! 'Let it go, Umma. If not this, then something else. There is a time for everything. We cannot expect everything to remain the same all our lives, can we?'

'Still, what the elders—'

'What elders?' Evron asked irritably. 'Didn't they all go their way? Let us look after those that remain.'

He had been like that for some time now. He became irritable very quickly. But though he seemed impossible to control when he lost his temper, he would cool down with the same swiftness.

'With her gone the family lost its grace,' Eshumma said, her hand against her head. She felt her body ache as though she was about to catch fever.

Evron went out muttering under his breath.

He was being defeated everywhere. Even Rebecca had defeated him. She had taken that tremendous decision without giving him the faintest hint.

No, he would not accept defeat. No one could defeat him that easily, he told himself.

Menahem alone said that it was good that the business with the palace was over. It should have happened earlier, that was all.

The younger one, Elias, generally did not comment on such matters. He, who read a lot and became involved in matters that concerned the world, was not bothered by affairs of the home and the neighbourhood.

With Rebecca gone Eshumma, who was rendered lonely once again, retreated into her small world. However, there was one person who brought her relief. Salamon, the bechor of the family.

Growing Up

Through Salamon's growth Evron was witnessing his own. The flailing of limbs, crawling on belly and then on knees, the attempts to stand up, the first tentative footsteps…

Through Salamon I, Evron, am beginning to learn to crawl, stand and walk. Learning to form words from letters, rendered sweet from being dipped in honey.

Vava must have done the same thing … watched him, Evron, grow up. Evron often thought about it. He was certain it had been so, for every man tries to rectify his own imperfections through his son. Unfulfilled desires, certain precious continuities. When one generation tries to impose its longings on the next, it thinks of many possibilities. The desire that the seed one sows should grow into a much bigger tree, spreading out into a world that extended beyond the palace and the Ernakulam market … a bigger world.

At times Evron even thought that it was fortunate that the flooded river took away Muthacha before he could see the future. Isaac had no idea of a world beyond his business. When Menahem went to study Hebrew and the Torah, and Elias went along a different path with his friends and his bundle of books, Vava said nothing. He was relieved that he at least had Evron. Evron's failure in business would have been unbearable for him.

Now Evron was expecting the same continuity from his son. When he bestowed the child with the name Solomon he had not thought of that great king's wisdom, but his immense capabilities, something he lacked. Muthimma often reminded him of it, and Rebecca too hinted at it during the early days of their marriage, not so much through words as through smiles and gestures.

Later realizing that it was pointless, Rebecca gave up. He did realize that the capable ones found it difficult to tolerate those who lacked that quality. But like most men, he was not willing to acknowledge defeat before his wife. As for Rebecca, instead of trying to defeat him, she gave herself up to be defeated because she recognized that it was the many truths within him that prompted Evron to draw back from several things.

'Give up business, undergo training and become a teacher. That will suit you,' she had once suggested.

However, Evron viewed it as an admission of failure, and determined to prove otherwise, got involved in some wholesale dealings in the Paravur market. He burnt his fingers badly there as well, lost quite a lot of money and was forced to draw back.

Evron had entrusted all matters concerning Salamon to Umma. After all, things had been more or less the same even when Rebecca was alive. However, as the boy grew, Evron's anxieties multiplied.

Salamon was an altogether spiritless boy. A loner, and a dreamer, he was often found in dark corners of the house or on the river bank, or in the shade of a tree, where no one would see him. Evron had hoped that his son would not be like himself, but learn to be a bit of a bully, so necessary to survive in this difficult world. So he took Salamon to play with the boys on the hill. Salamon stumbled and returned with a bleeding knee. Though he was sent back on the third day when the wound healed, he returned on the seventh with a number of complaints. Someone tripped him up, stamped on his buttock, aimed the ball at his chest when he was goalkeeper ... At that Muthimma intervened. My child need not go to play with that rough lot. Once Muthimma made a decree no one went against it. The goal that Evron had aimed at did not work.

A bit of a bully. Salamon too failed to understand the wisdom of Evron's belief.

However, her grandson's behaviour was a source of great relief for Eshumma. He did not create trouble in school like Evron or Elias, did he? When the teachers got fed up and ordered the boys to bring their guardian to school, Isaac Muthacha would skilfully avoid the summons. Finally when the children came home weeping Eshimuthimma herself would go to school and stand with a bowed head as the masters listed their complaints. Finally when this became too much she lashed out at her husband, 'Next time, you go. It is not enough to produce children, you should also know how to raise them.'

That day when Muthacha thrashed the boys with a stick from the guava tree, Eshumma did not even look that way.

'When mothers advise it is treated as a joke. Unless children get a thrashing or two from their fathers once in a while, they do not grow up well,' she said.

After that there were no more complaints from the school, and Eshumma got a reprieve.

'Isaac vaidyar's medicine should have been doled out earlier, isn't it, Evrone?' she had asked.

Stroking the swollen welts Evron had nodded. But the younger one, Elias, had a question. He had not understood some of the words that Vava yelled in fury when he caned them; were they English or Hebrew?

It was customary to hold the pidyon ceremony for the redemption of the first-born child on the thirtieth day. But from where would they get the kohen to perform the ceremony? The kohen would place his hand on the infant's head and mention a figure as the cost of the silver hip chain that the mother gave. She would then pay the money and buy back the child.

In the past someone would come once in a while to conduct the ritual for those for whom it had to be done. There had been no delay when Menahem was born. But when they couldn't get anyone to perform the rite for Salamon, the precious grandson born after such a long wait, Eshumma's anxiety increased.

But Evron did not believe in these rituals. My dear son is not something to be sold and bought back, he told Umma. But she did not agree.

If Rebecca had been alive? Evron saw the question on Umma's face and he laughed.

'You need not worry about that. I know how Simon master brought up his daughter,' he had said.

Yosef hazzan, who had great knowledge of the Jewish holy texts, guided Salamon to shape the letters. He made bread in the shape of a letter in the rabanim on the upper floor of the synagogue and dipped it in honey. As he fed it to Salamon he murmured, 'The letter is sweet. Bread is God. The sweetness of this letter, this bread, should remain forever on your lips.'

Eshimuthimma insisted that children should study the

Torah in childhood itself and recite the prayers in Hebrew. It was not often that learned rabbis came from abroad to the land. But the bearded old rabbi who came from Belgium five or six years ago fell in love with the land. He was seeing such a countryside and such a vibrant Jew Street for the first time. When many people approached him, during his two-week stay, with doubts regarding the Torah, he was fired with enthusiasm. His face was swollen from lack of sleep when he boarded the boat on the day of his departure. But he said again and again: 'I do not feel like going.' When someone tried to comfort him, he repeated with great determination, 'I will come, I will come again, most probably next year itself.'

But he did not come the next year. Nor the year after. He never came back. Not just him, no other rabbi came. When the elders in the street fretted about the new-age doubts that cropped up within them, the muliyar comforted them. Someday he will come. If not him, someone like him.

Salamon studied till the tenth with tolerably good marks. He was always ahead of his classmates Simon and Ephraim. He scored better marks in chemistry and zoology than physics. He knew how to make carbon-dioxide and nitrogen-di-oxide. He had learnt how to do experiments by heart, like the one using Kipp's apparatus. He could say where the appendix was located in the human body without looking at the diagram. Therefore the science teacher, Robert master from Pazhambillithuruthu, had good reason to call him the scientist from Kunnumpuram.

Every question in science has two answers. The first was a straightforward one, the other was complex. The one who gave the second answer was considered very intelligent or totally crazy. Since Salamon had not yet shown any signs of craziness, was it not wiser to call him intelligent? That is, one who had the ability to take his mind and intellect along hitherto unknown paths.

But Salamon knew he did not have that ability. He could study any subject, get good marks, but he had no particular liking for any subject.

There was one person in the school who was sure where Salamon's talent lay. The drawing master Appu Menon.

'Painting! That is your strength,' Appu Menon said.

He did not say this merely because Salamon won the first prize in drawing for three years in a row in high school. But because he had the eye to see many things others could not. This eye enabled him to find the right students to act in a play or take part in some cultural activity during the school's anniversary celebrations.

What the drawing master liked most was drawing portraits and painting landscapes using watercolours. When the headmaster Vasudeva Menon retired, Appu Menon drew a portrait of him, which still hangs on the staffroom wall.

'Just look at that! The eyes and the eyebrows, the cleft in the chin and the wart on the ear, all as in life ... the picture looks as though it is alive. It is a blessing, this talent, the reward for taking a bath and bowing before the lord at Kunnathol everyday,' the masters said to each other.

When they did that the drawing master would smile faintly and tell Salamon, 'Art is not drawing lifelike images, edo. Give life to the lifeless. See the unseen in what you see. Anyone can draw the hill and the river, the boat and the coconut tree. But one should be able to draw the world beyond that – situations, predicaments, agonies ... for that these two eyes are not enough. You need the real, inner eye. Colours too have their own layers, tones and cadences.'

Did he have that kind of inner eye? What were the layers,

tones and cadences of colours? How did one create the invisible from the visible? As Appu master said, the condition when hills and rivers talked to one...

For that...?

'A large part is innate talent. The rest is hard work. There are colleges that teach art, in Madras, Bombay and such places. But I don't know whether your people will support the idea.'

When Salamon said he wanted to go to college Evron felt a vague disquiet.

'What you have studied is enough to do business. Too much study creates problems,' he said.

'I want to study. I want to go to a college in Ernakulam,' Salamon insisted.

'Oh yes, you're going to study and become a magistrate, aren't you?'

Salamon was reluctant to look his father in the eye and say that he might not become a magistrate, but he would definitely not get into business like him.

Though Eliacha, who had studied till the intermediate course in the college at Thevara, tried to intervene, he did not succeed. When the boy was adamant, Muthimma entered the fray on Salamon's behalf, as usual.

'Let the boy study, Evrone, what is wrong in that? Is it shame that the boy will be more learned than you?'

Evron did not want to tell Umma that too much education was bad for business. It was dangerous to study too much because then lofty ideals got into one's head and going along with the tactics and crooked machinations of business would become difficult. One needed some cunning to prosper in business. He was determined that his son should not repeat the mistakes he had made. But how could he tell Umma all this?

The arguments stretched. The day to submit the application was drawing near. Finally Rebecca's parents, Simon muthacha and Miriam muthimma, arrived from Panayappilly to know what had been decided. And everything was turned upside down.

'Isn't it fortunate when the children say that they want to study, Evrone?' Simon master asked.

Evron remained silent. He could not talk about business to a schoolmaster.

'He can live with us. It will be convenient to go to college from our place.' Miriam muthimma supported her husband.

Eshumuthimma was quick to recognize the trap in those words. It was a neat tactic to get the boy across the river. They too had a right to Rebecca's son.

'But he is going to join the college in Aluva tomorrow, is he not, Eliase?' Eshumma interjected.

Though bewildered for a moment, Elias nodded.

Simon muthacha smiled as though he understood. He diplomatically walked towards Elias' room on the pretext of looking at the new books he had bought.

Very soon after joining the college in Aluva, Salamon lost his enthusiasm. Everything was taught in English; Malayalam terms for carbon dioxide and nitrogen were not used. Physics, chemistry … they were all English terms, an unfamiliar terrain. The laboratory was frightening. Gradually when Salamon was convinced that Robert master's prophecy of his becoming a scientist would not come true, he returned to the safety of home without writing the pre-university examination.

With that, Evron's anxiety increased. The boy had grown. He had an opinion on everything. It was dangerous to let him remain at home any longer. Unless he tied him down to something, matters could get complicated. Though Salamon had just a few friends he trusted them fully. Not having the ability to discriminate between milk and water he got carried away by everything they said. That's how he became friends with the communist comrades of Karimpadam and Vadakkumpuram, all of whom belonged to rabid communist families. He was not shrewd enough to recognize their machinations and calculations.

Evron remembered well how during the Paliyam struggle he too had been in danger of getting involved with the communists. When the struggle of the lower castes for the right to walk on the road adjacent to the temple gathered impetus, and the communists under the leadership of Jaleel took up the agitation, Evron would sometimes go and watch the satyagraha, not realizing the danger of doing so. Perhaps that is how he came to be on the police watch list. Or did someone in Kunnumpuram betray him?

It was Muthimma's presence of mind that prevented his arrest that day. An amin in the court warned them that the police from Paravur Police Station were looking for him. If he was caught they would take him straight to jail. There a constable named Ummar, notorious for his torture techniques, would take charge of him. Then court, sub-jail … Apparently Ummar told someone that it would be the first time he was getting his hands on a Jew.

One evening two policemen came in search of Evron. One of them was the son of Antony from Varapuzha, an acquaintance of Muthacha's. By the time she served them vellappam, duck's eggs and poovan banana, Eshumma had already hidden her son among the sacks of mangoes in the loft. When the policemen, having eaten their fill, were ready to depart, Muthimma handed them a bunch of poovan bananas and four duck's eggs, neatly packed.

From that day onwards every time Evron heard the word 'comrade' he was reminded of the thrashing expert, Ummar, known for beating people with a lathi and inserting needles under their fingernails. Evron decided he would not allow the groups in Vadakkumpuram and Karimpadam to corrupt his son, who was going to be the support of the family. Salamon might not pay any heed if he told the boy that to his face. Therefore he had to get the boy involved in something and not give him time to remain idle, Evron thought.

Thus it was that Evron thought of starting a small shop in Kizhakkumpuram. A two-room shop in a Konkani's building by the roadside was vacant. The shutter, made of numbered but warped and rotting planks arranged randomly – plank numbered three in charcoal was followed by seven, six followed two – didn't close fully. But a carpenter could easily repair it. They could start with some essential provisions and sundry stationery items. Evron did not have the resources, but he did not want the boy to be idle and get into bad company. He thought he would borrow from one or two places at first. Since he had wandered around the Kottapuram market for a long time he could get provisions on credit from the merchants there. The rest would depend on the boy's enterprise.

When Evron mentioned his plan Salamon laughed aloud. 'Shop? I do not want one.'

'Why, is it below your dignity?' Evron asked, stunned.

No answer. Instead just that cold smile. Evron did not understand it at all. He would never have dared to smile in that manner before Muthacha. Was one's traditional occupation such a shameful one? Ducks entered the water, didn't they? Does anyone have to teach the new-born sharks to swim?

The boy just stood there. He did not say anything. But it was unlikely that he would accept the key to the lock at the end of the iron rod that held the planks together.

Eshumma tried talking to him. Menahem talked to him. Relatives in Mala talked to him.

Finally, even Elias said, 'Business can be done in a straightforward manner too, mone.'

But no ... the boy would not budge.

When he realized that the shop would not work, a slightly embittered Evron began to consider other options. If the boy could not manage a shop, how about working in one?

Thus it was that a desperate Evron went to see P.C., who had a textile shop in the Paravur market. Their friendship went back to their school days when they sat on the same bench sharing peanuts, gooseberry and karuka leaves. A friendship that led them to fight over inconsequential matters. A friendship that prompted them to tackle difficult arithmetic examinations by copying from each other.

P.C. said, 'What is this, Sa'ib, you seem to have forgotten your way to this place.'

When P.C. voiced his complaint Evron grinned. The way to either of their places was the same. There was no variance in distance either. But when the need arises, shortcuts appear, distance becomes manageable. Thus Evron had walked all the way to P.C.'s shop.

Displaying unusual extravagance P.C. ordered salted sherbet and two glasses. He poured half the sherbet into the empty glass and extended it towards his old schoolmate. Evron sat there wondering how to broach the subject. But when the salty, sour sherbet reached his dry throat it gave him the strength to begin. 'How do I say this ... I have never asked you for anything till now, but as I have no other option...'

'What is this, friend, you speak like a priest…'

'That is how matters are…'

'How can this poor textile-shop owner be of service to you? I heard you were lording it around as a great Panchayat member!'

'All that is petty gossip. The Panchayat office is nearby so I go there to spend some time, that's all. I can help people too.'

'Good to hear about your social work, member. Anyway let that be. Tell me what you came for. You wouldn't have come without a reason. And you're a Jew, after all.'

Though Evron did not like the barb in that comment he decided not to let it ruffle him.

'My son is not okay, P.C.,' he said quickly. 'And he is the only male.'

'After all, he's your son. How can he be okay?'

'Stop joking P.C. Give my Salamon a job.'

P.C. stared. 'A job? For your son? Who do you take me for? Do you think P.C. is A.S. Bava or Chackola or some other business magnate? All I have is this tiny shop. What job can I offer him here?'

'Any job. If he is with you he will learn some discipline.'

'What are you saying, friend? What job can I give your disappointing son?'

'Whatever these girls do. Something like that…' Evron added, looking at the girls standing behind the counter handling bales of cloth.

'That is not "whatever". They are cutting cloth, that too expensive cloth.'

'He'll do that cutting.'

Make his old friend's only son cut cloth – P.C. found it unappealing. But Evron was ready for anything. He was determined not to allow his grown-up son to remain at home, idle. It is when there is nothing to do that all sorts of dangerous ideas crop up in the mind.

The salary can be anything. Evron was not concerned about that. He would be able to get the boy out of the house at dawn. That was enough.

'I suppose it is because you sit in the Panchayat office from dawn onwards that you are free from dangerous ideas?' P.C. asked, winking.

Evron smiled sheepishly as the past flashed across his mind.

Finally as they slapped each other goodbye, Evron dug into his pocket to pay for the sherbet. P.C. did not stop him.

'By the way,' P.C. said, and the grave tone of an employer crept into his voice, 'it is the first time that I am employing a boy inside this shop. I am responsible for the safety of the girls who work here. And they are all in that effervescent age. If your son says or does anything inappropriate, I won't consider that he's your son, I'll belt him.'

Even in their student days P.C.'s leather belt was famous. Now that he was older, its length, breadth and force might have increased.

Evron nodded. Salamon tried to argue his way out with Evronappa and Eshimuthimma; it led to several quarrels. Finally left with no choice, Salamon reached P.C.'s shop one day.

P.C. disliked the boy at first sight. The antipathy was mutual. Therefore, when on the third day, member Evron went to see his friend, P.C.'s face wore an oily look. 'Let's see,' he said casually.

On the sixth day he repeated, 'Not enough, not enough.' At that time P.C.'s face looked as though the bitter taste of the medicine he had swallowed lingered in his mouth.

On the ninth day P.C. boiled over. The boy was not in the shop. A barely suppressed grin was seen on the faces of the girls.

The moment he saw his old friend P.C. burst out. Spawning a son is not enough, you should rear him well. Take him away before he makes me unbuckle my belt.

Though Evron was a little relieved to see P.C.'s notorious belt still in place beneath his yellow voile jubba, the coldness in his voice made him lose heart.

P.C. had a lot of complaints against the boy.

He who had been running the textile shop for twenty years was astounded to discover that measuring cloth and cutting it were technical skills! At first, he had given Salamon the relatively inexpensive Jagannath mundu to cut. He tried to teach him several times how to use his arm to measure one muzham. When that failed, he took out the measuring rod, which his father had auspiciously gifted him when he started the shop. All he did was ask the boy to measure out one length of mundu from the Jagannath cloth – something even a child could do. By the grace of God, he gave him the expensive mull cloth from Aruppukotta only later on. The measurement was never correct; scissors never went along a straight line. He tolerated it somehow, remembering Salamon was his friend's son. But when he cut the cotton cloth for weaver Sumathi's blouse three quarters of an inch less than what was required, P.C. lost his temper. It was true that he had asked 'at whose breast were you looking when you cut the cloth.' Any employer could ask a question but the wayward boy did not let it go. He back-answered. Not just that, he threw down the scale and walked out.

Evron thought that was a good thing. He was more

frightened of Sumathi's tongue than P.C.'s belt. The stink of fresh cow dung would remain even if you bathed.

With that Evron realized that it was not wise to send Salamon to work.

'Well, you can't plant pumpkin seeds and expect gourds to grow, can you? After all, he is your son!' Eshimuthimma said, her hand on her breast.

Salamon was relieved. He was fortunate that Elsie had not come to know that the one who failed the pre-degree examination was employed in a textile shop; else she would have come to the shop to buy cloth without even a quarter coin to spend. She would have made him take down every bale of cloth from the shelf, spread it out, crumple it and finally leave haughtily, complaining about the defects. She tried her best to make him look small whenever she got a chance.

Veroni thathi's daughter Elsie. Devassy mapla's daughter Elsie. Salamon could not appear small before her.

Therefore, in a way it was good that he had severed ties with P.C. Evronappa would hesitate to come forward and speak of business again. Then when all paths closed he would be able to express at least some of his personal desires, wouldn't he?

His personal desires.

When he thought about them, Salamon smiled.

Ramanandan Recommends
a Replanting

Ramanandan should be the first to know about the dream he had had two nights ago – about the ship and the sea crows – Salamon was sure.

Comrade Pavithran and Varuthutty master looked at things very differently. Both had their justifications and both were stubborn. Varuthutty master, who had changed the name Solomon, which Evronappa had longingly bestowed on him, to Salamon; Makotha Pavithran who believed that the purpose of his birth was to guide the senseless locals. If Varuthutty master's shortcoming was that he had too much intelligence, it was too much reading that had turned Pavithran in a particular direction. Both were adept at holding on to their view, citing sundry arguments to prove themselves right, and succeeding.

Salamon wanted to know just one thing: why such dreams all of a sudden? He had never seen the sea or ships except in films. As for sea crows, he had only heard of them. How then did those scenes come in search of him one dewy dawn? He had not thought of anything specific when he lay down to sleep.

Was it a dream? Or just a feeling? If so, what did it mean?

Eshimuthimma was elated because she believed dreams one saw at dawn came true. She was all aglow in the belief that it was a call from the holy land directed at the non-believer.

This was not something he could tell comrade Pavithran or Varuthutty master. Not only would they laugh scornfully, they would also come out with some inappropriate interpretations.

But however large the bundle of doubts, there was a step that he could always climb, the one that led to the tiled house on the southern side of the Konkani temple. Once you stepped over the bamboo stile you would find Ramanandan somewhere in the yard or the grounds. In a soiled ochre mundu he would talk, his fingers playing on the sweat-smeared sacred thread that lay across his lean chest. When he got involved in the conversation, he would twist the thread around his finger and keep pulling at it. He would listen to everything patiently, untie each bundle carefully, weigh each one and suggest a solution. Ramanandan did not have his father Divakara Pai's cunning or his eye for trade. People generally called the Konkanis muthalali, as they were generally merchants, but Ramanandan would flare up if anyone called him that even jokingly.

'Oh, be quiet. One needs to have wealth to be called muthalali.'

'This shop, the business and the coconut groves on the island, aren't they wealth?'

'They belong to Black, don't they?'

'Black' was none other than Ramanandan's father, Divakara Pai.

Divakara Pai was a notorious miser. He acquired the name Black Divakara Pai when he sold rice and other essentials in the black market during the war. He made a lot of money that way. He, however, considered the nickname a compliment. Trade was the accepted occupation of the local Konkanis. There was no black and white in trade. It did not matter if the head on the rupee note was that of the king or the minister, the colour was the same. When he loaned half the money he had amassed to Muslim traders in Kottapuram, tripling it in the process, he had certain definite calculations in mind. He already owned almost fifteen acres of coconut grove on the island. They were all young coconut trees, the high-yielding variety. The rest of the land was in the hands of various people who had it from the Paliyam family on lease or else was freehold property. If he dug really hard they would easily come loose and become his. He had made the necessary moves and was now waiting for it to happen. Then there would be Divakara Pai's island on this side, like CR's vast coconut grove island on the other side. That was his dream.

Ramanandan feared that his father's nickname might descend upon him someday. Black Divakara Pai's son would become Black Ramanandan Pai. Black was a colour that spread easily. A colour that would spread through generations.

Though he was two or three years older than Salamon both were in the same class, perhaps because he joined school late. When all the other students were unwilling to sit next to him on the third bench, Salamon sat beside him. 'How can you sit near that muthalali? Doesn't he stink?' Ouso from the island often asked.

Salamon too was conscious of the various odours that surrounded Ramanandan. From his mouth came the smell of garlic, and his farts the stink of rotten eggs. By evening the whiff of stale gingelly oil from his hair was too much to bear. In spite of all this, Salamon became friends with him very quickly. He was more knowledgeable than himself, and had a definite explanation for every doubt. That is why Ramanandan enjoyed flinging certain complicated questions at Salamon and watching him struggle with them.

Once he had asked Salamon which weighed more – one measure iron or one measure cotton. Salamon had burst out laughing. 'Of course iron. Where's the doubt,' he had said.

Ramanandan remained silent for a while, thinking. He then said, 'True, I suppose it can be said that way as well.'

'Fine. Do you know the relative density of iron?'

Salamon stared at his friend. He had heard of it but could not recall.

The next question arrived: 'What about water?'

Salamon had no idea. Therefore, not bothering to ask about gold, Ramanandan gave the answer. 'The relative density of iron is almost eight, water one. From the point of view of density iron weighs more, but if you use a weighing scale both weigh the same.'

That was when Salamon was convinced that physics was beyond his grasp and that he would not become a scientist.

That day Salamon reached Ramanandan's house when the atmosphere there was slightly tense.

Ramanandan was guarding coconut halves that were spread to dry on a woven mat in the yard. Apart from the provision shop at Paliyam nada, Divakara Pai had a small interest in copra trade. He owned enough coconut trees on the island, after all. Exhausted from sitting under the sun and fed up with the cunning crows that managed to get under the net in spite of his vigilance, Ramanandan was in an irritable mood. Also, there was other work to do when watching over the copra was done. Salamon knew what that was without anyone telling him. There was damp rejected rice from the Kottapuram market to be dried, soggy from water seeping into the boat or from getting wet in the rain. Divakara Pai had people to get it for him at a low price. Once the rice was thoroughly dried in the scorching sunlight on the hill-top, third-quality rice became first-quality. Then Ramanandan loaded it into sacks and transported it to the shop. Though Ramanandan repeatedly refused to be part of the deceit, Divakara Pai knew how to tame him into submission.

Ramanandan's needs were few. In fact, he only wanted four annas to go to the cinema hall in Paravur the day a new film was shown. If it was an Anjali Devi film he might watch the first and the second show. He had still not had his fill of the movie *Kanavane Kankanda Deivam*. At first it was just two annas to sit on the floor but later, when he saw his friends sitting on chairs, he complained to his mother that he felt ashamed and somehow managed to get elevated to the four-anna bench.

Ramanandan knew if he loaded one sack and sent it to the shop he could see one show of an Anjali Devi movie; but if he wanted to see the second show as well, he had to coax his mother for more money. Fortunately, the mother, who had never liked either B.S. Saroja or Miss Kumari, was proud of her son's infatuation with the star. Regardless, Divakara Pai was confident in his elder son's compliance. He was not happy with the younger one, Sivanandan, who asked unnecessary questions. Therefore, it was his intention to hand over the shop to his older son after his sixtieth birthday and go on a pilgrimage to Kashi and Rameshwaram.

'Why this unusual arrival, Soloma?'

Though he sounded peevish, Ramanandan placed mirrors on the sides of the net to frighten away the crows and stepped on to the veranda. Fanning himself to dry the sweat on his chest, he let out two long belches, sat down and leaned back comfortably in a wooden easy chair.

'I was going this way, just thought I would come and see you,' Salamon said apologetically, realizing that Ramanandan was busy. 'I forgot that yesterday was market day.'

'That is okay. You come this way so rarely.'

Slowly Salamon began to speak about the dream, about the many doubts he harboured, about the many reverberations … Ramanandan listened intently.

'Say nothing, friend! A terrible dream, it was. The sea, the ship, the sea crows, the whirring sound of the engine … I was terribly frightened. Muthimma says I urinated in bed,' he concluded.

Ramanandan grinned. A coward who got scared on seeing the sea and the ship, and wetted his bed. He himself had done it only once – the night he saw the first and second show of an Anjali Devi film in Paravur Central cinema. He still remembered how his elder sister teased him the next day, saying that he had disclosed his years.

'It was not like the ones we see in books. A gigantic ship. An engine that made a terrible sound,' Salamon described, as though he had actually seen it. A myriad questions appeared on his face.

Ramanandan nodded as though he understood.

'It is the excitement in your street that lies behind the dream, nothing else,' he said. 'After all, that's all that one hears in the land these days, is it not? News of those who have left and those who are hoping to leave. It is not just the land and the trees that you are going to sell at a throwaway price when you board the ship, is it? Copper vessels and pots made of brass, tables, almirahs, and what not! There are people who know what all is to be had from each house.'

So that is what is being said in the village. Salamon sighed. Each one was eyeing the things he could get hold of as soon as the Jews began to leave. Though Ramanandan came up with an explanation, Salamon was not willing to believe it. He never thought about the reverberations in his street.

'You don't have to,' Ramanandan said. 'All those things are there at the bottom of your mind, in the minds of everyone in your street.'

'What are you saying, Ramananda?'

'The desire to go to the other side, just that.'

Salamon had said many times that he had no such desire but Ramanandan behaved as though he had not heard it.

'You all are lucky, you can escape from this cursed land!'

Salamon was stunned. Cursed land! He had never thought of it that way.

Things that had been smouldering within Ramanandan for a long time were gradually emerging.

'In all probability poor Ramanandan is destined to this shop and this trade and the Kottapuram market. In spite of all my longings I have not been able to go beyond Kodakara so far. And I have gone there only because an aunt is married there and because she does not have children. Therefore, for Ramanandan the other side is Kodakara. Sometimes it seems as though the end of Ramanandan's earth is Kodakara. We do not know anything of the world beyond that, do we?'

Earth's end!

That must vary from person to person, Salamon thought. For those who went to Bombay and Madras in early times that was the world's end. Later Rangoon, Penang and Colombo … Now it had spread to Jehovah's land.

Salamon was gradually becoming aware of certain things. Ramanandan was fed up with the business. He was fed up with the land. He wanted to go to some other land, do something else.

'I get quite excited when I hear the tales that the soldiers coming on leave from Punjab and Assam narrate. True, a lot of it may be exaggeration, but they have such diverse experiences!'

But what about the difficulties they face? Salamon recalled the stories Eliacha told them.

As thoughts filled his mind Ramanandan shook his head irritably. Sweat trickled down the creases on his forehead. The furrows were deepening.

'Had a lot of desires. To go to college after the tenth, study and become a chartered accountant, open an office on TD Road. I had even found a suitable name for it. Pai and Pai … The question Divakara Pai asked was, "Then who will look after the shop?" A business that had been in the family from the time of Divakara Pai's father Guna Pai…'

As Ramanandan paused and swallowed the spit in his mouth, the bulge in his thin throat moved up and down sluggishly. 'Do you know, Ramanandan learnt numbers before letters? Instead of the rudimentary words thara, para, I learnt to add and subtract. The struggle with numbers has been going on since then.'

Family business. Salamon thought about it. What Ephraim muthacha told Isaac, what Isaac told Evronappa, what Evronappa told him. What he might say to his son one day.

An unending chain. Was that what inheritance was? Shouldn't someone break that link and get out?

'I have had enough, Soloma!' Ramanandan's voice seemed drenched in sweat. The smell of garlic suddenly became overpowering. 'Divakara Pai is in a hurry to hand over the keys before setting off for Kashi-Rameshwaram.

Apparently, he has even found a girl for me from somewhere in Thuravur. An only child and therefore heir to the shop and the family business. One who can cook and serve ten, thirty people. I suggested that the marriage could wait for a while, but who will listen? Over and above the responsibilities here, Ramanandan will have to take care of the shop in Thuravur as well.'

Salamon could not believe it. True, Ramanandan was three or four years older than him, but was it time to get married?

'Divakara Pai wants to give up all his responsibilities. Then he can go around without a care, attending festivals, seeing Koothu and Kathakali. Even now it is hard to get him in the months of Kumbham and Meenam. He goes off to Trichur, Koodalmanikyam, Arattupuzha and Uthralikavu ... He needs to return only when it is time to pluck coconuts from the trees. If one asks if these are meant for Konkanis, there is no answer.'

Indeed, Salamon had heard it said that the only thing Divakara Pai was fond of was the temple festivities. He always went alone. He carried cooked rice with him so the only expense was the bus fare. Since he had acquaintances everywhere, finding a place to sleep was not a problem.

'Can't you hand over some of the responsibilities to your younger brother Sivanandan?' Salamon asked.

'Oh no!' Ramanandan grimaced. 'Divakara Pai does not trust him. He is not like me. At times he gives as good as he gets. That infuriates the old man.'

As all the bitterness within him began to come out Ramanandan shuddered.

'Shall I ask you something, friend? Can you take me along with you to your Israel?'

'What a foolish thing you are saying! Israel is the land of the Jews.'

'So what! I will become one of you. What do you say?'

'Oh let it be, Ramananda. How can a Brahmin become a Jew?'

'If you had something like the baptism rite of Christians, I would go through with it.'

'Oh stop it, mothalalee!'

'Just you watch. One day I will throw this bunch of keys into the river and plunge in. I don't care where I surface – Madras, Bombay, Burma, wherever … It is only the thought of Amma…'

Salamon tried to change the subject. 'Truth to tell, I have not really thought much about going, Ramananda,' he said quietly.

'What is there to think about?' Ramanandan asked, surprised. 'It's a great opportunity. You should go. Definitely you should go.'

It was late. Salamon did not want to delay Ramanandan's work. He got up. As he walked with him towards the gate Ramanandan placed his hand on Salamon's shoulder, surprising him. As the stench of sweat, stale gingelly oil and garlic hit him, Salamon averted his face.

'Let me tell you something, if you continue in this land, no one will value you. As your Varuthutty master says, here I am just blue black. But if you go to some other place, make money and return, you immediately become important.' There was an unusual resonance in Ramanandan's voice. 'If you remain in the land where you sprouted, you will wilt. It is good to be replanted when you grow a bit. It is true in the case of plants and in the case of people too. You need some time to take root, that is all.'

As he walked northwards without replying, Salamon's thoughts revolved around what Ramanandan had said. Replanting is good for plants and people. Some plants wither if they continue in the land where they sprouted.

Was this the reply he wanted? Salamon did not know.

Kunnumpuram Reacts

The Jews have a country of their own beyond the seas. It has a name and a flag. The people of the land came to know about it only when the Jews hoisted a blue flag in front of the synagogue and ceremonially chanted a few lines in an unfamiliar language. *Kol od balevav penima*…

Later they took out a procession through the main road to the town. Men, women and children took part in the procession, wearing their traditional dress and holding that flag. This is our new birth, they said. The birth of a new nation called Israel, which includes the holy land, Jerusalem. Today evening our president, Ben Gurion, will declare independence through the radio service Kol Israel in Tel Aviv.

The white flag, with blue bands above and below and the Star of David in the centre, had become the pride of a group of people.

Our country. Our flag. Our anthem. Our prime minister …

'What farce is this?' Shambu Namboothiri, a son-in-law of the Paliyam family, could not understand it at all. 'A group of harmless people who went about their sundry businesses quietly, have they too started going around with flags like the communists?'

The bare-chested Nairs who gathered around the banyan

tree near Paliyam nada in the evenings to chat were not pleased either.

'What you say is perfectly true, Thirumeni. How can a new country take shape just like that? Will the white man forgo everything that easily?' That was the doubt expressed by Panicker, the tax collector of Paliyam. As far as the tax-collectors were concerned, the biggest landlords in Kochi were undoubtedly the Paliath achans and the biggest landlord in the world, the white man. Land changed hands only when the landlord gave up a property, isn't it? How could a new country be formed unless the white men gave it away? Was the land around Jerusalem given free of tax? Was it given on lease or as freehold? What could the conditions be? Would there be bare-chested tax collectors there as well, to collect tax for the white men?

Almost everyone had to concede that such a country had been formed.

'That was why they walked about so grandly holding a flag,' K.P. master intervened. 'They did not just take out a procession. Some of them are actually trying to go there.'

'Go? Where?'

'There … Where else?' K.P. master said.

'Shiva! Shiva! What is this I hear! The Jews here leave for another country!' Shambu Namboothiri was trying hard to suppress the belch that was rising within him.

'That is what I heard.'

'Why are they doing something so senseless?'

'They say it is their land, don't they? Apparently they left that land a long time ago.'

'I too had heard something like that, but I did not expect things to happen so quickly,' Namboothiri said, quivering in relief as the gas escaped downwards.

'There was no need for this,' someone said.

Later, the Christians on the islands said the same thing.

'There was no need. They went about with their own concerns, doing no harm to anyone.'

'Besides, they never displayed any of the eccentricities of outsiders,' the Muslims from Anchamparuthy added.

'Though they were reluctant to mix with others they were dependable.' The Ezhavas of Vadakkumpuram, who gathered in Ashan maidan, had no doubts about it.

Surprisingly all the communities in the village were united on that point. They were an okay lot. Why should they go anywhere at all?

The next day the discussion spread to the staffroom of the Paliyam school. What has happened to the Jews all of a sudden? To live in one country, sing the anthem of another country, and take out a procession holding the flag of that country, wasn't that inappropriate? They too sang *Jana gana mana* on every 15 August when the national flag was hoisted in the school compound, didn't they? Will they do that after this? Though there had been rumours floating around, no one had expected anything to happen so fast.

What is the history behind it?

Mani Menon master, who taught arithmetic, knew something about it. He went through every bit of news in The *Hindu*.

Krishna Menon master, who taught history, knew even more since history was his favourite subject.

Meanwhile, everyone gathered around Moses master, the part-time Hebrew teacher in the school.

'It is true,' Moses master said. He looked faintly embarrassed.

Though he tried to withdraw without saying anything

further Mani Menon did not let him go. Many wanted to know where this new country was, and how it had been formed. By that time someone went to the headmaster's office and brought the globe and the large map that hung on the wall.

Mani Menon twirled the globe with his index finger and looked at Moses master, his eyes brimming with mischief.

'Your country must appear somewhere on this, isn't that so, master?'

'Of course.'

'Then show us where it is?'

'That … that…' Moses master was in a quandary. Truth to tell, he had no idea where the new country, Israel, was located.

'Is it possible that it is not on the globe?'Ambujakshi teacher joined in.

'But how can I say when the globe is round like this?'

'Master, how do you think the earth is flat, not round? Okay, never mind that.' Mani Menon spread the world map on the table and asked, 'You can see the whole world clearly on this map. Tell us where Israel is.'

Moses master was at a loss. The atlas based itself on topography, and topography was the source of the atlas. Every teacher knew that tiny little fact. That was why teachers who taught geography took the rolled up map with them to class. Sturdy nails were hammered into the walls of each classroom to hang it on. If anyone stood up to ask a question about a country the teacher used his cane to indicate the place.

In that case, there should be an Israel also at the end of the cane, should there not?

Moses master broke into a sweat. It would be a disgrace if he did not say something. If those who had celebrated the birth of Israel could not point out where it was…

'It is … a lot of land around Jerusalem, with hills and mountains and deserts.' Master tried to find a way out.

'But where is it – that is what we want to know.' Mani Menon was not willing to let go.

Thus, screwing his spectacles firmly into place, Moses master stared, searching for the town of Jerusalem on that huge map. The map lay like a many-coloured expanse. Where among those colours was his holy land hiding? Master's gaze became hazy. His eyes were tired. The glasses became moist. The holy land that had appeared so clearly in his dreams all this while, was it now finally distancing itself from him?

Seeing Moses master's gaze flit towards the wrong corners, Krishna Menon master felt sorry for him and intervened. Pointing to a black spot he said, 'Isn't this your Jerusalem, master?'

'Yes, yes.' Relieved, Moses master ran his finger over the map and added, 'Here on this side and that side, here, and there…'

'What this side and that side, here and there?' Mani Menon asked, putting the heat on him. 'Shouldn't a country have definite borders? What are they, that is what I asked.'

Gentle Krishna Menon master once again came to Moses master's rescue: 'Leave it, master, it is an old map.'

In the relief of having found a way out, Moses master declared, 'The new Oxford atlas is being drawn. When it is printed you will see our country, in a different colour. One day we will get on board an aeroplane and leave, then you will see.'

'Where?' Ambujakshi teacher asked.

'There, of course.'

'Oh yes, yes!'

There was an outburst of laughter. It began with Mani Menon and spread through the room. Moses master went out, bewildered by the manner in which a great dream had been rendered meaningless.

The bell rang. It was interval. Master moved towards the nearby paddy field in the hope of getting hold of at least a few of the students who had eluded his eye and had gone off to play.

Just as they knew the land, the land too knew them.

With the tenderness of a mother, with innumerable memories, the soil remembered the time they came, the wretched state in which they had been. For the travellers who were exhausted by their wanderings, the land offered shelter at first, then a transit point. Slowly, the breeze of this land became a source of solace, the water elixir. Thus a people whose feet were constantly on the move found a firm hold on this land. Grew roots. And those roots, they grew deep into the soil, unknown to anyone.

A people who had learnt to live without growing close or distant, without becoming friends or foes, remained in the background always, content to row with the current, and thus confined their world within the boundaries of a street. As for those boundaries, they were their armour of sanctity as well.

Then why suddenly this journey in search of salvation?

Why? The land asked. The people asked.

Though the same question was reverberating within them as well, the Jews were reluctant to admit it.

When the Panchayat met, the question echoed there as well. As usual Evron sat leaning against the wall in the veranda, listening to the arguments going on inside the office. It was then that the president sent word for him to come in.

'You at least explain to us, member, what is behind this sudden excitement?'

Though bewildered at first, the member who was not a member tried to be non-committal.

'All that is a matter of faith, isn't it, president!'

'We cannot make out this pointless fervour, that is all.' Shambu Namboothiri belched loudly.

'How do you know it is pointless, Thirumeni?' Comrade Kamalan intervened. 'Do you think they would show so much fervour if they did not see something to their advantage in it? Am I not right, Evron Sa'ib?'

'What advantage can there be in this?' Evron asked irritably.

'Then you tell us, member. Tell the truth.'

Once again Evron was in a predicament. What was the advantage in selling, at a throwaway price, everything that had been acquired through generations, and leaving with just what they could take for a land across the sea? Rumours abounded; what the muliyar in the synagogue said, what the Paradesi Jews in Mattancherry said, what Elias had learnt from his reading…

Where was the truth?

Elias often said, 'We are going there to suffer. Keep that in mind when you make plans.'

Evron did not argue with that. The history of the Jews was one of suffering. Challenges were not new to a people who got scattered when their blood was spilt, from the time of the Roman emperors to Hitler. But these people would not understand if he said all that. So he said quietly, 'We are not going there looking for gain. We will have to manage somehow, like we do here. But to be able to say that it is one's own land, that is a matter of pride, isn't that so?'

'So this is not your own land?'

'Of course, yes,' Evron said, scratching his head with the wooden ruler.

'We know, we know...' There was a note of sarcasm in Kamalan's voice. 'We have seen this before. Food here, loyalty there.'

The president knew the reason for Kamalan's ire. Evron did too. The day Israel got independence the Jews had taken out a procession in Chendamangalam and Paravur. Holding the blue flag, they gathered around the radio shops in the town to listen to Israeli Radio's broadcast of Ben Gurion's Declaration of Independence ... mechanic Luka having tried and failed to bring their dead radios to life ... Unlike Pavithran, Kamalan who had won the election from the third ward was an obstinate man. Even otherwise, it was inappropriate for the citizens of a country to take out a march carrying the flag of another country. Apparently the Jews had a radio of their own to listen to for news that could not be got in this country. What must they be saying in their language? Suppose the Jews tried to spy for their country?

During all that time Evron had one solace.

There is a belief that every Jew across the world holds close to his heart – the belief that someday almighty God will surely call his people back to their holy land, Israel. For that reason, when they celebrate Passover every year and read the holy Haggadah, the Hebrew words they utter – 'bashana haba'ah' Yerushalayim' – come from the heart. That is, 'the next year in Jerusalem...'

The saying from the holy Haggadah, handed down by the Jews through generations, commemorated their escape from slavery in Egypt. In a way it was both a reminder for coming generations and an attempt to assure themselves that they would be able to set foot on that sanctified soil in their lifetime. It was a matter of faith. There was no space for queries or counter queries.

'Hope you won't be forced to return.' Sarcasm tinged Kamalan's voice. 'You might go in style by plane only to return on foot. Like Daniel master from Paravur.'

Daniel master, who taught in a Paravur school, began to dream of going to Israel long before that country took shape. When after years of teaching, history and geography filled his head and the line between hearsay and facts became blurred, Daniel master was at first bemused. Later he began to prepare for that journey. The desire to be the first to set foot in the holy land. Not as an immigrant, as a mere pilgrim. Thus, when Daniel master and his friend, both of whom did not have families or other responsibilities, went to Calcutta to board the ship, they had made all the necessary preparations for the journey – a suit, cap, woollen clothes for the winter, dry bread, water…

They wandered around the streets of Calcutta for four or five days, armed with the addresses they had procured from somewhere. But their search proved futile. The money they had reserved to pay for the voyage was dwindling by the day. At the same time it would be a disgrace to return. They were wondering how to go on when the war broke out. That gave them an excuse to return. Were not all the whites in the world engaged in the war? Until the war ended, will there be any ship on sail?

Kamalan was reminding him of that Daniel master's story. Evron felt a sudden surge of anger.

'This is not like taking people to party meetings, comrade,' he hit back. 'Those who go and those who take them know how it should be done.'

'Yes, yes.' Kamalan could not stop grinning.

'Let it go, member.' The president tried to calm Evron. 'Tell me, does this mean none of you will return?'

'Who knows, president, it is about people, after all.'

'So does that mean everyone is willing to go?' someone asked.

'That is what I heard.'

A great silence spread over the gathered people. Everyone had something to remember. A people who had been there for generations, whom they had seen as they grew up, were about to disappear all of a sudden ... There was no surety that they would see them again. Even if they did meet after several years, they would have to reintroduce themselves to one another, search for words to talk...

In the meantime, Evron left the room quietly. He made his way through the people waiting for the meeting to end and walked out into the yard. Somehow he did not feel like remaining there any more. Something was churning inside him. Generally he sat on the Panchayat veranda till it was time for lunch. He would be surrounded by people who came for various things. Both acquaintances and strangers. They trusted him more than they did the actual members.

Elias was also in the veranda when Evron reached home. Seeing the disquiet on Evron's face he asked what had happened. But when Evron climbed the stairs without saying a word and lay back in the armchair in the veranda, Elias withdrew.

Evron was conscious of many things frothing up within him, things that had not been there before.

Why did they ask such disturbing questions to a people who stood wound taut by a hope, the purpose of which they did not know. Though they claimed that it was intimacy that prompted them, every word they uttered seemed to have a barb lurking within it. After all these years, for the first time the realization that they were outsiders was growing stronger within him.

Perhaps this is how the leader of the Jews in Kochi, Salem Kocha, must have undergone a change of heart. Salem Kocha, who was a true nationalist, had stayed aloof at first, without any show of interest, but later came forward, as though strengthened by some inner call, to aid the great departure. Even though he himself did not leave, he recognized that as far as the ordinary Jews were concerned, such a migration was unavoidable. And he worked hard to make it a reality.

Surely such a desire must have lain latent in at least some hearts, even before Eliahu Meir began to bring such news from Bangalore? The desire to step on the soil in Jerusalem, of which they had heard so much, at least in the form of a pilgrim. But the idea of permanent migration to a land they had never seen must have been beyond their imaginings.

Then, as things began to move forward gradually, desires grew wings. No one had to tell anyone anything. The decisions that took shape within the walls of every house in Jew Street had a clarity. As each one began to weave dreams around that decision, the desert they had never seen blossomed within them. In the sweetness of its fruits they realized a new bliss.

A sigh arose from somewhere.

Evron was not sure whether it arose from him.

The Corner Beneath
the Stairs

Kadavathu Aachi's double-storey mansion stood on the banks of the river. Gold and money that one could not lift, coconut groves and paddy fields across the land, dependants all around her; her husband, he had left long ago. The inheritor of all that wealth was the one sole daughter, a beautiful girl. Beautiful both to the eye and the ear. Several eminent suitors came hoping to take her hand in marriage but Kadavathu Aachi turned her back on them.

'Who in this town is worthy of my daughter's hand, tell me, girls?' she challenged her female attendants.

'No one, Umma. There is none,' the servants submitted.

'Then listen, one day one such lord will come from afar on horseback, riding down the hills, crossing the river...' she said.

Hearing her umma's words the daughter too waited, for the prince who would come riding a horse, faster than the wind.

That wait went on interminably...

Thus, several seasons of summer, rain and winter went by, tumbling over one another. The daughter, who had begun to lose heart, started to direct harsh questions at her mother. It was then that it happened.

Instead of the prince who should have arrived on horseback, it was the local chieftain who was well into middle age who arrived in a palanquin. He, who had many a time watched, half-hidden by thickly growing bushes, the pretty girl bathing with her friends at the bathing place in the river, went back with unbearable yearning. He wanted the virgin. Wanted her quickly. Kadavathu Aachi's daughter should live, not in a mansion, but in the palace. She should bathe, not in the open bathing ghat, but in the large pond inside the palace precincts.

Thus, a messenger went to Kadavathu Aachi's place.

Aachi on her part was unmoved. She scornfully spat out the remnants of the tobacco and betel she had been chewing and snarled, 'Young girls should live in well-ventilated homes, not in walled-in palaces; should bathe in flowing rivers, not in stagnant pools…'

Hearing this the chieftain, who had grown faint with ardour, boiled over with fury. 'Is that Jewish woman that arrogant?'

Immediately he sent an order: two days from now the girl should reach the palace before nightfall, or else. Recognizing the threat, Jew Street immediately packed its bundles and fled in all directions. When it was midnight, the ones who had hidden among the thick bushes by the river saw fire flare up and spread far away behind them. It was their street. It was their synagogue. As the tongues of flame spread to the accompaniment of the howl of foxes they entered the waters. They swam swiftly to the opposite shore. There were strong young men in their group who carried the ones who did not know how to swim on their backs.

'That was how we Jews migrated from Kodungallur,' binder Daveed chettan said. 'Since then no Jew who goes to Kodungallur remains there after dark. The night there is dangerous for Jews. I myself started a shop there when I came from Pandinadu. And what happened? I had to close it down in the third month … This is not the only one. There are other stories as well, you know.'

Another hard-to-believe story. Salamon felt like laughing.

Daveed chettan's place in Paravur town was four shops away from P.C.'s textile shop, in the landing beneath the spiral stairway that led to the upper floor. He spent his days in that damp and dark corner separating, with infinite tenderness, the dilapidated, moth-eaten pages of books that had changed hands several times, finding missing pages, putting them in order and stitching them together … the thoughts, the dreams of some writer.

A grizzled yet luxurious beard; faded kipa, the dome shaped cap, pulled down in front; a long, dirty tunic torn in several places; a face with more wrinkles than his tunic and red from sunburn.

Binder Daveed chettan himself could not recall at what point of time he had arrived at that tiny, square space beneath the stairs where neither wind nor sunlight nor rain could reach. When he left his reasonably well off ancestral home in Mala, as well as his homeland – after quarrelling with the elders and severing all ties with everyone – Daveed was a young lad. Later he travelled through several lands, saw several kingdoms and finally, when he retreated into the space beneath the stairway, all that remained on his lips was a parched smile.

A demeanour that seemed to say, ultimately everything comes to this: this place beneath the stairs. This damp and grey gloom. This bulb above the head that gave out dim light.

That was all that he had to say to Salamon as well. A

friendship that began when Salamon worked in P.C.'s shop.
Neither of them thought it would last this long. The like-
mindedness that they felt at first sight at their first meeting,
the affinity, often brought Salamon to the corner beneath
the stairs.

'Do not plan too far ahead … nothing is in our hands,'
Daveed chettan cautioned.

During the days when Salamon went about aimlessly,
thereby becoming cause for Evronappa's anxiety, Daveed
chettan would comfort him. Though he went to the synagogue
and believed in God, Daveed chettan was convinced that
our fates were not in the hands of gods. The days of our life
lie scattered like the faded, odd-sized pages that customers
bring him. Even as we desperately attempt to put those
pages, scattered by time and human hands, in order, the
flame of our life burns out.

'Some stringing together, some stitching together … is
this not what our lives are, mone?' he once said, stroking
his beard. 'If looked at that way, you, me, everyone in this
world is a binder, isn't that so? This attempt to match the
right things, is it that easy? It is all wishful thinking, isn't it?'

Nature is the greatest binder, he said another day. There
is so much cutting and pasting together that we are unaware
of. As it takes up the land and sea and plays with them, the
contours of continents change, rivers change their course…
As old landforms disappear new ones come up. Tell me, is
there a greater rhythm than the rhythm of nature? When
that rhythm goes awry, when nature explodes in fury, we
call it a natural disaster. Earthquakes, floods, the churning
of the seas, deadly diseases … so many things.

It took many more years for Salamon to understand the
significance of Daveed chettan's words.

'Many people hold me in contempt,' he had once said. 'Old acquaintances often ask, "You wandered around many lands, did you not get a chance to learn any other work? Something more dignified…?"'

True, he had learnt many other things during his wanderings. It was in a printing press in Pandinadu that he learnt to bind books. At first he was disgusted by the work, which involved crouching on the dirty floor, but later it began to fascinate him. The books he got in the beginning were new ones. Then, as different types of paper began to pile up in front of him, he was bewildered by pages that bore the fingerprints of time, that had the scent of mould, pages that had been thoughtlessly thrown away.

When Daveed demurred, Munuswamy who taught him binding said, 'Do not talk in that manner.' He gathered the pages Daveed had discarded and pressed them to his eyes.

'These pages are like God. There is nothing new or old about them. Everything is the same, and in a way, the older ones are better.'

Those words of Munuswamy's became the lesson Daveed chettan remembered for the rest of his life. Those who shape books are like God. There is nothing old or new among them. At times the older ones are better.

From that day on, whatever book he got, he first bowed before it, pressed it to his eyes in prayer and only then started to work on it. Thus, in a way Munuswamy became Daveed chettan's guru swamy.

Only one of Daveed chettan's eyes had sight. 'For this work of mine one eye is more than sufficient,' he often said. Even in that dim light he did not need help to thread a needle. The right eye had not lost its power even at this age. However chettan had greater affection for his left eye, which had been rendered sightless by the many sights seen during his endless wanderings. After all, it bore the weight of a lifetime of experiences, did it not?

The only regret he had was about the rare sights that had been trapped in the lightless left eye. Would he ever be able to regain them?

When Daveed picked up the pages of a book barely visible in the dim light of the bulb that hung above his head, he never looked at the letters. They were not his responsibility. All he needed were the numbers inscribed at the top or bottom of the page. It was through the coordination of these numbers that the pages blended harmoniously. That was the binder's fate as well.

'What if some of the pages are missing? Or if pages appear in between those with faded numbers?'

When he heard Salamon's cheeky question, Daveed chettan lifted his decorated checked peak cap, wiped the sweat on his forehead and smiled.

'That is the binder's fate, mone.' He sighed. 'It could be that that page is the most important one. We do not know the pangs of the one who wrote it or of the ones who read it. Sometimes I feel that we do not realize the value of the life of the one we bind. That is exactly what that Munuswamy said that day.'

He thus said many things without actually saying them.

The search for missing pages, the tiring work that it involved, the thrill of locating them, the understanding of the human predicament that is made possible through the coordination of pages...

It took much persuasion for Daveed chettan to reveal that he had once lived just three houses away from Eshimuthimma's home in Mala. That the distance of three houses grew into one of thirty was admitted with great reluctance. Finally, when it slipped out that they had been classmates and went to school together, Daveed chettan stopped his narrative abruptly.

'That's enough, Soloma. Who are you, a detective? Sherlock Holmes?'

Later, when Salamon approached Eshimuthimma to fill in the blanks of the story, she too hesitated at first.

'Those are old stories, mone. Why bring them up now?'

Why was Muthimma, who loved to slip back into the colourful memories of the old grandeur at Mala, trying to avoid this subject?

That aroused Salamon's interest.

'Truth to tell, mone, among us Malabari Jews, Mala Jews are superior,' Muthimma said. 'The old saying goes that anyone born to a Jewish mother is a Jew. But when caste and other prejudices began to surface among us Jews as well, the Jews from Mala alone stood together as a separate group. That was how a synagogue was built in Mala.'

Seeing Muthimma slide into well-worn tracks Salamon tried to reroute her.

'Muthimma, Daveed chettan!' he reminded her.

'Why, is he still alive?'

'Yes, Muthimma, in the town.'

'After he left the village at a young age there was no news of him. I heard that he fell ill somewhere in Pandinadu and died.'

'Nothing like that. He is still here. With a peak cap and a luxuriant beard. In a corner beneath the stairs of a two-storeyed building. He binds books.'

'Why a corner beneath the stairs? Doesn't he have a home or family?'

'He lives alone in a room near the synagogue.'

'Why? Didn't he marry?'

'I don't think so.'

'Oh God ... He was so handsome!'

The handsome Daveed of old now sitting in the corner beneath the stairs and binding old worn-out books!

Muthimma sat leaning against a pillar in the kitchen veranda, stunned. Salamon had no clue what was going through her mind. She was remembering, trying to recapture the brilliantly hued past.

'All that was a long time ago, mone.' She sighed.

'A childhood full of play, laughter and loud noise ... had a lot of friends, both boys and girls. As I was the longed – for eldest daughter, I was cosseted by the elders of the family. I played and went around mostly with boys. Once the holidays began, I would not sit in the house ... I would be in someone's grounds, yard, kitchen or on the branch of some cashew tree.'

Finally, she came to Daveed. But only when Salamon prodded her.

'Though they did not have much money their people were members of the synagogue committee. He was an impudent fellow. Though good at studies and games, he was the type who heeded no one ... impulsively got into fights. Handsome to look at. When he returned after playing ball his face would look flushed. In school he was always surrounded by girls. We all called him chongan.'

'And?'

'He was not wise. Though he had the means he did not go to college after the tenth; just idled around with friends. He had two younger sisters to marry off. This led to arguments and altercations with his family.'

'And?' Salamon asked avidly. Eshimuthimma became slightly more enthusiastic.

'And what? I do not know what happened after the quarrels began. By then Muthimma was married off.'

Eshimuthimma did not say when the distance between the three houses became that of thirty. Salamon did not ask her either. Later it was from Daveed chettan's tongue that he gathered certain bits of information.

Like Muthimma, Daveed chettan was reluctant to talk about the past. When Salamon reminded him of his nickname, chongan, the furrows on his face deepened. His beedi-stained teeth became visible in the gap in his grizzled beard.

'So she hasn't forgotten that!' Daveed chettan removed his cap several times and wiped his head with it, as though he could not believe it. Running his fingers through the remaining hair, he said, 'There's nothing to say, eda. She was a terribly self-willed girl! The colour of gold and just the right height. As bold and proud as a full-grown man. They should not have got her married that early. That too a totally unsuitable alliance. A girl who made people stare, such was her presence! And the one who married her – a dark, thickset Jew. And he looked a lot older. She wept and pleaded, saying she did not want to marry him. And what? The elders were enamoured by his wealth and grandeur. The wedding was a pompous affair, but did the man know anything beyond trade? A self-willed miser. She was like one confined in that house, wasn't she? Poor Eshu, she must have grieved a lot at that time!'

That is Daveed chettan's envy, thought Salamon. Muthimma loved Isaac muthacha dearly. It was mutual. Eliacha often said that it was after Muthacha's death that she became so thin. Even now the very mention of Muthacha saddened her.

'All he needed to do was carry on the business, which his ancestors had begun, properly. They could have lived comfortably. But that was not enough for the man. The more he got, the greater became his greed. That was how for the first time the business of pawning gold began in Kunnumpuram. A totally heartless transaction. Of those who came to pawn their gold, most were poor. The interest was very high. Shouldn't he have thought that when the interest mounted and the forfeited gold slid into his hands, the curses of all those people would fall on the entire family? A boorish, Shylock-like man!' Daveed chettan had several other things to say about Isaac Muthacha.

'It was the time of the Great Floods of the twenties. A time when the town and all the land around it lay submerged in the floodwaters. The only places that remained above water were the Kottayil Kovilakam hillock and its slopes. When people boarded boats of all sizes like ants clinging to leaves, and took refuge on the hill and the surrounding slopes, the entire place turned into a refugee camp.

'As people waited for the floodwaters to recede, they brought all the rice and provisions they had; cooked, ate and drank together, unmindful of social differences. The one person who very cleverly stayed away was your muthacha. You know why? To sell his stock at double the price when the water subsided.'

Though the cruelty in that voice hurt Salamon terribly, Daveed chettan was not about to stop.

'And what happened? Didn't the very next flood take him? That too right into the Arabian Sea ... the wind and the water are more truthful than the gods. Even if people forget the gods, they should not forget the fury of nature.'

Daveed chettan chuckled, remembering. It was as though

he was enjoying it. Perhaps he was trying to imagine the last word that the traveller called out as he and his boat swirled in the whirlpool near Palathuruthu and sank.

That day for the first time the corner beneath the stairs and the old man who had sat there for years and grown roots filled Salamon with intense hatred.

Later he recalled that what Eshimuthimma had narrated was the very opposite of this. Was it not the Isaac family that came forward to help the local folk during the flood of the twenties?

'Did he not empty all the rice bags brought from the Kottapuram market over there?'

Salamon did not try to find out which version was the true one. If Muthimma swelled up with pride whenever she spoke of Isaac, Daveed chettan seemed bent on denigrating him.

Gradually Daveed chettan's corner beneath the stairs became Salamon's haven whenever he went to the town. If Daveed chettan did not see him for several days he would ask, complainingly, 'What is this, Soloma? Can't you come at least once in a while to see if this old man is still alive? Even if I lie dying here no one on your hilltop will know. Fact is, though I have some friends there, I never go to see them. They do not come to see me either.'

True. Only a few people knew that the lone room next to the synagogue was occupied – the boy who came to sweep the synagogue, a few old men who came to pray and the muliyar in the synagogue.

'I plan to visit one day.' When Salamon said this Daveed chettan stopped him.

'No, don't. Everything is a mess over there. You will feel like vomiting.'

'That does not matter. It's not new to me.'

'No,' Daveed chettan said with unusual vehemence, 'I do not like anyone coming to my place. I am so used to being alone that I become uncomfortable when someone comes.'

'What about cooking and eating?'

'I have a stove, kerosene, rice and things. Sometimes I go hungry. Sometimes I boil something to eat. You may say that Daveed chettan mostly prefers to eat things raw. So I eat some fruit or vegetable. And, of course, there is a clay pot full of water. The taste of that water is something special.'

'What about fasting?'

'Fasting? What fasting?' Daveed chettan laughed.

Salamon could not understand that lifestyle. Daveed chettan was not eager for anyone to understand it either.

One's Own People

Chit Fund Veroni. Veroni's husband Devassy mapla, their daughter, Our Elsie. The younger one, Mincent.

The name that the mother fondly bestowed on her daughter was Elsie. Her father, on the other hand, always called her Lucy. Later, as the number of Elsies in Kizhakkumpuram and its surrounding areas increased, Veroni began to call her 'Our Elsie'. Over the years it became her pet name, and for Salamon it became a term to be used playfully. Our Elsie!

When Devassy mapla had gone to help fix the new thatched roof of the Kunnel house, a wooden beam broke and he fell. That is how he became a cripple. For a long time now he has been sitting in the veranda, leaning against a pillar. The parish priest Pathros achan firmly believed that it was Veroni's devout prayer and God's prompt response that had led to Devassy's fall. She had got disgusted with Devassy, who spent his evenings on the bench in the arrack shop. When the threat that Chathedam Thupran's arrack would scorch his intestines did not work, she first took Devassy to the altar by force and then made him take an oath. Though Devassy was not familiar with parish sermons, he gave in when wife and daughter put their arms around him and held him. Do not drink arrack; have toddy instead, that was the compromise the priest suggested. But three days later Devassy mapla reappeared on the old bench in the arrack shop. The bench with unsteady legs.

Thus, as a last resort, Veroni climbed the Malayattoor hill and lit a candle in the church.

'Still, what you did was an extreme step, Veroni.' Pathros achan expressed his regret when he heard the news.

'But Veroni only prayed that he should remain at home. I did not say that he should fall from the Kunnel rooftop.'

Due to someone's grace all he broke was his leg. If anything had happened to his spine or chest he would have become bedridden for the rest of his life.

That is how Devassy mapla came to sit in the veranda till he gradually put down roots. Though he could limp about in the yard with the help of a stick he considered it a disgrace to do it in front of others.

And the nicknames for the members of the family increased – irikkana devassi, Devassy who sits, nadakkana veroni, Veroni who roams, and of course Our Elsie and Mincent…

Apart from doing domestic work inside her house and outside, in two Nair households, Veroni undertook weaving palm frond panels and making vellappam. But her heart was in the chit fund business. Her elder sister, who was married off in Thuruthipuram, had introduced her to it. The sister used to keep telling her that the contacts made through the business would come to one's aid if the need arose. A few misunderstandings and arguments had occurred at the start, but by the time four church feasts had gone by everyone trusted Chit Fund Veroni.

Soon her member list grew. The types of chit funds increased. Most of them were weekly and monthly chits. When she started a daily chit fund, she had the weavers in Karimpadam, who received daily wages, in mind. When their payments became irregular, other daily wagers who did not have too many daily expenses – like toddy tappers, masons and carpenters – became her major customers. But once it was evening they would invariably go to some toddy shop or other. As Veroni did not know who went where she conducted the transactions with their women.

Though it was Elsie who managed the accounts, Veroni had begun to get tired of the never-ending running around that began at daybreak. She was waiting for the chit funds she had started to come one full round before she could quit work in the two Nair households and the sundry other jobs she had taken on. She had already given her word to the Virgin Mary at Velankanni that she would marry off Elsie to some prominent chit family in Trichur. After all, the Syrian Christians in Trichur were the ones who had introduced chit funds to the world. Though there were very few Latin Christians there, some boys might be willing to come over to this side when they saw the girl, so Veroni hoped. *She had the colour and elegance of gold, didn't she? If she went to attend the feast at Puthen church or Kuriyachira church would anyone say she was not a Syrian Christian?*

'If you wait for all your numerous chit funds to complete one round the girl will grow so big she will break through the roof. Wandering around the land, trying to get the entire population to subscribe, isn't that what you do?' Veroni did not believe she should pay heed to the words that emerged through beedi smoke from the veranda. At such times Devassy mapla was just a puff of smoke voiceless ... And she had a justification for it.

'In a family one should listen only to what one needs to

hear. It is when you listen to unnecessary things that you becomes distressed.'

For a long time now, Elsie too had stopped listening to her father. Only the words of her ammachi, who worked hard from dawn to dusk, mattered to her. And that is why even when her father said something excessively harsh she could walk off breezily, unmindful of it.

Devassy mapla got to know what was happening in the village through Salamon, who went there occasionally. So when Devassy mapla said he had not heard that the priests had started a resistance movement, the Vimochana Samaram against the communists, Salamon was surprised.

The whole land was in turmoil and this Christian alone did not know about it? Was it a small thing if bishops and nuns stepped out into the streets and organized protests? They claimed they were trying to liberate the country from the communists, didn't they?

'How long do you think it has been since I saw the threshold of the toddy shop?'

That was a reasonable response, thought Salamon. The toddy shop was the right place to know what was going on in the world. However, you would get some news about it when you went to church?

'Well, how long do you think I have been sitting like this?' Devassy grimaced, running his nails through the dandruff caked on his head. 'How can I, who never entered the church when I was whole, go and attend mass now, leaning on a stick?'

Salamon nodded. Devassy mapla was the kind who said things bluntly. If you wanted to know what was happening in the village you had to go to church and attend mass or to the toddy shop.

Devassy mapla often thought that, in a way, the younger one, Mincent, was blessed. None of these problems reached his ears!

Every time Salamon crossed the threshold of Devassy mapla's home, he knew that Mincent was somewhere inside the house. But he never looked in that direction. After all, Devassy mapla would be waiting in the front veranda, his eyes fixed on the road, eager to hear all the tantalizing bits of village gossip.

Mincent's sister Elsie did not know how the fondly chosen name Vincent became Mincent. Neither did Veroni, who gave birth to him. However, Mincent had learnt a long time ago to answer Elsie's long-drawn-out 'Vincenteee' with an equally long 'whaaaaat' in the same tone.

Though Mincent's bones had attained the growth of a ten- or twelve-year-old, he had never gone to school. Not because he did not want to. But because he could not be exposed to sunlight. If he went out his body would turn blue, as though he had been poisoned. It would be a many hued blue, depending on the intensity of the rays. Though Salamon had never seen him in that blue state he knew more or less how it looked, from Elsie's words.

'My Soloma, my ammachi has knocked at the doors of so many vaidyars carrying the blue-hued child on her shoulder.'

At times Salamon heard a peevish Devassy mapla curse him.

'It is when this Hindu god was born into our house that all the misfortunes began.'

How Mincent could become a Hindu god, Veroni did not know. But was there anyone who did not know that her husband fell from the Kunnel people's rooftop and was reduced to sitting in the veranda because of his own fault?

Just because it happened on the seventh day after Mincent's birth, was it right to blame him? Besides, the bluish hue had nothing to do with the skin – it was some deficiency in his blood. She distinctly remembered Anthappai vaidyar from Kottuli telling her this with certainty during the ceremonial feast at the Vallarpadam church. A long period of treatment was required for the disease to be cured, he had said, with ayurvedic concoctions and massage oils. This required a lot of money.

'You tell me, Chedathimare, does this Veroni have the means for all that?' As usual, Veroni bared her problems to the women in the neighbourhood. 'Don't you see the lone male support in the family sitting and smoking in the veranda, turning the beams black? There is only this Chitty Veroni to wander all over the land and struggle to feed the family!'

As usual, the neighbours stood, forefinger on nose, and listened to it all, knowing well that there was nothing they could say, and so confined themselves to some sympathetic noises. They knew that for a straight path to open up before this family Elsie had to study hard and start earning some money. But so many more years had to go by before that happened!

Whenever Sumana teacher, who had taught her in the third standard, hinted that she wanted to see the blue-skinned god and bow before him, Elsie felt a slight annoyance but she did not show it. 'What if he has not seen daylight or the school, my mon is smart!' She said this with the vehemence of two generations.

At first, Salamon hesitated to make friends with Mincent, who sat rocking and humming to himself in the inner room. Though Mincent grinned, revealing all his teeth when he saw Salamon, and beckoned to him to enter, Salamon felt something holding him back. Was it disgust, pity or lack of understanding that made him hesitate? Salamon did not know. Perhaps it was because of the bundle of complaints that the father held against the son he had longed to have.

If he starts eating he goes on eating, if he sleeps he sleeps on and on, if he starts crying … There were several such irritants and the father did not know their beginning or their end. A life trapped in the pointlessness between beginning and end.

'Curse the hunger and curse the sleep.' It was his father who cursed him.

Salamon knew that if there was no humming when he entered the veranda, Mincent was either eating or sleeping.

At first they thought he was mentally deficient but that was not the truth.

'My mon is too intelligent. That is his problem,' Elsie observed with great tenderness. 'The ashan just taught him to trace the alphabets on the sandy floor. And then? He slyly gets hold of Elsie's books and reads them. Some of it he remembers and disturbs Elsie by asking uncomfortable questions.'

Elsie was certain that someday he would be cured, and doubly strong, he would have the world at his feet. Mother Mary was her witness when Anthappai vaidyar had asserted that such miracles happened at the Vallarpadam church.

'These diseases follow their own path, Veroni. They come and go even without the knowledge of the Lord, our maker,' he had said.

'It is a princely birth, Soloma, isn't that what the blue blood signifies?' Elsie often said. 'Besides, a divine birth is always in a thatched shed, isn't it?'

Salamon maintained a neutral silence because he too had begun to feel that there was something hidden within Mincent, something no one had deciphered yet. He had once asked playfully, 'What is the colour of the sky, Mincent?'

'Blue.'

'You mean…'

'Many blues … ten, sixteen blues.' Sixteen blues within one blue.

That answer really stumped Salamon, who longed to understand the fullness of colours. Like the drawing master Appu Menon said, there were so many layers within a single colour, and Mincent had the inner eye with which to see them. That was when he realized that Mincent was special.

Mincent's vocabulary was limited but the few words he had tamed stood submissively before him. From these he would select a few that suited his tongue, sharpened them to a point and aimed the shafts. No wonder he astounded those who heard them.

'Why need many? What he has is enough. His words are like shafts with multiple points,' Salamon had often heard Devassy mapla mutter.

'What is wrong with this, Appa?' Elsie would say in a low voice. 'Can't he leave the child alone instead of provoking him?'

Over the few days following Salamon's visit Devassy felt his heart lighten. When it was time for Salamon to leave and he asked for the matchbox to light the bundle of coconut sheaves to use as a torch, Devassy mapla would pat him on the back and remind him, 'Come this way once in a while, Soloma. It is good to hear your voice.'

Each time Salamon nodded and tried to smile. He would also turn to see if Elsie was near enough to hear.

'A respectful boy. So what if he is a Jew? He is loyal,' Devassy often remarked.

As usual, Veroni did not hear it; but Elsie heard it and savoured it.

There was a time when the same Devassy mapla's voice had been listened to with great attention by the locals as well as the family.

At that time Devassy was the most loyal assistant to Adrumman from Kondotti, who was a wholesale dealer in the Kottapuram market. In those days the majority of the traders in the market were Christians except for a few Konkani and Muslim ones. Adrumman trusted Devassy, who had been with him from the start. To unload and store the goods that came from the north in huge boats, tally the accounts, keep each item separately, send them at regular intervals in boats and push carts to the retail shops in the town according to their requirements involved trust.

Adrumman had only one firm reply for all those who raised questions about the ties between Devassy, who could not stay away from his nightly intake in the arrack shop, and Adrumman, who kept all that was taboo at arm's length.

'He is a true Christian. He might destroy his heart, but he will not cheat. He is better than our people.'

Later when the cunning second assistant, Moideen from Mamburam, began to whisper things in Adrumman's ear and the latter began to teeter, Devassy could only look on helplessly. By that time Adrumman, who had crawled into the Kottapuram market a long time ago as a scraggy immigrant, had become Adrumman Haji, a man with an impressive pot-belly who wore silk shirts and gold chains. He had a lot of assets; three elephants to pull logs in the timber yard and adorn the front yard, three beautiful wives in three lands, and sycophants on all four sides to listen, respond and nod suitably.

Though at first Adrumman rejected everything that Moideen murmured in his ear, soon he fell for those honey-soaked words.

'The highs and lows in business are just like the tides in the Kallai river, ikka,' Moideen said. 'Now we are on a high. It is better to have one's own people around when one is on the rise.'

Moideen was related to the third wife in Kallai. When Adrumman could not dig out, in their entirety, the words murmured again and again into his ears, they lay there and grew hard. That is when Adrumman conceded defeat. Though he sifted and picked, measured and weighed the twenty-odd years Devassy had stood with him, he could not find the means to add him to his 'own people'.

'That, ikka, is the strength of blood,' Moideen told him.

The half-grunt that emanated from Adrumman Haji gave Moideen confidence. With that complaints against Devassy the Christian, who was not 'one's own people', increased.

When he got fed up, Adrumman Haji spoke.

'Do anything you want, hamukke. Just don't choke me with these infernal complaints!' he said harshly.

Before they parted Adrumman Haji embraced Devassy with genuine affection and said regretfully, in a tone meant to comfort him, 'You stood with me all this time, saw many highs and lows. They say from now on it is a good time for me. The maulavi says that in times of prosperity one should be surrounded by one's own people. Now that I am old, I too think that it is the right thing.'

Devassy mapla stood with his head bowed, not saying a word. He knew well that it was Moideen who had said it and not the maulavi, but he did not let it out.

One's own people!

This was the first time that such a thing had come up between them. The Christians in the market had taunted him so many times. Are you not ashamed to tag along behind that Muslim from the north? Come with us. A new thing that he had not thought of at that time had now emerged directly from Adrumman's tongue.

One's own people!

Adrumman said in a placating tone, 'Do not take this the wrong way. You can come any time you want, ask anything. Consider this threshold yours.'

How did Adrumman, who was not conscious of community divides when he was struggling, suddenly discover it when he became rich?

Thus confused by the new-age interpretation of highs and lows, Devassy stumbled into Chathedam Thupran's arrack shop. He was sure of one thing: the arrack shop was the only place that was unaffected by 'ours and theirs', 'great and small', where truth prevailed. The shaky bench, the love that frothed between the glasses filled to the brim. The oneness.

But Veroni, who roamed around collecting chit money, understood the rationale behind Adrumman's decision. 'How will you know what happens in the world if you drink and sit at home? You have to go out and meet people. Then you will know how the world moves and who helps whom.'

That is, Hindus for Hindus. Christians for Christians.

Muslims for Muslims.

Jews for Jews.

For some reason these new synonymous links did not

affect Devassy much. In all these years the Kottapuram market had not taught him such distinctions. In a place where many truths and falsehoods were exchanged, such a distinction had not put down its roots, till now. His heart resisted it.

Thus when Veroni's moral lessons began to lengthen, Devassy mapla slowly got up and groped for the bundle of beedis hidden somewhere in the recesses in the ceiling.

It was after that incident that he mulishly stopped going to church. When he was continuously absent for mass, Pathros achan sent sexton Mathai, but Devassy stuck to his resolve.

'Tell him that I will say whatever I have to say directly to Christ. Why should priests be intermediaries?' he asked the sexton.

Later, Veroni began to fear that by following the style of the Kottapuram market the father would teach Elsie his godless ways. 'When you make friends in school don't give importance to colour or lack of it, to caste or religion,' the father told the daughter. That was a mistake, for the lesson she learnt from her father in childhood lay entrenched in Elsie's mind till later.

That could be why among all her childhood friends she was closest to Salamon.

Elsie was slightly short of hearing in one ear, though the sharpness of her eyesight was four-fold. Therefore, what needed to be heard had to be said close to her left side, what didn't need to be heard could be told to the right. It was only when the argument about the ancestry of their respective religions grew heated that Salamon found himself wondering which side to address.

Salamon had no doubt that they were the first people in the world. Adam muthacha and Eve muthimma. The story

of human beings began from them. The other religions grew
out of the Jews.

When she heard this, Elsie would begin to get annoyed.
Man's beginning was from the Messiah and the Holy Book,
wasn't it? It is after the Messiah that we start counting the
years, isn't it? Or else, just count the number of churches. If
you were such great people why did you not build synagogues
all over the land? Are you claiming greatness with just five
or six synagogues?

'Don't talk about years, okay!' Salamon would interrupt.
He would then repeat Moses master's words. 'Our calendar
began 4,000 years before Christ.'

However, when she harped on the number of synagogues
Salamon was lost for an answer. Despite bending his
fingers to count without error, the number of synagogues
remained eight. Alright, the Christians were ahead of them
in numbers and the number of churches, but didn't the
Jews have greater antiquity? Christ was a Jew, wasn't he?
The Jewish era began four thousand years before Christ,
didn't it? He had heard Eliacha say that the exact number
was three thousand, seven hundred and sixty. But how
could he make this girl, who came shaking her horns at
him, understand all that?

But Salamon had another way to put her in her place.

'Anyway, your festival comes only after our festival. That
too just one day.'

'Oh, go away! Listing festivals!' Not willing to accept
defeat, Elsie made a face at him.

The knowledge that Christmas came after their Hanukkah
gave Salamon confidence.

Hanukkah, the eight-day-long festival of light. At night
lamps would be lit in a row in all the houses in the street.

The ceremonial lamp with the nine branches would be lit in the synagogue to the accompaniment of prayers. One horn for each day. A tall one in the middle.

Finally, Elsie said, 'We have more candles and lamps. But it is fun to watch you burn that Satan … looks exactly like our mathematics teacher Swami … eye and nose and *chatty* like head, they look the same.'

'It is not Satan, girl, it is Bagris!' Salamon corrected her. 'Bagris, who was the chief of the army of Antiochus.'

'Let it be any devil … it is nice to watch the crackers burst inside that Swami.' Elsie chuckled. She could not bear the sight of the mathematics teacher Subramanya Iyer with his tuft of hair at the back of his head.

They would begin to make the effigy of Bagris in the morning, wrapping it with dried grass and hay. The children would join into help. They would sprinkle salt over elanji leaves and stuff them into the effigy to make it crackle when it began to burn.

When the effigy of attacker Bagris explodes amidst children's shouts, it marks the victory of light over darkness, of good over evil.

It is said that Bagris was the right-hand man of Antiochus the Greek, who had taken over Judea. The Hanukkah festival celebrated the victory over the Greeks when, after a long and violent battle, the Jews regained control of the Jerusalem temple. Hanukkah began on Sabbath and went on for eight days. On Sabbath day – the day God took a day of rest after creating the world in six days – it was after reading the scrolls describing the history of Antiochus the attacker that the Torah was ceremoniously taken out of the arc and read. The scrolls were handed down from one generation to the next.

'Ours is just a one-day festival. Why do you have eight days?' Elsie asked.

Salamon then told her the story behind the festival.

'When they defeated and drove out Antiochus' army and regained the temple, there was just enough olive oil left to light the lamp in the temple for one night. Therefore, they lit only one branch of the lamp and enjoyed eight nights of light with that oil.'

'No wonder Jews are called misers,' said Elsie, her shoulders shaking with laughter.

The friendship that started in the third standard went on till the tenth. This friendship did not acknowledge gender difference, did not acknowledge religion either. As they went higher up Elsie became a girl and Salamon a boy. Elsie became a Latin Catholic and Salamon a Jew. But it was only much later that they realized that the ridges created by the differences were growing increasingly broader. Even the way they walked to school and back gradually changed. The one who walked ahead of the girls with plaited hair, with a lot of chatter and laughter was Elsie. Among the boys with close-cropped hair, the one at the back, and who did not talk much, was Salamon. If Elsie's group was made up of the Latin Catholic girls in the island, most of the boys in Salamon's group were Jews who sported colourful caps at the back of their heads.

There was a time when the eight- or nine-year-old Elsie would sit on a spathe of the areca tree, while Salamon pulled it all over the land, and command, 'Pull faster, Soloma. It is too slow!'

That would make Salamon fume.

'Of course! You're as grand as Elayadathu rani, aren't you, *penne*!'

But even when he grumbled, Salamon would hold his breath and run as fast as he could because he couldn't bear to see her pout with displeasure. Elsie, on her part, would not give him time to breathe. 'Pull faster, Soloma, you lame horse.'

During one such breathless dash, the spathe overturned and Elayadathu rani fell flat on her face. Though she grazed her thigh on a stone and drops of blood appeared, she just brushed away the mud and got up shouting, 'Pull, capped one; don't stand there staring.'

Salamon, who had brought porippu of the coconut tree to put on the wound, stood aghast.

Seeing his look she pulled down her skirt and yelled, 'Don't think you can enjoy this sight. I will teach you a lesson, you dirty Jew.'

'Oh, yes, yes.'

As she puffed up her face in anger and ran off, all he could do was stand and watch.

But the period of frigid silence continued only till the day of the school's anniversary celebrations. When she went on stage again and again to receive the first prize not just for studies, but for high-jump, sprinting, and singing, Salamon clapped loudly with everyone else. Finally, when he went to her, conceding defeat, she said softly, 'I knew you would come here one day.'

When he looked at her without a word, she added, 'That is what you call power of the female.' She paused, then said, 'After all it is the cock that runs after the hen, isn't it?'

At that time Elsie was ten, Salamon was fourteen. Later on, when he was eighteen, Elsie continued to remain ten, not willing to grow up. That was what bewildered him.

Though she stopped calling him 'dirty Jew', her

tormenting tactics intensified. When words fell from her mouth unmindful of time or context, Salamon became conscious of his lack of a suitable retort.

Later, she grew up. Salamon even more. By the time he joined the college in Aluva for the pre-degree course, she was in high school nursing the dream of joining a teacher's training course.

Though Salamon occasionally crossed that gate to see Devassy chettan, he knew that he would not see Elsie if Veroni was at home. From time to time Pathros achan took care to deliver lessons to the house regarding the norms of virtuous demeanour a grown-up girl should follow. The women in the homes where Veroni went to work – Ammaluamma and Dakshayaniamma – knew well that the reason for Veroni's anxiety was that her daughter was fair. That is exactly why both women advised her in one voice whenever they got a chance, 'Take care, Veroni, times are bad. You must always have one eye on the girl.'

It so happened that one day when Salamon met Elsie near the landing he decided to tease her.

'I heard Veroni thathi is looking for a groom for you.'

'Oh, really!'

'I heard it was a moustached army man or a hefty policeman, someone like that.'

'Yes.'

'After all, you need a trained elephant to tame a wild one, don't you?'

'Oh really? Let him come, soldier or policeman or whatever, to tame Elsie. I have seen certain bulls piss with fear at the sight of the female.'

'Why, are you going to join a convent?'

'Shhe!' She dismissed the comment.

'Then what? Don't you want to get married?'

'I want to study, become a teacher … I will marry after that.'

That was the first time she revealed her thoughts. She wanted to be a teacher like Mercy teacher, who was the moonlight of the school with a nice face, nice figure, nice smile, nice way of talking. She did not complain when Sugunan master from Pallanthuruthu tried to kiss her one day when there was no one else in the staffroom; neither did she complain when Eldo, who studied in the tenth standard, tried to give her a love letter. 'If you cannot bear your wife's bad breath, buy her the new toothpaste that has arrived in the market,' she told the teacher. As for Eldo, she corrected the spelling and grammar mistakes in the letter with red ink and advised him to improve his language. She gave each of them a scathing smile and walked off. That was Mercy teacher.

Salamon knew all this. Elsie too. Elsie had all the qualities to become the next Mercy teacher but she could do without Sugunan master's kiss and Eldo's love letter.

She thought for a while and said, 'Elsie just wants a school master. That will suit her.'

Though her plan made him feel slightly uneasy, Salamon retorted with spirit, 'He will need an extra-long cane to tame this one.'

'Go away, you Jew.'

'Or as they train a wild elephant, a tame one must stand on the side…'

'You!' Elsie stomped her feet and got on to the ferry, furious. But what she had said throbbed within Salamon for a long time.

School teacher! Elsie wants to be a school teacher.

If so he should reach one level higher than her teacher's

training course. He should be at least a graduate and then get trained as a teacher. The first one in the Isaac family to become a graduate! He felt a thrill go through him. No one in that family had studied beyond pre-degree.

With that Salamon discarded the desire to become a scientist, which Robert master had triggered in him. In Elsie's eyes the best thing to be was a school master. If it was in a high school, it would be even better.

But graduating in science would be difficult. There was no guarantee that at the time of the practical examination the attendant Khader would be around to tell him what salt it was.

He wondered if he could take up history after pre-degree. Let Robert master find someone else to train as a scientist.

As he briskly cycled away from the landing, certain thoughts were trickling into Salamon's mind.

Salamon master BABT Elsie teacher TTC. For her sake, he could perhaps revert to the old Solomon. Elsie Solomon. There was harmony. The names matched. He smiled.

The Call of the Land

Aliyah!

The return to the holy land!

Evron first heard of it from Eliahu Meir, who served in the Royal Air Force at Bangalore and had come home for the holidays. Though Evron had heard a lot about the holy land of Israel that had been formed in Jerusalem, migrating to that land was something that had not entered even his dreams.

Meir, who forgot to salute his white superior, was ordered by the controlling officer, a Jew, to appear before him. The intent was to punish him but when he found that Meir was a Jew, blood recognized blood, and it stretched into a great friendship. Thus, when Meir got a chance to spend a few evenings with him, he came to know of the largest organized migration in world history.

Perhaps the government did intend to create a place for all the Jews in the world to live together. But would the poor Jews of Kochi be included in that group? Would the black Jews, who were barely two thousand in number, become an irritant in their eyes? Eliahu Meir wondered.

What is there to doubt? The white officer smiled. There is no black and white among Jews. There is no differentiation between great and small. Those born to Jews are Jews.

There is no race within that. Is that not Zionism in the true sense?

That was not what Meir had heard. The Jews in Kochi, called Malabari Jews, were even now prohibited from entering the Paradesi synagogue in Mattancherry, built for the whites. Would a Malabari Jew get a bride from a white Jewish family? As Meir stood bewildered, unable to believe what had been said, the white officer stretched his hand towards him and asked, 'Tell me, would you like to go?'

Meir could not give him an immediate reply. Though the officer said all this there was no guarantee that it would happen. Besides, it was an important decision that required a lot of thought. It was a departure that meant leaving behind one's home and land. Such a thought had never ever entered his mind.

'I will tell you one thing. This is not a migration in search of a means of livelihood. Nor will there be a return. It is a breaking of all bonds, a total wipe-out of the past, whether you like it or not. You are going to start a new life in a totally new world.'

Eliahu Meir sat numb.

'There is no hurry. It is just the beginning. Bringing together the Jewish community spread all over the world is a huge process,' the officer reassured him. 'There is an agency in Bombay authorized for this. You will get more details if you get in touch with them.'

Though Eliahu Meir quickly forgot about it, it resurfaced like a call from within some time later. That was when he realized the strength of those old bonds that had been severed a long time ago. After that, he contacted the agency in Bombay. Endless correspondence queries, doubts, fears, vague disquieting replies.

In the meantime he received one specific piece of information: a mission called Magic Carpet had already taken a group of Yemenis to Israel by a special aeroplane.

Jerusalem had begun to spread the welcoming carpet.

What would be the colour of the carpet destined for the Jews of Kochi?

Though several days went by in this manner, the bits of information that came from various corners lacked clarity. But Eliahu Meir became certain about one thing: several people from Bombay had already left. Many were waiting to leave. One day it would be the turn of the Jews of Kochi. But nothing could be said about when or in how many groups they would be taken. Because Jews from all over the world were coming together in one small country, making arrangements for their journey and settlement was not a small thing.

Therefore try. Keep on trying … be patient…

It was through Meir that the news first reached the Jew Street in Chendamangalam.

The ones who heard it did not believe it at first. Even those who were willing to believe had many doubts. Was it easy to throw away everything they had and take root in unknown soil? What about the assets they had here? What job would they find there, without knowing the language? What facilities would be available to them? What about children's education, medical care, facilities for the elderly? So many details like these had to be looked into.

There was only one answer to all the questions. This was a great migration. The call of the holy land. The call of history. The call of sacrificial altars. You are not the only ones going; there are people from different corners of the world, of different nationalities, different cultures. They are all preparing to go with a willingness to suffer difficulties. This is not a sacrifice, it is a goal.

Later Evron took up the task of convincing others, based on the information he had received from Meir.

Meanwhile, fresh news continued to arrive from Mattancherry and Mala. Many people from there were preparing to leave. If this enthusiasm was sustained, then maybe the agency would open an office in Kochi as well.

The muliyar too received fresh information through the synagogue.

'Be patient. Wait for our turn. Our lives depend on it,' he repeated.

With that, those who had kept away till then began to crowd into Evron's courtyard. What is the next step? What should we do? What papers should we get ready? Should we send the children to the next class when school reopens? Should we buy books and other things?

Doubts were increasing in the street.

'I am not the person you should ask, friend.' When Evron could no longer bear the unending questions, he tried to escape. 'I just repeat what I hear in Kochi and Paravur. Maybe one of you should go to Mattancherry to find out.'

'Will it happen? Tell us that, member!' someone said harshly.

'It will. Why the doubt?'

It was Moses master, the part-time teacher of Hebrew in the Paliyam school, who said it. Word had spread that his son's name was included in the youth group that would go first. In fact, the fifty-odd families in the street bore a grudge against him because of this.

'Did I not tell you long ago that if you studied Hebrew, it would serve you well in the time to come? Did anyone pay heed at that time?' Moses master asked of the crowd in the street.

That, of course, was Moses master's constant complaint. Hebrew was taught during the noon interval. As the students ran out into the grounds to play, he would follow them and catch hold of at least ten children. Only then could he teach. Only if the report that the class had been held reached the authorities would he get his salary.

All this effort to teach Hebrew, the divine language! Master laughed, remembering it all. Wouldn't these people not have benefitted if they had learnt the language well at that time? And all due to the benevolence of the kings of Kochi! They had always shown a willingness to listen to the problems of the Jews. Besides, the kings had permitted the hapless Jews, who had wandered into the land centuries ago, to settle in the street near the palace, hadn't they?

Thus, the Jewish traders received several concessions. If there were ten students to study Hebrew the school must engage a part-time Hebrew teacher, that was the rule. The government would pay half his salary, the community would pay the rest. There was also a rule that teaching should be done in a manner that safeguarded Jewish religious rituals. The Jews were forbidden from doing anything on Sabbath day, the day God rested after creation. Therefore, if an examination fell on a Saturday, which was Sabbath day, the Jewish students would be herded into a separate room in the morning. They could answer the same question paper in the evening. Two seats in colleges and two posts in the government were also reserved for Jews.

Salamon watched the waves of excitement in Kizhakkumpuram and Jew Street. The young and old alike were in a hurry to go to the other side. Elders hurried about preparing their papers, and in spite of several tiring trips to Kochi and Ernakulam, no one wearied.

Soon the agency opened an office in Kochi and the excitement doubled.

When the first batch of seventeen people crossed the sea without paying any money, the fervour increased. Later a group of youngsters also went across to Israel. Thereafter there was a lull for some time. Though the agents in Kochi tried to discourage the people at times by giving all sorts of excuses, Moses master assured them that no one would be left behind. Though learning Hebrew was tough, everyone trusted Moses master.

Meanwhile, it was Eliacha who brought some fresh information from Kochi. Apparently, a prominent person from Israel was coming to understand issues related to the migration. He would first go to Kochi. After that he would probably come to Chendamangalam.

It was Ezriel Carlebach, founder editor of the Israeli newspaper *Ma'ariv* and well-known writer, who was coming. Generally, important people from abroad never came that way, save the rabbi who came to teach the older ones Torah and the kohens, who came for the children's pidyon ceremony. That too happened only once in a while. The usual practice was for such people to visit Ernakulam and Kochi and depart. Perhaps it was the reluctance to admit that the ones with a greater ancestry were on this side. Or was it the sense of superiority of the white Paradesi Jews in Kochi?

Elias took upon himself the responsibility of making the arrival of the journalist from abroad a great event. After all, as the first newspaper agent in the village he was the only one connected to newspapers.

So when Elias decided to visit each house in Jew Street

and talk to the people, even after the announcement was made in the synagogue, Salamon went along with him. 'The one who is coming is a very important person. Therefore his visit should not be treated casually. This is our opportunity to show our strength to those outside,' Eliacha kept saying.

'Will he take up our case and speed up our departure?'

That was what most people wanted to know. The journey to the other shore had taken that deep a root within them. Elias tried to evade answering that question.

'Isn't that what I said, we must show him our strength; when so many people come together, will the impact be small?'

At that time Moses master, who was with him, intervened, 'How can the Sa'ib not mention us when he returns!'

Eliacha and his group informed the nearby church, the mosque and also Paliyam nada. 'The one who is coming is an important person, a well-known journalist. He is coming from abroad. Therefore treat this as the welcome organized by the entire village and cooperate with us.' Elias also hung a large board in front of his type-writing institute in Paliyam nada – 'Welcome to Ezriel Carlebach'. The words were written in bold letters in red ink in English and Malayalam.

All of a sudden, the hilltop and surrounding areas were wide awake. Jew Street and its neighbourhood were decorated with flags and floral garlands. The entire Jewish population stood ready to welcome the guest, dressed in their traditional attire. The elders had definite rules for this. Violet trousers, white tunic and cap. The caps were of different colours for different occasions – white on the day of atonement, green for Sukkot festival, red for Torah...

When he heard that there were people of other faiths among those who had gathered to welcome him, Carlebach

was amazed. Such a grand welcome in such a small village!
For one who was used to cities, the goodness of Indian
villages was a novel experience.

'You are our guest!' When Pathros achan shook hands
with him and said this, Carlebach looked puzzled. A parish
priest in the group that welcomed him!

'That is the uniqueness of this land,' Eliacha struggled
to say in his broken English. 'Over there, on top of the hill,
you can see the Hindu temple. There, down below, are the
church and the mosque. Next to it is our synagogue. They
all stand on land given by the king who ruled at that time.'

Whenever Moses master tried to join the conversation
with his loose Hebrew, the guest would turn towards the aide
who had come from Kochi. Seeing this Eliacha was amused.
So that was the extent of Hebrew that Moses master knew!

The festive arrangements in that tiny village in a foreign
land bemused the outsider, who represented a race that had
gone through innumerable persecutions. He reiterated this
as he shook hands with them before he left.

Carlebach's visit shook not just Jew Street but the entire
region.

In the book that he wrote after returning to Israel,
Carlebach remembered Chendamangalam through the
words of Theodor Herzl, the father of modern political
Zionism and the one who dreamt of the fatherland of the
Jews. 'For the past fifty years I have been wandering among
the Jewish communities all over the world, spreading the
message to return to their own soil. But at that time no one
heeded my call. They did not willingly come forward to
return to the soil of their birth. Yet in the thatched houses
of this tiny village, a group of ordinary people are waiting
for the call from the holy land … Isn't this true Zionism?

Aren't these people the real Jews? Is this not Aliyah in the true sense of the word?'

Real Aliyah! Real Jews! What more did they want to hear? There were arguments about who first landed on the western coast. There were also arguments regarding the copper plate kept in the Paradesi synagogue in Mattancherry. Now a great writer in the holy land was saying that they were the real Jews. They, who yearned to migrate to the holy land without expectations. Was not the white man underlining the fact that a firm belief in Zionism was more important than white skin?

When friends who heard this came from Paravur and Mala, Eliacha did not have anything particular to say.

'I did not do all this so that he might praise us,' Eliacha said. 'I just wanted to show that if we try, we too can make things happen, that was all.' Though he did not mention names, those who heard him understood what he meant; because in the matter of their departure, the agency in Kochi was creating hurdles at every step of the way. They stalled the procedure for some time, making filariasis an excuse. Now they were saying that those who could afford it should sell all that they had and pay the fare in advance. What justice was there in that? Earlier they had taken people without demanding a deposit.

'After going all over the land telling everyone about it, will it finally end in embarrassment, Eliase?' Evron asked Elias in a doubtful voice, on a sweltering night in the month of Meenam as he walked about in the front yard after supper.

'It was not I, you were the one who went around saying it,' Elias retorted.

'Well, when someone asks for help I cannot deny it, can I? They are poor souls who do not know how to get things done in government offices, or prepare forms.'

'But you need not have stirred up so much excitement without knowing something for sure.'

'Well, when I saw all the bustle in Kochi at that time, I thought it would happen immediately. Anyway, they did take some boys as part of the youth programme, didn't they? Some of our boys went too, didn't they?'

'That is because they need young people who can work, that is all. Who will look after the old men and women? We can't leave them behind, can we?'

'That is true.'

Eliacha was getting irritable. 'Then there is that Moses master! To see him behave, you would think he is already in Jerusalem.'

'Poor man, he is making this an excuse to teach at least a few people Hebrew.'

'We saw the extent of his Hebrew when the white man came! Because of that man from Kochi we escaped without embarrassment.'

'Let that go. Tell me what you really think about it.'

'I think it will happen. But there is no point in hurrying the process. Everyone needs to be patient.'

'People just won't let me be. They think it is the member's responsibility. Do I have some government authority? I just come and tell them what I hear in Kochi and Paravur.'

'You should have thought of this when you went about pretending to be a member,' Elias said to himself.

'Calm yourself. Tell those who ask that it is not simple like the Panchayat affairs, and that it will take time. Let those who have questions go and ask in the agency office in Kochi.'

It was at that time that Eshumma entered the yard, wiping her hands on her cloth. She had just finished her work. Having heard the last part of the conversation she asked Evron, 'So will it happen, Evrone?'

Evron lost his temper. '*Olakka*!'

As Evron stamped into the house furiously she turned towards her younger son. 'What is the meaning of what the member said?'

'That it will happen, Umma,' Eliacha said soothingly.

Eshumma was bemused that olakka, the pounding rod, had such a meaning. 'If it's *olakka*, then so be it. I only hope it happens, Lord.' She raised her arms and prayed to the gods in the sky.

It was not the prayer of just one family, it was the prayer of so many families in that street, so many people…

A Lesson in World History

'Look, here comes the lord of queries! What is your new problem?'

Though Varuthutty master said those words with a wide smile, taking hold of Salamon's hands and pressing them warmly, the latter's face clouded over.

Master tried to correct himself at once. 'I did not mean to hurt you, Salamone. We need minds that can bear the load of doubt, don't we? Questions and the search for answers by perplexed minds are what take humanity forward, isn't it?'

Varuthutty master's house was on the banks of the river that flowed along the western boundary of the plot. Therefore, the master sat in an armchair on the veranda on the western side of the house. 'When one approaches the end of one's life it is good to sit like this and watch the river flow,' he often said. Watch the wind blow over the river, the mist spread, the darkness merge into it … then the various moods of the river – the rage that marks the months of Mithunam and Karkkidakam, the wanton fury of the water that flows from the hills, bringing down embankments during those months…

Seated in that chair he could see the landing place far away.

'It is fun to sit and watch the landing, Salamone,' the master often said. 'Watch those who come, those who leave, those who wait. At times I feel this landing place is the greatest truth in life. A witness to the comings, goings, waitings...'

The steps that led down to the bathing place built by the ancestors were slippery with moss. No one used them to enter the river. Due to continuous sand mining some parts of the river had become shallow while whirlpools had formed in other places. Youngsters were afraid to enter the water as they had no idea about the depth. It was only after four or five youngsters drowned in the unknown whirlpools the previous year that a yellow board with the danger sign was put up to warn the unwary.

When Salamon reached the house, Varuthutty master was, as usual, sitting in his armchair with a thick English book in his hands. He removed and put aside his silver-framed spectacles and the fan, even as he directed a sharp look at him.

'I have not seen you come this way for a long time,' he said. 'That means you have not had any anxieties of late. It is only when you are really agitated that you feel like climbing these steps.'

The same veranda. The usual manner of sitting on the half-wall, leaning against the pillar, his legs stretched out before him. The same evening hour. The same breeze. Salamon tried to smile. Master looked for new meanings in that attempt.

His parents had lovingly named him Varghese. Some time later, without telling anyone, he went to Ernakulam, submitted a request and changed his name to Varuthutty. Appan lost his temper, Amma wept. Master was unmoved.

While in school he had excelled in mathematics. His skill in unravelling even the most complex mathematical problems made several people predict that he would reach great heights. Of that they were certain. Though his parents too shared that certainty, when he went to join the intermediate course, Varuthutty master selected the third group, again without anyone's knowledge. Economics and history. After the intermediate course he chose Malayalam as his elective for the graduate course.

This time too Appan lost his temper, Amma wept.

'What, are you going to be a Malayalam teacher?' Appan asked. Here was a boy who could have become an engineer, but had been so wilful.

'What is so shameful about it? It is our language, isn't it?' The son was confused.

Later, when he joined the school in Gothuruthu as a Malayalam teacher, the headmaster asked, 'Won't you teach mathematics as well, at least once in a while, master? It is easy to get a teacher for Malayalam, getting one to teach maths is difficult.'

'Whatever maths I learnt I forgot long ago, master. Now even addition and subtraction seem difficult. I am always seized with doubts.' Varuthutty master turned abruptly. 'Another thing about these languages is that once they enter your head, they are like the devil; they just won't let go.'

Thus it was that the master learnt several Indian languages. Since there was no one to teach him, he learnt them with the aid of books.

'I have just one regret, edo. I did not have the luck to study in Maharaja's College during old L.V.R.'s time,' he often said.

Apparently, the learned professor L.V.R. Ramaswamy Iyer knew almost twenty languages, including several foreign ones.

'I have heard a story about him. I do not know whether it

is true. During the Second World War, the news, in German, about Hitler's decision to attack Russia was first caught by Professor Ramachandra Iyer's wireless set in the Physics lab. At that time L.V.R. was there to translate it. Thus even before the outside world knew about Hitler's reckless decision, Maharaja's knew,' Varuthutty master said.

It was his love for the authentic and the innate spirit of languages that made him call Solomon, 'Salamon'.

'Isn't this the authentic native name? The white men left a long time ago, didn't they? Then why should we bear their names?'

Though at first the call 'Salamone' irritated him, Salamon slowly got accustomed to it. Evronappa and Eshimuthimma had nothing against it. Evronappa in fact liked anything that recalled the past.

'It has the scent and vigour of our land in it, eda. It is not the foreigner's language after all,' Evronappa said.

But the name Solomon remained embedded in the school's records. It was Menahem mutha who was adamant that it should not be changed. Mutha had studied Hebrew so exhaustively, read the Torah so extensively, that his consciousness of sights and sounds outside these had dimmed. The great Solomon the Wise was unparalleled. How could they rubbish his name?

Gradually the names stuck – Varuthutty and Salamon…

Varuthutty master chuckled as he recalled the past.

'Tell me. What is the new problem that is worrying you?' master asked, looking intently at Salamon's face.

'Nothing specific, master.'

'That is not true. I know you would not come by the evening ferry if there was nothing bothering you.'

Salamon was in a quandary.

'Why, has your Evronappa found you a new job? Or has your mutha in Thoppumpady delivered some new moral precept…?'

'Aye, no…'

'Then?'

Salamon knew very well that Varuthutty master was adept at reading the expressions on his face and so he never tried to conceal anything. It was better to tell him everything rather than give him the chance to dig it out. Therefore, he always planned what he wanted to say.

He had made plans to say certain things this time as well. But most of those were no longer there within him. Recently it was like that – he forgot the important things while the unnecessary ones lay piled up within him. These trips across the river to Puthenvelikkara often brought him great relief. Varuthutty master had never taught him in school and he never tried to teach him when he came to the house. But when he unloaded the soiled bundles of thoughts and feelings on this veranda, Salamon felt a great sense of relief.

These days his mind was filled with doubts. When he freed himself from one, several others entered. There was no one to ask. The elders preferred to evade the questions of the younger generation. Some feared that the doubts would multiply till the people turned against them. Others had definite answers for everything. Answers that had been cut and shaped to suit their individual needs. But such answers did not satisfy Salamon.

'What are you thinking?' Salamon heard the master ask again.

'Shhe, just like that…' he said, unable to talk.

'Then I know what is going on inside you now. Knowingly or unknowingly you are bending your fingers and counting the days ... how can those fated to count days ever get relief?'

Why was Varuthutty master giving such broad hints? Was Salamon really counting the days?

Salamon searched within him.

Master continued to stare into his eyes.

'The great poet Vyloppilli has written an evocative poem about the return of Jews to their homeland. Have you read it?'

Salamon shook his head. He thought he had heard Eliacha mention it at some point.

'It is not enough to hear it. You should read it,' the master said. '"The exiled vagabonds of history returning to the home of their ancestors", that is how he describes the Jews. Do you understand the significance?'

'Some of it.'

'The poet also speaks about the persecution the Jews had to suffer at various points of time: Roman emperors who threw them to hungry lions; Hitler who gassed them to death ... The poem ends with the lines that they return to their own Israel with great knowledge, through grief and through empathy born of suffering. That means this is indeed the great migration. There may be differences of opinion. You just need to see them as lines that come from the heart of a sensitive poet.'

Varuthutty master then began to speak slowly. Salamon realized that, for the next few hours, his only duty was to listen. That was how it always was.

'The important thing is having a question to ask, not finding an answer. So you should not insist on getting answers for all your questions. At times, seemingly insignificant questions often relegated to silence become complex, bewildering ones.

'Look, Salamone, if you won't get bored I will tell you a bit of history. It is something that you and your people should know.'

Salamon nodded.

Varuthutty master's speech began to gain momentum.

'They came as groups, when they could no longer endure persecution – by Assyrians, Babylonians, Romans. As they scattered the world over, some must have reached our western shore through the familiar spice route.

'All these migrations have a common characteristic. When they wandered around in scattered groups they did not ask questions amongst themselves; they had learnt a long time ago to break and bend into passivity the sharp tips of the questions that sprouted within them. Because at that point of time the only thing before them was raw life. In the desperate struggle to live and go on living, the meaninglessness of their questions did not bother them. When they could not be certain of when they would get their next meal, or if they would remain safe in their new homes, other questions became irrelevant.

'Truth to tell, asking questions like where they came from, when they came, why they came, seems like a meaningless exercise, after all this time. Has anyone at any time had a place of their own? Stories of immigrations, isn't that what world history is all about? That is, stories of those who came, those who left, those who were driven out. A continuity that began from the beginning of human existence. Is it not through man's desperate struggle to safeguard himself, to assuage his hunger, by wandering across continents and invading another's land that communities and cultures take shape? Early man, in his zeal to invade and conquer, brought the land, the forest and the animal world under his control.

'Remember, migration is not restricted to human beings; animals, birds, other living creatures, even plants migrate. In this great migration, knowingly or unknowingly, intermingling takes place, of language, ways of life, culture. Therefore, in a sense, migrations were also transformations.'

Varuthutty master went on talking. Through those words uttered in an unfamiliar tongue with the river as their witness, unseen worlds were opening up before Salamon's eyes.

'To go in search of evidence and documents would be foolish because to confuse us with interpretations and untruths is the mischief that history plays on us. The scraps of history that reach us have undergone several additions and omissions, taken several turns as they passed through centuries and generations. Therefore, to ask what new light they shed will only confuse us.

'When the persecution in ancient Egypt became intolerable Jehovah said: "Let my people go." When Moses led the Jews through Mount Sinai … it was their first journey. But it must have been after the synagogue in Jerusalem was destroyed a second time that the large-scale dispersal of Jews occurred. Perhaps in the first century or so. Self-preservation, the need to satisfy hunger, the need to find a safe haven, these were their only goals at that time. Thus among the people who wandered off, one lot must have come to our western coast. I have heard that a large group came from Yemen. But of course they would not have all come together, at the same time. Like every other migration in world history this too occurred in stages, from one place to another.'

'One place to another?' Salamon asked.

'Why should you be surprised? It was a large world, wasn't it, without boundaries or fences. Like cattle wandering from one place to another in search of green pastures, water and safety.'

Still, from so far away, across oceans and seas, to come to this small place of ours ... Salamon found that hard to believe.

'It happened,' Varuthutty master asserted. 'The main reason for their coming to our land was the pepper trade. The pepper trade that existed between our shores and the countries of Europe some two thousand years ago. The spice route is mentioned in history. In those days they had trade with several ports, including our Muziris. Thus, through many goings and comings they must have seen this as a land where they could live without fearing anyone.'

'But were they all Jews?'

'Certainly a large number of them might have been Jews.' Varuthutty master laughed aloud. 'Because trade is in the Jew's blood, isn't it? Thus, they spread across Chendamangalam, Paravur, Kodungallur, Mala, Methala and Pullut. All these places must have been linked in some way with the maritime trade of those times. I have heard that years later the synagogue near the Jewish pond in Methala was burnt down by miscreants. In those days, Methala was the Jerusalem of the east. Therefore, when the southerners left the place they would take a handful of ash tied up in a piece of cloth to sprinkle over their coffins when they died. When they began to tie such a bundle at the edge of the tunic of brides who were married off to other lands, the northerners started making fun of them by calling them ash-binders.

'Some of it is history, some hearsay,' Varuthutty master added. 'In between, there is sure to be some truth.

'So it would not be easy to identify periods in history based on evidence. The arguments and counter arguments could go on indefinitely. One thousand years before Christ, in the days of King Solomon of Israel, gold, silver, ivory, sandal wood, peacocks and other things were taken from our land. It is said that the domed gateway of the town of Carthage was crafted from our sandalwood trees. The old folk songs mention one Habban who came from Jerusalem in search of a master carpenter to build King Solomon's synagogue. If that is so, Habban must be the first Jew who set foot on this land. Anyway, the copper plate given to Joseph Rabban, who was the leader of the trade group called Anjuvannam, by the Perumal of that day is significant proof. When the war between the Cholas and the Cheras went on interminably, Joseph Rabban helped the Cheras by providing men and money, for which the Perumal made him a regional overlord with seventy-two rights. That copper plate is now in the Paradesi synagogue at Mattancherry. If the Perumal was Bhaskara Ravi Varma then we get a tremendous piece of evidence that it was the tenth century. Methala, called Shingly in those days, must have been the centre of the Anjuvannam trade group.

'Later, when the Brahmins brought in caste distinction, among the Jews it was based on the difference in wealth. When economic distinctions like Pandikabhagam, Kadavumbhagam and Thekkumbhagam gradually became castes and sub-castes, arguments and quarrels became frequent among them.

'Finally, during the great flood of 1341, when the river Choorni called Periyar divided into rivulets and changed its course, the river mouth at Muziris was silted and ceased to exist. When an estuary, Kochazhi, formed towards the west, it became the present Kochi port. Thus, when Muziris was wiped out and Kochi developed, the king of Kochi welcomed the prominent traders of Shingly and gave them land on which to establish a market near the palace.'

Varuthutty master paused, spat into the yard, lighted a cigarette and continued, 'Do you know what is inscribed on that stone in front of your synagogue?' he asked.

Though Salamon had heard Eliacha speak about it, he had forgotten.

'"Israel's daughter Sara." The stone is dated 1269. That means your people had reached here before the thirteenth century. They must have brought it from some cemetery, following the tradition of digging up memorial stones of ancestors when they moved to another land. The Kunjakkari mentioned by Ibn Battuta, who travelled through this land in the fourteenth century, and Kunnumpuram, mentioned in the Everayi song, which describes migratory birds coming in search of the guava fruit, must be your area. Ibn Battuta has said that the Jewish chieftain of Kunjakkari paid tax to the Sultan of Kollam.'

Salamon too had heard some of this. Apparently, the present one was the third synagogue. While the Portuguese destroyed the first one, the second was lost to a fire. The first synagogue was said to have been a graceful structure modelled on the synagogue in Jerusalem.

'Famous carpenters who came from abroad built the synagogue,' Eshimuthimma often said. 'Instead of adding water to slaked lime do you know what they added? Water of the tender coconut! To maintain purity!'

Salamon recalled something else that Muthimma had once said: 'In the past, travellers used to get frightened when they saw lights and movement in the yard in front of the synagogue at midnight. Not ghosts or devils. Just dark Pandis, who had come to sieve the sand for gold. When the synagogue was destroyed in the fire, the thick covering of real gold also melted, did it not?'

'Anyway, you people bear a very ancient history,' the master continued. 'Kesari has written that what was called Vanchi in olden times is Chendamangalam.'

Salamon nodded like an idiot. He did not understand much of what was being said. But because it was Varuthutty master who spoke, he could believe it.

Master continued, 'The question is, do such migrations carry within them the possibility of a return. That is, before the call came from the new country called Israel, did your ancestors ever think of a return? It is not surprising that this land became native soil for those desperate people who had come in search of asylum at that time. Because those days the concept of nationality was alien to them.

'I will tell you just one thing. Whatever be the birth of that country and its politics, when this migration is complete your Israel will become the greatest kaleidoscope of races in the world. So many different races. A rare coming together of people across continental divides. Whether this is good or bad, only that great power, Time, can tell.'

Salamon sat with his head lowered. He was unable to say anything. Varuthutty master had said a lot of things, he heard a lot of things ... understood some of them.

Had he seriously thought of a return? Was going to Israel truly a return? Did they actually come from that land?

Having gone one full circle, when he reached the same pinnacle of doubt, Salamon shook his head, vexed. These questions seemed to be taking him nowhere.

Seeing the bewildered look on Salamon's face Varuthutty master smiled. 'What is it?' he asked.

'Shhe, nothing.' Salamon smiled like an idiot.

Dusk had begun to fall on the water. The wind too had a chill to it. It must be raining somewhere far away.

As Salamon prepared to get up Varuthutty master stopped him.

'I can understand the bewilderment you feel. Do not fret thinking of this and that. It is not going to happen immediately. When things become clearer take a decision according to the circumstances at that time.'

'What decision? When everyone in the street, the family, were in a hurry to leave, what decision could he alone take?'

Varuthutty master nodded as though he agreed.

'What can I say? If everyone leaves, you alone … Truth to tell, even getting a bride will be difficult…'

Master stopped abruptly, then stared at his face. Salamon understood what that meant.

'It is difficult to make a decision, isn't it? Sometimes that is how it is. It is only after taking a decision that you feel you need not have done it. I'll tell you one thing: this is not a bond that you can cut off easily. As long as generations of ancestors sleep under this soil at least some will be forced to return. That tiny bundle of ash in Methala is not a trivial thing. A great belief that we do not understand lies behind it.'

Salamon got up shaking his head idly. It was like that these days. He would come to this veranda hoping for an answer to a lot of questions, only to return with a greater burden of doubts.

The river had darkened. He could not see the light of the lantern that was hung from the lamp post near the landing. For a moment he panicked.

'Would Ittaman have left, master?' he asked.

'Aye, no, it is not time yet. Most probably he must have run out of kerosene.'

That happened to be the truth. Ittaman was waiting at the landing smoking a ganja beedi. The lamp was placed behind the stump of a coconut tree, its wick turned down.

'Want a smoke, mone…?' Ittaman asked conversationally.

'No,' Salamon replied, disgusted.

'It's fun, eda. You can see all four worlds and the world of the gods; and the women there, bathing naked.'

'I don't want it.'

'It is not a joke. Isn't this how youngsters learn things? I will not tell anyone, not even the member.'

Salamon went and sat on the cross plank in front of the boat, pretending not to hear. He said impatiently, 'Let's go.'

'Wait. One has gone towards the west in a hurry. We cannot abandon him,' Ittaman said placidly.

By the time the ferry reached the bank and Salamon hurried up the hill, it was dark.

Eshimuthimma would panic. He was never so late, Salamon thought.

Darkness lay huddled in the grounds around the synagogue. Somewhere submerged in that darkness lay a stone that marked lives. That stone too would have a story to tell. The story of Israel's daughter Sara, who was born here centuries ago, who grew up here … her desires. Agonies. Fears…

Israel's daughter Sara.

As he hurried into Jew Street, Salamon felt Sara's shadow following him through the memorial stone with an old tale to tell.

Remembering Rebecca

'Rebeccamma, Rebeccamma! Why are you crying, Rebeccamma?'

'I feel sad, mone.'

'Do you always cry when you feel sad, Rebeccamma?'

'There is no one here to listen and talk to, mone.'

'Why do you feel sad?'

'I don't know, mone.'

Mother and son would talk in this manner for a long time whenever she appeared in his dreams. For Salamon the very memory of Umma was sad. When Umma wept he felt unhappy and helpless. It was Umma of the dreams who told him not to call her Umma. 'Call me Rebecca or else Rebeccamma.'

During those early nights when he entered high school and shifted his sleeping space from Muthimma's room, he lay awake tossing and turning. It was Rebeccamma who kept him company then.

'Mone, haven't you slept yet?'

'Hmm, no.'

'Did you not hear the cock crow the midnight hour?'

'Don't feel sleepy, Umma'.

'Is it because you are away from Muthimma?'

'Hmm ... no.'

'Then?'

He did not have an answer to that.

'Then, mone, you put your arms around umma. Umma will put you to sleep.'

He felt her breath on his cheek ... an unfamiliar scent spread around him. As he lay snuggled against her breast he felt he was an infant once again.

'You have grown, mone. Now you do not need Muthimma. Rebeccamma is here as your companion ... I have not had enough of you.'

The faint feel of lips on his cheek. Then a slight wetness. Was Rebeccamma crying?

Salamon often thought that no one in that house remembered Umma. It was as though they were ever vigilant that the name Rebecca should not crop up in their conversations, not even accidentally. Even Eliacha, who knew everything, said everything...

The vague shape in a five-year-old's memory could never become a mother, could it? After all, wasn't mother a form that could never be complete? Therefore he preferred to create in his mind the picture of the umma he had not seen rather than the one he had.

There were no pictures of Umma in the house. When he asked why, no one had an answer. Evronappa would walk away as though he had not heard him. As for Eshumma, she would look stricken the moment she heard the name.

'Was she not the one who filled the void of a daughter? A girl who came from somewhere. And then what! One day she just swept the dust off her back and left, to make the ones who remained grieve.' This would inevitably turn into long sobs.

Eliacha recalled that there had been certain photographs

in the house, including a wedding picture. Where had they disappeared to later? Eliacha gave no reply. Did they throw them away or hide them somewhere?

When he saw even Eliacha evade these questions, Salamon would become angry.

'Those who have gone have gone, haven't they, mone?' Eliacha would say soothingly. 'Then why remember all that and torment yourself?'

Salamon wanted to ask: 'Is it not a son's right?' But when he saw Eliacha's face he could not bring himself to say anything further.

What really was Umma's illness?

Salamon thought about it a lot. Was it just fever that had shot up? Perhaps in those days they did not have many options for treating that kind of fever in rural areas. But from what he had heard, his mother was not the type who would waste away easily. Panayappilly Rebecca, who went about with her head held high, causing discomfiture to all the women in Jew Street! Some saw her independence as pride. Others kept away, suspicious. Many felt sorry for Evronappa. A noisy headstrong girl who was not the ideal mate for Evronappa! Malicious remarks were made behind his back.

Everything changed so quickly. The girl who provoked both locals and family to say many things retreated into the recesses of the house like a wet cat.

Did the changes manifest in Umma after she delivered him? Was it just the after-effects of the delivery?

Eshimuthimma was reluctant to answer these questions when Salamon asked. The moment she heard Umma's name her eyes would fill with tears, her throat would thicken, her voice change. The ones who perform pious acts, they are the ones God calls first. The whole earth is going to fill up with sinners whom no one wants, she would say.

As for Evronappa, a terrible frozen look would appear on his face when he heard all this. Was there a sense of guilt behind it? Salamon recalled that once it accidentally slipped from Panayappilly Miriam muthimma's tongue that even when the fever intensified they continued to treat her with local herbal medicines. Finally, when they took her by boat to Ernakulam it was too late.

When Simon muthacha, who came in hearing her words, stopped her, embarrassed, Miriam muthimma went inside murmuring something. Salamon had heard part of what she said.

'You all can say that. Only the womb that bore the child knows the pain…'

'It is okay,' Simon muthacha said as he placed his hand on Salamon's shoulder and led him out. 'Miriam says such things out of anguish. Don't let it upset you,' he said, trying to console Salamon.

In truth certain oddities of behaviour began to appear in Umma even before he was born. By the seventh month or so. She who had gone about doing the chores so enthusiastically suddenly became lethargic. She was reluctant to enter the kitchen; the smell of fish made her queasy, she said. She no longer helped Muthimma in outside work like sweeping the yard. She said she had back pain, that her legs ached, that it fatigued her. Muthimma never reprimanded her. She hardly ever complained to anyone either. She did all the work herself as before, inside and outside the house – cows, goats, chicken, ducks…

That was because she knew that the child growing in her daughter-in-law's belly was the result of her long prayers.

The male child that would carry the Isaac family forward. That it should be a girl from Kochi who made this possible was God's will.

Yet, sometimes, as they sat down for supper, she would burst out, 'Everyone thinks Umma is still young. Does anyone bother to find out how things go on in this house? Eshumma who gave birth to three sons, her fate is terrible indeed! When the neighbours say that, I feel my skin peel in shame...'

At times Eliacha saw her gaze lengthen towards him hopefully. He knew well what it meant. Eliase, you at least marry a girl and bring her home as a help to the mother who gave birth to you...

But Elias had learnt long ago how to steer clear of both the looks and the loaded words aimed at him. When they irritated him too much he would leave, his heavy footsteps pounding the floor either for the library in Paliyam nada, or to one of the three landings in the village. If not, he would take a thick volume out of the wall cupboard and seek asylum in his room.

It was Rebecca who fostered his love of books. At a time when he used to wander about idly with his friends she said to him one day, 'Can't you read something, Eliase, instead of wasting time like this?'

Elias was surprised. Was he not the only one in that house who read anything? Till then he had prided himself on his reading; sitting on the veranda of the library he would read all the newspapers that were there.

'True,' Rebecca agreed. 'But these papers tell you about happenings, give you information. But to know the world, to learn and understand the pain and agonies of human beings, of the human predicament, you must read books, that is what my appa says.'

The agonies of the human predicament! What's that? Elias was puzzled for a moment.

That was a new perspective for Elias. Reading to understand the world, understand the human predicament. All of a sudden he felt he had lost stature before Rebecca. After that he was determined to read.

The beginning was with detective fiction. Slowly, ever so slowly, the novels of more famous writers began to seem accessible – Thakazhi and Basheer and Keshav Dev. He made arrangements to get their works from various places.

'This is not enough, Eliase. You have to climb even higher...' It was Eldo master in Fort Kochi who said that.

Thus as the popular detective novels resentfully made their exit, Jean Valjean and Raskolnikov, Anna and Olan entered with their slippery Malayalam. When the master told him about the bookshop in Fort Kochi run by an Anglo-Indian and from where he could get old books at a cheap price, the passion for books increased. Thus he began to sidle up to Muthimma whenever she unwrapped the folds of silk at her waist, hoping for largesse. If he got money he would board the boat and go straight to the bookshop. Elias loved to wander around the shop, to touch and feel the books that were arranged in neat rows in the wall cupboards.

When, after a long search, Menahem did not find any religious texts among the books, he was annoyed. 'Why do you give money for such whims, Umma?' he lashed out at his mother.

'So? I am not planning to become a muliyar, hazzan or Hebrew teacher, am I?' Elias hit back.

But Eshimuthimma did not have the time to interfere in such arguments between her sons. She had more than enough work to do in the house.

Now after all these years when he tried to recall old incidents, Salamon thought that Rebeccamma knew all this. Umma knew many things – that the affliction that Achuthan vaidyar hinted at would direct itself not at the child, but at the mother. Wasn't that why she took on herself his scurf and his diarrhoea and took them with her?

Like any other woman she was fulfilling her duty to her birth. That is what the family expects from any bride who enters the husband's home. The means of taking the generations forward. A male child to the Isaac family which did not have any. Evronappa, who desired her, who held her hand and brought her here, must have wanted the same thing. That was the sole duty of being born a woman. Flowers that were fated to fade once they bore fruit.

Eshimuthimma knew its worth. Menahem and Elias too knew. The neighbours knew.

But by the time Salamon figured it out, it was too late.

Panayappilly Simon muthacha and Miriam muthimma lived for some more years after Umma's death. Muthacha died when Salamon joined college. Muthimma died within three months of his death. Until they became bedridden they would both visit once in a while. However, when they pleaded with Muthimma to allow Salamon to stay with them for a few days, at least during the vacation, it was with great reluctance that she consented. Salamon could not understand why Muthimma, who showed no reluctance in sending him to Menahem mutha in Thoppumpady, became unenthusiastic when it came to Panayappilly. And then what? As soon as five or six days had gone by she would become restless and send Evron. Apparently Muthimma could not sleep! Salamon on the contrary was reluctant to return. It was the time when the jackfruit and mango trees in Panayappilly were loaded with fruit. As for the jambu tree near the well, he knew exactly when it bore fruit.

It was not just that. He had a lot more freedom in Panayappilly. No one came after him, oozing affection.

The moment she saw Evron's head at the gate Miriam muthimma would start grumbling, knowing that he had come to take his son home, but gentle Simon muthacha raised no objection.

Simon muthacha had only one thing to say. 'Your umma always excelled in studies. She stood first in the class, right from school. She had so many longings! She wanted to get a first class for MA and become a teacher in a college, if possible study law; she wanted to be the first woman to get a master's degree in the community, to be the first female lawyer in the community, like A.B. Salem from Mattancherry, who was called Jewish Gandhi ... become a name everyone remembered...'

If only some of Umma's unfulfilled desires could be fulfilled by the next generation...

When Simon muthacha's eyes glowed with memories of Rebeccamma, Salamon felt his heart quiver. He wanted to be known as Umma's son rather than Appa's son. The Umma of his dreams was barely visible yet she towered over Appa whom he saw every day. But even as he yearned to be like her, Salamon was tormented by the disquieting realization that, academically, he was Appa's son...

Salamon had a number of questions within him, which he planned to ask Eliacha.

Quite unexpectedly, he got a chance to ask them on a stormy night when a harsh wind was blowing. Evronappa had gone to bed early as he was not feeling well. So had Muthimma.

Eliacha was sitting in the narrow rain-drenched veranda,

watching the coconut trees swing towards one another in the dark. The western wind was blowing low, announcing the arrival of the monsoon.

As he softly touched Eliacha's shoulder from behind, Eliacha looked up, startled.

'The month of Edavam has just begun, yet the rains have started,' Salamon began quietly.

'Hmm,' Eliacha grunted. His face bore the bewildered look of one suddenly jolted back into the present from some other world. Salamon guessed that in this state he could lead him to the very places he wanted him to go.

It was true. A light breeze continued to blow against his face. It had been after much effort that Salamon was able to bring him to talk about Rebeccamma. As memories tumbled out, Eliacha began in a low voice, 'It was actually my loss, mone, more than Evron's, more than Umma's, more than her parents.' Eliacha's cold voice froze.

Eliacha could not say with certitude what Rebecca – who was more or less his age – was to him; an older sister? A friend? A guide who directed him towards the right path? So many things…

What had amazed her when she first came there was that it was a house without a newspaper.

When Simon muthacha came to visit he could not believe it either. Not just in the house, there was no newspaper in the whole village.

'No paper in the area!' Simon muthacha's eyes widened with disbelief.

'It comes to some places. Some people buy and bring them from Paravur and Kodungallur. There is no newspaper agency here, that's all,' Eliacha intervened. 'I see it in the library. Evron has it in the Panchayat.'

'Appa insisted that we children should read at least two newspapers every day. One in English, one in Malayalam. It was not enough to just read The *Hindu*, we had to write a summary of the editorial in neat handwriting and show Appa in the evening. Only then would our English improve, he said.'

Embarrassed, the very next day Evron went to the town and made arrangements for a newspaper to be delivered to the house. The agent was amused to see Evron's urgency.

'When we came there and asked, you were not interested. Perhaps the Kochi bride wants one, member?'

Evron had no answer.

That is how gradually, unobtrusively, Rebecca began to fill the many deficiencies in that house. She told Elias to call her by name. 'Don't call me chetathi and add to my age,' she had said right in the beginning. The advantage of being born in a town, of having seen a larger world, of being the daughter of a wise man.

'Appa only told me to study. "Study till you touch the sky." That's all,' she would tell Elias. 'Never told me to study hard in order to get a well-paid job or to buy things. He believed girls should learn to do things by themselves, be self-sufficient. Money was not important in our house. We never threw tantrums for anything. Appa bought this cycle without my asking for it.'

That was the great difference she saw in the Isaac family.

No one told Rebecca to study. No one asked why she did not. When Eshumma heard that Rebecca was weighed down by guilt for not completing the masters examination, she was astonished. Isn't this much study enough for girls, mole? she often asked. Evron did not ask that question but it lay latent on his face. Most people there advised one to make money, as much as possible, as quickly as possible. Find some employment as soon as the eyes and hands are steady; the income earned from it was all that mattered. Grandchildren and their grandchildren should follow the path Muthacha took. That was the tradition of that land.

Rebecca felt like laughing when she thought of it.

'Eliase, have you read Shakespeare's *The Merchant of Venice*?'

'I know about Shylock.' Eliacha grinned.

'After all this time, Shylocks are still alive amongst our people. In many forms, many guises.'

Thus it was that Rebecca urged Elias to complete the course he had left midway and get a degree. Age is not a factor as far as education is concerned, she said. You just have to scrape through two more years...

Go to college once again! Be amidst textbooks? Elias could not bear the thought. He had sold all his books at half the price a long time ago. 'That is no problem,' Rebecca said. She could get him books from her friends in Ernakulam.

'Later, Rebecca, I will tell you when,' Elias said uneasily.

Elias remembered what Rebecca had said when she finally gave up.

'This is a cursed family. The conventional type of Jewish family that thinks money is the greatest thing. You don't realize that the world around you is changing. You still live in Shylock's time.'

The effects of having grown up as a non-Jew among Jews was visible in all her ways.

Elias told her repeatedly that he was not attracted by money, but she did not believe it. Soon, she stopped reminding him to study.

Though she was enthusiastic about writing the exams she could not do it for several reasons. She would have had to go to Ernakulam for tuition for two or three months to get a grasp of long-forgotten subjects. But she had become so involved in managing the household that she was reluctant to leave Muthimma alone. Determined to give back at least half the love that Umma showered upon her, she gradually forgot about her exams. Though Umma never said anything, it must have hurt her a lot at that time, Salamon was sure.

Salamon was thinking that the curse was now extending to him. If Umma were alive, she would tell him to study, acquire as many degrees as possible.

Eliacha paused for a while as though putting his thoughts in order, then continued.

Rebecca came to the house at a time when he was unemployed.

'Don't you get bored wandering about idly with your friends, Eliase? Can't you think of doing something?' she asked him once. 'You are wasting the best years of your life.'

He was willing to work, but at what occupation? He did not want to do business. Perhaps, something that benefitted people…

It was Rebecca who had a suggestion. 'How about a type-writing institute?' She had seen boys and girls walk to the faraway town to learn to type.

'But I don't know how to type,' Elias replied.

'Who said you need to know typing to start an institute?' Rebecca laughed.

When he heard about it, Evron too became interested. Thus, they ventured into it. There was a vacant room in the two-storey building near the main road. The monthly rent was ten rupees; three months rent to be paid as advance. Evron managed to get hold of four or five old Remington machines through his friends in Ernakulam.

As he ran his fingers along its unsteady keys, Elias could not control his laughter. 'Like old people's teeth, high and low.'

'That is how it is in the beginning. Let the children learn to type on these first,' Rebecca said, remembering the typing classes she had attended. 'If you give them new machines they will ruin them.'

'What about a teacher?'

'We have good old Rama Iyer Swami for that,' Evron said.

Evron had already spoken to Swami, who had retired from the Paliyam school.

Swami had looked at the Remington machines that stood on unsteady tables.

'These must be the ones Vasco da Gama discarded when he left!' he quipped.

'They are not that old,' Evron replied. 'About our age.'

'Havoo!' Swami sighed. 'If the Remington people saw them they would not leave us alone. These are museum pieces!'

'Let the institute start, Swami. We will make proper arrangements later on. Someone offered me an even older Underwood for free. I refused,' Evron said placatingly.

It was a good beginning. When a few students came forward to combat and win against the old Remingtons with their various defects, as well as Rama Iyer's irritability, the educational institute thrived and prospered. Later on, when there was not enough space, tables were lined up in the front and back verandas. When younger instruments and an even younger Damayanti teacher from Puthenchira arrived, half the boys who went to the town to study changed direction and came to the institute. Seeing the teacher's red earrings and even redder lips every day, even Swami became younger, gradually.

Fed up with the noise created by the students, the tenant of the adjacent room left, thereby providing the institute more space. Eshumma was very pleased with the direction in which Elias was going. 'He is not like the other one. He is smart,' she spoke aloud for everyone to hear.

When she heard it Rebecca laughed. The trouble she had to go through for this one to get smart!

The Newspaper Comes to Kunnumpuram

One day, when Rebecca asked him why not start a newspaper agency, Elias too thought it was a good idea. He went to the newspaper offices in Ernakulam and Trichur, taking Evron with him. When asked how many copies would sell, the answer they gave did not impress the manager. 'First create an interest among the people, then we will think of an agency,' he said. So they decided to pick up the papers from the agent in the town until they had established themselves.

Arrangements were made for the delivery of three newspapers, *Deenabandhu* from Ernakulam, *Express* from Trichur and *Mathrubhoomi* from somewhere in the north. Subran, who spent his time playing football in the paddy-field-turned playground, took on the responsibility of collecting the bundles of newspapers from the town and distributing them. He knew most of the side lanes and houses in Chendamangalam.

'Have an English paper as well, Eliase. It is good for students to read the *Hindu*. There are also sufficient advertisements for those on the lookout for jobs,' the agent in the town suggested.

The *Hindu*, which had advertisements on its front page, had an avid readership in the library veranda. If someone wanted the advertisement page, someone else asked for the sports page or the editorial. Reports from the sports page or job advertisements would be neatly cut out with a blade. Seeing the torn pages at closing time, librarian Kurup would grumble.

They said in those days that the *Hindu* printed advertisements on the front page, like the *London Times*.

Although what the agent said was true, it was doubtful whether anyone in their village would subscribe for an English newspaper.

'Not now. We will see later,' Elias told him.

'*Gomathi* will find readership among the Nairs,' the agent persisted.

Elias considered it for a moment. Wasn't it enough to have three dailies for the time being? If the number increased, Subran would start grumbling.

Gomathi was the favourite newspaper of the upper-class Hindus of Trichur. Printed the previous evening, boys hawking it on the streets, yelling 'Tomorrow's *Gomathi*' was a familiar sight of that town. When Evron suggested that they take it to please the Nairs of Chendamangalam, Elias agreed. So *Gomathi* became the fourth newspaper.

Thus, on an unusually bright and hot day two bundles of newspapers arrived in the village for the first time.

Deenabandhu from Ernakulam and *Express* from Trichur. Apparently, the other two dailies would be delayed by another week. Subran counted seventeen papers from the agent, tied them with string, and put them in a gunny bag. As he walked, the bag slung over his shoulder, the hot news he had seen on the front page was bubbling within him.

However, he was not willing to divulge it to anyone on the street. If they want, let them buy and read. They cannot get it for free. His left shoulder sagged under the weight of the responsibility he had undertaken.

The first newspaper man of the village! Subran was proud of that exalted position. From now on, the paper would be Subran and Subran's words would be the newspaper's voice. Till now Subran had idled his time away, but now onwards, the entire land would hearken to Subran's sharp bird-like voice. People would wake up seeing his face, the days would dawn with his footfalls. Subran felt his heart brim over.

He was going to be 'someone' in that land.

However, after a while the shame of going all over the village with just seventeen newspapers snuffed his enthusiasm. Though Elias was the agent it was to Evron he complained, since he had some influence in the village.

'This is not enough, member,' he said. 'There must be a wave in the village. For that you have to go into the midst of people and stir them up.' These were lines that party comrades had taught him to recite on some occasion.

Though Evron too thought that seventeen was too small a number, he was irritated that a mere newspaper vendor should dare to address him as 'member'. But because Elias had warned him not to say anything that might alienate Subran, he merely grunted.

It seemed as though the assurances given to the agent in Paravur and the newspaper offices would remain unfulfilled. They had a long way to go before they got their own agency.

'People need to have money, don't they, Evrone?' Elias asked. 'After the war, everything is so expensive. Coconut fetches as low a price as an areca nut. People can manage without a newspaper.'

Rebecca did not agree.

'But it is always like that, Eliase,' she said. 'The wealthy always have money to spend. But they don't spend it for a good cause. Anyway, the beginning is always difficult. Slowly it will become a habit; soon the women who gather near the fence and the men who sit on the compound wall to gossip will discuss what is reported in that day's paper. And gradually, when the elders insist on taking the newspaper to the toilet we will have won ... That is how it was in our Ernakulam.'

Though he did not like the way Ernakulam cropped up in everything Rebecca said, Elias believed she made sense. It was the initial stage that was difficult. After that it would become a habit; a habit of the land, of the people. But for that it was not enough to get the paper at noon as it was now. The newspaper should reach people with their morning tea, as it did in the towns. Though the newspapers reached Paravur town by the first bus, Subran would go and get them only when he was free. Moreover, Subran was unpredictable. Each day he had a different face. If Elias asked, 'Can't you start earlier?' he would have to listen to choice quotations from Marx and Lenin. Subran would then start about his workload. Elias had noticed that, of late, the word 'workload' was cropping up a bit too frequently in Subran's words. He was sure that someone had instigated him to say it.

'It is on just a cup of black coffee that I walk one, one and a half miles, and back. After all this walking my heels...'

As the number of subscribers increased not only did Subran's old enthusiasm wane, he also took to announcing certain hot news items along the way. Soon people began to wait to hear him announce the news, some even started asking him.

'What's the hot news, Subra?' or 'What's the latest news, Subra?' they would ask.

Subran had begun to enjoy this query. But there was a lot of news inside and outside. Which was the hottest?

At first, Subran was perplexed. This dilemma confronts the news desk at the newspaper office every day ... what to keep and what to discard. Now the vendor had to face it. Subran decided hot news was what startled people and forced them to stop and listen.

After that, it was a tornado of sensational news: 'A boat capsized in Cherai. Two believed to be dead!'; 'An elephant went berserk in Thekkinkad in Trichur! The mahout from Ashtamichira who tried to bring it under control is in hospital'; 'Has Cathrina who disappeared from Edavanakkadu returned?'

Though Subran's audacity in breaking the news on the road infuriated Elias, he never reprimanded him. If he left in a huff it would be difficult to replace him.

It was only later that Evron found a solution to the problem of late delivery. He decided to make arrangements to separate the bundles to the village in the town itself. If they were then sent by the first bus to the village, the subscribers would get the paper in the morning. Till they had their own agency, they would need the cooperation of the agent in the town. He would not refuse to help as he received commission for it.

Thus, when the newspaper began to arrive early the number of subscribers increased. Interest increased. As reading became a habit, complaints increased: the paper was delivered late the last two days; no inside page in yesterday's newspaper; the paper is all crumpled up; it is not enough to throw the newspaper near the gate, it should fall at the precise spot on the veranda as instructed; can't you get that Subran to appear a bit more cheerful? Will the paper be delayed once monsoon starts? It was an unending shower of complaints, queries and instructions.

'What do you say now? Where did the non-existent money come from?' Rebecca asked. Evron did not have an answer. Neither did Elias.

True, the difficulty is always in getting things started, Elias said to himself.

In the meantime when *Manorama* and *Deshabandhu* started arriving from Kottayam the number of newspapers increased. All in all a sizeable load. They arrived on the morning bus in bundles of different sizes.

With that Subran became more cantankerous.

'I cannot do it any more, muthalali,' he told Elias. 'One subscriber is in Arankavu, the other is in Vadakkumpuram. The third at Karimpadam. And you, muthalali, you are at Kottayil Kovilakam. Subran does not have wheels beneath his feet. All this trouble after forgoing my morning sleep, on just a glass of black coffee.'

Elias offered to increase his salary a little. Though the business would not run on the commission he got, he was willing to spend from his own pocket. After all it was for a good cause. He was not wasting his money on fripperies like Vava and Evron.

But salary was not Subran's only problem. It was the burden of work. He suggested a solution.

'Muthalali, employ one more person. One can go towards the south, the other towards the north.'

Though the word 'muthalali' annoyed him, Elias said in a conciliatory tone, 'Let the business take root, Subra. I am trying to get an agency for at least two or three dailies. Right now I am running at a loss. Once I can stand straight, I will get hold of a second-hand cycle from somewhere.'

But Rebecca was shrewd. She realized that Subran had his eye on her new cycle, not a second-hand one. For that very reason she never looked towards that side. Subran was a difficult customer. It was the job of the men folk to tackle him.

Though he had to shell out quite a bit of money from his pocket, Elias acquired fame as the one who first brought the newspaper to the village. Like electric Appu Menon who brought electricity for the first time. Like Anjalottam Chami who brought post for the first time. Like Krishankutty Menon who started the first handloom weaving mill.

Appu Menon's electricity, the wires that brought the electricity, and the teak poles, all became a matter of pride for the village very quickly. When a teak pole in front of the house and wires that tore the sky became symbols of prestige Appu Menon found himself in a fix. Everyone wanted it. Would he have to bring the entire Pallivasal hydroelectric project to the village? Appu Menon calculated the available electricity and prepared an estimate. He would provide electricity for the houses along the main road. Those living in the by-lanes would have to pay for the poles and the wire.

That was where Shambu Namboothiri found himself at a loss. The lane to his house was long and curved and three or four poles would be needed to draw the line to his house. He could arrange for teak poles to be brought from Chalakudy. But what about the wire? He was not willing to give up so easily. Certainly not when even the riff-raff lower-castes were erecting poles in front of their houses.

When Evron too expressed enthusiasm to draw wire to the hilltop, things became easy...

In the early days the anchal runner Chami, who got down from the boat from Kodungallur, literally ran to the post office to deliver the bag. Finally it was Shambu Namboothiri who told him: 'Just because you are called the anchal runner, you don't have to run all the time. You can walk once in a while.'

Though Chami was initially reluctant to give up what had become a habit, gradually he settled for a more rhythmic kind of a run, and from thence to a rhythmic walk. As for the pace of that walk, it became slower as time went on.

The post office and the anchal office were different. The post office was for British India, the anchal office for the kingdom of Kochi. The heads on the stamps too differed. One was the British queen, the other, the king of Kochi.

Later, when the magic of the telegram and the man who could tap the secret code on a wonder machine arrived, the post office wore a festive look. And Chellappa Menon who received the first telegram became a name in local history. His oldest son, Vishwam, who worked in a textile mill in Coimbatore, had sent him the telegram. 'Syamala delivered. Boy is a girl.' Menon was puzzled.

Finally it was Mani Menon master who interpreted the riddle: 'Syamala gave birth. The child is a girl.'

Thus the whole village was waking up. When Krishnankutty Menon, who studied engineering in Bangalore, started a huge handloom mill on the slope that led down from Kottayil Kovilakam, many were overjoyed. Evron was one of them. Though the mill was shut down after a few years, it was on that hilltop that the handloom culture of the land began...

After a while, Elias rented another room on the eastern side of the institute. He hung a blue board outside: Janata Agencies. Apart from becoming the direct agent for three newspapers, he also took on the agency for Nayak clocks from Mangalore. Depending on the school session, he began to order notebooks from the press at Kunnamkulam. Someone mentioned to him that the RMDC, the company in Bombay which ran the well-known crossword puzzles with handsome prizes, did not have an agent in the vicinity. 'You might get it if you try now,' he was told. 'The commission is good. If you are lucky you might even win a prize.'

Around the same time someone else arrived with an agency for a few other papers. The second newspaper agent of Chendamangalam.

Later on the village got its own reporter, Pilla Nambisan. When his first report appeared in print the unassuming Pilla Nambisan walked into the pages of regional history.

Elias left the house after breakfast. He returned only at noon. After a quick lunch, he hurried back to his office in Paliyam nada. He had found a place to spend the day.

When he grew older, Salamon too went there sometimes, but Elias would not allow him to linger for long. He would find some work to send him away. Only later did Salamon understand the reason for this. There were a number of young and attractive girls studying in the typewriting institute. He did not want the youngster roaming around in the building unnecessarily. The fame of Elias' institute had spread. Even conservative parents had no hesitation in sending their daughters to it. Elias had also given strict instructions to all concerned that discipline was most important, and not even a slight act of misconduct would be tolerated.

'Thus, our Elias is now on track, isn't that so, Evrone?' Evron knew at once that Eshumma meant it as a dig at him. In her eyes, he was the one who never did well.

'His time is good,' Evron said, directing a sharp look at Elias.

'It is not enough that the time is good. You need to have the ability for it.' As Rebecca came in with these words Evron felt her voice pierce him somewhere deep inside.He went out with lowered head.

'Managing things in the Panchayat is also a way of being on track, isn't that so, mole?' Eshumma intervened.

Rebecca's response was a faint smile.

Eliacha stopped with a long-drawn-out sigh.

'Because of what she said at that time, I have an occupation. Subran too.'

'The words she uttered had much greater significance,' Eliacha said. It did not just provide him an occupation. In a way Rebecca had provided that village a door to the world outside.

'As Umma says, the gods always pick the good ones. The ones no one wants remain,' Eliacha said. 'At times I feel like bringing back the past – slash off events and rewrite them. At those times it is the memory of Rebecca that appears first. Our carelessness. Our error. It is only when we lose them that we realize the worth of things.'

An unusual dampness spread in his voice. Salamon felt uncomfortable.

'And after a while that Esther,' Eliacha continued. 'It was a mistake on the part of the gods to bring together two people who were so ill-suited. And we carried the burden. At times I feel this is a house where women will not survive. As though someone performed black magic. In a way it is a good thing that I did not marry, isn't that so, Salamone? We were saved from seeing the tears of yet another woman.'

Esther...

Estheramma of Thoppumpady...

Salamon shivered. Memories were crowding into his mind. Unable to say anything, he quickly moved away.

'I need to go out.'

'Where?'

'Vadakkumpuram.'

'Why?'

'Just like that.'

'Oh...' Eliacha did not say anything after that.

Moses Master is Worried

In 1956 when states based on language were born, it was Moses master who rejoiced the most. At last, the state of Kerala had become a reality by merging the erstwhile Travancore-Cochin with Malabar. So happy was he that he took all the students who studied Hebrew to Sivan Moopan's tea stall and bought them black tea and pappada vada.

'Children, we are blessed that we have Panditji to rule the country,' he said. 'He is a writer and lover of books and, therefore, knows the greatness of language. What should you children learn from this?' he asked.

As usual, the children remained silent.

'What we call language is actually culture. Culture is what history is all about,' the master told them.

Though the students, who sat swinging their legs on the rickety benches in the tea stall, did not understand what he said, they realized that the event was something very important. The generosity of Moses master, known to be a miser, who did not offer even a cheap toffee to his students, surprised them. But a clever one amongst them, not willing to let go that easily, asked, 'Is language greater than everything else?'

'Why the doubt? Our language is the best, that which we heard on our mother's tongue.'

'Then our language is more important than us Jews, isn't it?'

'Quiet! Don't talk nonsense.' Moses master was roused. 'If all the people of a land speak the same language is there anything more blessed than that? There is only one such country in the world. Do you know which one it is?'

'This, our land.'

'No, eda,' the master corrected the boy. 'The land where we are going. From whichever corner of the world they come, whatever the language they speak, when they reach that land their tongue becomes one. The language that will emerge will be the holy divine language you learn now – Hebrew!'

When he banged the table for effect the glasses knocked against one another. The tea spilt. Sivan Moopan craned his neck from the kitchen to see what the commotion was.

Though they did not understand half of what the master said, the children nodded their heads. Their elders had already told them that if they wanted to go to the other shore and prosper they had to learn Hebrew.

However, when the communists came to power in the election to the Kerala assembly the following year, Moses master wondered whether the black tea and pappada vada had been for nothing. It was the first time in world history that communists had come to power through the ballot box.

'Things are in bad shape, member. Wonder what they are going to do,' Moses master said to Evron fretfully.

Moses master had a lot of concerns regarding the communists. More than that he feared them. They were the ones who did not hesitate to thrash and kill and throw bombs. They had perpetrated such terrible acts in Telangana! It was said that during the days when the police were on the lookout for communists, many had gone into hiding in Kunnumpuram and the nearby islands. Though they belonged to the same group as Comrade Jaleel, most of them were not friendly like him. They only travelled at night, going from place to place in great secrecy. Once the day dawned not one of them was seen. No one knew exactly where they went. It was easy to hide in the nearby islands. The policemen would find it difficult to get there fast enough by boat. That's why the parish priests constantly reminded their parishioners to keep a wary eye all around.

The communists were very cunning. If there was a police case against them in the state of Travancore they would escape into the state of Kochi by crossing the border at Andippillikavu or near Ayyappan's bridge. The reverse also happened. The boundary stone between the two states, inscribed 'KO-THI', stood like an alluring possibility mocking the policemen of both the states.

It was during that time that Eliamma chedathi's two plump cockerels went missing. One that she had vowed to offer at the church at Edapally, the other to serve her newly-wed brother and his bride when they came for the festive meal the following week. At first she thought a fox had got them; but Pathros achan had no doubt that the communists, who were on the prowl at night, were behind the theft. Eshumma too felt the same way. If the fox had caught them, wouldn't the other birds have screeched? But if it was communists who knew how to hypnotize chickens…

That was why Eshumma decided to have a large coop built next to the cowshed, one with thick wooden bars. Not just that, she moved the lambs from the enclosure next to the cowshed to the back veranda. What if the communists knew how to hypnotize goats as well?

And they were the ones who were going to enter the secretariat and govern the state!

'We did not need this new state, isn't that so, member?' Moses master asked.

'It is too early to say that, master,' Evron replied calmly.

'But there is a sense of instability.'

In a way what the master said was true. When Malabar joined Travancore-Cochin, a number of reds also came along. That is why they won the election. E.M.S. and A.K.G., they all came from the other side, didn't they?

'So what Panditji did, with the best of intentions, has become a curse for us, hasn't it?' Moses master lamented.

'Wait for a while, master. After all, Namboothiripad has just climbed into the chief minister's chair. Let him get accustomed to it, then let us see what he and the others do. After all, there are several great men with him.'

'We'll see.'

Moses master did not sound convinced. 'A leopard's spots don't disappear so easily. If not today, tomorrow its true form would be revealed.'

'True ... The cabinet included a line of eminent men. E.M.S. Namboodiripad, C. Achutha Menon, M.N. Govindan Nair, T.V. Thomas, Gowri Amma, Joseph Mundassery, V.R. Krishna Iyer, A.R. Menon ... men who had fought for freedom and were accomplished in various fields.'

Moses master was engrossed in his own thoughts, trying to assess each of them, making calculations accordingly. After a while he asked a little anxiously, 'Will all this bring our issue to a standstill? Will they create obstacles?'

'What issue?'

'That of our departure, of course.'

'Some have already gone, haven't they? And the

preparations for the rest are being made, master.' Seeing the master's expression Evron felt like laughing. 'There is still time,' he added.

Evron knew for sure that this was what was worrying Moses master.

To reassure him Evron said, 'Besides, the two are entirely different matters, master. The state government is not concerned with our departure.'

'Still…'

'Aye, there's nothing to worry about.'

'Suppose they bring up the old issue of filariasis…'

'What are you saying, master? All that was sorted out long ago. What is there to bring up now? The papers are already being processed.' After a pause he said emphatically, 'And there is no filariasis here!'

Despite this reassurance, certain doubts lay thick in the master's mind. The communists could do anything, couldn't they, since the government and the police were in their hands? Just as they were once suspects in the eyes of the government, suppose tomorrow they viewed Jews as suspects? He still remembered how the police kept a watch on them near the circle around the court when they took out a procession through the town, carrying the flag with the Star of David in the centre, on the day Prime Minister Ben Gurion of Israel declared independence. He also recalled several people telling him later that it was wrong to sing the anthem of another country and take out a procession holding their flag.

The only consolation was that Comrade Jaleel was still in Kunnumpuram. Jaleel was friendly with the Jews and was liked by all. He was a branch they could hold on to in case the party created any problems. A sturdy branch.

Moses master noted down two points in his mind, that too in the divine language that the *devils* did not understand –

One should always keep an eye on this group.

Try to reach the other side.

Also, the master subscribed for a newspaper. He made it a habit to go through the dailies that lay abandoned on the table in the staffroom. He had never bothered to do it until then.

Who knew what would happen, and when, or where ... He would not know that unless he saw the newspaper every day, would he?

Thus, Elias watched with amusement as the number of subscribers in Kunnumpuram increased, spurred by Moses master's various anxieties.

Veroni Seeks Salamon's Help

'**D**id you see our Elsie?'

As Veroni stepped into the yard, anger throbbing in her throat, Devassy mapla sat unmoved. For one who was used to sitting leaning against the pillar in the front veranda greedily inhaling the smoke of a beedi, his wife's anxious call was nothing new. He became truly conscious of the helplessness in it only when he began to spend the evenings in the house. And it was all because of Pathros achan's unwanted interference! He warned Devassy that the true and honest Chathedam Thupran's arrack would burn his intestines. 'No arrack, you can have toddy that is not too sour,' was his advice. Not just that, he threatened to drag Devassy to the altar and make him promise not to drink. He said he would take a final decision when the church's anniversary celebrations were over, based on Devassy's future conduct.

Thus, Devassy was forced into a situation where he could not walk along the road in front of Thupran's shop till the next anniversary celebration. But who went back on his word after the anniversary? What was the point in wasting money on freshly tapped toddy? It would just flow out with his pee. Though Devassy did not approve of his one and only daughter's habit of wandering around at dusk, he knew well that he lacked the authority to forbid it, because from the time he was crippled after the fall from the rooftop and forced to sit on that veranda, the girl knew exactly who she should obey.

Veroni, who went around collecting the chit fund instalments, did not view her sixteen-year-old daughter's whimsical wanderings on the hill and by the banks of the river as inappropriate because she too had run about freely in the market in Kottapuram and by the banks of the river without anyone keeping a watch on her. The arms and legs that gained strength in that manner had never gone astray either.

Crazed by the frustrating helplessness of sitting in the veranda, Devassy would grumble to himself, 'Whatever it is, can't the child come in at least when the chickens are put into the coop?'

But Veroni knew how to ensure that. Elsie had to be back before Chackalel Eli thathi's goats came home bleating, leaping over the bamboo barrier. After all the dumb creatures had a more precise awareness of dawn and dusk than human beings. Perhaps the girl sitting on the bank, enjoying the breeze that blew across the water, watching the western sun drop into the river like the ripe jambu fruit, would doze off, but the goats never missed their time.

But today the dark had started to descend early. The sound of Eli thathi's goats bleating was heard a while ago.

'Did you see our Elsie?'

Repeating the question, Veroni had stepped across the threshold and the yard and was already at the edge of the lane.

Devassy mapla continued to sit as though he had not heard her. Lost in the heady smoke of the beedi his heels tapped against the floor, the rhythm accelerating.

'Our Elsie…' Veroni was despairing.

Though the child's father did not move, Salamon who was coming along the lane heard and recognized the tremor in Veroni's voice. He thought that the emphatic utterance 'our Elsie' was directed at the community as well.

The moment Veroni saw Salamon she felt slightly relieved.

'The light is fading, Soloma,' Veroni said, distressed.

'Where do you think she went thathi?' Salamon asked.

'That…' Veroni scratched her head. 'Could be the landing, could be the hilltop, could be under the tamarind tree…'

As the list of possible locations lengthened, Salamon turned and walked back.

From which 'could be' should he start? He paused for a moment, thinking.

Then without saying a word he walked quickly towards the north. It was not dark enough for a full-grown girl to become invisible. Eli thathi's goats must have been blinded by the dark sky and the unexpected rain. And Elsie, seated under the tamarind tree on the slope of the hill enjoying the rain, might not have heard their clamour.

Salamon walked quickly in the fast-fading daylight. She would either be under that tamarind tree or by the river, he had no doubt about it. But first, the landing.

As soon as he climbed down the hill and reached the landing, he was sure she had not come that way. It was not safe for a young girl to loiter around there at that time. Most of the men who came across on the ferry after dark were drunk senseless.

He stood there for a while. It was exciting to watch the approaching dark and the faint daylight mingle on the water. He had heard that great artists often placed their easels on river banks to paint daybreak or the twilight hour. Not just on river banks but on top of hills, on slopes, on the beach…

Salamon saw the ferry coming from the other bank with its lantern lighted.

And suddenly he remembered. Elsie? A shiver went through him. Would she have reached home? Where should he look next?

On an impulse he once again climbed the hill.

What sort of a girl was this? Was she blindfolded that she did not see day had tumbled into night?

It had stopped drizzling and there was a slight breeze. It could start raining heavily soon.

Salamon walked fast. As he climbed the hill he saw Elsie, just as he had thought – sitting beneath the tamarind tree, lost in a dream. When she saw him she got up, pulling at the corban grass that clung to her skirt, a look of surprise on her face.

'So you were sitting here daydreaming, were you?' Salamon was furious. 'Veroni thathi is pulling at her rope in panic, crazed with fear.'

Elsie seemed amused. She said, 'Tell Appan to tie her up tighter. Suppose she sticks her horns into someone.'

Salamon said, 'Come, let's go.'

'Oh, you've come to take me home, have you?'

'What else?'

'I came here alone.'

'Grown-up girls should be home before dark, that is the rule.'

'Oh, so have you become old enough to quote rules for me?'

'Stop it, girl.'

'All right, tell me when does one become grown-up?'

'This one seems over-ripe,' Salamon murmured, looking nowhere in particular. Elsie seemed to have heard it.

'I think it is unwise to befriend these Jews.' She sounded annoyed.

Salamon began to walk, without bothering to reply. Elsie walked beside him.

It was quite dark by now. As they walked in the dim light, their shoulders rubbing each other, Salamon heard the pleats of her starched skirt crackle. The scent of stale gingelly oil. Elsie's scent. Earlier in childhood, when he used to lift her from the spathe of the areca palm, her sweat smelt like the Koori fish. She had grown up. Too quickly.

After a while he heard her mutter, 'Anyway, it is good to have a companion when it is dark.'

Searching for unspoken meanings in those words, Salamon quivered. As blood surged within him he felt an impulse to grasp her hand, to press it, just like that ... and to say something.

By that time Elsie's voice rose. 'Even otherwise, how can one trust these Jews?'

'Why not?'

'They are preparing to leave, aren't they?'

'For?'

'To their land.'

'Isn't this our land?'

'They say it's not.'

'Who says?' Salamon asked, bewildered. This girl knew too much!

'Everyone.'

Salamon was in a dilemma. Suppose he said he wasn't going anywhere? If he said that she would laugh mockingly. There was nothing that Veroni chedathi did not find out during her wanderings, through thickets and grasslands, to collect the chitty instalments. By now she must have got hold of the leaves and the roots of all the great preparations that were going on in Jew Street and Kizhakkumpuram. Not just that, there might be people in that group who claimed their chit fund money early for meeting the travel expenses.

So what reason could he give Elsie? Who would believe the words of a people who were selling all that they possessed and were preparing to cross the seas as a group?

Elsie waited for a while, expecting Salamon to respond. Then she probed, very skilfully: 'I heard that some people are to receive their papers soon?'

Again Salamon did not reply.

'Apparently, they are going by aeroplane, not by ship.'

'Who said that?'

'That old froggie woman who sells vellappam.'

'That woman is a liar. She will say many such things.'

'What about Moses master?'

'Master says different things at different times.'

'So what we hear are exaggerated nothings?'

Salamon evaded that question. 'Let those who want to go, go,' he muttered.

'So you are not going?'

'Who knows?'

'Why? Won't you get the papers?'

'Who knows?'

'Why? Aren't you a Jew? Then what about that old cap? If you discard the cap will you cease to be a Jew?'

Elsie always had a lot of questions. Questions for which there were no answers. He turned and looked at her as though wondering, how can I reply?

'But when all your people are leaving, why do you want to remain? To guard what? The graveyard of your ancestors?'

'All that you hear need not be true.'

'That means those people in Jerusalem don't want you!' She did not seem to be in a mood to put an end to her cross-questioning. 'Maybe you are a convert.'

Salamon wanted to speak about many things. Of things that tied him to that land. This soil. This hill. This river. These twilight hours. This breeze … then … then…

After a while he said slowly:

'I want to paint.'

Elsie stared at his face as though she did not understand. 'Really? Whose picture?'

Her eyes widened. Apart from the drawing master in school who went about chewing betel she had never seen anyone who painted.

'Whose?' she repeated with heightened curiosity. Salamon did not have a reply for that.

'Not of anyone.'

'Then you remain here and paint Elsie's picture. What can you find more beautiful than that?'

Salamon could not laugh. He was searching for something within him. Forms, vague ideas, unseen colours, that gained clarity when least expected. How could he give colour to his nebulous thoughts?

He coughed softly as his throat went dry.

Veroni was waiting at the gate. Salamon thought that she would scold her daughter or utter a couple of words thanking him, but nothing like that happened. Without looking him in the face she caught hold of Elsie's arm and went inside. As she entered the yard she said, a grave note in her voice: 'Go carefully, Soloma. There might be vipers on the path. These are bad times…'

It was Elsie who replied to that, her throat turned dry by the breeze from the river, 'But will snakes touch him? He's one of them.' It was then that Salamon remembered that snake was the nickname of one of the prominent members of his family. This Christian girl's tongue! The one who marries her is really in for it...

He bit his tongue. Something grew moist. Something was swallowed.

Comrade Pavithran Speaks

As usual comrade Pavithran was on the veranda of the reading room at Vadakkumpuram. Four or five of his cronies stood around him. The unusual seriousness on his face revealed that the topic of discussion was a grave one. Therefore, Salamon sat down in one corner of the narrow veranda, leaning against a pillar, so as not to bother him.

Evron disliked Pavithran intensely. One who loitered around without doing any work. He would leave home at daybreak, wearing a loose shirt, politician style, and it would be late in the night when he returned. Even at that time there would be two or three people accompanying him. An undisciplined, unruly group. In fact, the entire family were rabid communists. Wherever there was a flag and a procession one would find his father, Makotha, in the midst of it. Due to his skill in reciting long slogans in the inimitable rhythmic folk style, Pavithran got a place in the front ranks of the party in the beginning itself. When the lines penned by the leaders emerged from the front, with double their resonance, the ones behind took them up enthusiastically and repeated them. Later on as he began to read, his style changed. When he started adding his own juicy bits to the slogans given to him his followers became even more enthused. As popular party jargon like dialectical materialism, class conflict, disintegration of the state and Che Guevara entered the speeches that he delivered at street corners in an easy local style, there was no scarcity of venues or audiences. His power to use his tongue to capture the audience took him further forward later.

Afterwards during the 'Liberation Struggle' – popularly called Vimochana Samaram – against communist rule, when kathaprasangam artist Rajan conquered the entire region with his satirical tale *Bhagavan Macaroni* ridiculing the communists Pavithran had ready repartees for every one of his quips. Thus Pavithran followed the *Bhagavan* trail wherever it led. Because of the power of his tongue he received a fair amount of applause as well.

Party men often indulged in jealous gossip amongst themselves, mocking Pavithran's oratorical skills and the crowds he could attract. However toddy tapper Kunjappan, who always complained about the heavy language that the great leaders used, was all for Pavithran. 'Whatever it is, one can understand what he says.' Kunjappan was not interested in the complexities of Marxist ideology. After all, he was forgoing that evening's labour to sit before the loud speaker like a loyal follower and listen to the satire and criticism in words he could understand.

Pavithran was describing the community meal organized by Ayyappan master and his group in 1917. Ayyappan master, known as Sahodaran Ayyappan, had campaigned against the practice of untouchability in his community, the Ezhavas.

Pavithran's voice rose and fell according to the context. That was the usual style of his speech. Though Salamon was not really interested he sat there listening to Pavithran.

'Didn't we all go about abusing the upper class Namboothiris and Nairs at one time, in the name of caste?

During the time of the Paliyam struggle we were children. But I remember hearing the elders boast about the slogans they shouted in front of policeman Ummer's nose. And what! At one time pollution and untouchability existed even among us Ezhavas. Isn't it? With that in mind Narayanaguru Swamy advised Sahodaran Ayyappan when they met in the Advaita Ashrama at Aluva. After that master too became convinced that awareness of caste must first be driven out of the minds of our own community.'

Pavithran's narrative continued.

Gradually the crowd grew. A few going to the evening market and those who had come from the islands by ferry gathered around on the veranda and on the floor. With that Pavithran's fervour increased. Most of the youngsters had not heard of the historic community meal at Cherai.

Sit with people of those castes, whom they had kept at a distance till then, and have lunch with them. That was Ayyappan master's plan. But in spite of the elaborate plans he had made it was not going to be so easy. There was an uproar against the move from the powerful Ezhava community leaders and warnings were issued that anybody who violated their code would be dealt with severely.

'It was easy to start such a campaign. But they needed to get people, to eat and to serve, didn't they?' Pavithran laughed.

Then he began to describe the incident.

The idea was received with enthusiasm at first, but later many of those who stood with Ayyappan master drew back. The wall of evil practices was that thick. In the end only three people went along with him: his son-in-law Raman Pillai, Koru vaidyan and Karthikeyan. Though several others joined later on, that beginning was not easy.

The southwest monsoon season.

It had been raining since the morning. The arrangements had been made in Raman Pillai's house. With great difficulty they managed to find people to sit with them for lunch. Though many of those who had agreed earlier withdrew, intimidated by the threats of local bigwigs, two people came. An old Pulaya called Aiyar and his son Kannan. They stood by the gate, in the pouring rain, wet and shivering under a thoppi kuda, a leaf-umbrella, not daring to enter. Finally Koru vaidyan coaxed them to enter the yard.

And then to climb on to the veranda. Their cap-umbrella and torn mundus were removed, they were bathed, new towels were wrapped around them, sacred ash smeared on their foreheads. Finally they were made to sit down before the banana leaf. Rice was served with Bengal gram and jackfruit seed curry. Gradually more people arrived and the rice ran out. Many got just the jackfruit seed and Bengal gram curry...

Before he knew it, Salamon became engrossed in the story, for Pavithran was an adept narrator. As he continued the tale raising and lowering the pitch of his voice, using gestures and facial expressions, those around him sat open-mouthed, entranced by a period about which they had only a foggy idea. A period they found difficult to believe in today's circumstances.

'And then what, Soloma?' Pavithran turned towards Salamon. 'Things happened like a torpedo bursting out of a giant German ship. The locals, the church and the prominent citizens were furious. Things got really heated up – abuses, threats, prosecutions and judgements. Ayyappan master and his friends, who had spread poison by breaching the caste divide, became Pulayachovar. Twenty-two families were declared outcastes. They were prohibited from using water, fire, from washing clothes, shaving and a lot of other things…'

'Ente amme!' exclaimed a youngster with long sideburns, finding it hard to believe. 'Can such things be possible?' he asked, aghast.

'Do not say anything, friend.' Pavithran tapped him on the shoulder. 'The rage of some of our prominent people was worse than that of the Namboothiris. Can traditions that have existed from the time of their ancestors be ended by a few jackfruit seeds and Bengal gram curry, that was the question. Frightened by the threat of torture, some agreed to a compromise and re-entered the community. The next attempt was to round up the ones who continued to rebel and forcibly purify them; to seize them and take them to the entrance of the temple and douse them with holy water, force them to swallow panjagavyam. Those were the purification rituals, those were the techniques. Those who resisted had their mouths smeared with panjagavyam.'

Pavithran chuckled repeatedly as he recalled the incident. Strange times. A period when there were no flags, marches or slogans.

Salamon was waiting for the crowd to disperse. By the time it did, it was dark.

Pavithran's throat was parched. When sherbet appeared in Manuel's steel glass he became energetic once again. The bitter, tart taste of raw lime…

Salamon began hesitantly about the dream he had seen a couple of days back. The sea … the ship … the sea crows.

Pavithran chuckled softly, then laughed aloud, ripple upon ripple of laughter till he shook helplessly and his eyes welled up. When people walking along the cut road began to crane their necks to look, he controlled himself. Communists should not laugh so uncontrollably. Therefore he tried to summon as grave an expression as he could.

'This God's call of your elders!' Pavithran thumped Salamon on the back. 'Tell them to keep quiet, Soloma. If you lie down thinking about such unnecessary things, perhaps you will see all kinds of strange things ... ships, aeroplanes, ghosts, witches and what not ... That is how it is. I myself have dreamt of Comrade Lenin so many times at dawn. "What news, Pavithra, how is the village?" he asks, shaking my hand. That very moment his face grows dim ... The next thing I see is our Comrade Jaleel.'

Pavithran's shoulders shook as he laughed again. Salamon did not find that surprising. For the party members in Vadakkumpuram and Karimpadam Comrade Jaleel was Lenin and Comrade Lenin was Jaleel ikka. Besides, why did leaders need different faces? One face was more than sufficient for them, wasn't it?

There was a time when Evronappa was quite friendly with Jaleel ikka. But his opinion of Jaleel changed when he heard that he had donated all the wealth he inherited from his family to the party. After that, all sorts of adjectives and phrases like 'incompetent', 'one who has no sense of family', among others, were used to refer to him...

'We'll walk,' Pavithran suggested. Salamon nodded.

A light evening breeze was blowing. They walked silently. Pavithran's mind was still full of Ayyappan master.

'He was such a great man, wasn't he, Soloma?' Pavithran said. 'Isn't it because of the birth of a few such people that we can walk about swinging our arms freely, without fearing anyone? Do you know, during the time of our ancestors, the lower castes walked along this road howling, to make their presence known. If some Namboothiri or Nair appeared on the road they had to move aside to let them pass, that was the rule.'

'If they didn't?'

'They would be beaten. With a cane or a whip.'

Evronappa, who always talked about the past, had never mentioned this. Pavithran explained the reason for the omission.

'As Jews do not have castes there is no question of untouchability. Like Christians and Muslims, who also do not have caste, they could walk along Paliyam road or any road without taking anyone's permission. They did not have to move aside if they saw a Nair or a Namboothiri. We alone became lower castes, untouchables.'

That was new information for Salamon. Pavithran continued, 'That, of course, pertains to this land. Who knows, there could be such distinctions in the place you are going to. The whites and the blacks. It is the white man's law. The one with fair skin is always at the top. So is that not caste difference? You know about the Paradesi Jews of Mattancherry, don't you? They came so much later than your people. Yet because of their fair European skin they became superior and you all are just Malabaris. Do you know what they used to say about your people?'

Salamon shook his head. Though he had heard Eliacha say something about it, he did not quite remember what it was.

'In their eyes, you all are the offspring of slaves. That is why they deny you entry in their synagogue, do not allow you to marry their women. So isn't there caste among Jews as well? Maybe it spread from the Hindus here, I don't know.'

They had reached Paliyam nada by this time.

They sat on the culvert. By then Sankaranarayanan's news report from All India Radio Delhi had begun. It came to them through the aluminium loudspeaker of the Nair Samajam.

Pavithran seemed eager to continue with whatever it was he wanted to say. Perhaps enthused by Ayyappan master and the community meal! The subject could have been the Russian Revolution or the Edapally Police Station attack case. Impatient to bring the discussion back to his own concern, Salamon placed his hand on Pavithran's shoulder. As though he understood, Pavithran continued, 'Do you know what the justification behind this so-called migration is?' Confronted with Pavithran's booming voice Salamon cowered.

What justification? What migration? None of it made sense.

'In the past, many people from our land boarded the ship to Burma, Ceylon and Malacca. Not to gather ingots of gold from the streets over there. They went to work as coolies in the white man's plantations. The more educated ones became clerks. They had no other way out, for hunger and despair was ravaging the land after the war. Was it truly a migration?'

As Salamon's eyes widened, Pavithran himself provided the answer.

'Though some of the smart ones married the women of that land and settled down, most of them kept working till they grew old, their blood ran dry and they could not work any more; they then sold all their belongings and returned to their native land. Why? Because it was not a migration, just a desperate attempt to make a living. Is that the condition of the Jews here? You were born here, grew up here, became natives of this land. How can you grow roots in strange soil?'

Salamon nodded as though he agreed.

'Not just that, you are not leaving in ones and twos like those who went to work in the plantations. You are leaving this land, this country, as a group, every one of you, with your families, from Chendamangalam, from Paravur, from Mala, from Mattancherry ... An exodus, leaving an entire street free for cats and dogs ... What has happened here to cause such a departure? When your people were forced to scatter throughout the world, didn't this land stretch out its arms and welcome you? Didn't the king of Kochi give the desperate refugees land close to the palace? Didn't he extend his support when the attacks by the Portuguese increased? If so, isn't this ingratitude?' Pavithran's voice rose.

Salamon did not have an answer. In truth, what was the purpose of this mass migration? It was a question he had asked himself several times. He knew there was no point in asking it at home and to his people. They all had just one reply.

Yosef hazzan, who recited prayers in the synagogue, and David muliyar, who came to teach Torah, said the same thing.

The call of the holy land. The call of the fatherland. The true Jews around the world could not ignore that call.

But was the land of hearsay greater than the land where you were born?

'The call of the holy land!' When Salamon unconsciously said this, Pavithran was irritated.

'What holy land? Land that was seized from someone. Land you try to enlarge by a show of strength. And some Western capitalist countries to back you!'

What about the fatherland Vyloppilli master sang about? What about the atrocities that the Jews once suffered?

'Vyloppilli is a poet, isn't he? Poets see several such dreams. They also write about a lot of things. You need not read too many meanings in them. Then again, if Jews have been persecuted they themselves were responsible for it to some extent. The Jews in other lands were not the harmless ones we see here.'

Seeing the bewildered look on Salamon's face Pavithran softened a bit. He said in a milder tone, 'Look at this. This vast expanse of land that lies in front of our house till the edge of that road; who do you think it belongs to? Velayudan chettan, who trades in rice in the Kottapuram market. Money that he made by smuggling rice from Travancore when there was control over the import of rice. With that money he bought all the land he could, and encroached on some public land as well. Land that had high-yielding coconut trees. Enough wealth for two generations to live lavishly. Let that be. What about the thirty-six cents of land behind our house by the side of the river? It belongs to Hyder Ali of Vedimara, who owns a timber mill in Perumbavur. He bought thirty-one-and-a-half cents; acquired the remaining four-and-a-half from the river through land-fill. In my childhood the washerwoman Devayani washed clothes at that bank. Hyder Ali first began to come that way to see the birthmark on her thigh as she washed the clothes, her striped mundu lifted thigh-high. But Devayani was a sharp one. The moment she saw someone coming, she pulled down the mundu. She was determined not to provide such easy pleasure. Then what? When Devayani, whose husband had left her long ago and who had no children, fell ill and became bedridden, Hyder Ali came to see her with great concern. He saw the birthmark and got her to sign over the land at a throwaway price.'

Pavithran coughed, swallowed and continued.

'My grandfather often says that, at one time, all that land belonged to our relatives. The elders sold everything. And now all that we have is the ten cents of land we got merely because we tenant it. Not even enough land to provide a decent burial for everyone in the family. It is natural in such circumstances to eye the land that lies next to ours, isn't it? Now suppose one day I bring along four or five hefty thugs and grab ten cents of land from either side. If one is to cite rights, we too have the right of inheritance to that land. Our ancestors have been laid to rest in that soil. Isn't that so? Velayudan chettan, washerwoman Devayani, mill owner Hyder Ali, they are all outsiders, aren't they?'

As Salamon stood puzzled, wondering why Pavithran was telling him all this, the latter lit a beedi, inhaled deeply twice and concluded: 'Isn't the story of your holy land the same of one taken forcibly?'

Salamon understood nothing. What did that faraway land have to do with Velayudan chettan and Devayani? He could tell this story to Elsie. Or Eliacha.

After a while, Pavithran continued slowly, 'It is not a simple game that your people are playing lying amidst the Palestinians. It is the arrogance of having America to support them.'

Salamon just nodded his head.

'Therefore, your elders too might say such nonsense from time to time. It is wiser to think of it as their idealism and dismiss it immediately. But tell me the truth, do you want to go?'

Salamon did not answer. He was not sure about it himself.

'A land no one has seen or heard about,' Pavithran reminded him. 'I hear it is all desert. Maybe it is the fate of some people to be scorched to death in that heat!'

The party had a definite stand regarding the mass exodus of Jews from Kizhakkumpuram to the land across the sea. Comrade Jaleel had spoken about it to Evron when he went about enthusiastically to make it happen. You should not get excited over something the Paradesis in Mattancherry say. They are somewhat like the British. So you should have your own view point on the subject. After living here comfortably for so many generations, going so far away to a place no one has heard about…

Pavithran was repeating the same thing.

'When the Paradesis reach Israel they will wear coats and trousers, speak English and prosper. Of course, the country needs people to work under the whites who come from different parts of the world. So the dark Jews from Mala and Chendamangalam and Paravur will serve that purpose! A Sara who belonged to the Mattancherry group was with us in college in Ernakulam. You should have seen her colour! In those days, everyone was after her…'

That was true, Salamon thought. They were so fair! Truly, it was the caste difference Pavithran spoke about.

'There might be notions of pollution and untouchability there as well. Untouchables howling to announce their presence! However, there will be no Sahodaran Ayyappan to hold a community meal.' Pavithran laughed. After a slight pause he continued gravely, 'Difference of caste becomes a broader one of race, that is all.'

Whom did Pavithran resemble now? Jaleel ikka or Comrade Lenin himself?

Similar talk from Vadakkumpuram and Karimpadam had reached Evron's ears as well. Arguments on the subject had taken place on the veranda of the Panchayat office and at Malavana landing. At such times the misfortune of having no one to support him in the arguments often vexed Evron.

'That is why I tell you not to go along with that group of insolent ones,' he reprimanded his son. 'These communists who have neither temple nor church are always on the side of the Arabs. They are against us having our own country. When America aids the Jews, Russia is on the opposite side, on the side of the Palestinians. That is the way it works. Just think of it as God's call to us. Do you know what happened towards the end of '49?'

Salamon had heard it all several times. Apparently, as it was flying over the sea, one engine of the aeroplane that was carrying the first group of people from Kochi developed a leak in its fuel tank and stopped working. And it was the day of the holy Hanukkah. The arms of the sky were there to safeguard the people who had lost all hope. Not only did they return to Bombay safely, but the plane was repaired and they landed on the soil of Jerusalem on New Year's Day. At a time when snow was falling, they spent several days in a tent in the desert, without any woollen clothes. Now some two thousand people were waiting, ready to leave. Half of them were from Ernakulam and Kochi. The rest from Chendamangalam, Paravur and Mala.

Salamon was not interested in these old stories. He repeated to himself the question that had been echoing in him for some time.

Do I want to go to the other shore?

The vague reply that he had given Varuthutty master would not work with Comrade Pavithran. He was adept at asking piercing questions one after another.

'Tell the truth.' Salamon felt the grip on his shoulder tighten. 'Do you want to go?'

'Well, when everyone goes ...' The lack of decisiveness in his reply distressed Salamon. 'Evron appa, Menahem mutha, Eliacha, Eshimuthimma, Ephraim...'

'Enough, enough.' Pavithran stopped him. 'I did not ask for a roll call of all the Jews in that street. I want to hear what you think. You are a full-grown man after all! You must have gained some awareness and should have an opinion of your own, especially after going along with us for so long.'

'If everyone leaves Jew Street—'

'The world has been won by those who dared to tread a different path, Soloma,' Pavithran cut him short. 'That is being the lone soldier. Let those who want to go, go. That is their fate. You have a backbone and a strong body. Instead of being scorched in that desert can't you do some work and live here? Whatever it is, you have a house to live in. You could start some business next to it?'

'They are going to sell all that.'

'Why?'

'They need money to deposit in the agency in Kochi.'

Pavithran began to laugh when he heard it. 'Aren't the whites wealthy capitalists? Shouldn't they bear the cost of taking all the Jews who, having heard the call of the holy land, wait in every corner of the world to board the ship? Why should the poor sell all that they have and deposit money in the agency?'

Salamon did not have an answer to that question.

'Well, they say that those who have money must pay.'

'So you are among the haves, are you? And they are the have-nots?'

Even otherwise, in Pavithran's eyes there were only two castes in the world, the haves and the have-nots. How could the haves include the dark-skinned ones among them?

'That…' Salamon was faced with a dilemma. 'When the agency insists…'

Though Pavithran continued to talk, none of it fell on Salamon's ears. It was pointless to argue with Pavithran. As one who had mastered the art of interspersing hard and soft techniques in the party's study classes, he would have no problem forcing Salamon into a corner and tying him down.

It was growing late. If he delayed getting back too much Muthimma would be out on the street waiting for him. She might even walk to the ground in front of the synagogue to seek information from passers-by. She could be that worried. It was not just thunder and lightning, Jehovah might have prepared so many other ways of punishing the bechor.

'Let us go,' he said hastily. Pavithran nodded.

They got up.

The dark was thickening. Where could the treacherous hands of the gods of the skies be hiding? Though at first Salamon used to dismiss it as one of Muthimma's several tactics to frighten children, when Yosef hazzan, who conducted prayers in the synagogue, said the same thing, he began to think that there must be something to it.

He hurried along, considering plausible lies he could tell Muthimma.

Trapped: An Idle Ribbing
and its Aftermath

'Mothalatta, that girl is chattel indeed, isn't she?'
There was a sly grin on his face when Lohithakshan
from Cheriya Pallanthuruthu said this. Salamon flinched.

'And till now you have not done *anything* …?' Pushpan
from Kaitharam joined in.

'Shhe! What are you saying?' Salamon was embarrassed.

'What "shhe"? After touching and brushing against each
other for so long…'

'Nothing like that … It is not right.'

'Is it because you don't know how to go about it? If so,
I'll tell you in detail.'

'Let it go … Let's talk of something else.' Salamon tried
to change the subject.

Ouso from Thuruthu alone stood apart, saying nothing,
looking slightly uncomfortable.

'Don't feel shy, Soloma. All of us have gone through this.
But mind you, it's not enough to have the jaggery-sweet
mango within your reach. You should know how to aim a
stone and make it fall, know how to eat it. It may not be as
it appears. Some might be sour, some sweet.' Lohithakshan
seemed determined to go on.

'Indeed, you don't even have to throw a stone. She's the type that needs just one good shake to fall. Can't you see it in the way she walks?'

'Rubbish. She is not that type.' Even as he tried to put an end to the discussion, Salamon was vexed by the weakness in his voice.

'There is no typewriting and shorthand in all this. Let's say it depends on your being smart or not. Now tell the truth. Haven't you done anything till now, not even a little something?'

Salamon flinched once again. If he told them that his friendship with Elsie had nothing to do with sex, they would keep teasing him. Their belief that he was timid would be strengthened.

'No wonder she allows this innocent Jew to tag along behind her ... She need not be wary of him. If it had been some Christian boy you would have seen the difference,' Clement said annoyingly. 'It's always so. God does not put the stick in the hands of the one who can aim and strike.'

'Leave him alone,' Ouso said, tapping Clement on his shoulder.

Listening to all this, Salamon's anger and frustration were mounting. They were trying to humiliate not just him but his race. Suddenly, his voice grew louder. 'Enough, that's enough. Just stop this.'

'Then tell the truth.'

'Well ... one does not become friends just like that, after all...' The words were out before he could stop them.

'Meaning?' The eyes of the listeners glittered, their ears grew sharp. Some hands, he did not know whose, fell on his shoulder.

'Well, things have happened, you know...'

'Really! Go on, tell us…'

'Well, like … like…'

'Like what?' There was mockery in the tone.

Forced into a corner Salamon blurted, 'I have kissed her…' His voice sounded weak. He lowered his head without realizing it.

'Oh, yes … yes … that's a story!'

'Believe if you want to,' Salamon retorted.

'How many times?'

'Lots.'

'And she?'

'I think she liked it…'

'Oh Jesus!'

'Then?'

'Then what? Then nothing.'

'What do you mean?'

'That … that…' At his wit's end, Salamon said angrily, 'Don't get your hopes up. I am not going to tell you.'

Although the ribbing ended there, Salamon was smarting, on behalf of himself, on behalf of his race. The boys did not quite believe him. 'He must have bluffed when he found himself cornered,' they mocked. 'She is the kind who could confront two or three like him and lay them flat on their backs.'

Ouso alone said nothing.

However, the incident was a revelation for Salamon. Was there a grain of truth in what his friends had been asking? It was hard to believe that he and Elsie had been friends for all these years and yet nothing had happened between them. Had any such thought even crept into his mind? Truthfully? Even when he found her beside him, he hesitated to grasp her hand, let alone kiss her! Was he waiting for some overture from her side? Or was he scared of her? What if Veroni, with her one-and-a-half-measure-long tongue, got to know?

It was a harmless lie. Salamon decided to leave it as it was, at least for the time being.

But even as he thought about it, he felt a shudder pass through him. Like Lohithakshan and the others, did she too see him as a weakling, an unassertive good-for-nothing? Was her relentless teasing a way of saying the unsaid? Was there a hidden meaning in what she once said biting her lip, that Jewish boys were fit only for business? After all, what more could a young girl say? The male should make the first move, shouldn't he?

Then unexpectedly, on a day when Thupran's arrack shop remained close due to some strike and Devassy mapla wandered about in search of another and got trapped among the arrack brewing sheds of Gothuruthu, and Veroni, making her rounds to collect the chit instalments, went to see Devaki, who pounded husks to make fibre, got caught up in her problems and was unaccountably delayed...

It was evening when Salamon entered the yard.

Elsie was lying on her belly near the threshold, reading a weekly magazine. Mincent's loud snores could be heard in the lane.

Bewildered by Salamon's flushed face, tense voice and the strange look in his eyes, Elsie came out carrying a mud pot full of water. She found him sitting in the veranda panting.

'What is it? What happened to you? Aren't you well?' she asked.

Salamon could not speak.

'They say there is fever all over the village. It's so hot this year!'

He had come with a lot of plans. But now he couldn't even speak. He tried hard to scrape out the scorched words from his burning throat.

Suddenly, something flashed in Elsie's mind. The timing of his arrival was unusual. It seemed as though it had been planned. That he was aware of its oddness was evident in the confusion on his face.

'Appan?' There was a tremor in his voice.

'Ah ... Who knows? I saw him go out somewhere, leaning on his stick,' Elsie replied casually.

'Thathi?'

'Who knows?'

Inside the house the tune of Mincent's snoring changed.

When she stared hard at his face Elsie felt her heart waver ... but then a wick lit up within her, the wick that kind Mother Mary kindles to support vulnerable girls in such situations. She said gently, 'Soloma, leave.'

'What?' His voice broke.

'I said you must go now.'

'I ... I...'

'It is better you leave now ... for both of us.'

'Elsie, I want to say...'

As she saw his hand stretch towards her she quickly took two steps back and leaned against the door frame.

'I told you to leave...' Her voice rose. 'Come when there is light, and when there are people in the house. That is real manhood.'

'I want to say...' As he once again began to stutter an explanation, the door was shut with a loud bang.

He stood in front of the shut door stunned, unable to say a word. As he began to walk back he heard loud laughter and

mocking howls within him ... there were several voices ...
Ouso's, Lohithakshan's, Pushpan's, and many others.

Was there a female voice amidst them?

Salamon shuddered.

Call Me Estheramma

For some time now Salamon was becoming aware that Estheramma was intruding into the broken strands of his memory, mostly during the heavy monsoon downpour and the chilly winter months. Estheramma, the wife of Menahem mutha in Thoppumpady. Younger than Rebeccamma. Much younger than Evronappa. Much, much younger than Menahem mutha.

At a time when he was wondering how he should address Menahem mutha's wife, it was Estheramma herself who suggested that he call her that: Estheramma. 'Or else, call me Esther. That too is fine,' she'd said.

Right from the beginning, for some inexplicable reason, Eshimuthimma did not like her oldest daughter-in-law who entered the house as the second.

'Her red colour and her walk!' she often muttered.

There was nothing wrong with Esther's gait. She was not impetuous like Rebecca. Yes, she did walk with her head bent forward. There was an air of helplessness about her. As for the red skin, it was a frothy pinkish hue. After all she was born in Baghdad, and grew up in Bombay. So when she first came there her way of talking was weird, they said. She spoke a mixture of Hindi and Marathi with a sprinkling of Malayalam words, so the elders found it difficult to make sense of what she said. It was after she lived in Thoppumpady for some time that her language became somewhat better.

Her attire too was different. A kind of 'town' style with a low-cut blouse and knee-length frock. These must have been the things that made her seem improper to Eshimuthimma.

It was after much waiting that Menahem brought home a girl. Eshimuthimma had begun to believe that the eldest was fated to follow the path of God, when suddenly on a Passover day he announced: 'I am going to get married.'

Those who heard it were stunned at first. Later, they were relieved.

'He has affection for his mother, after all; concern for her well-being. With Rebecca gone he has indeed found someone to be a support for his mother in her old age!'

However Eshumma asked searchingly, 'You went about saying repeatedly that you did not want a girl; why the sudden change?'

'No particular reason.' There was an embarrassed smile on Menahem's face.

'What, did they throw you out from God's path?'

'Shhe!'

It was much later that Eshumma realized that he had already chosen the girl. Some Esther. Stubborn, just like his younger brother, she thought angrily.

Eshumma tried to wander through pathways familiar to her, to find details about the girl and the family, but there was no hint of an Esther anywhere.

'She is from Thoppumpady,' Menahem told her.

Gradually things began to come out. Esther was half-foreign. Her father was from Thoppumpady. Her mother was Persian. Though she was born in Baghdad she grew up in Bombay because when his Persian wife died, the father returned to Bombay to work in a textile mill. After his retirement, he returned to his native land.

'That is how it always is, Umma. Once the stalk is clipped, it falls near the root,' Evron solemnly repeated the old saying.

'Still, ente Evrone.' Eshumma was inconsolable. 'What great sin did Isaac muthacha's sons commit for a foreigner to be brought into the house as a bride?'

'But she is not a foreigner, Umma. She speaks our language fluently.' Evron tried to soothe her but failed.

Esther's vava was against the marriage. A villager who went about preaching about God was not his idea of the perfect husband for his daughter. Such an alliance did not suit his status. Besides, he already had in mind a smart young man he had met during the festivities at the synagogue. A good-looking man who was employed at the court in Ernakulam. He was attracted to Esther the moment he saw her. Esther's vava was waiting for her to become more pliant to broach the subject.

When Umma too objected, Menahem became anxious that things could get out of hand in the beginning itself. Therefore his first attempt was to get Evron on his side.

Though Evron tried to shrug off the responsibility by saying that Umma was adamant Menahem did not let him go.

'You go about solving the problems of all the villagers, yet when it comes to something that concerns your own brother, you are not interested. That is not right, is it?'

'No, it's not like that.'

'That time when it was your problem I was on your side,' Menahem reminded him.

'All that is true, but this time Umma is really angry.'

'What can I do, Evrone, I gave her my word.' Menahem looked pale. Evron quickly understood Menahem's anxiety.

The agony he had gone through when he had sent Manuel to find Panayappilly Rebecca! The tension on Menahem's face was twice what he had suffered. He was generally a grave man whose words went dry the moment he crossed the threshold of the house; but now he appeared drained of all strength as well.

'Therefore you should somehow straighten this out for me, Evrone.' Very much unlike himself, Menahem stood before his younger brother and pleaded. He also pointed Esther out to him in the synagogue at Thekkumbhagam. Though Evron was now convinced that she was not a foreigner, he knew it would not be easy to persuade Umma.

One day he approached Umma as she was grinding chillies on the stone in the kitchen veranda.

'Isn't your work finished yet, Umma?'

Eshumma straightened, stretching out her hand smeared with chilli paste. There was displeasure in the eyes reddened by having blown on the damp coconut fronds to light the fire in the stove.

'What is it, member, you have come to your Umma all sweetness and honey? Generally, you are like a buffalo about to gore someone!'

'Nothing, Umma, just like that.'

'There is something … you are out to get me into a fix.'

'It's about our Menahem.'

'What happened to him?'

'Let's agree to this marriage, Umma,' Evron said gently.

'Go away. It's time for the Panchayat meeting … There will be space on the veranda.'

'Please listen, Umma. Poor Menahem will be upset.'

'Poda! Upset!' Eshumma's voice rose. She did not look up from the grinding stone. 'The mothers who give birth and watch their children grow, they too are upset. Just because you behaved in a self-willed manner, Menahem, who goes about with his synagogue and his preaching ... You should know better...'

'My wilful behaviour did not cause you pain, Umma. You two were like jaggery and bees, weren't you?' Evron asked crossly.

'That was because she was from heaven.'

Eshumma stopped abruptly. Her hand shook, scattering chilli paste all around. But Umma did not seem to notice. Evron knew that any reference to Rebecca ended in weeping.

'How do you know Esther is not like that?' Evron asked.

'Onnu poda got himself a Persian ... As though there are no girls in this land!'

'It was her mother who was Persian. She is dead, isn't she?'

'There are such lovely girls in our Mala.'

'Then why didn't you get him married before?'

'Because he said he did not want to.'

'That is what I am saying, Umma, now when he says he wants to marry it is our duty to arrange it. The family is well-off. Menahem is lucky to get such an alliance.'

'Still, Evrone, there should be some sameness...'

'All that will happen gradually. As it did with Rebecca.'

The unsaid meaning in Evron's words distressed her. Why was he bringing up her name again and again, quite unnecessarily?

'If we don't arrange the marriage, they know what to do,' Evron warned.

Eshumma looked at him enquiringly.

'They will go to the registrar's office, that's all.'

'A man who goes about preaching the holy book go to a registrar's office? Ha! What a joke!'

'Why? They don't allow Jews to enter the registrar's office?'

Eshumma knew that such a marriage was unlikely. Marriages are not between a boy and a girl, but between two families. That is why it is always the community which solemnizes a marriage. It should take place in an atmosphere of friendliness and gaiety, where the whole community celebrates. She had never heard of any Jew who had antagonized the synagogue, and the community, and crossed the threshold of a registrar's office. Umma however realized that things were moving in an unacceptable direction, so she said nothing more. As she gathered the paste from the stone, her eyes looked redder than before.

Thus, the wedding that no one was happy about took place. It was a short ceremony which left out many of the customary rituals. As a result a feast was arranged in the house that night for their friends.

As Menahem entered the house in the bridegroom's garb and holding the bride's hand, heads appeared above the fence as usual. There were many among them who had heard the news and come to see the spectacle.

The day Esther entered the house, Eshumma realized the problem lay in the bride's language. By the time one figured out what she was saying from the alloy that emerged from her mouth, one would lose patience. If the bride who enters the house does not have a tongue to speak to the mother-in-law or a ear to listen to her, the mother-in-law shrivels up. The daughter-in-law, who can hide behind the barrier of language, wins.

Two days later the women in the neighbourhood cross-questioned Eshumma.

'From where did our Menahem get this foreigner, Eshumma?'

'Who knows? I think she got into him in a synagogue in Bombay,' Eshumma replied without enthusiasm.

'We heard them talk charupira ... with each other. She doesn't know our language, do you think?'

'It is not that she doesn't know. Just acting smart, the arrogance of growing up in a town.'

'What a fate, Eshumma! Now you will have to learn French in your old age!'

The women were peeved because the bride did not come to the fence to chat with them. Esther did not know that making friends with those on the other side of the fence was the first lesson a bride in a village should learn.

It was not Esther's language that was the problem for Eshumma. Unlike Rebecca, Esther did not know how to tune her behaviour according to the mother's ways and moods. Esther always wore a sweet smile, a smile that could be read in different ways, that could make those who received it feel big or small. When she smiled, her face would be flushed and look round like the jambu fruit. Salamon felt like standing and staring at her. He was studying in the primary class at that time.

After Esther's arrival Salamon gained some importance in school. No one had seen a foreigner, except in the news reel in the cinema hall.

'Is she really a foreigner?' Ephraim asked.

'Of course.'

'She speaks English to you?'

'Of course.'

'Does she wear a skirt at home?'

'You can see that, can't you?'

'Do they eat what we eat?'

'Sometimes we have special dishes.'

'They say they don't wash after they shit. Is it true?' Ouso from the island wanted to know.

That was news to Salamon. But since he did not know for sure he replied solemnly, 'Umm ... sometimes it is like that.'

For the local people, Menahem mutha's sudden marriage was a matter of surprise.

How did someone who said he did not want to marry and went about with his preaching and his duties at the synagogue suddenly descend into worldly affairs?

'Must have used some kind of black magic. From her face you can tell she is cunning!'

When someone said this nastily, Muthimma nodded. How else could one who was going along God's path experience such a change of heart?

But there were others who wondered who had cast a spell on whom. How did the brown-skinned, gaunt and shrivelled Menahem get such a beautiful bird-like girl who was so much younger than him?

Evron alone knew the facts and he told them to Elias.

'This connection dates back to the time Menahem was in Bombay,' he said. They were close for a long time. Menahem's sudden return and his decision to go along God's path were the result of dejection caused by some trivial misunderstanding between them. What he told us earlier, that he had returned because the company he worked in closed down, is not true. Similarly, the girl's vava wanted to continue in Bombay after he retired but they too returned to Mattancherry at his family's insistence.

It was the couple's fate that after so many years they should meet again in the grounds of Thekkumbhagam synagogue.

In a way is that not God's plan?

Eshumma's grumbling never ceased. She had good reason for her complaints. A mother who gives birth to three sons always expects support from the women they bring home. But here...

'Without saying one word to their umma, both her older sons had brought home a woman – one from Kochi, and the other from abroad. Two totally different types. If one was over-friendly, the other did not seem to notice anyone at all.' Unfortunately, Eshumma did not have the insight to recognize that the roots and the ways of the two were very different.

Though Esther could read some of the mother's misgivings from her face, she had no idea how she should adapt herself to please her. By the time she came, Rebecca had gone. Therefore she knew no tricks to win over her mother-in-law or become friendly with the neighbours.

Every time Eshumma saw Esther's white skin she wondered whether she could enter the Mattancherry synagogue.

She often asked her son, 'Evrone, do you think they will let her enter the Paradesi synagogue in Mattancherry? She has a white woman's colour.'

'She got it from her umma, didn't she?'

'But can she go in there because of that?'

'If they let her, she can,' Evron replied indifferently. 'If she was truly a foreigner would they have allowed this marriage?'

'I already told you she is not a foreigner, Umma. So why all this fuss?'

'Must be Thekkumbhagam. That is why she is so arrogant.'

There were many stories underlying that comment. People of Thekkumbhagam did not generally give their daughters in marriage to those in Kadavumbhagam because they thought themselves superior to the others.

'Just let it be, Umma. Times are changing.' Evron's voice rose.

'Still…'

'They have got married, haven't they? What is the point in searching for roots and branches?' Evron snapped and walked off.

'Whenever I speak the truth the member bursts out angrily!' Eshumma muttered to herself.

Whatever Eshumma's reservations were, one thing Esther had gathered very early. The shadow of Rebecca, who preceded her, lay vertically upon that house. Everyone loved her. Her presence was everywhere. After all these years, even Evron had not been able to get away.

What had Rebecca looked like? How had she managed to get around Eshumma?

She had once heard Kallu Moopathi, who came to sweep the yard, say that Rebecca was a big support to the mother and that she went about briskly, doing the household chores. But how could Esther go about doing chores if Umma did not give her any work to do? If she went to help in the kitchen Umma's face would puff up with displeasure. If she prepared fish or cut vegetables, they were not evenly done. If she washed vessels they were not clean enough. Esther was not used to such covert fighting strategies.

'She criticizes everything. What shall I do, Menahem?' She once asked her husband.

'Don't let it affect you,' he tried to comfort her. 'It is just that she measures you against Rebecca in everything.'

That made Esther angry. 'Those who have gone have gone. If you continue to...'

'Try to get along with her. After a while she'll cool down and become friendly.'

Esther did not know how else she could get along with Umma.

Once, when he got tired of hearing Eshumma's grumbling, Evron too tried to comfort Esther.

'She's old, Esther. How much longer will she live? You all have seen the world. Just pretend not to see or hear certain things. That is all you can do.'

Though she did not wholly understand what he meant, she gradually got into the habit of doing whatever she wanted without being openly rude to the mother.

But Menahem was watching. So was Evron. Both knew that if they said anything against her, Umma would bring the conversation back to Rebecca. As long as memories of Rebecca remained unhealed wounds, such disapproval could not be avoided.

Thus one evening when, without any forewarning, Menahem and Esther went down the steps with bag and baggage, Eshumma did not stop them, did not call after them to come back; it appeared as though she had not seen them. After all, she had mentally rejected her eldest daughter-in-law a long time ago.

But when he watched them leave without looking back even once, Evron was upset.

'Umma, if you had said one word they'd...' he said sadly.

'Oh, really.' Umma pursed her lips. 'If they want to go, let them. I am spared the strain of cooking and serving two more.'

'Still, my Umma, it must have hurt Menahem terribly.'
Evron's voice rose.

'If he wants to leave the house where he was born and
the woman who gave birth to him to go and live in his wife's
house, who am I, a magistrate or muliyar, to stop him?'

When Pathros achan asked if he should try for a
reconciliation, Evron said that he should not. Eshumma was
Eshumma. Once something was engraved in her heart it was
difficult to erase. There had been instances when even headstrong Muthacha had lowered his head before her.

The truth was, Esther's vava had been unwilling to
leave Bombay. For one who had seen the city grow before
his eyes, both the bright and dark sides of city life were
equally appealing. Even otherwise, those who are used to
the conveniences of city life fear the countryside. However,
when certain relatives in Thoppumpady suggested that he
should return, it was Esther who had protested at first. She
had many questions. Were there theatres that showed Hindi
films? Do new films come there? Do they get Radio Ceylon?
Because a world without Madhubala, Suraiya, Dilip Kumar,
Dev Anand and Ameen Sayani was a jungle. Even after
seeing *Mughal-e-Azam* thrice in Maratha Mandir, Anarkali's
pain still haunted her.

'Yes, they do,' the relatives in Thoppumpady asserted
with conviction. 'You can also get Radio Ceylon and Ameen
Sayani. Films of Dilip Kumar, Madhubala and Suraiya come
to the nearby Patel Talkies. If that is not enough, there is
Menaka Theatre on the other side of the backwaters. Quite
a few English films come there.'

Vava still hesitated. What life would it be, without the
tram and the local train, the pushing and shoving, the noise

and bustle, the sea breeze and the night lights and the unending traffic along the roads! After all this time he had forgotten how to walk. The ordinary Bombayite's gait is a sort of running, isn't it?

But the relatives insisted. Times are becoming bad, they reminded him. For those who are few in number, strength lies in togetherness. The Jews in Kochi, who were the first to come to the land, had a history there. It was the responsibility of everyone to safeguard it.

That was how Esther's vava bought a plot of land near Patel Talkies, renovated the existing house and shifted there. At that time, Esther did not think of Menahem, with whom she had quarrelled and separated in a cafeteria in Dadar. He too did not know that they were coming.

In a way, was it not God's will? Was it not the holy grounds of the synagogue in Thekkumbhagam that brought them together once again?

Though Menahem married her and brought her home Esther continued to be the paradesi girl from Thoppumpady in Eshimuthimma's eyes. Both the sons tried hard to prevent the distance from growing but Eshumma was not willing to give in.

There was one question that always bothered Salamon. How did the totally unsuitable Menahem mutha marry Esther? How did the beautiful Esther agree to marry him?

Esther herself provided the answer one day. He had gone to Menahem's house as usual for the summer holidays.

'Fate. What else can I say, Soloma?' She laughed loudly. However, after a while she corrected herself.

'At that time your mutha was not like this, mone,' she said. 'Clean shaven, long hair plastered with Brylcreem to keep it in place, white shirt, white trousers, white shoes, he was very stylish. When he donned his hat he looked somewhat like O.P. Nayyar.'

When he tried to create that picture in his mind Salamon bubbled over with laughter.

But Mutha's present gaunt form – with his shaved head, long grizzled beard, the curly payot above the ears, the coloured round cap, the loose tunic and trousers – resembled the rabbis who came from other countries. Carrying a thick book he walked fast, as though he carried the weight of the whole world on his head. He talked very little, even at home, even to Esther.

Was this the same man that Estheramma was talking about? Salamon was amazed. Where had they met in Bombay? How did Mutha find a place in her heart?

Estheramma loved to tell old stories. Sitting close to him, running her fingers through his curly hair, her warm breath falling on the nape of his neck, she would talk...

'Honestly, Soloma, in those days this Esther too was not bad-looking. When boys called her Madhubala's younger sister Esther thought that there was some truth in it.' As the scent of her perfume hit his nostrils Salamon tried to move away slightly. 'Actually, it was Esther who went after Menahem; he did not come after me.'

Her shoulders shook as she laughed. Salamon sat there stunned. This attractive Esther, who looked like a foreigner, go after the odd-looking Menahem mutha!

'In those days, if there was any programme in or around Colaba, Menahem would be there. If he got a chance he would get on the stage and speak, without invitation. His English was so perfect, even the white men clapped.'

'Did Mutha talk in English about the Torah?' Salamon had often seen Mutha slide into a kind of trance when he got into the interpretations of the Torah.

'What Torah?' Estheramma broke into a smile. 'All that got into his head much later. In those days he would speak about anything on earth. It was very interesting to listen to him.'

They first met at some function in the synagogue. They grew close. The intimacy later spread to walks on the beach and in parks, and to cinema halls.

Menahem liked to watch English films. So they became regulars at Metro, Eros and Regal Cinema. Gregory Peck, Peter O' Toole, Richard Burton, Elizabeth Taylor, Sophia Loren, all became familiar faces. Occasionally, they went to Maratha Mandir, Liberty, and Opera House to watch Hindi films.

When Salamon asked if they went to see films now, she shook her head.

'That was a different time, Soloma,' Estheramma sighed.

Didn't she, being so attractive, have other friends? Salamon wanted to know.

'Of course. There were many boys who came after me, following my scent. From our college and other colleges. But Esther was no fool! After a while, they realized there was no point in wasting their time. Even then two of them continued to follow her. It was in their group that Esther once smoked a Players cigarette. I coughed so much my face turned red, as though I had spat out blood.' She paused, savouring the memory. Then continued, 'Those two were really crazy. One was a Parsi, the other a Sindhi. The Sindhi boy was handsome, like a film star. When one invited me for a matinee show in Regal, the other one's eye was on Juhu Beach. The trees in Malabar Hill, the string of rocks in Worli Sea Face ... "no one will see us"! You should have seen the look on their faces when I asked what for!'

'Then how did … Menahem mutha…?'

Even before the question was asked, Estheramma came up with the answer.

'He was decent, very decent. He did not flirt. Like the others. That was what attracted me.'

As she continued to speak about those exciting times Salamon was conscious of the smell of her perfume drawing closer. The scent of hair oil, Cuticura powder … Estheramma's scent. As she grew engrossed in the telling, her fingers caught in the strands of his hair, then moved down the nape of his neck and Salamon quivered as though he was tickled.

It was when he was studying in the eighth standard that Eshumma ordered him to be sent to Thoppumpady during the vacation. Instead of roaming around with friends here, let him learn about godly ways and worldly matters from Menahem. There was Esther as well, to teach him some English and mathematics.

There were three vacations. One after the quarterly exams for Onam, the other after the half-yearly examinations at Christmas; then the summer vacation at the end of the year. The Onam vacation was just one week long but they got two weeks for Christmas and three months during summer. Though he was reluctant to go to Thoppumpady during the Onam holidays, Menahem mutha would make arrangements in advance for him to stay for one week during Christmas and one month during summer.

At first it was Menahem who awaited his arrival, but later it became Estheramma. When he began to pack his bag to go back after Christmas, she would become sad. She would hold him close and say, 'Do you really want to go, that too today itself? Make it tomorrow, Soloma.'

When he stood quietly she would say in a hoarse voice, 'Esther feels sad. The days went by so quickly.'

At first, he thought it was because she did not have children of her own. He had heard that women who had not known birth pangs loved children a lot.

But as time went on and he grew older Salamon felt that for some strange reason Estheramma was growing younger. Esther noticed it too.

Though the stay and food were good, for some reason Salamon did not feel sad when he bid her goodbye. The Jew Street in the village, the rows of houses, the women who tried to listen to what went on in the next house from across the fence, the friends who gathered on the hill slope, the evenings spent on the banks of the river, those were the things that he liked.

Therefore when she asked whether he was sorry to leave he did not feel like saying no.

But Estheramma became sad.

'Why, don't you like Esther?'

'That is not it.' Discomfited, he quickly found an answer. 'School will reopen soon.'

'That's a lie! There are many days left before school reopens.' Estheramma tried to smile. A dull smile. 'Besides, who is waiting for you there?'

He stared at her, surprised. What kind of a question was that!

'Muthimma and Appa.'

'But you don't have Umma, do you?'

But how can this woman be my umma? After all, who is she?

As he grew older, certain thoughts took shape in Salamon's

mind. New pictures, colours, things that he could not quite decipher, taboos.

For some time now he had been noticing changes in Estheramma's behaviour when he visited. Most of it he did not understand. Mutha was always away. Even if he was at home, he would be in his room most of the time, with the door closed. You knew he was there only when Estheramma knocked on the door at meal times.

Perhaps that was why he would sometimes hear her complain, to no one in particular.

'When I was studying in Bombay I had lots of friends – boys and girls. That was what Esther liked, to go out with her friends, to enjoy. You may assume that I was a bit of a trouble – maker in college. In those days, I would joke to Vava: get me married into a family where there are a lot of people – old men and women, youngsters and children. A house full of people.'

'I have heard that there were a lot of people in our family as well at one time,' Salamon said. 'Then they left, one by one.'

'When I lived in the tiny flat in Bombay, I longed for a three-bedroom house. Now we have three bedrooms but there is just me living in it.'

'What about Menahem mutha?'

'His being here or not makes no difference. It is only when you come that there is some noise and movement in this house.'

Estheramma liked to tell stories of old films. Most of them were tragedies. Stories about the sufferings of beautiful women. Ashok Kumar's *Mahal*, Raj Kapoor's *Barsaat*, Waheeda Rehman's *Pyaasa*, films that she had seen, that she had heard about.

Though Salamon liked to listen to the stories, he did not like some of Esther's antics when she sat down close to him to tell them.

Then the Hindi songs on Radio Ceylon.

On Wednesday nights, when there was Binaca *Geet Mala*, she would finish her work early, before eight o'clock, and come and sit in front of the old National Echo radio. She had been a fan of Ameen Sayani from childhood. In those days she would say that if anyone were to tie the sacred minnu around her neck, it should be him. Similarly when it was usual to use Colgate toothpaste in the house, she alone insisted on Binaca.

At such times Vava would tell her teasingly, 'What can I do, Esther, he got married long ago and his children may not be old enough for marriage yet.'

Though Salamon liked Ameen Sayani he did not like the way she praised him to the skies.

'Oh, really! He just reads the script.'

When they argued about which songs made the top two, Estheramma would challenge him. 'Place your bet.'

What bet if you did not possess a single coin? When she saw Salamon draw back, Esther would become sad. Perhaps that was why once, when he was leaving after the vacation, she called him to her and held out her closed palm.

'If you can tell me exactly what there is in this hand, I will give you double the amount.'

When he failed as usual, she chuckled and said, 'Here, take it.'

She had tightened her palm into a fist.

'Take it...'

After hesitating a bit he forcibly prised open the plump, ringed fingers to find a small plastic purse. There were five one-rupee coins in it.

'What is this for?' he asked, bewildered.

'Keep it. You are young. There will be needs.'

Whenever she made such attempts to get close to him, the old questions would crop up in his mind. Who is she? Why does she behave like this?

When the answerless questions twisted and turned within him, Salamon shook his head, irritated. It was a relief when some dirty flakes fell off each time he shook his head.

Once or twice he even considered making up some excuse and leaving early. But he gave up the idea immediately because Mutha was set in his ways. Salamon did not know how he would react or what he might tell Muthimma.

If earlier he feared the holidays because of Hebrew now it was different. Though some questions continued to trouble him, he gradually began to look forward to the vacation. Because there would be an Estheramma waiting for him, who longed for noise and fun to resonate in that big house with his arrival. But he was frightened when she began to enter his dreams. Each time a different form. Many hitherto unseen meanings surfaced in each dream. With that, the taboos thickened.

Esther wearing a short frock and a silk upper garment with the neck cut low, so fine you could see through it. As they sat close together he stared at the large birthmark on her red-hued thigh; it seemed to have grown bigger. He experienced a sudden urge to touch it, 'accidentally'.

During the summer holidays after the tenth standard exam, he wandered around idly, relieved after having written a public examination for the first time. When she did not see him preparing for the usual vacation trip, Muthimma reminded him.

'Later. I want to learn Hindi,' he replied in an offhand manner.

Therefore, when a week later Menahem and Esther came for him, Muthimma was bewildered.

'What is this, edo, we have not seen you our way?' Mutha removed his cap and wiped the sweat off his bald head. He began to fan himself.

Estheramma did not utter a word. She just sat there staring at Salamon's face. Instead of the usual full smile he saw a different kind of smile on her face. Unable to bear the piercing stare he looked down.

Evronappa was not at home. Eshimuthimma was saying something. Esther on her part looked as though she did not hear her. Her face looked pale; she had become thinner than when he saw her last...

'How else can it be, Umma? She should eat and drink at the right time, shouldn't she?' There was reproof tinged with love in Menahem mutha's voice.

'If she doesn't eat, make her eat. That is where a man's smartness lies,' Umma persisted. 'If she becomes ill and bed-ridden, it will be your burden. You haven't forgotten the past, I hope!'

Why did Muthimma bring in Rebeccamma for no reason? What did she gain from bringing up old forgotten things? Was it guilt?

All that while Esther continued to stare at Salamon without saying a word. A faint enigmatic smile played on her lips.

After a while he heard her say in a low voice: 'Esther is not ill, Umma. I eat what I can.'

'Whatever it is, it is not good to be anaemic, mole. This is the time when you should be healthy and energetic. By your age I had three children, Buy some iron tonic or something. Let the flush of blood appear on your face.'

That was when Salamon noticed her face. What Muthimma said was true. The old flush had disappeared. The eyes too had lost their glow. She looked fatigued.

He wanted to move closer, to ask, 'What happened, Estheramma?' He read some kind of a question on her face as well. 'Why didn't you come our way this time?'

'Listen, Menahem, if you go around with your synagogue and your preaching unmindful of your responsibilities, finally like Rebecca ...' Muthimma swallowed the rest, as though regretting her words.

Salamon was stunned. Why was Muthimma bringing it up again, for no reason?

'What can I do? I suggested going to the hospital but she just will not listen. She won't go to see the vaidyan either. I said I'll go and tell the symptoms and get the medicine, but she must remember to take it at the right time.' There was more frustration than regret in Menahem's voice.

'But there is nothing wrong with me, Umma.'

Salamon thought that Estheramma's voice had lost its old firmness. The strain of weakness had appeared in her voice as well as her behaviour.

They sat talking for a while. Finally, when they got up to leave Estheramma paused for a while. Staring into Salamon's eyes she asked, 'Are you angry with me?'

'Hmm ... no.'

'Then?'

'Nothing.'

'Why are you behaving like this with poor Esther, mone?'

Without waiting to say anything further, she wiped her

face with her handkerchief and began to climb down the hill quickly.

Down below Menahem mutha was walking towards the landing to catch the evening boat, carrying a bag full of moovandan mangoes and pieces of jackfruit. Above, Esther was following, trying to catch up with him. Salamon stood for a while watching them leave.

Mon! Salamon was distressed. Like a child who has done something wrong before his mother. He searched for a long time in the darkness within him.

Rebeccamma ... Eshimuthimma ... Menahem mutha ... Evronappa. Eliacha.

Then, somewhere, Estheramma. Just Estheramma.

That night he could not sleep. As he lay tossing about in bed, Estheramma once again came in search of him as various sights and sounds.

Young Esther walking along boisterously with friends in the streets of Bombay. The low-cut blouse and short frock. The four-anna-coin-sized black mole on her plump thigh just above the knee...

Suddenly Rebeccamma appeared. She staggered through the rooms, the yard, a wan smile on her face. Rebeccamma.

'Umma,' he woke up with a cry, startled. He was covered in sweat. As he gulped water from the mud pot he felt his throat burn, sting.

Raw Desire

When Salamon made haste to leave on the morning boat, Evron was surprised.

'You said you were going to study Hindi?'

'Let him go, Evrone,' Muthimma intervened. 'After all they are a childless couple. Yesterday her face looked like that of a dead fish.'

There was a new tenderness in her voice.

Without saying a word Salamon walked quickly towards the landing. It was time for the boat to arrive. The helmsman Anthappan was very particular that the first trip should be on time.

'Delaying the first trip is inauspicious. The whole day goes waste if one doesn't start on time,' he often said.

Salamon sat down as usual on the wooden plank next to the engine, staring at the waves in the water, when he heard the helmsman call out, 'Why do you sit there inhaling all that smoke? There is space in the front.'

When he did not respond, the helmsman muttered, 'Are you scared I will sink the boat? Don't worry, Anthappan will do that only when your father is on board.'

He had heard Anthappan say the same thing once long ago when he and Evronappa had got into the boat to go to Varapuzha. The moment they stepped in, Anthappan had said in a low voice, 'Get the child out, member ... There aren't too many people today. Anthappan is going to sink the boat.'

Salamon had moved closer to his father, frightened. Evronappa shook his head to reassure him.

'He will not sink the boat. He is just a little crazy,' Evronappa whispered to him.

Salamon was appalled. Was he really crazy? Then why did they entrust him with the boat?

Later it was Eliacha who explained Anthappan's eccentricity to him. It began after his only daughter, whom he loved dearly, eloped with a Tamilian lad from Thakkala. The boy had come there to drive the roadroller when the road was being laid. Months later, her body, half-eaten by fish and rendered grotesque, washed ashore Thangassery beach near Kollam ... Three night later, Anthappan's wife who was taken by the police to identify the body was found hanging from a mango tree nearby. Helmsman Anthappan was shattered. He had hoped that his daughter would study well and be a support for the family. His son, who was a porter in the market, was totally unreliable, and he kept getting into fights and so was in and out of the police station.

'But why is Anthappan angry with Appa?' Salamon asked.

'Don't you know that?' Eliacha laughed. A series of questions and answers followed. Eliacha asked the questions and answered them himself.

'Who owns the roadroller?'

'The government.'

'Who employed the Tamilian driver?'

'The government.'

'So who should compensate for the loss he caused?'

'The government.'

'Who represents the government in our village?'

'The Panchayat.'

'Who is the one who gets things done in the Panchayat?'

'Your appa.'

'So who should be the one who should get compensation for Anthappan?'

'Your Evronappa himself.'

As the questions and answers cleared the path from the roadroller to Evronappa, Salamon's fears grew. How would they enter that boat again? When would the helmsman sink the boat? If he did sink it, would his daughter return to him alive? What about the others travelling on the boat? On which beach would they be washed ashore?

'Don't be afraid,' Eliacha assured him, 'he only threatens. He is a poor soul. But his self-willed rascal of a son is capable of sinking two boats at one go.'

'For some time, Anthappan went after the president of the Panchayat, demanding that he should get him compensation from the government. Then he started stalking him with a knife. When the police found out, they caught him and gave him a warning. After that, he left the president alone and began to threaten Evron.'

Anthappan, who had been sitting on the roof of the boat singing the film song *'Kayalarikathu...'*, suddenly stopped as though he remembered something, lowered his head and yelled, 'Tell your Evron Sa'ib that Anthappan helmsman has not forgotten the past ... that he will drown him someday.'

Salamon saw two or three people sitting in the front of the boat laugh, their hands covering their mouths. They must know the old story.

But it was as if he couldn't hear their laughter, as if his ears were blocked. There was just one thing on his mind

right then: the empty house in Thoppumpady, the dry leaves
that lay in the yard, the crows cawing their heads off on the
grafted mango trees … and a woman who stood waiting on
the veranda…

Estheramma…

Salamon found her exactly like that. As though she was
waiting for him. As though she knew exactly how much time
it would take to get from the jetty to the house. A shiver ran
through him as the thought popped up in his mind … she
must have waited like this for several days.

A tiny patch of sunlight lay wearily in the yard where
the jambu cast its shadow. Green leaves, yellow leaves, dry
leaves lay scattered all over. The yard had probably not been
swept for three-four days.

Estheramma's gaze seemed fixed on something beyond
him. Then without saying a word, she turned and went in.
The usual cheerful look was absent. Salamon followed her
like a criminal, his head bowed.

He looked around as if he had come to a new place. The
same old photographs adorned the wall. Young Menahem
mutha wearing coat and cap, pretty Estheramma standing
close beside him … There was one new item – an old clock
with a marred face, picked up from somewhere, dusted clean
and hung on the wall. Its needles lay motionless against some
bygone moment.

'It is not here to tell the time. Menahem likes old things.
Cannot resist collecting them. At times I too feel old ones
are better. How do you trust the new ones?'

Salamon was in a quandary. What should he say?

He heard her voice behind him. 'You will come only if
you are invited, is that it?'

It was aloofness rather than reproof that Salamon

detected in those words. As though she thought he would never come there again. Perhaps that's why there was more relief than joy at his unexpected arrival.

Salamon was idly looking at the thick books in mutha's almirah. Estheramma sat sideways in a chair some distance away. His discomfiture seemed to amuse her.

'If we had not come there to invite...' she began after a while.

Salamon felt a lump form in his throat. This voice was not Estheramma's. She looked terribly weak, as though she had not slept. There were dark patches under her eyes. She was finding it difficult to raise her swollen eyelids.

'I was busy preparing to go to college,' he said hesitantly.

'What is there to be busy about?' Her eyebrows curved. 'If Menahem recommends, you'll easily get a seat in Thevara college. Or else in Albert's. There is just the two of us here. Esther will find a companion that way.'

'Simon muthacha too invited me to stay here.'

'And?'

'Muthimma said no.'

'So you plan to go by boat every day?'

Salamon did not reply.

'Esther has become boring, hasn't she?' Estheramma's voice quivered.

He could bear it no more. Suddenly he moved forward, grabbed her hands and squeezed them. Estheramma jumped up, as though she had been waiting for it.

For some time, they stood looking at each other. Salamon was like one lost, gazing at images never seen before. Estheramma suddenly seemed to grow younger while she felt he had grown a lot.

A myriad hues, as when glass falls and shatters ... the

shards reflecting countless shades ... Salamon searched desperately among them. So different from the box of paints Eliacha had bought for him the first time, the thought flit across his mind. Dazzled and blinded, he groped. Voices hitherto unheard came from he didn't know where.

Suddenly, Esther held him close, panting, crushing him as though oblivious to everything else. Salamon felt himself suffocate. With a passion that pulled down barriers, with an untamed vigour, she kissed him hard, on his forehead, his throat, his cheeks, eyes and then lips...

Salamon felt himself explode, become pliant, loosening into nothingness ... floating about like bits of cotton. Over the backwaters, across the flowing river, above the valleys, buoyant with freshly sprouted untrained wings...

His lips felt bruised, his throat seared. Parts of him felt swollen. Estheramma was clutching at him, holding him tight, afraid that she would lose him if she let go.

She was murmuring, 'Ente mone, Soloma...'

He felt his sight, his memories, blur.

At some point, he became aware of the dim light in the bedroom. He did not immediately recognize the new form beside him.

They lay pressed together. He felt every atom in his body split and explode in the fiery heat that rushed into his head. The impulse to pull away submitted to the vigour that the female body aroused in him, drawing him back. Pressing his head against those full breasts, he panted.

When jerked out of slumber sometime later, he gazed bemused at the female form that lay entwined with his own. He felt sweaty and sticky all over. The throbbing and searing pain had not abated. He could not remember what had happened. The light seemed blurred. Half his blood had been in his head after all. He heard something. Groans he did not recognize. Faint laughter. Subdued sobs.

Estheramma lay beside him, watching his face, with a faint smile on her own.

'Are you spent?' she asked, running her fingers through his hair.

He could not say anything. His throat felt blocked.

'You're not what you seem. You've become an adult, haven't you?' She touched the hair sprouting on his upper lip.

'You are angry with Esther, aren't you?'

'Aiye…'

'You must be thinking Esther is crazy.'

All of a sudden, she began to shake with dry sobs, rubbing her face against his chest.

'Esther is such a miserable creature, mone. Esther has no one to call her own.'

Fearing that her sobs might turn into weeping, he covered her mouth. 'Mutha?' he asked fearfully after a while.

'Who knows?' Estheramma wiped her face with the edge of her frock. 'He must have gone to preach somewhere.'

When he tried to get up, she stopped him. 'Don't be frightened. He said he was going to Mala. It will be dark by the time he comes. Besides, so what if he sees? You're not a stranger.'

Salamon was stunned. You're not a stranger! Was the woman insane?

He sprang up. He gazed with bewilderment at the checked mundu he had hastily wrapped around himself. It was Mutha's. Traces of Mutha's scent still clung to it. How did it come to be on him?

As he carefully folded the mundu and hung it on the

clothes line, and wrapped his own around his waist, there was a faint smile on Estheramma's face.

'Why did you smell it?'

'Just like that.'

Again the same smile. The old smile seemed to be returning to her face.

'From now on, you will sleep here, mone. Esther can sleep without fear.'

'No … no…'

'If you are shy, I'll spread a mat for you on the floor.'

'Mutha?'

'He sleeps in another room, doesn't he?'

'Mutha … if Mutha gets to know…'

'So what? You're not a stranger.'

Salamon stared. What was this woman saying? He couldn't understand anything.

As she spoke, Esther got up and began changing her clothes.

'I got some good river fish. Should I fry or cook?'

Salamon shook his head. Whatever. Right now he was not thinking about any of that.

'I just asked. I know you like it as a curry with kokum in it. I will also fry some of it. If you want beef or chicken, I will send someone to buy it.'

'Anything will do.'

'That's not right. At this age you should eat well … Esther likes to cook. But there should be someone to eat! Moopar says no to everything.'

Without any sign of discomfiture, she walked towards the kitchen humming the song '*Suhana safar*' from the film *Madhumati*.

Later when they sat down for lunch, Estheramma seemed

to be completely transformed. The exhaustion he had seen in the morning had vanished. Her face looked rosy and plump. With fresh enthusiasm, she was remembering and retelling the jokes of her college days. He had heard most of them. The Parsi and Sindhi boys returned, as did Players cigarettes on Chowpatty Beach.

'Do you know, I wanted a house full of children? Boys and girls. One of them like the baby in the Murphy radio ad. A house full of their laughter and tears, pee and poop.'

Estheramma sighed as if remembering something.

Salamon was thinking only of Muthimma's barbs.

'Whatever it is, Evrone, you gave me a grandchild. Some others ... but how can that be? All coconut trees do not bear fruit, they say. It is only when you have some sterile coconut trees that you realize the worth of the good ones.'

Good ones!

Salamon had seen Evronappa stamp out of the room angrily whenever she said this. He was sure Eliacha would never entertain such comments. 'Why do you blame that poor woman for every little thing?'

Crows had begun to caw on the mango tree outside the window with some fruit still on it. A fat crow was ripping apart a ripe mango and other crows were swooping down for a share.

'The mango season is almost over. This time it came early,' he heard Estheramma saying.

She sat on the other side of the table, eagerly serving him food. She kept loading curries on to his plate even when he said no. Apart from fish curry, there was beef. Eshimuthimma would not allow beef to be brought into the house after she kept a cow. As Salamon had grown up playing with the calf, he too did not relish it.

Finally he pushed away his plate feeling stuffed and slightly nauseous.

Cooking had become a simple make-do affair at home. Muthimma constantly complained that her sons did not care that she was growing old and was no longer energetic as before. The frustration made her threaten to lock up the kitchen. They would have to make their own arrangements then.

'I feel ashamed when people say, "Eshumma has three hefty sons, yet there is no end to her suffering." One day you'll see, I will fall on my face somewhere and become bedridden. Then you will learn!' she would warn.

As Esther picked up the plates and walked towards the kitchen, Salamon went back to the cupboard where books were arranged in neat rows. Among the thick religious books, he found a book as big as an atlas. Curious, he picked it up. *The Secrets of Jerusalem*. It had pictures of Jerusalem, the city of peace. The holy city that not just Eshimuthimma and Menahem mutha but an entire street dreamed of. The city where memorial stones lay scattered, many mysteries of the past hidden in them. He did not understand the text since it was in English, but the pictures spoke to him, told him many things.

Next to the book lay another bound album-like volume, thicker than the first. As he turned the pages, Salamon's eyes widened. A whole world of colours. Unknown forms, shapes ... Having finished her work in the kitchen, Estheramma returned, wiping her face, humming the rest of '*Suhana safar*'.

'They are the remains of Menahem mutha's youth,' she laughed and said. 'Prints of paintings by great masters.'

She was wandering among the gaps between old memories.

'At one time, Menahem used to visit all the art galleries of Bombay. It was a kind of madness. His friends were a few bearded men who gathered in the Jehangir Art Gallery and the tiny restaurants in Kala Ghoda. Most of the men had a horrible stink. Though I knew nothing about painting, I liked to wander about there. That was a long time ago…' Estheramma sighed.

'Did Menahem mutha have such a colourful past?' Salamon could not believe it.

Esther did not know how and when Mutha became obsessed with religion and the synagogue, but the changes took place swiftly. Many new interests cropped up to replace the old ones. Many things that he had held close to his heart till then became taboo. Estheramma recalled that the speed at which it happened was bewildering, so much so that she feared for her own mental stability. One thing led to another, and they had arguments which led to fits of stubborn rage and days spent without talking to each other. But she always believed that someday everything would be back to normal.

When that hope dimmed, Esther decided to sever all ties and go back to Bombay. It was Vava who stopped her. Don't be foolish, mole, he said. I told you once that you can bring together only those things that match. You did not listen to me at the time. Anyway, be grateful to God that you realized it now, even though it is too late. But going back, trying to find a new life … aren't all those just wishful thinking?

That was the day she saw a wall rising in front of her, Esther said. As the days went by, the wall grew higher and higher. Though she longed to bash her head against it, to bleed, all she did was retreat into herself.

'Wonder whether you heard anything I said.' Salamon

was startled when he heard Esther's voice near him. He had been engrossed in those pictures.

'Ah…' he answered vaguely.

'Take the book if you want. Mutha never looks at it. It will just gather dust here.'

Pointing to the magazine that lay on the teapoy, she said, 'I read only *Filmfare*. It is a habit I acquired in Bombay. I leave it here even after I finish reading, to irritate Mutha. After all, isn't this enough to lead a Jewish girl astray?'

Again the same laugh that made her body shake.

As he continued to leaf through the pictures, he heard her say, 'Esther needs to lie down for a while after lunch. I suffer from backache. Today the pain is more than usual.'

Salamon grunted.

'If you have finished reading, come and lie down. Esther will have some company.'

Once again he did not reply.

After a while, she called out to him again from the bedroom. Salamon did not budge. The pictures in the album had all his attention.

So this was how great artists painted. Art was not about painting pictures of hills or rivers…

Suddenly a long, impatient cry came from the bedroom.

'Solomaaaa.'

He did not move.

Soon he heard a gentle snore. Estheramma had fallen asleep.

He heaved a deep sigh of relief and put the album in his cloth bag. Softly he walked into the bedroom. Esther lay stretched out on the cot, the old milk-froth-like sweet smile stuck on her face.

He stood there looking at her for some time. He felt a sudden urge to kiss those full lips, but he stepped away startled, as though someone had pulled him back.

He could not stay there anymore. He turned and quickly walked out of the room, changed his clothes, got out of the gate and hastened towards the jetty. He did not know if he would find a boat at that hour.

'It does not matter,' he said to himself. There will be a boat to some place – to Varapuzha, to Ernakulam, to Vypeen.

Anywhere. He had to get away from there.

Eliacha Explains

Salamon watched the waves of excitement wash over Kizhakkumpuram and Jew Street. Many of the fifty Jewish families that had lived there had already left. Those remaining were running around, getting the papers ready, to leave for the other shore. The umpteen trips to Kochi and Ernakulam were exhausting, but no one seemed to mind.

It was when the first lot of seventeen people crossed the sea without spending even an anna that the desire intensified among the others. After that, some youngsters went as part of a youth programme. Though every now and then the agency in Kochi tried to discourage them, Moses master assured the people that every one of them would be taken; no one would be left behind. Though learning Hebrew was tough, everyone trusted Moses master. But Varuthutty master laughed when he heard it.

'Moses is a good soul. In all probability, he himself does not understand the language he takes such pains to teach. It has softened his head to the extent that he will believe anything he hears.'

Salamon nodded.

'Why does he try so hard to teach an outsider's language which no one understands, I want to know.'

Salamon did not like that statement. It was their divine language that Varuthutty master was dismissing so casually.

'Eda, isn't the language that you first heard, the language spoken by your parents, your own language?'

Salamon merely nodded his head. He did not want to antagonize the master.

'These are just games played by those Paradesis in Mattancherry; isn't that so, Salamone?' Master observed, then continued, 'When you all come together, the whites will all be on one side. They will be served the best, the rest will get the leftovers, if there are any.'

That is exactly what Comrade Pavithran and others in Karimpadam had said, Salamon recalled. There are only two castes in the world, the haves and the have-nots. That is the whites and the blacks. Whatever be the issue, the ones that get sidelined are the have-nots. The ones who stamp over them and march forward are the haves. What does Changampuzha's *Vazhakkula* say? The low-caste farm labourer nurtures the banana tree and the landlord takes away the fruit. Thakazhi's *Randidangazhi* and Keshav Dev's *Odayil Ninnu* don't fade away from the mind.

With that, the doubts in Salamon's mind multiplied. Wasn't that why the agency people were creating new obstacles every time – to avoid taking them? Suppose, in the end, they said that they needed only the white-skinned ones?

At one time, the Ephraim family had many coconut groves in and around the village. But they had lost them all because of Muthacha and Evron's many failed business ventures. No doubt Muthacha had amassed a lot of wealth in his heyday, but his last years were a financial disaster. Starting a chit fund and a gold loan business in Kodungallur with some people from Pullut was a blunder. A chit fund was not something he was familiar with. When those who won the lump sum stopped making their monthly payments, the partners escaped to Pandinadu with whatever money they got and half the deposit. The entire burden of the loan fell on Muthacha's head and he was shattered. The decision to expand the flourishing gold loan business in the village by accepting partners and shifting it to Kodungallur was a bigger mistake.

Kodungallur was not good for the Jews. What binder Daveed chettan said was right.

Now Evronappa was running from pillar to post to sell the remaining one and a half acres of land, the outermost part of their property. What would remain after that was the house they lived in and the land surrounding it. If that old house were to be demolished, they might get some laterite blocks and wood. Apparently the best quality teakwood brought from Chalakudy had been used when the upper floor was renovated during Muthacha's affluent times. The carpenter who came to examine the wood from Cherai struck a couple of places to examine the wood and nodded in approval, but his group left, saying they would return. Eliacha was sure they were biding their time, waiting for the day when the permit would arrive from Kochi, hoping that the family would be caught unawares, and they would get the wood at a throwaway price.

There were some ten, twenty young, good quality coconut trees in the thirty cents of land surrounding the house. Some were on the verge of bearing fruit.

One day, when the men had gone around to the front of the house after supper, Salamon asked Muthimma secretly, 'Why are we in such a hurry to sell all this?' He knew that if Evronappa heard him, he would snarl.

'Shush.' Muthimma lowered her voice and said, 'It is no longer possible to go like Ephraim and Simon, who went as part of the youth group. We have to deposit the travel expenses in advance at the office in Kochi. They are demanding two thousand rupees.'

Two thousand rupees! From where would they get so big an amount in these hard times? No wonder Evronappa was running around madly.

Salamon was puzzled.

As Pavithran said, 'Why deposit the travel fare in advance? We are not going on charity, we are responding to the call of the holy land, aren't we? It is not just us, Jews from all over the world are being taken to the land by that government, aren't they?'

'At times I wonder, why go to the other shore at all. The soil we first felt on our tongue, isn't that our own soil? Isn't the language that the woman who gave birth to us spoke our own language?' There was a slight quiver in Muthimma's voice. 'But when people come and say this and that, the mind falters.'

The soil that we first felt on our tongue. The mother's language.

So that was what Muthimma really felt. Salamon was surprised. Words that he had heard several people speak, not just Varuthutty master.

Later on Eliacha explained the agency's stance. 'That is how it is, mone. It is a new country and a new government, is it not? They do not have the resources to take everyone. There are a lot of people from Africa and other such countries who are very poor. They have to take care of them as well. Is it a small thing to feed all the people who arrive there? That is why they insist that those who have the resources should pay at least the fare. They will consider the cases of those who cannot afford.'

Salamon thought that was reasonable. Let the ones who have money pay. How could those who did not have money pay?

However, when he thought of the young coconut trees, he felt sad. He could not bear to see their parched look when the summer heat ripened and scorched the soil. True, the nearby well was very deep, and its water never dried up even in the harshest of summers. The only problem was drawing the bucket from that depth. Earlier Chathan Pulayan would dig a shallow trench around the trees and make a drain for the water to flow into the trench. But when Salamon grew up, Evronappa stopped Chathan from doing it. 'Let Salamon do the digging. It'll keep him fit,' Evron had said. Salamon did not mind at all since he liked to work with the spade and draw water from the well. True, at first he found it difficult to lift Chathan's heavy spade, but gradually he got used to it.

But when calluses formed on his palms, when the skin split and became red, Eshimuthimma got upset. But she was unwilling to express her disapproval to Evron. After all, his constant complaint was that she spoilt her grandson with too much mollycoddling.

Instead she told Salamon, 'Why do all this, mone? When it is time to flower, the trees will flower on their own and bear fruit. Why are you working so hard?'

'What about Evronappa's orders?'

'He will say a lot many things like that. Men just have to go around giving orders and showing their authority. It is the woman who looks after the children and takes care of their growth. You don't bother listening to all that. When your appa comes to roost at night after his Panchayat duties, he should see a bit of dampness around the trees, that is all that is needed.'

But Salamon could not be persuaded to cheat or do shoddy work. The coconut trees on the hillock were in a pitiable state. They did not get the moisture of the river bank. Nor did they benefit from the silting caused by the floods from the southern hills which the low-lying lands received.

'You need not worry, Salamone,' Varuthutty master said one day. 'No one is going to buy that land. You are not going to sell it, either.'

When Salamon looked at him questioningly, the master laughed.

'You are not leaving, that is why. As for the ones who have already gone, well, perhaps it is their fate to be scorched in sand.'

Salamon did not like these disparaging remarks that Varuthutty master made. If one did not want to go that was fine, but why belittle those who wanted to go?

Once again he approached Eliacha.

It was always like that. Salamon needed Eliacha to tell him the stories. Stories that Eliacha recalled and narrated, those that he interlinked and narrated. Some he had heard, some he had been made to hear. What he heard from Evronappa contained extraneous elements, that too unsuitable ones.

'It was because he did not know how to cheat that the member's business ventures failed,' Muthimma often told him confidentially. Salamon agreed. That is precisely why he had been reluctant to pursue business like his father.

Eliacha was talking with ease. 'What your Comrade Pavithran says is partially true. At one time, there were differences of caste and creed among our people as well, just like the Hindus. The dark-skinned ones were Malabaris, the white-skinned ones Paradesis. Though we were the ones who came first and were greater in number, they, who came much later, became superior. That is, they, who had come five hundred years ago, became superior to us, who came two thousand years ago. They also appropriated the copper plate that the Perumals had granted us.'

Salamon couldn't believe it.

'It is said that all those who are born to a Jewish woman are Jews. But if we go to attend prayers in the synagogue at Mattancherry, we are not allowed to enter the main hall. We must stand outside, towards one side. Similarly, however great you may be, you cannot marry a Paradesi woman. If anyone violates the divide and goes over to the other side, his entire family is declared outcastes.'

Apparently that was how it was at one time. Prayer could begin only if ten adult males assembled. That was the rule. The discrimination was so intense that even if they had to forgo the prayers due to the lack of the prescribed number, the Paradesis would not call the Malabari who was standing outside. Whenever Malabari Jews tried to enter the synagogue as a group, the Paradesis would inevitably leave. There was discrimination in the manner of seating as well. The tallest benches were for the superior Paradesis. The lower ones for those who had converted. The lowest were for families whose members were born out of wedlock.

A complaint had been sent to the diwan of Kochi once, but it was of no use. The Paradesis were that influential. Finally an edict was issued from Jerusalem that anyone born to a Jewish woman was a Jew. But things were not easy. As marriage between Malabaris and Paradesis was prohibited, the penalty that the Paradesi who defied the ban paid was to become an outcaste forever.

Eliacha continued his narration till he reached A.B. Salem of Mattancherry. Abraham Barak Salem, otherwise called Salem kocha.

'Evron and Menahem once went with him to stage a satyagraha,' Eliacha said.

In those days, Salem kocha, the first lawyer among the Jews, was part of every progressive movement led by the Malabari Jews. He began a satyagraha before the Paradesi synagogue, protesting against discrimination based on colour, which was against the tenets of the Jewish faith. That was when he became Jewish Gandhi. For a long time, he represented the Jewish community in the Kochi assembly. When the people's government took away the assembly seat that had been reserved for the Jews by the king of Kochi, the Jews of Kochi staged a satyagraha before the assembly hall. Salem kocha, who had been Rajaji's classmate in Presidency College in Madras, was invited by the government to go to Delhi, but he was not willing to leave Kochi. He preferred to work among the common Jews of the land. In fact, he would place clippings from English dailies in the tiny window on the wall of his house to inform the people about things happening in the world. Those who read those clippings could go in and talk to him directly and clear their doubts on that or any other topic.

'At that time, there used to be a grass-covered mound in Rajendra Maidan in Ernakulam,' Eliacha continued. 'In the evenings, people would gather there to hear Salem talk on a variety of subjects. Soon that spot came to be called Salem mound. In the end, he must have realized that it was better for our people to cross over to Israel, for he began to look in that direction. From the very beginning, there were obstacles, weren't there? Salem kocha went to Israel to straighten things. But let that be ... Do you know on what some of the great Paradesi Jews had their eyes fixed when the migration began?'

Salamon shook his head. 'America and Europe and such rich countries!' Eliacha burst out laughing. 'The poor Malabari Jews had just one place to go, the deserts of Israel. No one else wanted them, did they?'

This is what Pavithran describes as racism in a masked form, Salamon thought. In each country, it appears differently, that's all. If that was true, what fate awaited them in Israel?

'When you think of it, what Pavithran says is correct,' Eliacha said. 'There were obstacles right from the start. Each contributed its bit. When the travel documents arrived, Bombay Jews were listed above Kochi Jews, and in Kochi the Malabaris were listed below the Paradesis. In short, our place was at the bottom.'

Salamon too had heard something like this.

'It was after the first group left that the agency began to make excuses. There was filariasis everywhere in Kochi!'

And then another story began.

When a few youngsters went across to Israel as part of the Youth Programme, Jew Street suddenly came alive. Even the elders, who till then had been unwilling to believe Eliahu Meir and withdrew on some pretext or other, became enthusiastic.

'So it is not a lie,' they said amongst themselves. 'Some did go across, didn't they?'

'They were young-blooded ones. Who wants old men?'

'No, it's not at all like that. Everyone will be taken, isn't that what our Moses master says?'

'That master will say things that are easy on the ear. When it happens, we'll know it did.'

News from Mattancherry generally came through helmsman Anthappan. He made two trips to Ernakulam jetty every day. Morning and evening. He did not board the boat after dusk. He spent the remaining hours in a toddy shop near Thattukadavu where he had a regular account. Generally he did not bring good news.

What had begun as a grievance against Evron later extended to the entire community.

'Claims to be a straightforward man ... phoo!' he would begin his diatribe, spitting into the distance. 'One day I will take the whole lot of them and dump them in the backwaters.' He knew very well that the Jews who were not used to the waters around the village did not know how to swim.

That was the helmsman's only weapon. For him, the river and the backwaters were his empire. As long as he sat in his cabin above the boat and turned the wheel, its rope was in his hand.

The news about filariasis also came through him. 'So don't think your going will be smooth, sa'ab,' he told the old man sitting by the landing and enjoying the sun. 'Doctors are coming from that land to tear and examine the bodies of those planning to go there.

'They will take your blood, then make you lie on a table, turn you this way and that, and place a tube on you. If necessary, they will cut you open. Who is there in this land to question the whites?

'Filariasis is the worry. God alone knows who all have the germs of the disease in them. Suppose when they reach that land the germs reproduce and multiply, and the legs of the people of Israel too begin to swell...?'

'But who in this land has filariasis, helmsman? All that is in Fort Kochi and Mattancherry, is it not?' asked toddy-tapper Thankappan. He was friendly with the Jews as he leased their coconut trees for toddy-tapping.

'Go away!' the helmsman shouted. 'Coming to plead for the Jews!'

Later it turned out that what the helmsman had said was true. Someone in Kochi had planted the suspicion in the mind of the doctor who had come from Tel Aviv to conduct a health check. Based on his report, the government sent out an order stopping people from Kochi temporarily.

'And?' Salamon unconsciously raised his voice.

'What is there to say, Salamon? The decision came at a time when people here were preparing to sell all their belongings and leave. Some had agreed to sell their land and homes to Muslims and had received an advance, others had taken their children out of school. It was one big mess.'

'And?'

'Salem kocha and two others went to Israel and met a number of officials, but to no avail. They were forced to return without resolving the matter. Finally, when things had come to a standstill, some of our people who were already there went and met Prime Minister Ben Gurion. They explained everything to him. He listened patiently to all that they had to say. People have come from all over the world, they said. Anyone could be carrying disease-causing germs. Does the state have the equipment to detect all those diseases? The prime minister acknowledged that it was a logical argument. He agreed to lift the ban. Thus after great effort, migrations began a second time.'

Eliacha saw fresh doubts form on Salamon's face.

'Of course there will be difficulties everywhere. The important thing is that we do our work without quarrelling with anyone. That is all,' he said.

Menahem mutha, who has studied the Bible and Torah extensively and who takes classes on the grounds in front of the synagogue, will not have a problem, but what about Evronappa, who goes about taking care of public affairs?

'Everything will be okay. It has to be,' Eliacha comforted him. 'Think about it as the fate of the seeds blown about by the wind. They sprout wherever they fall. We must have spread throughout the world, survived in the lands we reached, whatever be the soil, because of this power to endure.'

Salamon stood listening attentively.

'So which is our country then? Do we have anything we can claim as our own with certainty? We are a kind of exiles, aren't we? So look at this journey as yet another change of abode. For some time, we will have to bear the heat and the sting of this change. You need not have any deep feelings about this village or this street.'

Somehow Salamon could not agree with that. This was not just a change of domicile, this was a migration ... But then, what about the holy land, Jerusalem? Was it not the desire of Jews all over the world to be buried in Jehosafat's soil in the Kidron Valley, near the gateway to Jerusalem, where the resurrection of the dead would begin when the Messiah came? Every year, during the festival of Passover, didn't they read the sacred Haggadah with the prayer 'next year in Jerusalem'?

Eliacha smiled slightly. What holy land? What Passover? He did not believe in those rituals.

'Those are words uttered by the rabbis. Wherever you are, you should be a good Jew; that is what is important. So the place where I can dwell peacefully is my holy land. What holy land for a people who wandered all over the world?'

If that is so, will Eliacha not go with the others to Israel?

As though he read the question lurking in Salamon's eyes, Eliacha said in a firm voice, 'I will go. Certainly I will go.'

'It is not like joining a group of blindfolded sheep. It is the wish to be together. As one who has read a lot about the suffering of generations of Jews in Rome and the cruelties perpetrated in the Nazi camps, I have just one thing to say: Our survival lies in numbers. Wherever we are, we Jews have to be together. Or else concentration camps will rise up again. Our people will be persecuted once again. Just remember that we have always been alone. When bad times come, no one will be there with us. Even now Israel is surrounded by enemies, isn't it? I heard that a book called Anne Frank's diary was published recently. It is about some Jewish families who lived in a hideout in an old building in Amsterdam during the time of Nazi atrocities. Anne Frank's diary was discovered after she died in a Nazi concentration camp. It describes the cruelties the Jews had to suffer at the time.'

Salamon merely grunted.

'Do you know, during the Spanish inquisition, thousands of Jews were forcibly baptized? Some of our Paradesi Jews apparently belong to the group that escaped. So you see, all we have to tell is stories of atrocities. Did we get relief even when we came here? Though there was the king of Kochi to support us when we moved from Kodungallur to Kochi, was persecution by the Portuguese any less? They burnt down all our synagogues, didn't they? There was a saying: if it is a synagogue that is gutted, the perpetrators are the Portuguese. Why did the Jews who landed in Palayur escape from there? Because of the problems created by the Zamorin and the Muslims. The Muslims in the north were jealous because Jews in Kochi were prospering through business. As for the Zamorin, he always favoured the Muslims.'

Salamon said nothing. He did not understand any of this.

'They say our first synagogue in Paravur is a thousand years old. Do you know that it was burned down many times? First by the Portuguese and finally by Tipu Sultan? The songs our women sing describe a ferryman abusing the Portuguese as they returned after setting fire to the synagogue.

'That is why I say, even though I love this land and its people a lot, I will certainly go. Not for anything else, just to be together. Not to stay back alone...'

The pain of loneliness, the thought of abandonment. It made Salamon shudder.

That must be the reason behind all social institutions – the fear of being alone.

That day, Salamon felt that a number of his questions regarding the return had been answered.

Eliacha's answer was valid, and important – even if one did not entirely agree with it.

And perhaps that was the answer of everyone in that street.

Liberation Struggle

It was Comrade Pavithran who first told Salamon about Vimochana Samaram, the 'Liberation Struggle' started by the Congress against communist rule, laughing as he spoke.

'These Congress men, they are the limit! They cannot bear to stay away from the chair even for a little while. They think this thing called power is forever. Even a slight break is intolerable. They call it liberation struggle. Liberation from whom? From a government the people elected? The days when they could frighten people with references to Russia and China are over. The new generation is politically aware. They won't be frightened by these devils.'

But soon Pavithran's became grave.

'It was when the agricultural labourers and factory workers began to organize themselves to protect their rights against the arrogance of landlords and employers that they began to feel the heat, isn't that true? After enduring a long period of persecution, the labourers woke up and decided to hit back, isn't that the problem? Were the landlords and employers deluded that they could continue their system of exploitation till the end of the world? We won the elections, yes. It was the people's reward for a struggle we never let go of. No point in being green-eyed about it.' As usual Salamon walked beside him, listening open-mouthed.

Pavithran had caught hold of Salamon as he was walking down Ayyappan's bridge after buying ayurvedic arishtam and tablets for Muthimma from Paravur. Pavithran had been arguing fiercely with some weavers on the veranda of a shop. They were members of the weavers' union and they were angry with Pavithran. 'Before the election, you had showered us with promises. Two years have gone by since the party came into power. What has it done for us poor weavers? Our industry is collapsing; if at such a time the party cannot do anything for those who stood by it, then say it openly...'

As the argument went on, Pavithran was feeling increasingly embarrassed. No leader likes his authority to be questioned in public.

In a loud voice, he said, 'Look, Pushpa, the government is facing so many burning issues right now ... they are solving them one by one, aren't they? Our ministers do not have magic wands to solve a problem instantly. It will take some time for things to get sorted out. Whatever it is, you all should not forget one thing: who led the co-operative movement into this industry and gave you all a respite.'

For once Pavithran's words failed to make an impact. The accusations continued. The weavers seemed unwilling to accept his flimsy explanations and show of authority. When two newcomers, who had heard the argument, joined the others, Pavithran was forced to change his stand. He saw Salamon at an opportune moment.

'Then, let it be that way. Red Salute! Come, Soloma, you are late, aren't you?' Pavithran waved his hand.

The weaver comrades who knew Pavithran's tactics did not say anything further.

As he walked with his hand on Salamon's shoulder, he

said, 'You must have got bored listening to our party talk, isn't it?'

Salamon shook his head. He was thinking about the Vimochana Samaram Pavithran had mentioned earlier.

He did not really know what this struggle for freedom was about. He had not been to Varuthutty master's house for some time now. He was reluctant to go there frequently for fear of disturbing the master's reading.

For what is this strife? Who is agitating? For what?

He remembered how Evronappa evaded the questions by walking away when Eshimuthimma went to him with her doubts. Later Eliacha explained. 'The other political parties cannot bear to see the communists in power,' he said. 'The commotion is to push them out. It is not just politicians; the Church, the Nairs, the Muslims, they have all ganged up against them.'

Though Eshumma did not understand completely, she nodded. The moment she heard someone mention the communists, her mind went back to the chicken story when they had been in hiding. Whenever she saw the big coop that had been built at the time, her memories became clearer. Do the communists still come out of their hideouts at night to catch chicken, she wondered. Kallu Moopathi, who swept the yard, and Chathan, who came to till the grounds, were both staunch communists. No matter what anyone told them, they would just not budge from their stand.

Therefore, whenever Kallu Moopathi spoke proudly about the election rally she had taken part in, wearing a red blouse and holding a red flag, Eshumma never demurred. One could not dismiss the communists as inconsequential. Were they not the only ones who knew how to hypnotize chicken?

Generally the Evron family and other Jewish families in the street were right wingers, but on the matter of the Vimochana Samaram, Eliacha did not agree with them.

'What they are doing is wrong,' he told Salamon. 'It is just two years since the reds came to power. Let them also see whether they can do something. If their policies are wrong and there is no other way out, one can get the people on the road at that time, isn't that enough?'

Evron tried to wriggle his way out, unwilling to take a stand in the matter. He could not entirely forget his earlier friendship with Comrade Jaleel and his leanings towards the party. Yet he was reluctant to acknowledge it. Though the days when the communists had to go into hiding were over and they had become respectable, he was unwilling to say that he was on their side. Therefore when the arguments in the Panchayat office became heated, he slowly withdrew.

Pavithran said the same thing that Eliacha said, only more loudly, with a note of authority in his voice. That a bit of party language and expressions crept into his words was inevitable. Whatever Comrade Pavithran said, phrases like 'capitalist monopolies', 'class enemy' and 'regressive bourgeoisie perspective' would come in for sure. He had more or less given up mentioning Che Guevara because he knew people had grown tired of hearing the name. However eulogies of the 'oh so wonderful China' often crept into his speeches.

Anyway, the communists were now the ruling party. A rumour had spread on the hilltop that the change could be seen in Pavithran's gait, his behaviour and the manner in which he talked. He wore a neat white shirt, free of creases, walked with his shoulders drawn back, and was reluctant to smile. He had gone a lot further than the old Pavithran. The haughtiness on his face had, to an extent, intruded into his voice as well.

Someone said spitefully that it was the chair that was offered to him when he went to the Paravur police station and taluk office on some business that had given him the new face.

Had Pavithran, who had proudly vowed to keep away from power politics, also succumbed to the sweetness of authority?

But Salamon did not notice any of these changes in him. Perhaps because he was always humble before Pavithran. One reason for it was that he did not understand three quarters of what Pavithran said. The other reason was the feeling that Pavithran always pleaded for the poor. For Pavithran's part, it was Salamon's subservient stance that prompted him to take him along whenever he could. This closeness was what Evron found disturbing.

'The ideal party for Jewish boys to make friends with! Who knows when he'll be put in jail,' Evron would often mutter, making Elias laugh.

Finally Elias had to remind Evron that the days when communists were looked upon with suspicion by the police were over. Now they had special chairs not just in the police station but also in government offices. Not just that, it was rumoured that certain special cells of the comrades controlled matters in the police stations. Apparently the party had prepared a list of those with whom there were old scores to settle.

A small group of people had gathered in front of the toddy shop in Karimpadam. The residue of some old argument must have spilled over to the yard in front of the shop. When Pavithran saw some familiar faces in the crowd, he quickly turned away and gestured to Salamon to walk faster. The leader knew that to intervene in such tawdry cases would be demeaning.

'So what were we saying, Soloma?' Pavithran paused, then continued as though he had remembered, 'Yes, this liberation movement. I ask you this because I don't know. Who told the priests and the nuns that if they took out a procession E.M.S. will vacate the chair? The US or Britain? It is said that a lot of money is already entering the country through the church.'

Salamon did not answer. He found it somewhat amusing. The US and Britain on the side of the right wing parties and Russia and China on the other side. But he was sure of one thing. This was not something limited to the cities of Kochi or Thiruvananthapuram. There were powerful nations behind the curtain backing both sides.

'Anyway, Comrade Pavithran was not worried. The right wing party might be able to persuade the Church and the landlords and umpteen others to join the fray, they might pour foreign money into their slick liberation struggle, but it will all fizzle out in the end,' he told Salamon confidently. 'The protestors would not be able to hold out against the organized strength of the people. The communist organization had been built on the sweat and blood of lakhs of people.'

'They can get some of their sheep into the street and have them beaten up, that's all.' Pavithran's lips twisted contemptuously.

The police always have a grand time. Salamon smiled to himself when he thought about it. They always find someone or the other to beat up. If earlier it was the communists, now it was the Congress men.

By the time they reached Bharani Corner, the evening sky had darkened.

As he said goodbye to Pavithran, Salamon was sure of one

thing. The atmosphere in the land was turbulent. Everyone was in a hurry to take sides. The sides in themselves were a mixture of various vested interests and stances. Many things that he had learnt while growing up were eroding from beneath his feet.

Would politics in Israel be the same? Would Israel too have its share of communists, churches and priests and a liberation struggle against its elected government?

Who would give him an answer? Varuthutty master? Eliacha?

A Return or A Migration?

When they reached the shores of River Jordan on their journey from Babylon to Palestine, the rabbi became impatient. The holy land that he had yearned for, since the time he began to understand things, lay on the other side. Despite resistance from all sides, they had reached this far. But how could they cross the river, the bottom of which could not be seen? After waiting for a while, the rabbi entered the water, without even taking off his clothes. When the people saw this and made fun of him, he said, 'Why should I fear, I who received the call of God, the call that Moses and Aaron did not receive?' And so without looking to the left or right, he began to swim to the other shore. Binder Daveed chettan was narrating the story of the holy Rabbi Zeira of Babylon, the one who spread the light of the Torah to generations of Jews in Babylon. The soil of Jerusalem had always been his great dream. It was his dream to reach Palestine someday, to spread the light he had gained through a lifetime of labour in other lands and to find new interpretations for the lessons he himself had learned ... His goals were many. But everyone, even the teacher who had taught him the holy texts, was against this migration from the land of one's birth. It was then that he had a dream in which he heard a voice proclaim that all

265

his sins were forgiven. With that, the rabbi gained courage to journey into the holy land, but he kept it a secret. Meanwhile, hiding himself from sight, he listened to some lines his teacher uttered while bathing. He treated them as holy and prepared for the onward journey.

Rabbi Zeira was determined that the Babylonian practices that had crept into the study of the holy text should be abandoned completely and a new beginning must be made before they started for the holy land. As one who had suffered severe persecution by the rulers to retain his purity, as one who longed to keep free whole days and nights apart for the study of the holy text, the rabbi knew only too well the price of the time spent on caring for one's body's needs. He was envious of the earlier generations, who did not have to strive for their daily bread when they lived in the desert, who lived on manna falling from the sky.

Finally, to escape from the living hell, Zeira Rabbi decided to forgo food and drink, and fast for a hundred days...

Leaning back in his foldable chair, Daveed chettan lit a beedi. As its terrible odour filled the room, Salamon covered his nose.

It was a small room, very much like the space at the foot of the stairs. Only, there was no spiral staircase going up. The fan that whirred atop a tall stool sang a distinct tune. One end of the room was partitioned off by a metal sheet. It might have been a bathroom. A kerosene stove stood in one corner, with some aluminium vessels arranged neatly beside it. A string cot placed against the damp wall as well as the rolled-up cotton mattress exuded the smell of the monsoon gone by.

The room was not as messy as Daveed chettan had described it that day. In fact, Salamon thought, it was quite tidy. As he looked around, he heard Daveed chettan's words.

'That day you asked me, did you not, about what I ate, whether I starved during my fast? To tell you the truth, Daveed chettan does not believe in such rituals. To forgo the comforts of life, to try and purify the body by making it suffer, these are practices that people from all religions follow, but our law does not say anything like that. Certain rabbis did observe such fasts, but it was not for salvation or to appease the gods. Rabbi Zeira was against his disciples fasting. However, it is said that such things may be done when the Jewish community faces threats. But that is group fasting in which everyone joins. Not for oneself, but for the entire community.'

Daveed chettan scratched his beard as though he was trying to remember something, then asked, 'What is the significance of having light food on the eve of the Sabbath, do you know?'

Salamon did not have an answer.

'It is when the stomach is hungry that you enjoy the taste of the food you eat, isn't that so? Thus, food eaten on the holy day becomes manna…' Daveed chettan chuckled.

As usual, Salamon only listened and did not ask any questions.

'You must be wondering why I am telling you all this. There is a reason, mone. From childhood onwards, I grew up learning the Torah. Do you know that at one time your Daveed chettan used to read a lot? I would also go to Mattancherry and Ernakulam to listen to a lot of speeches … a time when I used to swallow as is the words uttered by rabbis who came from across the sea. Though there were very many twisted questions churning within me, I was scared to ask. My travels began after that. Saw, heard, came to know many things. I thus became the eccentric Daveed chettan you see today. People who see me now, will they even believe that I was born in a respectable family?'

He continued to talk about his past as he stroked his beard.

After endless wanderings, he finally reached Bombay. Someone took the starved, exhausted, nameless, unknown youth who lay in a faint in front of a shop to the synagogue nearby. A youth who had grown up in relative comfort ... all that he now desired was a roof above his head, and some work to keep away hunger. He therefore stayed at the synagogue for a long time, doing odd jobs.

Later, after he came to know Rabbi Gabriel who had come from Africa, the direction of his life changed. An old bearded man, with the face of God and the voice of a dove, Rabbi Gabriel had said he had come for a short stay but stayed on in the synagogue in Bombay for a long time, for reasons he himself did not know, as though fulfilling a divine purpose.

From him, Daveed learnt Hebrew, learnt the Torah as it ought to be learnt, learnt religion ... learnt life. He made discoveries, became aware of things beyond the religious precepts and beliefs he had heard while growing up. The rabbi liked doubts and questions ... he encouraged Daveed to think for himself, not to believe all that he heard in its entirety, to ask more and more questions. Thus Rabbi Gabriel changed the world view of a young man who knew nothing about the world.

'Do you know, many rabbis hate those who ask questions, especially when it is the youth? But Rabbi Gabriel was not like that. He had immense patience and affection. When people saw me with him, they addressed me as Rabbi Daveed teasingly. Rabbi Daveed! This eccentric Daveed chettan, who has no idea about anything, Rabbi Daveed!'

He laughed as he recalled this and continued to laugh till his eyes filled with tears. As the laugh turned into a long cough, he wiped his face with his hand.

What caused him to leave Bombay?

Salamon saw Daveed chettan close his eyes for a minute. As he tried to make sense of the deepening wrinkles on Daveed chettan's face, he felt his head go numb.

'Honestly, Daveed chettan does not know, mone,' came the soft reply. 'What do I say? From childhood onwards, I was like one bitten on the arse by an ant; I could never remain for long in one place. A few years after Rabbi Gabriel returned to his own country, my mind sort of died. I stayed on for some more time, having nowhere else to go, but I was sick of the place. Then one rainy day when I woke up, I found myself on a bench in Victoria Terminus station, with two cloth bags stuffed with my things beside me.'

'How?' Salamon could not believe it.

'Who knows how and when I got there. After a while, I saw a train arrive. I saw it was going south. It was relatively empty. I felt like boarding it.'

'Suppose some other train had come first?'

'If it was towards the north, I would have travelled north. If it were going to the west, then westward...' Daveed chettan laughed.

Thus it was on a bright sunny scorching day that he reached Pandinadu.

Daveed chettan shook his head as though dispelling unwelcome memories. He took his cap and wiped the sweat off the top of his head. He turned the fan towards him. Its sound changed.

'Just like the journey to Bombay, reaching Pandinadu too was fated, mone.'

Daveed chettan looked exhausted. Salamon looked at him with pity. Was this the ideal time to ask about going to Jerusalem, he hesitated.

After a while, when cooled by the water in the mud pot Salamon began to talk about it, Daveed chettan turned away with a jerk of his shoulder.

'At first it sounded interesting. Now I have heard so much about it that interest has waned. I came here not in the name of the synagogue or religion … only because I had already seen a lot of places. This was a new place, with new surroundings; that's all. But now, for some reason, I no longer feel the old curiosity. I will tell you truthfully, Soloma, I am a Jew through and through, and I am proud of being one. But I cannot be just a Jew, can I? There is a world outside of being a Jew. A strange topsy-turvy world that we do not understand.'

He thought for a while and then said, 'All the people I saw and came to know during my travels were people of other communities, weren't they? There is good and bad everywhere. You will never be able to get me to say that one is superior to another. In a way, the kind of coming together that they speak about is good. But is the knot of religion the greatest one? Is the firmness of belief the sturdiest? Isn't it more difficult to be a good human being than a good Jew? Are there not people in our group who say it is more important to follow religious tenets than believe in God?'

Daveed chettan smiled faintly. 'They say that all those who are born to Jewish women are Jews. But can we say for sure that all the Jews here were born of Jewish women? Surely some sort of intermingling took place in the two thousand years that went by. If you look at it in that way, wouldn't it be more accurate to say that those born to Jewish men are Jews?'

Salamon suddenly felt that his gaze was reaching nowhere. It seemed to fall somewhere beyond the whirring fan, the walls dampened by rain, the unsteady chairs, the face scorched by Pandi sunlight...

'Even otherwise, why should I go?' He heard Daveed chettan's voice. 'Isn't this our land? The committee people came here, they came twice or thrice to ask. Each time I told them firmly to count me out, yet I saw them jotting down something and leave. Perhaps they need a certain number. When we resist, they seem to view it as personal insult. Some become furious.'

'Why? It is a personal choice, is it not?'

'Who'll listen? "Doesn't that answer go against our faith?" was what they asked. You should've seen their faces when I countered with "Is our faith that small-minded?"'

'And then?'

'When they asked me, "When everyone leaves, won't you be alone, chetta?" I said, "I am alone even now, aren't I?" The ones who came with the papers were prominent people who had never climbed these steps before. They must be thinking, when everyone is running this way and that in a frenzy to cross over to the other shore, this old man alone behaves like this! But how can this poor binder understand all this? What does he know other than pasting pages together? Crazy, no doubt about it. At times I too feel what they think is true.'

'I ask this because I do not know. Is this truly a return? Or a migration?' Salamon asked. 'Is there a difference between the two? They say it is a return, don't they? To Jehovah's holy land,' he added.

'Who knows from where we came? Return means going

back to the place you came from, is it not? How can you say for sure it is the place you say it is?'

Salamon had no answer to that.

'And if it is migration, there should be sufficient reasons for it. As far as I can see, there is no such thing.'

'So it is final, you have decided not to go?'

'More or less, yes. I said I don't know the reason for going. Then, of course, there is the fear of being alone. But surely there are other people in the land! If I fall ill, someone will dump me at a hospital for the destitute. Once I die, it is the problem of the municipality. If they do not remove the corpse to some place and bury it, won't it stink? Even otherwise, what is left after death; just a lot of stink, isn't that so? Then what is the difference between the synagogue's cemetery and vacant land, Salamon?'

Chettan's face wore the same dry smile.

Salamon thought what Daveed chettan was saying was true. Our anxieties last only till the life breath remains. Shorn of it, the body belongs to others. They will decide what to do with it.

As he walked away from the tiny dark room, Salamon was sure of one thing: even if everyone else left for Israel, one person would remain to guard the corner beneath the stairs. One who awaits the missing pages of unknown texts. One who prays for the bliss of bringing them together and filling the gaps, were he to come upon them by accident.

Binder Daveed chettan.

The one person who did not desire any part of Jehovah's soil, that which they called the Promised Land.

The Locked Room

Eshimuthimma had three money pots made of clay. Two of them were ordinary ones, bought from the local market before Vishu and replaced once they were cracked open. The third one was different. Made to order by potter Nanu, it was quite big, almost like a charity box. Watching Muthimma pick up the two pots and insert coins through the slit on the top, listening to the jingle of coins inside the pot, was something Salamon had done from childhood. One of the pots would be broken for the Hanukkah festival, the other for Vishu. At first Muthimma used to say, 'What Vishu for us?', but when the sound of crackers and the iridescent glow of fireworks rose from the houses in the valley even before Vishu, she, like the others, had to give in to the demands of the children on Jew Street.

That was how crackers, which did not distinguish between race and religion, arrived in Jew Street as well. High quality crackers from Brahman's shop in the town.

But the pot covered with a red cloth in the corner of the topmost shelf of the cupboard in Muthimma's bedroom remained intact. No sound of coins being put into it was heard either. Why so much secrecy around this one pot? Salamon often wondered.

'It is a secret, mone,' Eliacha once told him. 'Have you ever heard the sound of a coin fall into it?'

Salamon hadn't.

'The slit on it is bigger too. Do you know why?' Eliacha paused, then lowered his voice, his eyes gleaming mischievously. 'It is rupee notes that she puts in it. At times a single rupee.'

Salamon nodded. The potters made a narrow slit on top of ordinary money pots so that no one could take money out of it. But that Ouso from the island often boasted that he had nicked four anna coins out of his mother's money pot, using a twig of the tapioca plant.

Anyway, why was it such a big secret? Like the many others Eshimuthimma held close to her heart, Salamon wondered. 'It started when Rebecca was alive,' Eliacha had told him once. 'Umma must have something in mind. You know her, she does not do anything without a plan.'

'But from where does Muthimma get the rupee notes?'

'From your appa's pocket, where else?' Eliacha had no doubt about it. 'Since he has a generous hand and a deep pocket, Umma must have thought, let some of that money come this way as well.'

Like the rice Muthimma stored separately in the huge copper pot during the time rationing of rice loomed large in the land, Salamon thought. Every morning and evening, he would see her enter the kitchen and take two fistfuls of rice. There, in that generations-old copper pot with its misshapen rim, rice from various lands, of varied hues and different sizes, came together.

'I'm tired of eating wheat and maize, eda. I crave to eat a bit of rice,' Muthimma used to say.

Salamon still remembered those days. Though the war

had ended, everything was scarce, everything was rationed. The rice that was received as ration lasted for just one day. The other six days of the week, they had to make do with wheat, maize and bajra.

Things were slightly better if one crossed Ayyappan's bridge and went to Paravur, which was part of the state of Travancore. There, rice could be bought in the black market. But it was terribly expensive. During Isaac muthacha's prosperous times, sacks of rice smuggled from Paravur used to reach the hilltop regularly.

'All that was a long time ago, mone.' Muthimma sighed as she recalled those times. 'It was not like what it is now. He had a lot of people he could call and command.'

As always, Muthimma's eyes filled with tears as the memory of Muthacha came to mind.

'One basket of rice in return for one fistful of tobacco; that was how it was done.'

When the tobacco tax collectors at the border became stricter, smuggling became more rampant. The tobacco that came across one river from the north was sent along another river to Travancore, where the tax on tobacco was stiff. Rice, which was as expensive as gold, was transported to this side much the same way.

Surely, Muthimma would break the money pot covered with the red cloth one day, wouldn't she? It had to fill up someday! If she broke it, who would make another one for her? Nanu had disappeared after he went to Pandinadu for a festival.

'I know she will. You just wait,' Eliacha told him.

Was it an offering to some synagogue? If so, on which festival would she break it? Suppose he asked her tactfully...

'Try, by all means. But I warn you, it won't be easy to get

your Muthimma to reveal what she doesn't want to.' There was a sly smile on Eliacha's face, which was unusual. He repeated, 'The time for it will come one day. Did I not tell you it came during Rebecca's time?'

Though the unending anticipation of that momentous day excited Salamon initially, later on he forgot all about it. Along with several other things.

Then one day, as they sat talking, a chance reference to the side room next to Muthimma's came up, sending Salamon's thoughts in another direction. Muthimma had been searching for the key to it for a few days now. She had been doing it quietly, without talking about it to anyone.

'Where can it go? It must be somewhere in her room. She is growing increasingly forgetful. It's not surprising. After all, her every thought is focused on going to the other shore,' Eliacha said.

Salamon had never seen the beautifully crafted, moth-eaten door, with its brass inlay work, open. Though a discoloured lock hung from the ring on the door, Salamon was sure that if one pushed really hard, the hinges would give way.

This lone room, without light or air in an otherwise open sunlit house, was a constant source of mystery for Salamon. What had Eshimuthimma hidden inside it? It must be something valuable. Otherwise why lock it so securely? Muthimma must be entering the room when no one else was in the house. Salamon prodded him with questions several times, but Eliacha always evaded him.

'Who knows, mone? Your Muthimma keeps a lot of things locked up within her, doesn't she?'

Salamon knew immediately that it was a lie. Eliacha was Muthimma's eyes and ears. When her two older sons went their separate ways, it was inevitable that the youngest should become her anchor. Therefore, whenever she wanted to discuss something, she always turned to Eliacha.

'Shall we go in and have a look?' Salamon asked, hesitantly.

'Don't you have anything else to do, mone?' Eliacha asked, laughing. 'Do you think there is a treasure inside? There might be some broken chairs and tables and some utensils we no longer use. That's all.'

'What about the lock?'

'Look, Soloma.' Eliacha's voice rose slightly. 'A locked room means that which is not meant to be opened. In other words, no one should enter it.'

'Still…' Salamon could not contain his curiosity.

'Oh, there might be gold and money inside! Is that what you think?' There was sarcasm in Eliacha's voice. 'True, it is said that during his heyday, Moopar accrued a lot of wealth. Though towards the end he lost quite a lot of it, knowing Umma, she must have kept aside something, without his knowledge.'

'But why is it locked?' Salamon repeated the question.

'She trusts her darling offspring that much.' Eliacha began to laugh.

The questions ended there for the time being, but the gold and money that Eshimuthimma was supposed to have hidden began to enter Salamon's dreams. Would there be gold or green-coloured rupee notes printed at the government press? If it was paper, wouldn't it become damp and crumble? So many floods from the hills had come and gone after Muthacha's time. So in all probability, it was gold. After all, Daveed chettan had said that during the time he ran the gold loan business, Muthacha had often cheated the poor of their gold. He must have melted it into ingots. If so, there must be gold ingots wrapped in silk in that room!

Muthimma herself had told Salamon stories about a treasure being hidden in the ground, and particularly about lame Elayathu, who forgot where he had buried the gold and went mad thereafter.

'He told me. I don't know whether it is true.' Most of Muthimma's stories began like that. It was always Isaac Moopar who told her the stories. 'Tall, fair, thin Elayathu. They brought him from somewhere in the north to work in the kitchen at Paliyath. Though the limp was barely noticeable, he came to be called Lame Elayathu. He had worked in the kitchen for several years and during that time, he had collected quite a lot of gold ornaments. Either the Paliyath family entrusted him with them, or else he stole them … who knows? Finally when he heard that the Zamorin's army was coming, he took fright and decided to bury them.'

Muthimma continued, 'Apparently he planted a njalipoovan banana sapling to mark the place. By the time the war was over, the plant had grown and was about to bear fruit. When the first bunch of bananas appeared, Elayathu thought he would wait till they ripened. Just as the fruits grew lush and golden, Tipu's army descended upon the land. An even more valiant warrior than Hyder, and cruel as well. A sword in one hand, a cap in the other! Sword or cap used to be the question! Poor Elayathu was so frightened he waited for Tipu's army to withdraw. And what happened then? Tipu did not cross the river; he never arrived and the workers who came to till the land in summer dug up and levelled the grounds. When Elayathu who had gone north to take part in a festival at his in-law's place returned, there was not even the sign of a spade where the plant had stood. Anyone would go crazy after that. He began to walk along the ridge, chanting Sanskrit shlokas.' Muthimma chuckled again and again as she thought of it.

After Lame Elayathu went crazy, his older son too began to show signs of insanity. That was when his younger son eloped with a girl from a lower caste.

'If he forgot the place where he had buried it, he could have dug up the entire land, couldn't he?' Salamon asked.

'It was the Lord Almighty's gold. That is why it was lost in the soil.' Muthimma lowered her voice. 'Besides, these hidden treasures contain a hidden truth as well. Only the one who is fated to find it will get it. It is like the tree with fruit. One to sow the seed, another to eat the fruit.'

What about our treasure? How could something extorted from the poor by charging huge interest rates be called legitimate? Salamon wondered.

Where would Muthimma have hidden those bags of gold? He had often heard her say that everything in a family should be safe and secure. The war had ended long ago, but the problems it had created were not yet over. It was rumoured that notorious thieves from Travancore in the south crossed the stream to Kochi sometimes. When the police tried to catch them, they would cross the border at Andippillikavu and go back to Travancore. The Kochi police did not have the authority to cross the border.

Would the insanity that overtook Elayathu catch those who touched the treasure and those who touched the ones who touched the treasure? If so, who all in the family would go insane? Salamon shuddered. Even at this age, he was afraid of two things, snakes and mad men. The king cobra and viper that slithered in the thick forest on the hill slopes were said to be highly poisonous. As for crazy Thomman, he wore a tattered coat and cap, and hurried along, muttering Hindi words that he had picked up when serving in the army. Salamon still remembered how once, when he was a child, Thomman had chased him through the bylanes until Salamon had fallen down exhausted. Poking him in the back, Thomman had chanted 'touched you, touched you' and run away, laughing raucously.

Anyway, why did Muthimma, who was frank about everything else, keep this alone a secret? Salamon was determined to find out what lay inside that room.

But to open it, one needed the key. Where would she have hidden it? He would need Eliacha's help for that.

Eliacha just stared into his eyes with a faint smile.

'I don't understand … why are you so anxious to enter that room?'

'I am not anxious. Just…'

'Just what?'

'Just like that … for fun.'

'Isn't it better to avoid unnecessary fun? To know just what you need to know?'

His tongue itched to ask: in this house, what are the things to know and not to know?

After a while, as though recalling something, Eliacha said, 'Okay. Let's see. But there is a time for everything.'

As Salamon waited, the right time arrived. A wedding, that fulfilled all the traditional requirements, was to take place in Mala after many, many years. Eshimuthimma was very excited. They were friends who were distantly related to her. So she prepared to go for the feast and, if required, stay for a couple of days. Eliacha made his excuses. 'Let Evron take you this time for a change. I am the perennial escort after all,' he said.

Thus when Eliacha appeared jangling the key he had taken out of Umma's wooden box, Salamon stood transfixed for a moment. He could not believe that the magical world he had seen only in his dreams was about to open up in front of his eyes.

Seeing him breathe fast, Eliacha laughed.

'Relax! No need to hurry. Let the boat leave the landing.' He added, 'I have read about the white men who went in search of treasure among the aboriginals. Your excitement reminds me of them.'

The damp mouldy doors opened with a great groan. It sounded as though if pushed hard, the hinges would come off. There was a terrible musty smell in the room. A sort of putrid smell.

'Like the room of the dead; seems like that, doesn't it?' Eliacha murmured.

Salamon was startled. Did the dead have a separate room? Why did you need a room after you were dead?

After a while, he thought there was truth in what Eliacha said. There was a cold numbing something about that room.

'Rebecca loved this room. "If you do not find her anywhere else, you will find her here," Umma used to say,' Eliacha told him.

Salamon thought, yes, a room to sit in all by oneself, to tell one's sorrows to oneself. Rebeccamma's private room.

It seemed as though the memories and sorrows of a hundred years lay cold and frozen in there. The desires, the regrets of how many people, God alone knew.

When Eliacha opened the window towards the west, the breeze that flowed in had the smell of overripe, rotting kashumanga. The dim light that seemed bewildered by the presence of human beings looked terribly old.

There wasn't anything much in that room. Two wall cupboards. An old table. Two chairs with wobbly legs. A bench. Some stools, some empty wooden crates...

In one corner stood an armchair made of rosewood with a woven cane seat. A chair that had forgotten the prints made by hands. Covered in mould, it was a dark green colour.

'The chair in which your Ephraim muthacha sat. Would you like to try it?' Eliacha asked.

Salamon stared at the chair, slightly scared. It was broad enough for two large people to lie stretched out on it.

'I have heard he was big-built.' Eliacha's voice held the reverence of a descendant. 'Why don't you sit, see how it feels? Aren't you fortunate to be able to do so? A third generation sitting in the chair of a great man.'

'No.' Salamon's voice shook.

Suddenly, when he heard the sound of feet shuffling above the wooden ceiling, he jerked back with a start.

'Toddy cat,' he heard Eliacha mutter.

Salamon remembered that he had once seen Karumban, who had come to clear the grounds, climb up to the attic and listen intently. Later there was a great deal of commotion when he descended the stairs with his friend, the bloody carcass of a toddy cat hanging from his three-pronged pole. It was Karumban's older brother Velumban who had incited him to kill the cat by saying that the meat of a toddy cat had medicinal value. 'You know people talk so much about tuberculosis. It will vanish. But the problem is finding the elusive animal.'

The room was filled with dust. Muthimma must not have entered it for ages. Eliacha thrust his face between the iron bars of the window, inhaling the air outside.

Salamon felt dejected. They had gone through all that trouble for nothing. Muthimma must have used the room to dump old things that no one wanted. But then why keep it locked? What was she trying to hide?

There was a faint smile on Eliacha's face. A smile that said, I told you so. At the same time his eyes seemed to be saying something different; they held the glimmer of a hint that there would be something. Not that he, Salamon, wanted anything. It was just curiosity. He had heard stories about treasure hidden in vaults – in palaces, royal houses and the houses of the rich, or else hidden safely underground, wealth amassed by the ancestors and kept secure for posterity. Later on, at some point of time, when the deserving successors appeared, it would be discovered unexpectedly. Thus every treasure had a fate. It came only to the deserving. It had the skill to slip away, beyond the reach of others who went after it.

Such a treasure in Isaac moopar's family…

Eliacha had noticed Salamon's face fall. The look of disappointment.

'Now that we have entered the room, we might as well look in the almirah as well. Anyway Umma is sure to see our footprints in the dust,' he said.

The door of the almirah opened with a slight creak. Just some old clothes that had begun to fall apart, and newspapers with holes in them. In one of these, there was a picture of young Muthacha wearing a suit and cap. Or it could be his vava.

They replaced the things they had pulled out, carefully, in neat bundles. They found nothing.

Finally when they opened the left drawer whose frame had begun to crumble … Glass bangles in many colours. Kamala Vilas bindi and kohl, products of Iyer Company from Trichur, fragrant cream, some hair clips, necklaces made of coloured beads and stones – all arranged in rows in a square toffee-box.

Salamon looked at Eliacha. Eliacha returned the look.

'Rebecca's,' he whispered. 'Bindi, kohl, bangles – she was crazy about them. Her friends were Hindus, weren't they? But Umma hated them. Jews have their own distinct style, the Hindus have theirs, Umma used to say.'

Paths that will never meet, thought Salamon.

In the other drawer, there were two long books in which newspaper clippings had been pasted. The rice paste that had dried at the edges reeked of decay.

'Pictures of athletes, footballers,' Eliacha said. 'Emil Zatopek, Ferenc Puskas, Mewa Lal, Neville D'Souza. She brought most of these cuttings from the homes of her friends.'

Then pictures of some theatre actors and actresses, a big bundle of matchbox labels.

The short almirah next to it was full of dust-laden books. They included the Bible, Bhagavad Gita, Quran, *Arabian Nights*, Kahlil Gibran…

'Simon master's tutoring…' Eliacha murmured.

Salamon became aware of something flaring up and spreading within him. It was as though his mother Rebecca filled the room. The treasure that had eluded him for long, he became aware of it. A wealth he would never get back, however deep he dug.

At the bottom of the drawer, he found a white silk handkerchief folded in four. The letter R was embroidered in red on the edge. Even though so many years had gone by, the white had dulled only just a little.

'This is the treasure Umma kept safe.' Salamon slowly picked up the handkerchief and smelt it. The scent of other worlds that time had not let go of remained. Umma's scent. Rebeccamma's scent. He closed his eyes and stood still for a while. It seemed as though the scent were spreading through the room.

'Let's go.' Eliacha touched him on the shoulder. Without saying a word, his head bent low, Salamon went out of the room. Eliacha followed him after locking the room.

'Rebecca loved a lot of things. One might say she liked everything,' Salamon heard Eliacha say in a low voice. 'But when she realized that Muthimma did not approve of many of her "town ways", she laid them aside, that was all. She did not want to offend Umma.'

So things that she desired greatly, that she procured through her friends – chanth, kohl, glass bangles, necklaces with stones, she must have kept them hidden. The things that she had hidden away were now painful memories for Muthimma. After Rebeccamma died, Muthimma herself must have searched them out and locked them away in that room.

Muthimma who had taken care not to keep even a picture of Rebecca where it could be seen, why did she bother to take so much trouble and keep her things safe?

'To remember, to lament,' Eliacha said softly.

True. For Muthimma, Rebeccamma was memories, regrets...

'What about Estheramma?' Salamon asked suddenly. 'Won't Muthimma have such scraps of memory about her as well?'

When he saw the expression on Eliacha's face change, Salamon regretted asking the question.

'That is another story altogether, mone,' Eliacha said in a low voice. 'Umma is a creature of moods. Of contradictions. If she likes someone, she likes them a lot; however if there is even the faintest cause for antipathy, then it is all over. Your Estheramma too was a nice person.'

Rebeccamma, Estheramma. Two people who went away leaving behind a whole lot of memories.

Perhaps Eliacha too was thinking on the same lines.

When he heard Eliacha's loud sigh behind him, Salamon thought they should not have opened the room. A locked room is one which is meant to be so. At various phases of one's life, one is forced to confront such closed rooms. It is better not to open and look inside these recesses of memories.

As he came out into the sunlight-patterned yard, Salamon was concerned about just one thing: the dreams that would come to haunt him in the nights that were to follow.

The Album

S alamon saw Varuthutty master's eyes widen as he went
through the light-brown album.

'My Jesus! What is this? And so dusty. From where did
you get it, eda?'

'It's Mutha's. Menahem mutha's,' Salamon said quietly.

'And you did not tell me about this till now?'

Salamon looked away with a shrug of his shoulders; he
was reluctant to confess that he had kept it somewhere and
forgotten all about it.

Varuthutty master cast fleeting glances at him from time
to time, as though he could not believe it.

'Your Menahem mutha is very different from what he
seems! There's a whole world within him. This collection is
unique. I feel as though I have walked through some famous
art gallery, through centuries of inspiration.'

'That is true, master,' Salamon said. 'When Estheramma
told me there had been such a phase in Mutha's life, I did
not believe it. Apparently he used to wander around the art
galleries in Bombay. He must have got this album during
that time from someone who had come from abroad.'

'Look, from Michelangelo and da Vinci to Salvador Dali
and Picasso. These prints are of famous paintings by so many
great artists, from the time of Renaissance to Cubism and

Surrealism … Van Gogh, Cezanne, Rembrandt … so many artists. Though I have seen copies of some of the famous paintings of these artists, I have never seen such excellent reproductions on such high quality art paper … I just can't believe it.'

Salamon recalled a similar surprise on Eliacha's face when he saw the album.

'Honestly, Salamone, it is only now that I realize that Menahem had such interests. How quickly he changed! Anyway, you show this to that Varuthutty master. He will recognize its worth.'

That was how Salamon had boarded the ferry and reached Varuthutty master's haven.

'I am not competent enough to comment on art, Salamone. True, I have read pieces here and there, have heard people talk about it, that is all. However, I might find something to tell you by looking at these pictures closely because to understand the journey made by these masters through centuries and through various transformations, it is not necessary to read the notes at the bottom. Seeing the pictures is enough.'

Salamon sat there, listening silently.

'Sometimes I feel that those who want to paint must first see the murals and sculptures in our churches and temples, and the cracked walls of old palaces. What the artisans created with their ancient mixture of paints continues to exist even after centuries, as though challenging time. Aren't they even more magnificent than what the largest art galleries display? Celebrating the joy of artistic expression, isn't that what Michelangelo did in the Sistine Chapel and St. Peter's Basilica in the Vatican? Why go that far, aren't the sculptures in the temples in Tamizhakam or Ajanta and Ellora enough?

Then there is our Ravi Varma and the painters of Bengal. Looking at them makes one feel like a worm, particularly when we view their work against the times they lived in, the challenges they faced.'

There was an enthusiasm in the master's voice which Salamon had never heard before. He lit a cigarette and continued, 'Do you know Van Gogh's life was one of hardship and disappointment? He died without getting the recognition he deserved; even his major paintings were unsold. Van Gogh, who went about searching for an ideal, admitted that he could live without God but he could not do without life and creative energy which were greater than the self. Like many great intellectuals, Van Gogh too committed suicide. When he shot himself, he said it was for the benefit of everyone.

'Though there have been many self portraits, it is difficult to see one like this.' Turning the pages, the master pointed at one of Van Gogh's paintings. 'The crazed eyes of the artist who has lost his mental peace, they are trying to say something ... There are so many stories about all these painters. Some of them may have been made up at a later date. But they are all people who burnt themselves out to give light to the world.'

The master sat there, his eyes closed, a wry smile on his lips. Saying all this to one who knew only the basics of painting. Opening his eyes, he said, 'Do you know why I am telling you all this, Salamone?'

Salamon shook his head.

'It is just a reminder of the depth and expanse you wish to achieve. Anyway, it is a good thing our times are different from those in which these great people lived. Think of all those who faced threats from governments, religious leaders and other forces of authority, who turned their lives into a battle to protect their beliefs and, through them, their art.'

'Hmm,' Salamon responded as usual. What was it that was frothing up within him, fear or a lack of belief? As the master said, the inner eye has to see what others cannot. Give life to the lifeless. Layers of colour, rhythm, tone...

'Anyway, it is only now that I realize religion, religious beliefs and gods can be so dangerous!' Varuthutty master seemed to be speaking to himself.

'What, master?'

'Just look at your Menahem mutha. Can religion stifle a man's innate creativity to such an extent?'

'Estheramma too used to say that. But Mutha himself chose the present path, didn't he? It was not the synagogue that told him to do so.'

'Who knows? That is how some people change their paths,' Varuthutty master said. 'I have seen him only twice. What struck me both times was his inflexibility. Stubbornly determined that his word should be the final one in all matters. Unwilling to retract even a little bit from his stand, he would rigidly hold on to what he said ... at times it was comical.'

'I don't know. He was that way. It was poor Estheramma...' Salamon stopped abruptly, then asked in a slightly anxious voice, 'Master, do you think I can become an artist someday?'

Varuthutty master laughed. 'First ask that question of yourself. When one is young, one desires to do a lot of things. You must have the courage to ask yourself harsh probing questions, try to understand yourself through them. These are not things that someone else can tell you.'

'When I go there as a student...'

'Do not form opinions beforehand. Learning is a continuous process. One never stops learning,' Varuthutty

master tried to console him. 'Anyway, do not try to draw
boundaries for an artist's world. They write and paint and
sing in a world that is beyond space and time, don't they?
Therefore, try to look at the world around you with an open
mind, with open eyes. If the inner eye opens, even a desert
will bloom.'

That day, for some reason, Salamon did not make haste
to leave even when it grew dark. Even when time went by
talking of this and that, as night unburdened itself around
them, and kerosene lamps began to glow, he did not move.
It was during his occasional visits to this house, when he
sat on this veranda, that he remembered that he had a
tongue and a pair of ears. The peace he gained from that
awareness, the brightness it spread through him – would
anyone understand it if he explained it to them? No one
would. Not even Eshimuthimma.

Finally when he heard a shout, louder than usual from
the jetty, the master reminded him.

'That's for you, Salamone. Do you not hear a note of
warning in that call? It is the last ferry.'

'I don't feel like going, master.'

When he saw Salamon get up reluctantly, the master
smiled.

Master often said that these landings were a relief for the
loners who could just sit and watch the world go by. 'These
three landings are this land's wealth. They bring different
winds and memories. We'll know their value only when they
are gone.'

'There are two landings in one's life that one cannot forget.
The first and the last. Life lies like an ocean between the two.
It is the belief that there is another shore, and a ferryman to
take us across, that makes us go forward, isn't it?'

As he walked away fast without saying a word, Salamon thought the same.

At the jetty, Ittaman was waiting, leaning against a coconut tree, having made the last call.

A life that lay between two unknown landings. The ferryman who stood waiting for the last lone traveller. The shout that had a threat in it.

After a long time, Salamon experienced a sense of lightness within him.

Haunted by Memories

As Salamon faltered among old memories after a long time, he felt a searing pain spread within him....

Estheramma. Estheramma with her many faces and her many moods.

Of late she had been intruding upon his shallow sleep, with memories he preferred not to remember. He could not understand why. What was the meaning of that soft and low call, 'Soloma,' that the wind brought him from across the river?

In his childhood, as soon as the vacation began, Eshimuthimma would start reminding him, 'Aren't you going to go to Thoppumpady? You are going, aren't you?'

She was determined that every footstep her grandchild took should be under her watchful eye, a grandchild who had grown up clutching at her bosom. Even when he became an adult, she would not give up the mother-hen vigil that had become a habit for her. 'The child does not have a mother. That is why,' she explained to her neighbours, adding that some of the stern ones complained that Muthimma had spoilt the child by indulging him too much.

Life with Menahem mutha was totally different. He stressed too much on being systematic and precise even about little things, Salamon thought. In that house, everything had a definite place. A piece of cloth could not be left anywhere other than in the cupboard or on the clothes line. Books, paper, anything that was out of place would end up in the dustbin, Estheramma knew, so she too was careful to some extent. In fact, Salamon had felt Mutha's watchful eye on him at the dining table, in the reading room, in the bathroom, why, even in the toilet! It had made him uncomfortable at first.

Mutha often said one could tell how a child was raised just by looking at his study table. 'One should be neat and tidy from now, Soloma,' Mutha would say. 'It is difficult to change habits after a while.'

Though Salamon, who had grown up in shabby and untidy surroundings, found the military discipline in Thoppumpady a strain, he learnt to go along with it.

He recalled with a tinge of guilt that he had never gone back after that incident. Not because he decided not to. He just did not feel like going, that's all.

No one from there came this way either. Soon after the incident, Estheramma had become bedridden. She remained like that for two or three weeks. Then she was taken to a hospital in Kochi. From there, to the general hospital in Ernakulam.

Evron went to see her. So did Eliacha.

'Can't bear to look at her, mone.' Eliacha dabbed at his eyes. 'She was so beautiful. Now her face looks all pale, like the underbelly of a fish on land. Apparently blood is made up of red and white cells. When the red cells decrease and the white cells increase, this illness strikes.'

Salamon stood still, a terrible numbness overcoming him.

'And yet, you alone ... We always ask you when we go.' Eliacha sounded more perplexed than displeased. 'If nothing else, she fed you for some time, didn't she?'

'I have a lot to study,' Salamon said. As usual the weakness in his own voice annoyed him.

'You and your studies! I don't want to hear it anymore,' Eliacha said angrily. 'Just because you have reached college, do not forget your roots. She has great affection for you. Your name crops up in everything she says.'

Salamon said nothing. He felt something throbbing inside him.

'I don't know why, but this time she did not ask about you. Maybe because she was too unwell and tired to speak,' Eliacha said.

All that time, Salamon kept thinking about the changing expressions on Estheramma's face. A different face each time. The shift from the brilliance of early days to the dull inner spaces in Thoppumpady was not easy. Perhaps she had read the bewilderment on his face as he gazed at the varying shades of her face, for she once asked:

'Honestly, Soloma, what blood is my blood? Vava's? Umma's? A native's? An outsider's? I was born in Baghdad, grew up and studied in Cairo and Bombay. Now I am in your land. So to which land do I belong? Does poor Esther have any land she can call her own? In a way that is good, isn't it, Soloma? I am free from the burden of citizenship. I can tell the Iraqis that I am from Bombay. To people in Bombay, I can say Thoppumpady. In between, thanks to Menahem, there is Chendamangalam as well.'

At that time, he was unable to say to her, whatever be the land, the colour of blood remains the same. Confronted with her confusing questions, he could only stand as he always did, with his head lowered.

Now an equipment in the hospital was trying to separate her blood into red and white. White decreased, red increased … red decreased, white increased. In her last days, she must have repeated that question to the hospital walls. 'Which is the real blood, friend? Red or white?'

Truthfully, who was she to him?

Mother. Elder sister. Friend … then … then…

How did he, whom she repeatedly referred to as the son who was not born to her, later become the male companion she never had?

When memories began to well up within him, Salamon felt drained. You should not be so cruel, Soloma, someone was reminding him. You should go and see her, show that you care. People yearn for comfort when they are ill and vulnerable.

When she was young, Esther had many friends. She, who always longed for new friends, was finally alone, in the hospital bed. All alone, fated to recognize the meaninglessness of companionship and retreat into herself.

'She is not responding to treatment. They are not sure how long she can go on. Menahem is always at her bedside. I cannot bear to look at his face.'

When he got off the boat in the evening, Eliacha's voice was trembling.

As usual Eshimuthimma began to sob. She unrolled the Torah and began to pray to the gods in the sky with an aching heart.

Salamon was packing his books for the next day's class.

'Just go there, mone,' Eliacha suggested again. 'All you need to do is catch a bus from Aluva after class. Umma and I are going in the afternoon.'

'I am not going.'

Eliacha stared at him, bewildered, not knowing what to make of him.

'There isn't much time left. No point in regretting later,' Eliacha reminded him.

'Let him be, Eliase,' he heard Eshimuthimma's voice break behind him. 'We can only pray to God to make him see sense.'

As he quickly walked out into the darkening yard without looking at anyone, Salamon was aware of the weakness in his legs.

Now, as he remembered it all, he felt something grow taut within him. One of the many mistakes he committed. A grave mistake for which there was no forgiveness. That day, when he stood in the cemetery with his head bowed, was it not guilt that was crushing him? Why did he avoid meeting her even in her last moments? From what was he trying to escape? As he slept that night, why did he listen for those low voices that came on the breeze?

Estheramma who had come from somewhere and then disappeared somewhere – she seemed to follow him even now, unwilling to let go.

The house where she lived for a few years, where she spent her nights. The veranda where she sat to feel the breeze in her face. The yard where she walked.

The house was full of memories. What memories was he going to leave behind?

Memories of Ephraim muthacha and Isaac muthacha that had taken root within him through hearsay and myths. Then those of Rebecca, and those of Esther. Even if he crossed the sea, would it be easy to escape these memories?

Suddenly he remembered Evronappa's words. 'He walks like a chicken bewildered by the moonlight! If he is to do well, he has to leave this place. Another place. Other friends. Other surroundings.'

That day, for the first time, he searched for new meanings in Appa's words. But with that, the doubts within him increased. He remembered Ramanandan's words. 'No point in remaining here, my friend. You will prosper only if you leave. If you want to do well, go abroad. See the world outside. See life. Moreover, who is valued in the land of his birth?'

To be successful, he must go to the other shore ... no one is valued in the land of their birth.

It was Ramanandan Pai, the son of the wealthy Divakara Pai, who was in a frenzy to discard everything and leave.

But he, Salamon, was not going to the other shore to do well or make something of himself. It was not the land that he was trying to escape from.

Then what?

What was he trying to escape from?

He continued to ask those questions.

He was not sure whether he would ever get a reply, from the twilight on the slopes of the hill, from the breeze that came across the river.

Resistance Intensifies

Varuthutty master held A.K. Gopalan in great reverence. 'When A.K.G. got up to speak in Parliament, there was absolute silence for some time. Even the greats like Nehru and Patel would listen to every word, words that fell from his tongue with precision, as though sculpted from stone. His was a strength gained from working for long years amidst people,' the master would say.

Master was friends with the comrades in the village during the early days, but later they became estranged during the Vimochana Samaram. When the parish priest Emmanuel achan instructed the people to join the march to Angamaly police station after Sunday mass, and the master's wife Mary got ready to go, the master told her firmly,

'Don't go.'

'What about Emmanuel achan's instructions?' Mary asked.

'Let priests confine themselves to Church matters. There are laymen to take care of public affairs.'

'What about next Sunday, when I go to attend mass? Achan will call out the names of those who did not take part in the march.'

'Why? Is it a school that you will have roll call?' The master lost his temper. 'Tell him you are Varuthutty master's wife. Tell him I stopped you from going.'

299

Though that episode ended there, as the protests grew more and more heated, every parish was in tumult. Students and teachers in the Church-run schools took to the streets, shouting slogans.

Around that time, the priests in the Koonammavu area organized a march followed by kathaprasangam, a musical narrative called *Bhagavan Macaroni*. The story was directed at the communist party. It satirized the distribution of macaroni instead of rice during the days of rationing. Since the event was announced in the nearby churches, there was a fairly large gathering to watch the performance. *Macaroni* Rajan was a real crowd-puller. Besides, there would also be speeches by Vadakkan achan, Wellington and others. Although no one invited him, Varuthutty master went to hear Bhagavan. He went when the march and speeches were over, and *Macaroni* was about to begin.

But the comrades heard about it and were furious.

'Whatever the reason, you should not have gone there, master,' Comrade Jaleel said firmly.

'Why? Can't I listen to what Bhagavan has to say?'

'You, who don't go to church, go to hear Bhagavan?' Jaleel mocked.

'Why, can't I listen to what he has to say? Democracy means to hear what others have to say. Isn't it better to limit Stalin's style of functioning to those who are members of the party?'

'You need not teach us democracy, master. Anyway I don't think Varuthutty master will change two buses to go to Koonammavu just for the musical. And there is no bus to return from Paravur.'

'What if I went by cycle?'

'You travelled all that distance on a cycle?'

Just then, a youngster wearing a red jubba intervened.

'Besides, we know,' he said, rolling up the sleeves of his jubba, 'when it is time to hammer the hot metal, the ironsmith and his wife become one! It is the same with the lambs; the priests' words are edicts.'

Lamb! the master's face turned red with fury.

'Look here, mone,' the master said, trembling with rage. 'I read Marx and Engels before the likes of you were born … Do not bring on your junior-comrade voice before me.'

'Master, what he said…' Jaleel tried to lighten the tension. 'The party's line…'

The master stopped him. 'That is enough, Jaleel. We will separate before we lose whatever affection is left. This thing that you call line is something that you can curve and straighten as it suits you. Another thing: whether it is the Catholic church or the communist party, Varuthutty master decides what he should follow, or not follow. Even the priests here know that very well.'

The master still remembered how he had walked out of the reading room with firm steps. Jaleel and the others could only watch aghast. After that, for some time, both parties took care not to come face to face.

'Do you know, Salamone,' the master said, 'the Vimochana Samaram is the greatest stain on our democracy. An unscrupulous game played by some people behind the façade of priests and Nairs.'

Salamon sat listening. True, he had often heard Evronappa and Eliacha argue vehemently about it.

'Do you know what offends the priests most?' Varuthutty master chuckled. 'It is not criticism of Jesus Christ, but a mention of the Church's assets. Do you know why priests are so against communists? Because of Mundassery master's education bill, and of course the agricultural policy. There is no great politics in it.'

The master had a lot to say about the oppression in schools managed by the Church.

'If a teacher signed for one hundred rupees in the salary book, what he received was seventy-five or eighty rupees. That too when the manager felt like disbursing it. If anyone waited for that money to buy rice, they would go hungry. The state of those who plough the field or climb coconut trees is better. They at least get paid at the end of the day. But the situation of teachers who stand before students and tear their throats teaching them is miserable. That was the time when there were no specific rules about when teachers would be paid or how much they would be paid.'

Salamon could not believe what he was hearing.

'Mundasserry master had experienced it, that is why he took up the matter as soon as he became education minister. Have you heard of M. P. Paul? He was from our Varapuzha. A great writer.'

Salamon shook his head.

'He was a college professor. Want to know why he was dismissed from service? He questioned the management for reducing his salary. He wanted them to give him straight answers regarding just two things – what his salary was and when he would get it. But the Church's managers were not used to such questions...'

Varuthutty master paused, then continued, 'They were great people. M.P. Paul, Mundassery and Kuttipuzha. People who had the courage to say what they wanted to say with a straight back. Yet, Paul sir, who was a fervent believer in Jesus Christ, was buried in a part of the cemetery that is not consecrated.' The master paused and added, 'Perhaps that will be the fate of Varuthutty master as well, who does not go to church or bow down before priests. Sometimes I feel that, in some ways, the Catholic church and the communist party are one and the same. Both have priests and unblessed graves; and a large number of lambs to listen to everything they say and nod their heads submissively.'

Varuthutty master chuckled at the thought.

'Anyway, once one is dead does it matter what cemetery, which pit ... People will try to bury the corpse quickly before it starts to rot and stink. If the priests don't come, someone else will do it.'

As the days went by, the Vimochana Samaram became more and more strident.

The bishops' palaces and parishes were in turmoil. Pastoral letters and exhortations flew about in the wind. Colleges and schools remained closed. Students had a field day in the streets. Processions towards the south and the north. Marches with lighted torches to the east and the west. Speeches resounded in street corners and at crossroads. Furious tirades. New slogans every day:

Education is in danger. Agriculture is in danger. Religion is in danger. God is in danger. Everything is in danger.

As the list of dangers grew longer, the number of banners and slogans on the walls increased.

Beneath the banyan, in tea stalls, in barber shops and in toddy shops, there was just one topic of discussion:

How long will the Namboodiripad government be able to hold out?

If Mannam, Sankar and the bishops hold hands, will the communists be able to withstand their combined strength?

Does the Church have any shortage of money? Money comes in dollars from the United States, doesn't it? Weren't the CIA and MRA behind it? Earlier they played the game with milk powder and wheat which no one wanted. Now they are throwing around actual currency notes.

'Of course!' shouted Shambu Namboothiri in a shrill voice from under the banyan tree. That all the Namboothiri from the north would support E.M.S. was a given. 'The Thirumeni is sharp. He will not do anything without a strategy in mind,' he declared.

'Why are you arguing for the communists, Thirumeni?' K.P. master interrupted immediately. 'By passing the land act, they made a real dent in Paliyam's income, didn't they? Goodbye to rent on land given on lease and freehold! Same thing about the property of temples. Gowri Amma and Krishna Iyer together have destroyed the families of Nairs and Namboothiris, haven't they?'

'And of some Christians too,' someone added. 'Isn't that why they are agitating?'

Though he knew that all this was true, Shambu Namboothiri, who revered E.M.S., was unwilling to give in.

'It was that Mundassery master's bill that created the problem. It was when he touched their schools that the clergy became agitated.'

'Well, that is because he suffered a lot in the college managed by the Church. They told him his salary was one hundred rupees, but did he get the entire amount in hand? The management has the authority to induct anyone, dismiss anyone, as per its whim. It is all a game of money, you see. Money! When compared to that, our Paliyam school is run so decently!'

Though the ruling party was at first stunned by the series of accusations levelled at them, they soon woke up to the danger. They too began to march towards the south and the north. Torch-lit marches towards the east and the west. Speeches and furious tirades at street corners and crossroads. Comrade Pavithran was very busy. He had not gone home for weeks. At this time, the party needed his tongue, his throat, his vigour.

E.M.S., our leader, govern courageously!

You idiots, you bulls, Mundassery is not alone!

As the commotion increased and the police descended on the streets, canes twisted and swished. Then canes gave way to lathis, and lathis gave way to rifles. Blood splattered on the roads and on the front pages of newspapers. Lamentations and pastoral letters became more impassioned than ever.

'That is how it always is,' Ramanandan explained to Salamon. 'When there are party members to rule the police station, the police will descend upon the streets to beat up people to their heart's content.'

Salamon did not understand. How can a party rule a police station?

'That is how it is now, Soloman.' Ramanandan smiled. 'Party cells conduct the enquires, try the cases and determine the punishment.'

'What cells?' Salamon's eyes widened with surprise.

With a slight smile, Ramanandan tugged at the sweat-soaked sacred thread across his chest, as though saying, you will not understand all this. Salamon suddenly felt small.

Though he was against the Vimochana Samaram, Eliacha, like Ramanandan, had no affinity for the reds. Communism to him was the moustachioed Stalin. Through Stalin it was Mussolini, it was Hitler. How could Stalin, who supported Hitler who killed poor Jews, be a leader of the poor?

As the struggle intensified several groups emerged.

'What is your line in this, Evrone?' Shambu Namboothiri asked him one day when he met him on the street.

'Many asked that question, Thirumeni – the president of the Panchayat, the comrades, the priests – and several others...'

'And?'

'We have no line, and no circle, Thirumeni.'

'But Jews side with the United States, don't they? That is the Congress...'

'Who said that? We do not take sides. We just want to continue here without any hassle.'

'Whatever it is, finally the priests had to carry our leader Mannam in a palanquin. That is something, isn't it?'

'Because they needed his support.' Evron laughed. 'The moment their need is over, they will drop him, just wait and watch.'

'True. Though I am with E.M.S., some of the things these reds are doing is pure arrogance! They think we are all rich landlords. First they grabbed the land that we used to let out on lease and rent, now they come up with a new law. If everyone decides to build huts on whatever piece of land they fancy and then claim the land as their own, how will we get the money for the daily expenses of the nearly fifty temples under the Devaswam from?'

Even as he supported E.M.S., Shambu Namboothiri was filled with a faint uneasiness. E.M.S. was a good man, but suppose the ones who stood with him got him into trouble?

The Christians and Ezhavas in the village had their own stance, and Mannam was in the forefront of the struggle, but the Nairs who were fewer in number were waiting as usual, ready to move to this side or that depending on which way the wind blew. It was always like that. If there were ten Nairs there would be twenty opinions. It was difficult to bring them together. Besides, the NSS of Travancore had hardly any base in Kochi. And the Nair Samajam of Kochi had decided to stay out of the fray.

Pathros Achan Comes to See Elias

Things were going on as usual when one afternoon the parish priest Pathros achan came up the hill, accompanied as always by sexton Mathai. Assuming that he had come to see Evron, Elias quickly said, 'He has gone somewhere. I think it is Kodungallur. Saw him leave at dawn.'

Pathros achan pulled forward the cane chair in the veranda as though he did not hear him and sat down. He took the towel that hung from his shoulder and wiped his face and balding head.

'Ho! It is so hot!'

Elias generally avoided Pathros achan. Once Achan came, he would not leave soon. For him everything moved at a slow pace. There were too many hours in his day, too many minutes in his hour and too many seconds in his minute. In this largesse of time, he never knew his throat to tire. The briefest issue was turned into an elaborate, epic sermon, and to describe something that happened in the evening, he would start with waking up in the morning and brushing his teeth. Elias often watched with amusement Evron's expressionless face as he listened to the priest's ramblings.

Because he had gotten used to the idle chit-chat that went on in the veranda of the Panchayat office, perhaps the member had more ears and less tongue. 'What if I have come to see you, not Evron?' Flicking off the red ant that was crawling along Elias' shirt sleeve, Achan smiled. His words emerged through the gaps in his betel-stained teeth with a slight lisp. Sexton Mathai always stood at a distance, afraid of the bits of tobacco that could fly out along with them.

'What is it?' Elias asked.

'I went to the shop twice but did not find you. That is why I came here.'

A frown appeared on Elias' face. One could call it an office or an institute, certainly not a shop. There was nothing there to sell except perhaps a few clocks. But for priests from Ollur all open rooms were shops!

'I do not go to the institute every day,' Elias replied curtly. 'Besides, I need to go to the town today. This is an unexpected visit … anything in particular?'

'No, nothing specific. I just felt I should tell you that kaalam, the times, are becoming really bad.'

Elias looked enquiringly. What had happened to kaalam? Was Achan referring to the departure of the Jews?

'Didn't you see the newspaper today, Elias? It was on the radio as well.'

Pathros achan always began his conversations with such expansive introductions. It was difficult to guess what was coming.

Elias smiled. Achan was asking that question to the agent who had brought newspapers to the village.

'The police beat up people with lathis at the Ernakulam jetty and on Banerjee Road. I heard that the boys who were beaten up are now in the general hospital. Boys from good families, studying in Thevara and Albert's colleges.'

Elias got the drift of the conversation.

It was about the liberation struggle, Vimochana Samaram. He too had heard that a lathi charge had taken place near the boat jetty the previous morning. When the ones who were beaten were from reputed and well-to-do families, it hurt the priests. Who were the people who herded these youngsters into the streets to get beaten up? Youngsters who had had an easy life with all the comforts their parents could offer? Moreover, different newspapers reported the news differently. In fact, one newspaper reported that the police did not beat anyone, they merely swung their lathis to disperse the crowd. Which paper should the agent who arranged for several papers believe?

'Is it enough that we remain like this, Eliase?' the priest asked.

Elias did not immediately get the meaning of that question. What was he supposed to say?

'No, when the entire land is in turmoil, everyone wants to know what line the Jews will take?'

'We do not address such issues in the synagogue, Achan.' There was a bite in Elias' words. 'No sermons from the pulpit either. Every person follows his own personal line.'

'That is true, but in Kottukadu, Thuruthipuram and Gothuruthu...'

'Those are your places, aren't they, Achan? Many of the Jews here have already left. The others are waiting for the papers to arrive. It could happen today or tomorrow. Anyway the Jews here are not much into politics.'

Achan's face dimmed. He thought for a while, then said, 'Another thing. These communists are against Israel. Now that E.M.S. is in the chair, we have acquired a bad name, of being a communist land, haven't we?'

Elias understood what Achan was trying to say. 'Thousands have reached there from wholly communist countries,' he replied.

Elias too had heard the rumour that Pathros achan was hinting at. For some time now in Mattancherry, Mala and some other places, it was said that black Jews from red soil might not gain entry into the holy land. The officials in Tel Aviv had stalled the migrations from Kochi for some time, citing various reasons, filariasis among them.

They who jabbed a needle into Malabaris to see if their blood was filarial, what would they jab to measure the amount of communism in them?

Would they be able to prove that he was not a communist if he took part in the Church-led rallies in Koonammavu and Angamaly? Elias felt like laughing.

'Our people are not such cowards,' he said emphatically. 'Have any other people in the world suffered as much persecution as we have?'

'But can we give in tamely if things continue like this? Should we not do something?' Achan asked anxiously.

'You are doing more than what is necessary, Achan.' Elias did not bother to conceal the sarcasm in his voice.

'But you too are people who grew up drinking the water of this village.'

'Are we?'

'Why the doubt?'

'I have heard people say something else.'

Pathros achan realized that it was a dig at him. One Sunday, when he was totally caught up in his speech, had he not warned the people to be wary of the Jewish money lenders who extorted heavy interest from poor Christians?

'Be careful, Antoni, Paulo, Lonappa. They are true Shylocks. You know the old stories, don't you? When they have sucked out all your blood, they will throw you away like this,' he said, snapping his fingers. 'Besides, they are outsiders. What loyalty do they have towards our soil?'

Those words were heard not just by Antoni, Paulo and Lonappa, but the entire hillside. Later when he realized that it had reached the veranda of the Panchayat office as well, Pathros achan arrived to apologize to Evron. He had his permanent witness, the faithful sexton Mathai, with him.

'You know how it is, Evrone,' he said, a tinge of embarrassment in his voice. 'When I stand at the pulpit and begin to speak, I sometimes get carried away, say something inappropriate. It is the style of these sermons, alle? The people would have forgotten it then itself.'

As usual, Evron must have sat there listening to it all and nodding as though nothing had happened, Elias thought wryly.

Pathros achan knew he was on weak ground. He looked intently at Elias, then said smoothly, 'What I am saying is that we should all stand together. Things like religion and caste, Church and priest should not come into this. If we want to live peacefully in this land we have to make some kind of noise to register our protest. That is the way of the times. If it is our Church that is the target today, it will be your synagogue tomorrow. Then the temple. Then the mosque. After all, the communists do not believe in God, do they? Then why should they care about churches and temples?'

'What happened to the churches and temples here?' Elias asked, puzzled.

'They say people are being brought from Telangana to throw bombs at churches,' he said agitatedly. 'The Church is their greatest enemy now, isn't it? Those who escaped the police over there and now work underground are rumoured to have crossed over to our state. That is what they will do, won't they, throw bombs and kill the innocent? Our police will not be able to rout them. Moreover, since the police are under their government, how can we expect them to defend us? They will listen only to what the party bosses say. They thrashed our children like stray dogs near the jetty yesterday, didn't they?'

Elias began to get fed up with the rant. These things did not affect him. He would move away whenever he heard the topic being discussed; he refused to get involved.

'Achan, did you talk to Evron?'

'Of course I did. He is unwilling to commit himself. Why should Jews interfere, he says.'

'That is reasonable, isn't it, Achan?'

'Perhaps it is embarrassment! He went and hid like a mouse among sacks of mangoes when he took part in the Paliyam march with the comrades, and the police from Paravur came looking for him.' There was a sly smile on Pathros achan's face.

So the whole village knew about the incident that Eshumma had tried so hard to keep secret. That was the reality. It was impossible for the hillside to keep anything secret.

Pathros achan continued, 'It is better for the Jews that we all stand together. Have the communists come to the aid of Jews anywhere in the world? You have read some history and geography, haven't you? I do not have to tell you all this, do I?'

Elias was amused. The ideal person to talk about history and geography! He doubted whether Pathros achan had read even the holy book properly.

'Why are you telling me all this, Achan? Isn't Evron the person to whom you should talk? Or else the muliyar?' Elias got up. 'Anyway you can count Elias out of this. I do not interfere in things I do not know. Politics and public affairs are the member's concerns. His family is lucky he has not developed a crick in his neck from carrying the affairs of the whole village on his head,' Elias said sarcastically.

It was obvious that Pathros achan was unhappy with Elias' response.

'It is true that there are only a few of you. If it is just numbers you do not matter. But this is not like politicians asking for votes. It is our way to stand together when we face a danger, isn't it? I am not telling you to take part in the march or shout slogans. Just stand with us. At a time when such a big upheaval has struck the land, if your community alone remains uninvolved, everyone will think you are on the communists' side.'

'Community does not enter into this, does it? We do not practise excommunications or declare a person outcaste like you do. And no one is going to listen merely because it is announced in the synagogue. We are just harmless people who came here from somewhere, we live here quietly minding our own business. If anyone from our group wants to join, let them. It is their personal choice.'

'Yours is a prominent family in this village. If you speak, people will listen.'

'That is why I told you to talk to Evron. He is the leader, isn't he? What can this poor newspaper agent do in this matter?'

Achan got up hurriedly. He looked annoyed. Smoothing the creases on his cassock, he said in a grave voice,

'If you do not pick the right side at the right time...'

Elias had never felt the urge to take sides in such matters. Why were the priests so impatient? The communists had just started governing, after all. And during that brief period, they had done quite a few good things, hadn't they? Why not give them some more time?

'What good things?' Pathros achan's voice grew loud. 'Trying to ride over school managements! Grabbing people's land! Forcing people to give away the wealth that their forefathers had amassed to some nobody. It is not going to work.' The underlying threat was unmistakable.

So that was the issue. The government was trying to lay its hands on the wealth that the fathers and grandfathers had saved for future generations! No one had bothered to find out how the forefathers had got hold of all that land.

'Anyway, we voted them to power, didn't we? That is democracy, isn't it?'

'What democracy? Did you vote for them?'

All of a sudden Elias was at a loss.

'Just because they managed to get the chair, it doesn't mean they start asserting power that they do not have ... Do you know why they are after the schools?' Achan lowered his voice. 'To teach their party literature. To force their ideas into our children's heads. Thus by studying the red books our children too will become red. They will disobey their parents, go about waving flags and saying ungodly things. Then who will be able to control them?'

Elias was tired of this talk.

'Aren't you leaving, Achan?' He pretended to be in a hurry to leave. 'I have some work in the town.'

Pathros achan leaned against the pillar, visibly displeased. He gave Elias a hard look. Then he turned to the sexton. He did not notice the sexton making signs for them to leave.

'What is the point of saying anything? What do they care if people here are persecuted by those devils? Their one leg is always on the other shore,' the priest muttered under his breath as he climbed down the steps.

Elias' face reddened. He said in an unusually loud voice, 'What did you say, Achan?'

'Hey nothing.' Mathai the sexton made haste to leave. As for the priest, he had already reached the yard. From there he walked quickly into the lane.

'Wait, say that once again…' Elias said, hastening down the steps to follow him.

But Eshumma, who had been standing inside listening, hurried out into the veranda. 'Eda Eliase, come inside.' She slapped the pillar and shouted, 'Why are you trying to pick a fight with that priest?'

Elias was trembling as he walked back slowly. Umma was puzzled. Elias, who generally managed to remain aloof in such matters, was getting unusually worked up.

'Let it go, eda. Leave that old man alone.'

'If he is old his tongue should remain in his throat.' Elias' voice shook. He was trying hard to control himself. 'I have been hearing this for a long time. Whatever be the topic of discussion, this comment always crops up. One leg is on the other side, after all! Why? Isn't this land ours as well? We don't need anyone's magnanimity! What we have here is what our forefathers made through toil and sweat, isn't it?'

'Let it go, eda. How many more days do we have left here? Be patient until then. No matter what, we have a land to call our own. No one will call us outsiders there.'

'Keep quiet, Umma!' Elias said sharply. 'I am not going anywhere. This is my country too. Let me see who questions it.'

As Umma stood indecisively, not able to understand him, Elias stomped into the house.

The youngsters of today! Umma thought. Anger sits on the tip of their noses. Ready to lunge at each other's throats at the slightest provocation.

Let it go. How much longer can such skirmishes last? Whatever it is, they now have a land to go to.

Their own land. A land of their own. Their own holy land.

The Burden of Awareness

'I saw Umma in my sleep.'

Salamon remembered telling Eshimuthimma jubilantly several years ago about a dream he had had at dawn in which he had laughed a lot, cried a lot...

He also remembered that Muthimma had flinched.

'What did you see?' she asked.

'Several things.'

'Tell me what you saw, mone.'

'I don't know.'

'Good or bad?'

'Some good, some bad.'

'Henceforth see only good things, all right?'

How do you control your dreams? Dreams come without an invitation, don't they? Salamon looked at her, puzzled.

'Ummm, er...'

'Then you shouldn't see Rebecca any more. No one needs to see her. It makes me sad.' Muthimma's voice broke. Dull tears coursed down her wrinkled cheeks.

Salamon did not understand this at all. What was wrong in dreaming about Umma, who died when he was very young, leaving behind no clear memories? Umma didn't come because I called. She too must have desires.

Muthimma, realizing that she should not have said what

318

she did, tried to quickly correct herself. 'I just don't want you to be sad.'

But Salamon had not felt sad. How could he block the dreams that came in search of him? He had had so many dreams, both good and bad. Some dreams he longed to see again but they never returned. Others followed him, though he wanted to be free of them. As a child, he had often wondered who it was who shaped dreams and threw them into his head. Was everyone subjected to such visions?

When he voiced these questions, his friends laughed at him.

'It is fun to have dreams, isn't it?' Ouso from the island said. 'Sushila, Lilly, Shanti from Thekkumpuram and then of course our Clara, and...'

It was difficult to change the subject as the list grew longer. By that time Pushpan and Lohithakshan had joined in. Talking about girls was their favourite pastime.

'Clara's proportions are impressive, every part of her ... Sure, her face is covered with pimples, but still she's something! The one who marries her would be definitely lucky.'

'But I have already married her. Not once, thrice. That too in three different churches.'

'Oh yes, yes. Her soldier father in Assam is coming with his rifle to get you two married.'

Ouso, Pushpan and Lohithakshan then went to watch Kuttikrishnan, the Paliyam family's elephant that had gone berserk, killed its mahout and was circling the banyan tree, trumpeting. Salamon stayed back. The elephant had torn Ammunni Nair apart, like one tears the spathe of a banana tree, and trampled on him. The railway-engine-shaped silver talisman around his waist lay on the ground nearby.

Salamon did not even dare visualize that scene.

He had seen Ammunni Nair so many times, enjoying his betel as he sat near the elephant with his legs stretched out in front of him, his prodding stick resting against the elephant's front leg. As soon as he saw Salamon, he would call out, scratching his arse,

'Athei, what is the price of eggs these days, Sa'ib?'

Though Salamon had respect for the mahout who could control such a huge animal with just a rod, that question irritated him. Did he think all Jews in the village only sold eggs? So many of them were educated and well-off. And there were some, like the relatives of Pambu, who had a lot of land.

Though Ouso later whispered to him a suitable reply to the mahout's question, Salamon knew it was a vulgar abuse. Anyway Salamon preferred to steer clear of the betel-chewing, arse-scratching Ammunni Nair.

Salamon disliked Ammunni Nair, it was true, but the horrible incident that transformed his means of livelihood into an instrument of his death made him lose sleep for several nights. No one deserved such a gory death.

In all probability Thupran's arrack must have gone to the mahout's head and he must have tugged the back of Kuttikrishnan's ear with the curved end of his rod and hurt him. The animal must have already been in musth, which enraged it even further. As the horrified crowd watched, the elephant lifted Pashnam Raghavan up with his trunk and flung him towards the granite water tank. Muscleman Raghavan had thought he would show his valour by taming the elephant. Seeing that Pushpan fled.

Though Salamon had not actually seen all this, it all came vividly in his dream later. Not just the scattered remains of Ammunni Nair, but even the silver talisman with its broken string that lay in the grass on the northern side of the banyan, and the string of rudraksha beads that he used to wear around his neck.

That night too he had wet his lungi. Wet his bed. For the first time, Muthimma had scolded him.

Night after night, the same ghastly scenes haunted his dreams and frightened Salamon. Kuttikrishnan's rage. Ammunni Nair's piteous cries, his bloodied body thrashing about on the ground. The giant foot raised above his battered body...

Who was pouring these sights into him, sights he had not even seen?

'Let us tell the muliyar. There must be some way to avoid bad dreams,' Muthimma tried to comfort him.

It was not just this one incident. There were so many other kinds of dreams: Ephraim muthacha sliding out of the framed photograph on the wall, swinging the sword that the king of Kochi had presented him. How did Eshimuthimma's calf running down the hill acquire Elsie's face? Binder Daveed chettan sitting cross-legged with old books lying scattered before him. When he got fed up with pasting the flitting pages together, he inhaled snuff and sneezed loudly, cursing someone.

Salamon was certain about one thing. The landings that appeared in all these dreams were very clear. So was the water. The ferry lay abandoned. The boatman Ittaman waited for the lone traveller...

When Salamon used to sit before his open school books, lost in his dreams, Muthimma regretted the fact that she could not follow his thoughts. Whenever she complained about it, Elias would laugh. 'For God's sake, Umma, leave him alone. The ability to dream is God's grace. It is those who have dreams that no one else sees, become great men. What if he is not good at studies. The road destined for him must be a different one.'

Muthimma would be amused. Let him sit and dream. Those who study with him would have reached their destination by then.

However, as the days went by, Eshimuthimma was forced to acknowledge that the infant that had lain in her lap had become an adult. He had reached the age when the words uttered by elders could become a burden. He had his own ideas and views about everything, and obstinacies which no one could understand. So when she was certain that he would not tread the path of his forefathers, she gradually loosened her hold. Perhaps he knew what he wanted. Let the good Lord grant him enlightenment.

Therefore whenever Evron asked her sorrowfully, what should I do next, Umma, she had just one reply:

'Let him go his way, Evrone. Remind yourself that a saintly woman gave birth to him. I am sure he will not do anything foolish.'

Rather than comforting him these words infuriated Evron. Was it enough that he did not do anything foolish? Was he not the male child who should take the family of Ephraim and Isaac forward? How could he be so dull and lethargic at an age when he should be brimming with energy? Either he should study and strive towards a goal or he should find a means of livelihood like the rest of his age group. How he went about incapable of doing either is what Evron could not understand. It made him anxious about the boy. Of late, Evron was careful of how he talked to his son. If one thing led to another and ended in a quarrel, it was Umma who would be hurt. For Eshimuthimma, her grandson took precedence over everyone else in the family. That is why she would interfere in whatever anyone said to him.

'You keep quiet! You and your anxieties! Who were you at this age?'

Evron never tried to argue with Umma because no matter where it started, it ended at his own inadequacies. At times he tried to discuss it with Elias, but he too would raise his voice.

'Oh, leave him alone, Evrone. He is smart. He became an introvert due to circumstances. You just wait and watch what happens when the right opportunity comes. The boy will make everyone take back their words.'

Evron was now slowly recognizing the truth in those words. The boy was not as incapable as he appeared. Unfavourable surroundings and undesirable friendships had made him that way. What Elias said was true. There was some hidden talent in him. If he were in a different place, in different surroundings, he might follow the right path.

The right path. The right path for his son.

Thereafter Evron began to view the journey to the holy land as a journey of reformation for Salamon. Every bit of news, every piece of paper that arrived from Mattancherry by boat, brought a glimmering hope that illuminated the right path.

When after a long time he met his old schoolmate P.C., the shopkeeper near the court, he hinted as much.

'I'm telling you frankly, I am doing all this difficult work for the boy's sake,' Evron had said ruefully.

There was a look of embarrassment on P.C.'s face.

'We were the ones who made the mistake, Evron,' P.C. countered. 'Do you think this thing called art is something

insignificant? A few years ago, a boy came from Kuriachira
to draw the pictures of Jesus and the saints on the walls of
our church. Must have been twenty or twenty-one. A slender
thing like an unformed coconut on a stick. He climbed the
church wall like a lizard. You should see the pictures he
painted in some two, two-and-a-half months. Even the
drawing masters said that if they hear about him in Rome,
they will immediately snatch him away.'

'True,' Evron nodded. He too had seen those paintings.

'Only those on whom the grace of saints and angels has
fallen are fated for this. He is not like us, he is a good lad.
Christ has designed a path for each one of us. We were fools
to place a measuring rod in the hands of a boy on whom
God's grace has been showered.'

As P.C. had seen more of the world than him, his words
comforted Evron greatly. However, it heightened his
determination to somehow get Salamon to the land where
destiny awaited him. With that, his boat rides to Kochi and
his appearance on the veranda of the agency office became
more frequent. Besides, for some time now no one came to
the Panchayat office asking for Evron Sa'ib. The rumour
that his eyes were fixed on the other shore had spread thick
and fast by now.

Though Salamon was aware of some of Evronappa's
plans, he himself was unsure about them. What inspiration
would he gain in an unknown land that he could not get in the
land of his birth? You needed familiar, suitable surroundings
in order to dream…

A change from these surroundings. A change that Evron
and Ramanandan desired. Was that what he needed?

When as usual he stumbled into that formidable question
for which he did not have an answer, the words that

Varuthutty master had often said to him appeared like a disembodied voice:

The burden of awareness.

The torment of awareness.

What was awareness? What guarantee did he have that he would get it in some foreign land steeped in darkness? Even as he repeatedly asked that question to himself, Salamon felt himself descend even deeper into gloom.

Fences

'Looks like the Thuravur knot might tighten, Soloma.' Tension was writ large on Ramanandan's face.

Salamon did not immediately grasp what he meant.

'That same old alliance, eda,' Ramanandan said. 'I thought it had passed, but they seem unwilling to let go. I heard that someone had even come from there yesterday.'

'And?'

'The only question is whether the wedding should take place before Divakara Pai's seventieth birthday after which he goes to Kashi and Rameshwaram or when he returns from the pilgrimage.'

'And what did you say?'

'That I did not want to marry so soon.'

'And?'

'Black said he had given his word. That traders have just one word.'

'So this too is trade?'

'For traders everything is trade, isn't it, Soloma?'

'So?'

'If the Thuravur alliance is not grand enough, a better one has come from Lokamaleswaram. Only daughter. Lots of land. Prominent family.'

'What about the word given to the Thuravur people?'

'In business it is possible to go back on one's word if one gets a better deal.'

'Oh…'

'Apparently they are going to buy a cinema talkies outside the town. Right now it is just a shed with a thatched roof and sand floor. They plan to cement the floor and use asbestos for the roof.'

'You are lucky. Now you can see Anjali Devi whenever you want, that too for free.'

'Shut up. I lost interest in all that a long time ago.'

A faint flush of embarrassment appeared on Ramanandan's pale face. Salamon thought about it a great deal but still could not understand what was wrong with the whole thing. Divakara Pai had enough wealth for two generations to live comfortably. A provision store that was doing well, coconut groves on the island, a thriving copra business, a huge stationery shop by the roadside and rent from a row of buildings which the Thuravur girl would bring, lands and cinema talkies of the sole inheritor from Lokamaleswaram.

The moment Divakara Pai acquires the remaining coconut groves, the island will become his. Likewise if Ramanandan buys his incompetent brother's share after his father's death, the entire island will belong to him.

Ramanandan Pai's island.

The island of the male child which the Thuravur girl or the Lokamaleswaram girl gives birth to. Through him would come a long generation of rulers of the island.

Definite, precise roads. Perhaps that clarity, that certainty, troubled Ramanandan – the thought flashed across Salamon's mind.

'What are you thinking?' Ramanandan asked.

'I was wondering whether the problem lies in Thuravur or in Lokamaleswaram?'

'There are only problems. You do not have the eyes to see them, that's all. Does money make up for everything else? If that is so there are so many other ways of making money.'

So then? What else did Ramanandan want? Salamon had no clue.

Ramanandan leaned forward in the wooden chair under the shady canopy of the huge tamarind tree, holding a fan. Salamon sat nearby on a stool.

Ramanandan watched two labourers gathering the dry coconut halves spread on a mat and stuffing them into a sack. For a moment he was distracted.

'This year the coconut yield in Makaram is low, so copra is too less. It is three years since the flood water entered the land. On top of it the disease that infected the trees...'

These things did not concern the people on the hilltop, Salamon recalled. Earlier, every alternate year, muddy waters from the eastern hills flooded the lowlands during the months of Mithunam and Karkkidakam, leaving behind rich silt that was sufficient for two or three years. But when dams were built, the rivers dried up. The hills were displeased. The rivers were unhappy. The rivers were frightened. They dared not overflow their banks even during the monsoon. Suppose someone blocked the water that broke the embankments and flowed into the land...?

Even now the village was surrounded by the river. The surging floods and the tempestuous wind unconsciously crept into every sentence uttered by the elders.

'What are you thinking?' Ramanandan asked irritably.

'About what you told me just now. After all, Divakara Pai is doing all this with good intentions, isn't he?'

'That is not the issue, Soloma,' Ramanandan said, mollified. 'I cannot carry this burden, that is all.'

'Then?'

'I want to go somewhere.'

'What do you mean by that?'

'I want to leave this place ... leave this shore, just go away.'

Salamon was perplexed. People were always in search of a place to take root. Those who had no other option were the ones that left the land. What more would someone who had so much wealth want? Why would he want to leave this land? That was the question on Salamon's face.

Ramanandan countered it with a question.

'Then why are your people uprooting themselves and planning to leave? Is it because you are in dire straits because of financial trouble and persecution? Is anyone forcing you out?'

'You know very well why. I don't have to tell you.'

'You are leaving because you do not belong here, you are outsiders. Suppose I say we too are outsiders?'

'What do you mean?'

'We too were forced to flee from our land. We did not cross the sea, that is all; we came from another region.'

That was news to Salamon. Though their customs were different and they had their own language, he found it difficult to believe that the Konkanis had come from some other place.

Ramanandan began to tell Salamon the story of Konkanis who fled their land a long time ago. They had suffered many atrocities. First at the hands of Muslims, then the Portuguese. During the time of the sultans, conversions and destruction of temples happened systematically. But the greatest cruelties were perpetrated by the fanatical Portuguese. They committed unimaginable, heinous acts on. The notorious Goa Inquisition, a terrible stain on the history of Goa, saw the persecution of Hindus and Jews. A trial was held, the biased judge would pronounce the verdict, and the punishment could be anything. No one dared question it. Then they made the use of their language compulsory so that the Konkani language and culture were edged out.

'Do you know how they gathered people for mass baptism?'

As usual Salamon shook his head. Ramanandan continued, 'Priests would go around towns accompanied by black slaves to capture people. They would forcibly rub beef on their mouths. As a result, the victims became outcastes. So they, poor things, had no other option but to convert. And then, the ones who were converted became lesser people in the community. Like your black Jews...'

Like the Spanish Inquisition Eliacha had talked about, thought Salamon.

Ramanandan pulled at the sweaty sacred thread sticking to his chest and fanned himself vigorously.

'Do you know, at that time even wearing this thread was a crime? Not just that, many Hindu rituals were prohibited.'

Salamon nodded as though he understood.

'I have heard of people fleeing to save their kuduma,' Ramanandan said.

'Kuduma?'

'Yes, kuduma, the tuft of hair at the back of the head we call shendi. People had to pay shendi tax in order to retain it. That's what the elders say. I don't know if it is true.'

Ramanandan ended his story by saying, 'Thus many natives migrated to different corners of the country to escape the invaders who came from across the sea. Some families must have followed this road and come to settle here. That's all. Like your ancestors, they too must have found the conditions here at the time favourable.'

He and Salamon fell silent for a while. Then as if he had recalled something, Ramanandan said,

'However, my desire to go is not because of a call of any holy land. I have heard that during every Passover, your people pray "next year in Jerusalem". Our ancestors might not have made any such promise when they left their Konkan. So Ramanandan has no particular destination. Any place beyond Kodakara is acceptable to Ramanandan.'

'Then?'

'A small piece of earth to lie in when I am dead. What does it matter where it is – here or anywhere else.'

Ramanandan's gaze turned towards the workers who had loaded the sacks of copra on to the weighing scale. Crows lined the branches of the nearby trees, crows of different sizes, crows that cawed in different ways. Their eyes were on the woven mat. The eyes of the workers were on the crows. One moment of distraction and the birds would swoop down and fly off with the copra. One would not even notice, they were that swift…

'I hope the halves are perfectly dry, Kutta?' Ramanandan asked, brushing off a spider that had got trapped in his fan. Unconsciously his voice reflected the tone of the concerned and efficient muthalali.

'Perhaps a little too dry, I think.'

'I heard that the mill owners in Kottapuram complained last time … said they would send back the load if it was damp.'

'All part of their tricks, muthalali. They don't want to pay the rate of the Kochi market. Our coconut is rich in oil. Even twenty rupees more than the current rate is not enough, if you ask me.'

'Then what about the last time?'

'...*moochu*, what else? They get huge quantities in the month of Makaram. But whatever it is, the mill owners in Kottapuram have not become so high and mighty that they will send back Divakara Pai's copra.' There was pride in Kuttan's voice.

Without saying more, Ramanandan took Salamon's hand and walked towards the veranda. Salamon pulled his hand away from the sweaty oily palm in disgust. Sweat trickled down Ramanandan's chest. Why can't he wear at least a vest, he thought. What was the point of having all this wealth? For whose sake was he being so miserly?

Ramanandan wiped himself with a dirty towel and sank back into the soiled cloth-backed chair.

'In a way, everyone is an outsider, isn't it, Soloma? People came from different places at different times. Some who had fled; some who came in search of better living conditions, greener pastures. If you look at it like that, who can claim to belong to this place?'

As Varuthutty master says, and as Eliacha says, it is the land of people who came and went. It is these goings and comings that have taken place through the ages that create history, that shape cultures.

Salamon thought, then which is my land? Where is Ramanandan's land?

What was one's own soil? What was the price of that pinch of soil that the ash-binders of Methala tied to the edge of their tunics?

'I have had enough, Soloma,' Ramanandan continued, looking at something far away. 'I have told them, they will not get me to watch out for crows from next year. Kuttan is Divakara Pai's trusted servant. More trustworthy than me. Let Divakara Pai hand over the responsibility to him. If he wants he can make him wear the sacred thread, for all I care.'

After thinking for a while, he continued, 'I say I want to leave not because I do not like this village. I do like this land and its people. But do we need another Divakara Pai to lick his finger and count dirty notes? Is that my duty? I want to see the world which lies beyond this land. See people I have not seen. Learn about lives I do not know, want to become a part of all that. Ramanandan's birth is not to be wasted away, watching out for crows, and writing the accounts for provisions.'

Salamon nodded. This he understood.

'Divakara Pai knows it. That is why he is trying to burden me with a woman and family and the business. If he hangs them around my neck and weighs down my hands and feet, then I can no longer raise my head or move my leg, can I?'

Salamon was suddenly reminded of Varuthutty master's words. The eagerness to know the world outside is good. But can the roots firmed up by time be that easily uprooted? The desire to return, won't at least a little bit of it remain? At some time, in some form, perhaps even as an atma, a soul?

Almost as if reading Salamon's thoughts, Ramanandan said, 'I am not thinking of a journey only to consider a return later, Soloma.'

'Then?'

'Why return? For whom should I return?'

Salamon sensed the resolve in Ramanandan's voice. As though he had made up his mind.

'That is why I told you that day, that I am willing to come with you all. If you will take me, that is.'

Ramanandan laughed. 'I am even willing to marry a poor Jewish girl.'

Salamon stared at him blankly.

'Do you know, ours too is a closed community like yours. We mingle only within the boundaries of our group, a small group that takes pride in the purity of its blood. I want to get out of it. I know it is not easy. Still, the desire remains.'

At a time when everyone was increasing the height of the wire fences around them, here was a man who was trying to do away with fences, straining to thrust his neck out. Was there so much inner strength in this sweaty body? This mournful looking muthalali is rupturing all my ideas about the future, Salamon thought.

Aren't our people too confined within another wire fence? Though the question raised its head within him, Salamon quickly suppressed it.

Ramanandan was crazy. No wonder Divakara Pai was in a hurry to get him married.

Suddenly Salamon felt he could not take this conversation any longer. Perhaps he could tell Varuthutty master about it. Tell Eliacha. They might be able to explain it.

He got up and stepped into the yard without saying goodbye. Ramanandan did not seem to have noticed it. He was still in some distant world. Thinking that it was not right to call back someone who was preparing to go along a thorny path with no thought of return, Salamon jumped across the bamboo barrier and entered the cut road.

Parting

When Salamon saw Elsie on the hilltop in the evening, there was a frown on her face.

'So you are leaving too, aren't you?' Her voice sounded husky.

Salamon did not reply.

'Till a day ago you said you were not sure... Then?'

Salamon's throat went dry. She too must have heard that after three or four days there will be no lights on Jew Street at night. After all, for some time now, there was word going around about all the things that were up for sale in Jew Street.

Expensive copper vessels, wooden furniture, iron articles, household goods ... Those on the outside did not notice that the lively group of people who had lived amidst them for so long had suddenly turned into a jumble of lifeless articles. That was because they had been waiting for this. Their eyes were on objects they could get cheap. As carpenters from Manjali roamed through the houses with their measuring rods to assess the value of wood, some housewives plaintively asked,

'Will you take them down?'

The carpenters laughed.

'When you sell an old bull do you ask whether it will go

to a slaughter house or a shelter? Do you bother to find out whether the buyers are from Mala or Varapuzha?'

For them a house was just a mass of laterite bricks and wood.

Veroni, who was in the habit of telling all that she heard to the first one she met, thereby lightening the burden on her own heart, forgot all about the Jews leaving, but Devassy mapla who was fated to sit guard from dawn to dusk in the veranda heard and saw everything.

Thus one evening, as he sat staring at the crimson of the setting sun that spread in the lane in front of Salamon's house, he said to his daughter,

'For some days now, we have not seen our Salamon come this way, mole.'

'He must be busy, Appa,' the daughter replied.

'What busy ... the boy has no work?'

'Aa ... Who knows?'

'Must be busy preparing for the journey, I suppose?'

'Aa...'

Devassy mapla looked intently into his daughter's eyes. She stared at the crimson that sheathed the lane.

'This is what human life is all about! Just think of it that way. No point in brooding about it and hurting.'

Not sure what the father meant, the daughter looked at him questioningly.

'No, I was just talking about how things work in this world.' He quickly tried to change the subject, but she was wandering alone through the layers of meaning that his words had evoked.

Salamon noticed Elsie's breath quicken. After a while, he said in a low voice, 'I heard some people in Paravur have received the papers.'

'After that they will be coming here too?'

'Perhaps.'

'Then you too will leave.'

'Who knows?'

'So finally you decided to be a Jew.' Elsie's voice grew huskier. 'I always knew that you were cheating Elsie with your lies, that you too would leave in the end.'

She was striking off certain calculations in her mind. Though several people had told her not to count on those who were preparing to leave she did not pay heed, hung on to that old friendship, and as time went by, mingled many hopes and fragrances into it. And finally this ... She should have viewed the one who had pulled the areca spathe on which she sat and shown her the soil and the trees as just that – a friend. She should not have grown up from the time when she had sat clutching the dried spathe. Then she would have had at least a spathe to hold on to.

On an impulse, Salamon stretched his hand towards Elsie, but she moved away. No, I am returning to that old areca spathe, after all, she thought. That vehicle would suffice to see the world I need to see.

Salamon's face dimmed.

He stared at her intently for a moment, but did not say a word. Finally he muttered,

'I have not yet decided to go.' Even as he said it, the uncertainty in his voice made him cringe.

'You need not lie. We are no longer children,' Elsie said. 'Yesterday Mincent too said that you will go.'

How did Mincent, who could not speak clearly, acquire the voice of a prophet? The same old question was rising up within him once again.

'Well that ... I told you, didn't I, it is a mind that does

not know deceit. The Lord confers thoughts in him at the right moment and they turn out to be true. The day appan fell from the roof, he held on to his hand weeping, don't go.'

'Elsie, what I was saying was…'

'Elsie can understand certain things without your telling her. We did not grow up putting every thought in words, did we?' Elsie was trying hard to control herself. 'Elsie does not believe everything that people tell her. That is easier. If I begin to believe, it will cause heartache.'

Unable to withstand the piercing look in her eyes, he lowered his head. He knew she was trying to read his face, desperate to get some answer. He tried to put on a blank face, but realized that any such attempt would be a farce. Finally he murmured,

'Even if the papers come one doesn't have to go.'

'So these Jews prepare documents merely for fun, do they?'

Her gaze was still fixed on his face.

'I am coming to the house tomorrow morning to see Devassy mapla and Veroni thathi.'

'To say goodbye?'

'I did not say that.'

'Then Amma will not be at home. Appan has gone for meditation.'

'Elsie…'

'Those are things that are meant for strong-minded men, Soloma. As you said, for policemen and soldiers who will suit Elsie.'

A policeman, soldier coming for Elsie … Salamon's heart missed a beat.

'What I am saying…'

'Another thing. Just because you leave, the hillside will

not collapse; neither will the Malavana jetty be flooded. Elsie is not the type to feel sad or eat othalanga and commit suicide. I'll just think that this is what life is and it will go on as before.'

Though her words were harsh, Elsie could not wholly control the anguish within her. It was as though she was struggling to prevent the pain that flitted across her face at intervals from appearing in her voice as well.

Salamon too was aware of something frothing up within him. He stood limp and sagging, unable to say anything. He was in a quandary as to what he should say. True or false, she would not believe it, that was certain. The intimacy of many years was melting into nothingness. Chitty Veroni's daughter was no longer the little girl of old. She had begun to grasp facts with the maturity of an adult.

Suddenly, as if a new path had opened up before him, he asked, 'Will you come to the hill side tomorrow?'

'Why?'

'I want to tell you certain things.'

'Then say them now. You do not say things after checking whether it is the appropriate time or not, do you?'

'That is not it. I have to think out certain things.'

'So you have started to think before you speak, have you?'

'Elsie, I…'

'You need one whole night to make up a new lie, don't you?'

'Elsie, if you behave like this…'

'Enough, Soloma. This is more than enough. Elsie has not vowed to wait for you under the tamarind tree every evening.'

'Just one day, tomorrow,' he pleaded.

'Why, is it your festival?'

'No.'

'To say goodbye?'

'Elsie, what I am saying…'

As he stood stupefied by the weakness in his voice, she began to walk down the hill. He waited, hoping that she would turn back at least once. But she did not. He stood watching the blue of her printed skirt merge into the darkness that was climbing up the hill. He heard the muezzin's call from the mosque, the bell from the temple on top of the hill.

Then he too began to walk down the hill, his head bent low.

The First List

Finally, after a very long wait, the papers arrived for seven people.

The first group of seven. It included the old frog-like woman who sold vellappam, Simon whose one leg was paralysed and Ibraim whose eyesight was poor. What amazed everyone was that the list did not include the Evron family. It was Evron who had run around to get the papers ready for all the people in the lane. Then how did it happen that when things finally began to move he was left out of the group?

Though he did not let it show, Evron was upset about it. He found it difficult to stand straight before people, difficult to find answers to the barbed questions flung at him. However, when he enquired about it in Kochi, he was relieved. The process had just begun. There had been a long lull after that episode of filariasis. It was only now that things were beginning to warm up. Besides, none of the lists were final. It just hinted at the many that were to follow. This was a cumbersome, long-drawn-out affair. Large groups from different countries and from different backgrounds were waiting, ready to leave. There were elderly folk among them, there were those who needed help, there were women and children. If the leader himself left first, who would look after such people? The first list included the needy ones. After all, it was the call of the sufferers that the gods hearken to first. Was it not for them that the doors of Jerusalem should open first?

'It is not over, eda. There will be three or four other lists like this one,' Evron told Elias. 'They will have to take everyone. This first one is just a notice for us to be prepared. However many lists come, everyone will leave together.'

Elias was amused. Why was Evron getting so jittery? How could they not take their family who had paid half the fare in advance? Moreover, shouldn't the organizer always remain at the back? He should be the last one to leave, after helping everyone else to do so.

'You're right, Eliase,' Evron admitted, feeling better. 'Everyone belongs to the same religion, at least in name. So what, each one is different. If there are ten people, there will be fifteen curves and turns. When one turns left, the other turns right. And comes with it a load of crookedness. It is a mammoth task to take them along.'

Well, the cap of being the leader of the Jews in the street was one that he fashioned for himself. So let Evron wear it, Elias told himself. Leaders are fated to bear such loads.

Helmsman Anthappan sat on top of the boat to Varapuzha and laughed his head off watching all the commotion.

'More papers will come, so they claim! Yes, oh, yes. Just wait,' Anthappan called out to those who sat near the landing to bask in the sunshine. 'Just this lot will leave. Maybe some more. The rest will remain here, you wait and see. Why, have the people in that land taken a holy vow or something that they will give room and board to everyone from our Kunnumpuram? Do they have that much space over there? Won't they have to feed this entire lazy lot that hates to do physical work?'

When he found no one on his side, he became even more strident. He jumped down from the boat on to the landing. There was time as people were just beginning to board.

'If you want, watch,' Anthappan continued. 'This Evron Sa'ib's pride will end with this. He thinks he represents the people on the hilltop in the government! Who is he, Comrade Jaleel? Or Minister Panampilly? He went about getting things done for everyone else, yet when it came to matters concerning his own family it is gopi, zero. How else can it be, when those in Jerusalem know everything that happens here the moment it happens?'

'How can that be?' someone asked, offering Anthappan a beedi.

'No, I don't want. Anthappan uses his own special brand.'

He sat on a tree stump and opened the bundle tucked in the folds of cloth at his waist. He took a beedi and lit it. As the smell of ganja mixed with the scent of the moisture-laden breeze, the nostrils of the elders flared.

'Seems like a grand thing,' someone remarked.

'It's from outside. Pandinadu,' the helmsman laughed. 'You asked me, didn't you, how they get to know all that that happens here? Isn't that why they installed that live thing called wireless? Do you think those people in the Kochi office are sitting idle? They have big eyes and even bigger ears. They send every bit of news from here across the sea as and when it happens.'

'So?' Ahmed, who brought bunches of bananas from places like Cheriyathekanam and Parakadavu and sold them in the village, asked.

Ittaman lowered his voice and said, as though sharing a great secret, 'Finally they will strike off some of the names, I am sure.'

'Will our Evron Sa'ib be in that group?' It was ironsmith Nanoo, who had a smithy near the road in Karimpadam, who asked that.

'Do you need to ask? That will shatter his pride, won't it? Will anyone in that family be able to hold up their head if that happens? In such times, the present counts above all other matters ... Saints and angels are forgetful,' Anthappan muttered cryptically.

Though everyone knew it was helmsman Anthappan's malice that prompted him to talk thus, no one said anything. They could not antagonize him. They needed him. His anger against Evron was something the two of them had to settle between themselves. The landings had nothing to do with it. Anyway, no one wanted to enter the helmsman's list of those he wanted to drown. After all, Anthappan was the king of their journeys across the river, to Varapuzha, Kochi, Vypeen; he was their link to those shores. It was through him that hot spicy news first reached their village.

'He is a mischief maker. But every village has such nuisances. Life is incomplete without them,' Ahmed said.

'Though half of it is exaggeration, it's fun to listen to his lies once in a while.'

'As exhilarating as drinking two hundred millilitres of toddy along with some green chilli chutney,' ironsmith Nanoo salivated, as he thought of the hot spicy chutney from Thupran's arrack shop.

Evron never heard about any of this chatter. He was busy going around the lane, explaining things. Some of the people refused to believe however much he explained. Most of them thought it was a shame not to be included in the first list. Particularly some of the prominent families. Some said that there were less people from Chendamangalam in the list because Evron had not put in enough effort to push their case in Kochi. Most of the people in the batch were from Paravur.

'There is no point in saying all this,' Evron replied. 'They do not determine whom to include looking at the name of the village or town. They give priority to the more deserving and needy ones.'

'How then did that Eliahu Meir go?' someone asked.

Evron knew the reason for it. Meir, who worked in Bangalore, had put in a lot of effort that led to the beginning of these migrations. It was he who first heard and spread the news of the possibility of such a migration. It was he who went about getting the papers ready at the higher levels. He and his family got themselves included in the first list in order to make arrangements for the people who were to follow. They should not include such a great man among ordinary people.

Moses master too was displeased with the list. In the matter of knowledge and position, was he not the one the people in Jerusalem should be most interested in taking in? When all these people landed there, when they needed to open their mouths and speak a few words in Hebrew, they needed a Moses master amidst them, didn't they? If there was no intermediary who knew the local language, would they get even a glass of water?

'That is true.' When someone on the veranda of the Panchayat office agreed with Moses master, Evron retorted, 'Oh really! Do you think the Jews who come from Russia, Germany and Africa were Hebrew masters in those countries? Ones who ran after students to teach them Hebrew during the transition? Some of them do not even know the language of the land they live in.'

Evron laughed as he thought about it. 'Besides, what does Moses master really know? That day when that Ezriel Carlebach came, did you not see him following tamely, tail between his legs? Do you know what that white man finally said? Leave Hebrew alone, Moses. Speak Malayalam, I will understand it better.'

When things slowly cooled down a bit, the next list arrived.

Another seven people. The list, which Evron directly brought from Kochi, did not include his family. But Moses master, his wife and his son were on it. A useless idler of a son!

'Well, that is how it is,' this time Evron was forced to assert firmly. 'We will be in the last list, after everyone else has boarded. That is the decent way to do it.'

'That is if there are any seats left. Isn't that so?' someone tried to pull his leg.

'There is no question of there not being seats. If the agency people do not provide seats after taking money for them, will they be allowed to continue to function over here?'

For some time now, Eshumma had begun to have ominous feelings about this departure. There was something wrong somewhere. If they failed to get in the first list, they would surely be included in the second. That is what she had thought as they waited for the second list. But when that too failed to include her family, she became disheartened.

'Will they cheat us, Eliase?' She turned towards her faithful son hopefully.

'Umma, don't fret unnecessarily. Things will follow their course. Those people have a certain system. Things will move only according to that. Let all the initial hurry-burry settle down a bit, Umma. We will go without haste.'

'They say the best lands will be seized by those who reach

there first. We signed the agreement to sell this house and paid money in advance, and now we allow others to depart before us. Isn't that a shame? It's like breaking the pot at the final moment.'

'No pot is going to break over here. You be brave, Umma. Even if no one else goes, we will make you board the plane first and make you sit in the window seat.'

That really scared her. 'How can that be, Eliase? Your Umma who has never even boarded a train, how can I go alone in a plane?'

'We will be there with you, of course.'

She was somewhat relieved but one doubt remained. 'Do they not know that we paid money after signing an agreement to sell our land here?'

'Of course they know. The member must have told them that in the beginning itself. Besides, everyone is selling all that they have before they leave, isn't that so?'

'I have these doubts because it is your older brother Evron who is involved. He said similar things when he took a loan on the sixty cents of land in Pazhambillithuruthu to begin trade in the Ernakulam market. He said he would return the title deed before the next Hanukkah. And then what? The Gujarati got hold of that precious coconut grove. He sold it to some Christian at double the price. At that time he had Moopar to cover up all his misdeeds, so he escaped. It was on that day that I was convinced that half of what he says is lies. Now I feel it is more than half.'

'It is not because he wants to, Umma. Trade is like the eastern waters. No one knows how money comes and goes. If it comes to that, even Vava made mistakes, didn't he?'

'So what, he bestowed on us ten times more than what he lost, didn't he?'

Eshumma could not bear to hear a word of criticism about Isaac moopar. She firmly believed that her sons were unfit to even mention his name. Conversations which went in that direction only ended in lengthy bouts of weeping. It was as though the knot of that old relationship grew tighter as time went by. For that very reason, the unexpected flood that took him away continued to cleave through her inner consciousness.

For a long time after the tragedy, she was even scared of the river, let alone the ferry. Only after a very long time did she agree to step into a boat. That, too, only by holding on to faithful Elias' arm.

'This water, mone, is a dangerous one. How can you be sure that she who was treacherous once will not do the same again?' she had once said to Salamon. 'Whether it is water from the river or the hills, it is like some bloodthirsty woman. It takes as little time for it to get possessed as it does to return to normality. Once enraged, it has no idea of all the havoc it creates. After dragging off a full-bodied man, all she returned was two gold-capped teeth. Who wants that bit of gold? Couldn't the greedy witch consume that as well?'

Eshumma never again bothered to open the discoloured box kept safely in the cupboard in the drawing room wall.

The river that flowed just below the hilltop, reflecting myriad faces through the seasons, was always a woman for Eshumma. She had the same elusive mood swings of a woman.

Umma too was not all that different, Elias often told Salamon. She did not need a time or reason to love or to rage. She did not need summer or rain. If angry, she would tremble with fury. She became another person altogether.

The ripples that the papers from Kochi created on the

hillside did not upset Salamon in the least. A lot of things were happening. Some people were going somewhere. Or trying to go. Some were shouting, quarrelling, arguing. What did he have to do with all that?

When the entire Evron family packed their bags and left, did he not have anything to do with it? Someone from within flung that question at him.

He did not feel the need to find an answer to that question. As Varuthutty master said, he should not insist on getting an answer to every question. Some questions would remain unanswered for ages, evading one's grasp, countered with other questions. Through the years, new questions would continue to sprout. It was such questions and the search for their answers that took humanity forward.

Therefore, let there be more questions. More doubts, anxious misgivings and counter statements. That was the fate of being born human. That was its price.

Eliacha Has a Question
to Ask

'What have you decided finally?'
There was an unusual strain in Eliacha's words.
Salamon bowed his head without saying anything.

'Some more people will be getting the papers soon, I heard. Many have already started packing. There is no time to think,' Eliacha said.

On an impulse Salamon asked, 'Will I be able to paint over there?'

For a minute Eliacha was speechless. When he got the boy his first set of crayons a long time ago and later on a box of water colours, he did not know what an impact they would have on him. He had seen Salamon draw on the walls with colour pencils so he got the crayons and paints. But he noticed some of the shapes and pictures that Salamon had painted on the wall of Umma's room only when Paily came to whitewash the house. Umma had placed the cupboard in her room against the wall so that Evron would not discover them.

He keeps so many things secret, Elias thought. So diffident about everything!

When he recovered from his surprise, Elias replied, 'It might be possible after some time. Initially, however, we will be allotted work like rearing sheep, or working on a farm, or something from which we can earn some money to meet our daily needs.'

'But we know nothing about farming.'

'We will have to learn.'

'And grazing sheep?'

'Not just that, we will have to learn to carry loads of soil, and dig holes … We don't come out of the womb with a knowledge of all these, do we? Everyone will have to work. We will soon get used to it.'

'Everyone?'

'What else? It is the land of workers.'

That means Eshimuthimma who is past seventy and the old hunchbacked woman who has no clue as to her age … so many like them … Salamon was stunned.

'What, did you think it would be heaven over there?' Eliacha laughed. 'This is life, mone,' he said, patting Salamon on the back.

He then began to talk about what Bezallel, who was one of those who had gone to Israel in 1955, had told him. 'Do you know what he took with him when he went?' Eliacha asked.

As Salamon shook his head, he said, 'You won't believe it if I tell you. Fifteen kilograms of pepper and five hundred balloons. That is what they told him to bring. He spent his initial days selling them.' Elias burst out laughing when he saw Salamon's face. He then began to narrate the story he had not told anyone before.

The people coming from different countries were sent to settlements called kibbutz and moshav. Bezallel and his group first went to a kibbutz. Sandy plains all around. Patches of green here and there. During the day when the sand heated up, it was terribly hot, but at night it was so cold one could feel the chill pierce through the body. The kibbutz was governed by people's committees. Everyone was equal. There was no personal wealth. Since everything was common property, everything was shared and everyone had to work. Sleeping, eating, everything was done together. There were even some ministers who were part of such community living. But by the end of the first year, the elders in the group were fed up because they too had to work. There was not much freedom either. The first job that Bezallel was assigned was grazing goats. Gradually he got used to feeding the animals and milking them. He also made friends with school children and began to learn Hebrew. But the ones who had never done a day's work in their lives really suffered, particularly the older ones.

The moshavs on the other hand centred around families. There you could own land. You could join collective farming and take a share of the profit. Though there was government control, the situation provided an incentive to work more and produce more. Thus Bezallel's family moved to a moshav called Shahar. The Negev desert where Abraham and Isaac and Jacob had grazed goats. There was not even a proper house. A family of six or seven lived in a barrack made of wood, without rooms or privacy, between paths of red mud. Since there was not enough water for farming, Bezallel began by grazing goats there as well. It took two years for water and electricity to reach the place.

Thus Bezallel, who had never touched soil, learnt the first lessons in farming. When he was allotted some land, he built a small house. The government gave free seeds, fertilizers and water, and provided officers who taught farming. The settlers thus began to grow vegetables in the yard on a small scale. Later, when they got a bit more land, Bezallel was able to grow not just tomatoes, carrots, potatoes and red chillies but even sugar cane and cotton. It was then that he began to dream, to progress step by step, till he became a horticulturist.

When Elias concluded, Salamon looked at him, astounded.

This was the story of people who were successful. Surely there were also those who reached nowhere...?

'Need you wonder?' Elias smiled. 'Their numbers will surely be greater. Apparently when there was no work in the fields, people used to be taken in lorries to other places, to blast rocks, repair roads, and with the five lira they got for this, they would buy two loaves of bread and two packets of soup powder. In the intervening period, they would also get work in fields where cotton and groundnuts were grown. They worked ten to eighteen hours a day, without even a minute to waste, happy with what they got.'

'Entamme!' Salamon was shaken.

So what Comrade Pavithran and Varuthutty master said was true.

'You feel scared, don't you? It's all right,' Eliacha tried to reassure him. 'After a while things will straighten out. We are not lazy, we are just not used to doing that kind of work. It is a country of people who live in the midst of challenges. It is important that those who go there understand that.'

After a pause Eliacha asked again, 'Are you frightened?'

Salamon shook his head, but his face mirrored his misgivings.

As for Eliacha, he chuckled softly when he thought of the life that awaited one who wanted to paint!

Perhaps such harsh experiences might help to mould the

future artist, who knows! All great artists have grappled with life and struggled their way through.

Elias recalled that when he got his first box of water colours, Salamon's complaint was that it did not have enough shades. At that time he was forced to say, do not be in such a hurry, start with the colours you have. We will get the rest later.

But then Salamon discovered how to create new hues by mixing basic colours. With these exciting shades that emerged, he gave form to his innermost thoughts. He painted on paper and on bare walls, and no one bothered to try and decipher them, or to give him the necessary direction.

Now, after so many years, was the boy discovering his path? Eliacha looked at him in wonderment. Like Bezallel, who knew nothing about agriculture but became a successful horticulturist in Israel, Salamon might go there and become a great painter. Who was to tell?

There or here…? Something was making Eliacha uneasy. It was as though all questions were hitting a wall and falling down.

'You decide for yourself. I will not say anything,' he said in the end.

'Evronappa, Eshimuthimma?'

'You decide.'

'They will be sad.'

'That is why I said, you decide. You have reached the age to decide what path your life should take instead of…'

As usual Salamon was lost for words. His life seemed to be a series of such unexpected blocks in communication, he thought regretfully. He always needed someone before him, to show him the way – from Varuthutty master, Ramanandan and Pavithran, to binder Daveed chettan.

After a while he said, 'Whoever goes, there will be one Jew left in this land, that is certain.'

'Who is it?'

'That Daveed chettan.'

'Who is that?'

'The binder.'

'That man who sits in the corner beneath the stairs?' The derisive look on Eliacha's face surprised Salamon. Did Eliacha also see David chettan in that manner?

'Why, is binding books an inferior job?' he asked angrily.

'Hey, no. That is not the reason. I too have gone to him with some of Rebecca's college books.' Eliacha tried to smile. 'Okay, tell me, why is he so against going?'

'He is not against it. He does not feel like going, that is all.'

'But who does he have here to feel that way?'

'No one.'

'Then?'

'That is the very reason he has decided not to go. Why should one who has been alone all his life need someone now, is what he asks.'

'Oh,' Eliacha grimaced.

'The second reason is that he wonders whether this is a return or a migration.'

'Tell him it is both,' Eliacha retorted. 'A feeble excuse to stray away from the group, isn't that what it is? He does not understand the strength of the group ... It is very easy to remain aloof. But you should remember the magnitude of problems that those who attempt it confront. No one seems to understand that this is not just a migration, that there are deeper things underlying it. Isn't that the reason why I too joined it? They say such things because they have no sense of history, because they have not been taught our ancient history the way it should be.'

'He said the committee people there told him several times.'

'It must be their rough way of speaking that puts off people. This call should not come from the synagogue or the committee members. It should come from ordinary people. It is not enough that he binds books with his eyes closed. Once in a while he should open his eyes and read.' There was sarcasm in Eliacha's voice. 'If he had read the lines of that master poet Vyloppilli, your Daveed chettan would not have had such doubts. Vyloppilli sings that the children of Jehovah, who were fated to submit to the cruelties of religious fanatics and dictators, were born to testify through fire. A poet who follows another belief system feels it, yet the doubts of our own people do not cease … that is what I cannot understand. You need to see this journey as part of that test by fire. That is, to suffer, perhaps a little, perhaps a lot. Let those who go across the sea like this create a garden of roses in the soil of Israel, that is the poet's valediction. Is that not what our Bezallel and others achieved?'

Salamon did not argue further. Eliacha's belief in the journey seemed to have got stronger over the days gone by. One who had been in doubt in the early days was now wholly for it.

After a while Eliacha continued, a tinge of doubt in his voice, his gaze directed at something far away. 'Let that be. I wanted to ask you something else. It has been on my mind for some time now.'

'What is it?'

'That chit fund woman Veroni has a daughter, what is her name?'

Salamon froze. Who told Eliacha all this? He could not prevent the name slipping from his tongue.

'Elsie.'

'Aah ... Elsie. Though the mother's tongue is all around her neck, I have heard that the girl is well behaved.' Suddenly a grave expression spread over his face. 'I did not have the courage to do the right thing at the right time. You at least should...'

Salamon stared at him blankly.

'She was a Nair girl. This one is a Christian. It is not easy for us to accept either of them. In your case, you can at least go over to their side. Or else the two of you should have the courage to accept the difference and be together. At times I feel there are only two castes in the world, male and female.'

Salamon just stood and listened. That Eliacha had such a past! He was hearing it for the first time.

Eliacha wanted Salamon to have the courage that he himself did not have at that time. And after that? He had not thought of marriage till now. Not merely because he was young. How could he think of it when he had not been able to stand on his own feet yet?

His family. Her family. As Eliacha said, it was not possible to bring her over, but he could go to the other side. Did that mean changing one's religion? Was it that easy, changing from one to the other? Should the beliefs and awareness that were part of one's growing up be rejected for the sake of a girl? Was there such a binding knot between him and her? Had the intimacy that began in childhood grown that much?

He was not sure of it himself.

'What are you thinking?'

Salamon started as he heard Eliacha's voice. 'That ... that...'

'That you have not thought that far, is that it?'

'Aah…' Salamon nodded his head like an idiot.

'Shouldn't you think of it someday? Suppose suddenly one day everyone starts to pack?'

'That … that…'

'There is no place for hesitation, Soloma.' There was an unusually grave note in Eliacha's voice. 'You will have to make a decision, either way. Within eight or ten days.'

Salamon stared. Eight, ten days! What could he decide within that period?

'Veroni thathi?'

'There will be several such thathis and thathas in between. You must learn to ignore them. Forget what your appa did, what about Menahem? Umma was so much against Esther's entering the house. What did she lack for Umma to go after her?'

Salamon could not speak. What was Eliacha saying!

'She is studying. She says she wants to undergo training and become a teacher.'

'Let her. Who said she shouldn't?' Eliacha laughed. 'When you think of going across the sea, you should remember these ties as well, that is what I meant.'

Salamon could not say anything further. There was a turmoil within him. What would you call a relationship that had not grown beyond jokes, play and laughter? By asking these pointed questions, Eliacha was taking it to undreamt-of lengths.

'Everything will sort itself out.' He was aware of Eliacha's breath near him. 'If you keep your mind fixed on it, you will learn to do the right thing at the right time.'

Evronappa came in just then and Salamon was able to escape without giving a reply. Evronappa was carrying a bundle of papers soaked in sweat. It must be related to someone's departure. These days the member had just that one concern.

'They are wet. I think I'll have to put them out in the sun to dry,' he said, panting.

By that time Salamon had reached the yard. He had not seen his friends in Paliyam nada for some days now. It was as though a barrier that had never been there before had sprung up between them; many of them were avoiding him. Even when they saw him, they did not ask about the departure. They behaved as though they had already slashed his name off. Only Ramanandan whom he saw very rarely asked enthusiastically about the progress made.

Perhaps he was the only friend who stayed with him in this matter. The one who had decided that he too had to leave this land someday and escape into the world outside.

Salamon headed towards Malavana landing. He must sit alone on the shore for some time. He must spread out in his mind the things that Eliacha had said, sieve through them, weigh them.

There was no one near the landing. The flush of dusk had finally melted in the river, giving way to a murky darkness. In the thickening gloom, a boat moved over the water, its lantern throwing circles of light. He sat there for a long time, staring at the cleaved slices of water that moved along with the strokes of the paddle.

A Blot on Democracy

The first of August. The beginning of the month.

The newspaper arrived late that day. Apparently the bundles had been loaded on to another bus by mistake. By the time they reached Chendamangalam, climbed the hill and reached the agent's home, it was almost noon.

Eliacha, who had been waiting at the gate since morning and had finally given up and returned to the armchair in the veranda, was furious.

'What is this, Subra, has the day dawned for you now? A good beginning for the first day of the month.'

Subran did not like this kind of remark by the muthalali. Besides it was a shame to go around with that day's newspaper.

'Ask that question to those who loaded the bundles on to the wrong bus,' he retorted. 'If the newspaper meant for this place is sent to Perumbavur, it means those who sent it do not want us to read today's paper.'

Honestly, that was what Subran desired – that no one should see that day's paper. Something that should be burned without even unfolding it. When he thought of his miserable fate – that he was the one who had to go to every house with the paper that contained the unpleasant news item – he was filled with self-loathing. For the first time he hated his job. Till now it was the pride of being the one who brought news to the village that had kept him going. Now it included such ruinous news.

He should have said he had fever and remained huddled up in bed. The load of papers should have remained on the cracked floor of the veranda in the bus stand, like an abandoned corpse.

Elias grew suspicious that Subran had deliberately delayed delivery of the paper. Subran was a staunch party member. A trusted associate of Comrade Pavithran. An expert at sticking and tearing down posters. Though he was often moody and irritable, Pavithran never alienated him because of his expertise in climbing to the very top of any tree like a squirrel to hang the party flag. It was difficult to get such loyal followers these days. It was for that very reason that Elias too continued to keep him even though his occasional audacity infuriated him.

Elias quickly spread out the paper, pretending not to notice Subran grumbling as he went out.

The news was on the front page, announcing in bold letters: Kerala assembly dismissed, President's rule imposed. A Central ordinance had been issued according to article 356 of the Constitution, the article that empowered the president to dismiss any state assembly without soliciting anyone's opinion. The government was confident that the ordinance could be presented and passed in the parliament.

Though Kunnumpuram had heard the news in the morning itself, Elias got the news much later. On most days he would return home only after hearing the evening news on the radio, but he had not done that the previous day. Evron too had gone somewhere and had missed hearing about it.

As people began to snatch the paper from one another's hands in the Panchayat office veranda, Evron hurried home.

'Did you hear, Eliase? E.M.S. fell.' Evron's generally soft voice sounded excited.

'He did not fall, he was made to fall,' Elias corrected him.

Evron continued as though he had not heard.

'That day, when the shooting took place in Angamaly, at that moment, I said, Namboodiripad's time is over. Seven people died that day. That too poor folk who went to the police station to ask about someone who had gone missing. Didn't another eight die in Pulluvila and Vettukadu? The curse of that child that died in Flori's belly is enough to destroy an entire family.'

'Isn't it the priests who should provide an explanation for those incidents? They were the ones who incited the poor folk to take to the streets!' Elias countered. 'Isn't it because the priests announced in the church that religion was under threat that the people became furious and marched to the station? Honestly, did any of them know what this Vimochana Samaram was for? Just tell me, Evrone, will the Hindus run out of their houses without looking to the left or right if they hear the bell ring continuously in the temple? Would we Jews do that? We'll wait to ask what it's all about, won't we?'

Evron was amazed. When did Elias become a communist?

'What are you saying, Eliase? It was not just the priests, the Nair Service Society and the Muslim League all joined them, didn't they? They shut down schools and colleges, didn't they? Such turmoil did not occur even during the freedom struggle!'

'That is because the church felt threatened. Similarly, it was when the Nairs realized that their landholdings were in danger that the NSS became involved.'

'Didn't most of the panchayats and municipalities pass a resolution for dismissing the government? Isn't that true people's support? Then again, aren't several thousand people lying in prison? Is there any space left there? Do those who profess a great revolution confront people with batons and revolvers?' Evron's voice was full of fury.

'Lack of experience. They were forming a government for the first time,' Elias said. 'Where is the justice in evicting them after just two and a quarter years when you have voted them to power for five years, that too all of a sudden through an order from Delhi? Can you call this democracy?'

'When did you become a communist, Elias?'

'I am not a communist. Neither do I share their ideas. But what we did here is wrong. This should not have happened in a democracy like ours.'

'Oh, please don't use the language of the comrades of Vadakkumpuram, Elias. We are not so great as to teach Panditji democracy. In truth, the ordinance provided E.M.S. an easy way out. He can escape further notoriety by blaming the Centre for his failure.'

As he stood listening to the unusual political argument between the brothers, there was one thing that Salamon did not understand. Just like Eliacha was not a communist, Evron did not favour the Congress. Then how did the Vimochana Samaram become a topic for such a heated discussion between them?

Though he was not interested in learning more about it, he was relieved about one thing. From now on, the people who sat near the jetty, and under the banyan tree, in tea stalls and the veranda of the reading room, would have a new topic to discuss. He was that fed up with their intense political discussions.

At that time, he did not know that within two or three days the village would get a hotter topic to debate.

On Trial

A small crowd had gathered on the veranda of the government hospital. They were discussing something in a low voice. When they saw Salamon, their voices dropped. They moved to one corner, exchanging meaningful looks. A form crouched against a pillar which had a vertical crack along its surface and flakes of old whitewash peeling off. The face hidden between the knees could not be seen clearly. But as he drew near, he saw Devassy mapla's stick leaning against the pillar, and then his dishevelled hair.

Hearing Salamon clear his throat, Devassy raised his face reluctantly. A wet tear-stained face. The bulge in his lean throat with the interspersed veins appeared more prominent than before.

Salamon thought Devassy mapla saw him, but though he waited for a while for some kind of response, the latter did not shift his gaze, which seemed trapped in a group of trees farther away. He was in some other world. It did not seem as though he would return.

What has happened to everyone? Salamon wondered, bewildered.

It was then that he saw Ouso from the island emerge through the dark corridor that lay between the rooms tucked away on either side. He carried a flask and a bowl. There was a strained look on his face.

'Gruel for thathi,' he said, looking towards a corner of the compound where some dogs were barking and tumbling about on the rubbish heap. 'They have no one else to run errands, after all.'

Salamon was confused.

Seeing him, Ouso called, 'Come' with a reluctant gesture of the hand.

Ignoring the crowd gathered on the veranda, Ouso walked towards a mango tree in the hospital grounds.

Salamon followed him hesitantly.

Ouso's face looked terrible. He cleared his throat and spat out the phlegm several times, as though searching for words, then looked upwards and moved towards a spot where there was less chance of bird droppings falling on him.

'Why are you here?' There was an unusual sharpness in his voice.

'I heard people say something; I didn't really understand. So I came.'

'Oh!' Ouso grunted. He stared at Salamon, as though measuring him with his eyes, then said: 'So you were not fibbing!'

Salamon looked at him, perplexed. 'What are you saying?'

'Enough. Don't try to fool me further.' He paused and then continued, unable to stop himself, 'That day, even when you said what you did, I thought you were just reacting to their provocation. Never did I think that you would do such a terrible thing.'

'Ouso, what are you blabbering about?'

'Oh, I'm not blabbering, trust me! And don't act innocent. I know, the whole village knows what you did,' Ouso retorted angrily. 'If you go in, you can see your handiwork. She is lying in that room, dead to the world. Her mother sits next to the cot, sobbing her heart out. It's a terrible sight.' Ouso paused and muttered, 'Everyone together destroyed a family.'

'I was in Ernakulam,' Salamon said quickly, as though trying to explain his delayed appearance. 'The moment I got down from the boat at the jetty and heard it, I hurried here. I did not really understand.'

'So you came to take part in the excitement, did you?' Sarcasm tinged with sorrow laced Ouso's voice. 'You crossed the line, Soloma. I did not expect this from you. She is a foolish girl, says a lot of things without meaning it. You should have understood that.'

'Ouso, you...' Salamon said, totally bewildered.

'In a way she is related to us. A distant relative of Appan's. I never told you, that's all. Even when I thought you two were getting a bit too close, with all your silly jokes and teasing, I never tried to stop it, because I never thought things would go this far.'

'Look, Ouso,' Salamon's voice broke. He placed his hand on Ouso's shoulder, pressing it. 'Our friendship dates back to childhood. Tell me, please. What really happened? I don't know anything. I came running as soon as I heard.'

Ouso did not look convinced. Instead of looking at Salamon, he kept shifting his gaze between the birds flying towards the group of trees and the rickshaw pullers hollering on the other side of the wall.

'Ouso, look at me,' Salamon pleaded.

After a while, Ouso began to speak, looking searchingly into Salamon's eyes. As he talked, his voice thickened with emotion, sorrow and anger alternating. He was cursing a lot of people – Devassy mapla who sat leaning against the pillar in the veranda, trying to confine the world around him into that tiny space, Veroni thathi who wandered around the land, confident that the world was in her fist, without caring about her own family, neighbours, relatives, everyone.

Finally he cursed Salamon.

'Poor child.' Ouso's voice grew moist, brittle. 'I'd like to thrash, even kill someone … Point is, I don't know where to start.'

Salamon had never seen this side of Ouso, who always went about laughing and cracking jokes. Looking at him now, he felt that the hands calloused from holding the paddle might fall on his back any moment.

'Ouso, thrash me if you want to, if it will give you relief.'

The words seemed to have struck somewhere, for Ouso's face softened a little.

'Look, Soloma,' he said. 'You know how poor they are. They somehow eke out a living from what Veroni thathi makes by wandering all over the place collecting chit money. Only if Elsie studies and gets a job will that family have some hope. Our people know the struggle that her mother goes through to make both ends meet as well as to save up something for the girl's marriage. Our people know, but they are too proud, so no one says anything openly, that is all.'

He paused to shoo away a bird that swung from the bough right above him and continued, 'Just like us, girls too become volatile when they reach a certain age. They might say something without really meaning it. It is our duty to behave with propriety. That is what love is all about. When such things happen, it is the woman who has to bear the stigma.'

Salamon shuddered and said, 'I don't know anything,

Ouso. I'm telling the truth. I have not even touched her. She is not that type.'

'That's a lie! The kind that would wash away a grinding stone,' Ouso almost barked. 'This one will not be washed away even if there's a flood during the Pallipuram church festival.'

'It is the truth, Ouso … I will swear not just on your Christ, but on any god; or else on my muthimma. No one in this world is more important to me than her.' Unable to continue, he wiped his brimming eyes.

'Then why did she … Why are the villagers saying all kinds of things linking the two of you?' Ouso asked in a milder yet sceptical tone.

'They'll say a lot of things. It's our village after all. It has too many tongues. Tell me, did she say anything?'

'Who?'

'She.'

'How can she? She is barely conscious. Keeps muttering unintelligibly. The only thing that we hear clearly is your name. Isn't that enough for people to jump to conclusions?'

'You at least must believe me, Ouso,' Salamon pleaded. 'I swear, such a thought has not even crept into my mind. That day, after you all teased and provoked me I felt an impulse to embrace and kiss her. It is true, I admit it, but that is all. Just think, Ouso, can anyone look at her face and do anything indecent? It's the face of innocence.'

Ouso seemed to be in two minds, wanting to believe, yet unwilling to be convinced.

'I don't know, Soloma. No matter what we say, if anything falls from the girl's tongue, it stays. Like a chisel falling on granite. Even if all the Jews in the land come together, you will not be able to wipe off that mark.'

A tremor went through Salamon.

What would she say when she came to? Would people believe that even after going out with her for all these years, he had not even touched her? Forget touching, he had not even been able to understand her. She often boasted about it: 'In spite of his height and weight and the moustache, this devil called male is an idiot, Soloma. All he has is the size and weight of his body. His head is empty. Isn't that why moustachioed women lead them like mahouts lead towering elephants, that too without the stick?'

She had no doubt whatsoever that she was a moustachioed woman.

If she decided to display her skill like the mahout Ammuni Nair, who was torn to pieces by Kuttikrishnan...

'I'm innocent, Ouso.' Salamon's voice grew hoarse.

'What did they say at home?'

'I don't know. I came here straight from the landing.'

'Eshumma?'

'I don't know.'

'Evron Sa'ib?'

'With the kind of commotion you describe on the hillside, it will be difficult. There will be only one person to listen to what I say. Eliacha. But I don't know if even he will believe me.'

'True.' Ouso nodded his head. 'That is the problem with issues involving women. If the blot smears your forehead, it will remain forever. It is not easy to erase it. Whatever we say, our side is always weak. If a girl gets into trouble, every male who followed her scent will fall under suspicion. This is not a town after all. It is a small place, everyone knows everyone else. Then there is Pathros achan. True, he is a generous soul and he is also close to your appa. But when it comes to matters related to the parish, the members will become one. You people will be out. I heard that it was after his arrival at the scene that people became enraged.'

'What should I do now, Ouso, you tell me,' Salamon's voice broke.

Ouso looked at him kindly. 'Don't do anything now. Don't try to convince anyone either. Let us see what happens. Let her regain consciousness. Then we'll find a way.'

The realization that Ouso somewhat believed in his innocence was a big relief for Salamon. He had always been like that, right from childhood. It did not take much for him to lose his temper or to cool down. For that very reason, those who were close to him always treated him with caution. One never knew when he would lose his calm. If he did, he could get really angry. The kind who could crush you to death.

'Let it go, eda. True, I was upset when I first heard it. After being together for so long, such a treachery from your side...' Ouso softened.

Salamon asked impulsively, 'Can I see her?'

'Not now. Later. Let things calm down a bit. Let her begin to talk. If you go in there now and someone lays a hand on you ... When such issues crop up, everyone becomes a guardian, and a morality keeper. If something untoward happens, it will be a shame not just for your family but everyone in Jew Street; that too when you all are planning to leave.'

'That is what hurts me.'

Salamon stood with his head bowed for a while, then asked, 'How is she?'

'They say it is not critical. She escaped because some people heard Mincent crying loudly from the veranda and came running. Usually he sleeps in the evening. By the grace of God, he was standing at the threshold when it happened. Mother Mary's kindness.'

'And?'

'You know their well. There wasn't much water this summer. Because of a branch that broke her fall, she did not sink. However, by the time that cross-eyed Sivaraman rushed from the toddy shop, she had swallowed a lot of water. He was drunk. We were worried that he too would drown. I was the one who brought him. I had gone to see the stonemason and was on my way back. I was talking to old Paily when I heard the commotion.'

Ouso was breathing fast. He seemed quite shaken.

'When they pulled her out, they handed her to me. She was breathing like fish thrashing about on land. Her hands and feet were trembling. When we laid her in the veranda, we thought she was gone. But there was an old compounder among the group. He pumped her chest and got out some of the water. Then we carried her to the hospital. It was one big struggle.'

Seeing Salamon cover his ears, Ouso stopped.

'We hear and talk about such incidents unthinkingly. It is only when it happens to our own that we realize the horror of it. I could not sleep for two nights. Though I have seen fist fights and stabbing, this is a first. It is difficult to stand and watch. I do not enter the room. I don't even look in through the window. Even from outside I can hear her groan. And the mother's sobs. She was such a pretty girl. Everyone fussed over her and made a mess of it.'

As he paused to take a breath, his tanned face looked bloated.

Salamon found it hard to come to terms with that face.

He saw some people watching them from the veranda. They were pointing towards them and saying something.

'You'd better go now,' Ouso said quickly. 'Do not linger here. I will talk to them.'

Salamon nodded and turned back reluctantly.

Ouso reminded him, 'Go straight home. Don't go out for a few days. If there is any news, I will come and tell you. First try to explain things to your family. We'll think about the villagers later. The first place where you should find relief is your home, then your street.'

Without waiting to hear more, Salamon walked away with his head bowed.

Avoiding the main road, he entered the narrow lane that edged the canal, only to see Umma's tear-stained swollen face before his eyes. And Rebeccamma, who usually appeared only in his dreams. 'Oh my, Soloma, you ... and such a deed...'

Then Eshimuthimma.

However hard he tried, he just could not read the expression on Muthimma's face.

Waiting

The days dragged.

The atmosphere within the house was heavy. No one asked anything, said anything. Salamon noticed that when Evronappa left the house as usual every morning to take care of public affairs, he avoided looking at him. Salamon had thought that at least Eliacha, who knew everything, would ask him about the incident, but that did not happen. He walked with his usual laboured footsteps as though everything was normal. Somehow Salamon felt terribly let down.

If only someone asked something, said something, even cursed him.

Unless someone broached the topic, how could he say anything about it.

Ouso's words came to his mind. 'That is the problem with pennukesu, issues involving women, eda. If the blot smears your forehead, it remains. It is difficult to erase. Whatever we say, our side is always weak.'

Pennukesu! Salamon shuddered. There had been such stories involving male and female teachers in school, many of them fabricated by malicious tongues.

He had somehow managed to convince Ouso, but it would not be that easy with the people in the village. These were bad times. No one would believe in a smoke that emanated without a fire. By now, enough stories and more stories sprouting from those stories must have spread throughout the hilltop and its slopes.

Even otherwise, how many people could he try to convince? Was this something that he could announce publicly, going around the village on a bicycle, megaphone in hand?

Until Elsie opened her mouth, most people would mix stories they had heard with fabricated ones, exaggerate them and spread them. It gave them a thrill like that of scratching a half-formed scab. It had been long since such a juicy bit of scandal had fallen into their laps, Salamon thought bitterly. For that very reason, the news must have gone down the hill, gone beyond Paliyam nada, Thekkumpuram and Karimpadam, and reached Paravur town. Taking similar routes, it must have crossed the rivers and reached the islands, Puthenvelikkara, Gothuruthu ... Hot news that the wireless might take up and circulate. Salamon squirmed at the thought.

Even if Elsie declared him innocent, would anyone believe her? Even if everyone else did, Veroni thathi would not. She did not like Jews much. She would think that Elsie was only trying to protect him.

Suddenly another thought entered his head and Salamon shuddered. If, as these people said, she had done something wrong and did not say his name, wouldn't the question of who it was arise? Would she not have to give an answer for that? Something that any girl would hesitate to do.

Was there such another person between them? Someone who could get that close to her, whom he had not seen?

Who could it be? He could not bear to think of such a

possibility. The thought seared through him. Was it pain, mere jealousy or helplessness?

If something like that had happened, was it not better that she said his name? They did not need another name between them.

When his thoughts moved in that direction, he shook his head vigorously to get rid of them. He tried to divert his thoughts in other directions.

He wondered what problems Pathros achan would create. He would surely have discussed the issue with Evronappa. If so, what would he have said? Would the people of the parish tolerate the outrageous crime committed by a Jewish lad who was preparing to leave the country? Even if her family was willing to let it go, would the others agree?

He had heard that a neighbour had indeed informed the police station. But when Veroni went weeping to Pathros achan, he went with some parishioners, met some influential people and hushed it up. Ouso said that if a case had been filed, he would have been called to the police station, asked questions that would have made his skin burn, then threats and maybe even torture tactics to extract the answer they desired...

Salamon's thoughts were taking wild, circuitous paths.

Would they do something drastic to prevent him from leaving? Suppose Pathros achan and prominent members of the community insisted that he could leave only after they found something definite? What if they took him by force and converted him? Was it a small thing to get a follower from a famous Jewish family?

Wouldn't Elsie too desire such a move? If so, would she not support such an attempt?

Salamon thought and thought but could find no end to the

problem. He felt his heart throb in quick spasms. As though something untoward was about to happen.

With whom could he discuss all this openly? If only he could go out, he could go to Varuthutty master's house. But Ouso had insisted that he should not go out.

The hard expression on Eshimuthimma's face showed no sign of softening. It was the distance she kept that troubled him the most. Let others say whatever they want. But when Eshimuthimma who knew all his flaws and mistakes and yet had always stood by him … when she too…

When the first lightning flashed heralding the monsoon, Muthimma used to keep him, the bechor of the family, safely hidden in the folds of her tunic. Now when Jehovah's sword was about to descend on him in a season when there were no rains, did she not have any tunic to hide him? The more he thought about it, the better he understood her reaction. It must have hurt Muthimma terribly. For her, it was the honour of Ephraim Sa'ib's family that always came first. He had often seen her insist that whatever they embarked on, they should have one eye on that figure on the wall.

If they looked with a sincere heart they would get a reply, she would say. Isaac muthacha had many things to say from that aged wall to those who came after him.

Salamon was slowly beginning to grasp the meaning of that look that the sons did not recognize.

Suppose he were to go and tell her even if she did not ask?

He was in two minds. Even as he yearned to go and unburden his heart before her, a nagging thought prevented him from giving in to that impulse. She who had touched and known all his states from the time he could remember, should she not realize the turmoil in his mind without his telling her? Then why did she not ask? Again, being a woman, surely she would understand Elsie's feelings better than anyone else!

Finally he decided. Whatever the consequences, he would initiate the conversation, tell her all that had happened till now, hide nothing. Perhaps she might be able to show him a path that no one else could. After all, she was the one who had led the Isaac family both in prosperous and in hard times, in summer and in winter, wasn't she? He had heard that many a time she was the one who made the final decision even when Muthacha was alive.

But if he had to talk to Muthimma in that open manner, it must be at a time when there was no one else in the house. These days such chances were rare.

The servant Kallu Moopathi came regularly these days. Perhaps, for some time now, her husband had not fallen from the rooftop like before. Similarly her son must have realized that the chances of performing in Lavanasuravadham were slim and stopped going around with his guru's box of fineries. Anyway, when Moopathi began to come regularly, Muthimma too became energetic. The whisperings between the two, in the kitchen veranda or on the western side of the yard, had increased. If they saw his head anywhere near that side, they would pretend not to have seen him; Muthimma would stop talking and move towards the cowshed and Moopathi would go to pluck the leaves of the jackfruit tree for the goats.

With that, Salamon was certain of one thing. They were discussing him. Kallu Moopathi must have got some fresh news from Kizhakkumpuram.

Days went by.

He heard that Elsie had left the hospital only when Kallu Moopathi mentioned it while sweeping the kitchen veranda, this time loudly, so that he too would hear. There was nothing wrong with her physically, but she sat crouched on her bed, talking to no one. Though Veroni thathi and several others and finally Pathros achan tried to make her talk, she was not willing to open her heart to anyone.

Evronappa was becoming increasingly busy. He was running from pillar to post to get the last batch of papers ready. As usual he was taking care of matters concerning others more than his own.

Elias was mostly in his office at Paliyam nada. The agreement for the sale of the institute and the paper agency had been signed, but he had made it clear that he would be there till the last minute of the last day. He would then hand over the keys, shake hands with the new owner and walk out without a backward glance, climbing down the stairs with a bowed head. 'Because I built this with my own hands, I cannot bear to see another sit in that chair.'

Things were going on in that manner when one day a lad came from Puthenvelikkara bearing a note from Varuthutty master. He stood on the veranda hesitantly, then, after making sure that no one else was around, he gave Salamon the sealed envelope.

A few words in Varuthutty master's shapely handwriting, in the usual violet ink, gave Salamon a lot of courage.

'Heard everything. Do not worry. As one who knows you well, I am not willing to swallow whatever I hear. And even if there is some truth in it, it does not surprise me all that much. It is just one of the phases of life that one passes through. In the meantime, let me say one thing. You should have the courage to face all this. Never try to escape. Even if anyone advises you to do so, do not pay heed to it. Leave this land only after things clear up a little. Your departure is one where a return is uncertain. Even if you return as a tourist someday, we all would have gone. Therefore I tell you once again, do not leave things unresolved. Good and bad, it is better to leave behind everything that you received here. Then you can start as another person in a new place, live another life. To get the chance of a new life within this life is not a small thing. Whatever it be, let your future actions be directed towards that goal. Wish you the best. If we are lucky we will meet again, somewhere. They say the earth is round, isn't it? Let us see if that is true.'

Unload here whatever you gained from here. Was that easy?

In another place, live as another person, another life. Was that possible?

Varuthutty master was bidding him farewell. Salamon felt his eyes sting.

The letter was a real comfort. At least, the master understood him to some extent. The same logical, penetrating tone, courage-inducing words, a pointer that had many meanings … a pat on the back.

The boy who brought the letter had left as though he did not expect a reply. Salamon was relieved. Writing a reply was not easy. What could he write to Master, who always talked about weighty matters? Let Master himself find the answers. As one who knew him well, Master should be able to understand his regrets.

Not just Master, others as well. I have nothing to announce to anyone, all of a sudden Salamon decided. Let those who can, understand. I am not a prophet that I will explain everything to the world.

Ouso's Advice

Ouso continued to visit him, to tell him things that were neither frightening nor reassuring. Salamon did not hear half of what he said, and he did not understand half of what he did hear. He was floundering in the desperate attempt to keep together the scraps that had slipped out of his hand. Something was burning within him. A fiery heat was rising up that could consume all the water in the deep well in the yard and yet remain unquenched.

Why was it like this?

She who had tried to belittle him by saying that she would not need either the depth of the well or the poison of the othalanga fruit to deal with his departure, how did her heart waver so quickly? When all the arms in Kunnumpuram stretched towards her with yearning, why did she turn her own towards him? At a time when people were just waiting to get hold of something that fell from her tongue and stir up trouble, why did she evade an answer? Could she not open her heart to someone? Wasn't it because of the way she sat, hunched on her bed, her face a dark mask, that the smoke that shrouded that house did not lift?

The questions were many. The answers could come from only one person.

So many people asked her one after another – parents, neighbours, other well-wishers...

Finally even Pathros achan. As he prepared to receive a lengthy confession, Elsie smiled at him faintly and said, 'There is nothing in Elsie's mind that needs to be confessed. Whatever Elsie has to say she has said to Christ and Our Mother of Perpetual Sorrows several times.'

As he gazed at her, sitting with a somewhat empty mind, a relaxed face and a lost look, Pathros achan did not know what to say. His eyes grew moist. He put his hand over her head, blessed her, patted the grinning Mincent on the back and left the room. He woke up Devassy mapla who sat hunched in the veranda, waved at Veroni – who stood leaning against the guava tree panting, defeated in her attempt to get hold of the chicks that were running this way and that – and left. Any parish priest would pray to the lord to take away the burden of such a moment...

Ouso sat staring hard at Salamon's face.

'I tell you, Soloma, there is a serene look on her face, as if she has been blessed by Mother Mary. You won't believe it when I tell you. Her first words were to me. It was as though she was waiting for it. Do you know what she said? Tell that Salamon not to stay on here, to go away somewhere, escape. Pavam! He is without guile. He will prosper only if he leaves this land. Whenever he tried to remain aloof, I was the one who hung on to him.'

Salamon was stunned. Saying something like this ... that too in such a situation...

Salamon couldn't make sense of it.

Anyway, finally Veroni thathi too was convinced. Though her feet stumbled momentarily. 'My daughter has not committed any indiscretion.'

Elsie did not have anything to say against her friend from childhood. Not just that, she vowed that he had talent, that he was not one who should be confined to this land.

'He is different from our people on the hilltop. He paints. He should see a bigger world, become famous. Artists are people on whom God has showered his light. If he remains amidst us, he will perish,' she told Ouso.

Then why did she do it?

The same old question continued to whirl within Salamon.

Just then Ouso said, 'The human mind is like rain clouds, eda. It does not take much time to flit this way and that. In fact, when she was talking to me, she seemed more concerned about Mincent than you. Have you seen him at close quarters? His head seems to have shrunk. His body too. I don't think this is something that the doctors or vaidyars over here can cure. He might be cured if he is taken to Madras or some such place. But where do they have the money for that?'

'Entamme!' Salamon's hand went to his heart.

'I want to see her, Ouso,' he said, urgency in his voice.

'No,' Ouso said. 'Everyone has somehow got that thathi under control. If she sees your head anywhere near the house, she will get worked up all over again. The asthma she used to suffer from in the past, it had become less intense over the years. She would get an attack only when the moon waxed or waned, or when she was upset. After this incident, it has started again. It is a terrible sight, the way she sits and wheezes at night, after her hectic wanderings through the day.'

'Whatever it is, I want to meet Elsie,' Salamon insisted obstinately. 'Let them thrash me or kill me if they want. After all, everything will end with that.'

'Look, Soloma, listen to me.' Ouso placed his hand on his shoulder. 'Do not act impulsively. The people around us are foolish, quarrelsome. And you belong to another religion. If a drunk grips you by the neck, there will be others to join him.'

Ouso looked around, then lowered his voice and said, 'If you have anything to say, write it. I will somehow give it to her.'

Salamon shook his head. These were not things you could confine in writing. He did not have the suitable words for it. He did not want to say anything, hear anything. He just wanted to see her ... speak without the burden of words, hear without hearing.

But there was no point in telling Ouso all this. There must be some way. One evening without anyone's knowledge, without anyone seeing...

As though he sensed the plan from his expression, Ouso warned, 'Do not do anything foolish. What has happened has happened. You leave this alone for the time being. She is a foolish girl. Impulsive, that's all. Let that miserable family carry on somehow. You Jews have a place to go. Where can they go? As she says, you are destined to be famous. You go abroad, become famous, then return to this hilltop wearing a suit. Then we will see Salamon's grandeur! We will see all those who tell tales about you now follow you wagging their tails. Though this place would have changed somewhat, some of us will still be around, without any change or any prospects.'

Ouso's voice broke. Salamon's face dimmed.

Ouso, like the others, was bidding him goodbye. Even though he was still undecided about the journey, he had already become an outsider in their hearts.

One leg on the other shore. Not much time is required to pull up the other one.

Prompted by a sudden impulse, he put his arms around Ouso and said, 'I am not going anywhere.' He was on the brink of tears. 'Where will I go, leaving you all behind?'

'Then?'

'I am not going anywhere.'

'Oh, be quiet,' Ouso grimaced.

'It is true. I told Elsie about it.'

Ouso stared at him with disbelief.

'When those to whom you belong leave...?'

'I don't know.'

'How will you live?'

'People are living here, aren't they?'

'You are not like them, are you? You came as a group, you leave as a group.'

Seeing Salamon's face change, Ouso stopped abruptly.

'So no one wants us here, is that it?'

'That is not it, Soloma. Try to see things straight, without blabbering impulsively. The pangs of separation will last just for a day or two. After that it will be a new place, with new friends. How many days will you need to forget us poor souls?'

Salamon's face reddened.

'So you count me among that sort of people, do you?'

They did not see Eshimuthimma come out, hearing those words. Seeing the strained look on their faces, she asked Salamon, 'What is it, Soloma? What happened?'

'Oh, nothing.' Salamon wiped his eyes.

'No, there is something.'

'Nothing, honestly.'

'There is.' She turned towards Ouso. 'What is it, Ouso? Why is he upset?'

'Hey nothing, Muthimma,' Ouso responded. 'We were

remembering old times and suddenly he became emotional, that is all.'

'Why, what happened for him to become emotional? Did one of the buffaloes die or did the fox catch the chicken? What is it, Soloma?'

Sensing that Eshumma was not in a good mood, Ouso went down the steps without saying anything further. He quickly crossed the gateway and walked into the lane.

Eshumma watched him leave, a stormy look on her face, then burst out angrily, 'You went around with a worthless set of friends, created unnecessary complications. Now you feel sorry! There is just Ephraim moopar's family on the hilltop to bear the shame.'

She looked hard at Salamon's face, then, letting out a deep grunt of displeasure, turned and went inside continuing to mutter. Salamon stood immobile for a moment, then slowly stepped into the yard. He did not want to stand there any more. As usual he would go and sit near the landing for a while. Sit there in the dark, without anyone knowing, without anyone seeing.

Muthimma did not try to stop him as she usually did. She did not call from behind to ask where he was going.

Finally she too had given up on him. Salamon sighed as he thought about it.

Let it be. If that was how it was going to be, so be it. He tried to find consolation within himself.

The Eve Before Departure

Hectic preparations were going on in Jew Street. Salamon went about seeing nothing, hearing nothing. Some people were going somewhere. What did he have to do with it?

They should catch the first boat to Ernakulam tomorrow at dawn. The train for Bombay was from the Harbour Terminus in Kochi. Then from Bombay to Tel Aviv by plane. There were seven families in that batch, including the Evron family. Some of them were those who were still in Chendamangalam. It was because they had sold all their belongings and paid the money that the agency had relaxed its aloofness a bit. Once they reached Israel, they had to pay the remaining part of the fare within a year, from the money they earned over there. Evron kept the payment receipt carefully. At least they could go there and say with a straight back that they had paid their way, and not come on someone's charity.

What job would they get there to enable them to pay off the debt? No one knew. People who were not used to being in debt were now in debt, that too to the custodians of an unseen land.

Salamon noticed Eliacha looking at him intently. He did not ask why because he knew the answer.

After a while, Eliacha broached the subject in a low voice.

'That child Elsie, she should not have done such a drastic thing … that too now of all times.'

Salamon felt a sudden surge of anger. After all these days, he was bringing up the matter today! At a time when he was boiling inside. When he longed to talk to someone, Eliacha had not felt like asking. It was not because he was ignorant of Salamon's predicament. Then why was he bringing it up now, when things had settled down a bit?

The day when Salamon returned from the hospital, Eliacha's face had mirrored his doubts, but he had not asked openly.

Questions had lurked on Eshimuthimma's face as well.

After holding back for all this time, Eliacha was directing the questions at him now.

'Did you go to the hilltop that day?'

'Yes.'

'Saw her?'

'Yes.'

'And?'

'Saw her, just that.'

'Didn't she say anything?'

'She said she was not sad. Said she would not eat the othalanga fruit.' There was anger in Salamon's voice.

'Othalanga?' Eliacha stared. 'What can that do? It is not poisonous enough to kill.'

'I don't know. I have not tried eating it.'

Irritation throbbed in his voice when he said it. What was the sense in asking these questions? Ouso had said, hadn't he, that she had said everything to those who needed to hear?

Ouso was confident that once everyone left for Israel, this too would be forgotten. What more did they want? If the

Ephraim family's good name was more important to them
than his pain, they need not worry; it had not been tarnished.
Then why ask him these pointless questions?

Eliacha's face wore a dissatisfied look. It seemed as
though several things lay hidden in that sharp intent look
that seemed to pierce through Salamon.

'This should not have happened at this moment, mone. I
feel uncomfortable when I think about it.'

Salamon turned away with a shrug, as if to say that he
was not the one to answer that question. Without waiting
to hear anything further, he walked towards the doorway.

Evronappa was in the veranda. Seeing the strained look
on his son's face, he asked, 'What is it, eda?'

'Nothing.'

'Regret leaving?'

'Hey...'

'I think everything is ready. Pack only what is absolutely
necessary. They have to load it into the plane, remember.'

'Aa...'

'I wanted to meet several people and say goodbye, but
then how many can I meet! We talked about it for so long,
yet when things began to happen they happened so fast,' a
hitherto unheard coldness in Evron's voice.

There was no brightness on anyone's face.

The day they had waited for, for so long, had finally
arrived, but something lay taut and heavy in their hearts.
The land where they were born, where they grew up. Their
ancestors had not come prepared to leave. One of the rare
doors that had opened for a desperate people. The place they
had been given to settle down in later on became the asylum
for the generations that followed.

That afternoon Eshimuthimma did not eat anything.

Even at night she said she was not hungry. As she prepared for bed early, someone in the neighbourhood brought a big vessel filled with black coffee and some boiled yam.

The packets of biriyani that Pathros achan had sent with the sexton lay untouched. No one wanted them. No one was hungry. So the black coffee in the vessel got over fast.

As Salamon approached her bedside with a glass full of coffee, Muthimma hugged her grandson and wept. Salamon too wept, for the first time since he could remember.

'Now I feel I don't want to go. That I want to die here. This place where our ancestors are buried, isn't this our land?'

'Don't worry, Umma.' Eliacha, who had followed Salamon into the room, held her close and stroked her back. All this will last only for a day or two. When we reach there, it will be a new place, new people...'

Eshimuthimma wiped her eyes without replying.

'I wish we could go after the festival.'

'Now, this is a joke,' Eliacha laughed. 'The actual festival is there, isn't it?'

'But it will not be as grand as it is in our land, Eliase.'

Elias did not know how to respond to that.

'Do me a favour, Eliase.' She caught his hands and held them together. 'That picture on the wall...' Her voice broke. Elias ached as he heard the request that had been made several times before. When they began to pack the things to take with them, Eshumma wanted just one thing. The picture of Isaac that hung in the drawing room. When he heard it, Evron burst out angrily, 'We are going by plane, not in a large country boat.'

When he saw Umma's face grow dim, Elias intervened.

'We cannot take all that, Umma,' he said gently. 'They

said the luggage should not weigh more than a certain load. That picture is so large.'

'But we cannot leave him here alone.'

'No, we will get a ticket for him,' Evron's voice rose.

Elias once again intervened, gesturing to Evron to stop.

'I heard that certain things from the synagogue will be brought over later on. We will make arrangements for it to be brought along with them. Not just that, the old Moopar's as well.'

Though Eshumma was not wholly convinced, she nodded her head, staring into the dark outside the window. Elias was relieved. In some unseen corner of the darkness, the ancestors too must have nodded their heads. They at least must have understood facts the way they should be. Their reign was ending here. With their being abandoned on these walls, all ties with the family would be broken. That they were freed from the confines of the soil in the cemetery, that they could continue on those walls, providing light and guidance for the family for so long, was in itself a great thing.

When they saw Eshumma's eyes close, they crept out of the room noiselessly. Let her sleep for a while. It was going to be a long journey.

After a while, when Salamon came to the door and peeped in, she was lying with her eyes wide open. She beckoned to him. She took a packet from under her pillow and held it out to him. A bit of soil wrapped in a piece of violet silk which had begun to tear.

'A little earth from the cemetery. To sprinkle over my face. Now that is all that Muthimma has to take from here.'

The ancient tradition was to sprinkle soil from Jerusalem over the eyes of the dead. For her the soil of the land of her birth was transforming itself into the sacred soil of Jerusalem...

What about the clay pot hidden in the wall cupboard? They were the savings of her lifetime.

He wondered. Does she know that the money in the pot has no value abroad? Eliacha did not say anything. Salamon did not ask either. Maybe like Muthimma, the pot too was preparing to return to some alien soil.

'We came without anything, we leave without anything. Isn't that so, mone?' He heard Eshimuthimma's reed-like voice.

Her voice thickened. That which she meant to say lay trembling in her throat.

The sons did not understand the sorrow of Eshumma who had not seen the world beyond that lane. Neither did the neighbours who sat in the veranda trying to sort old memories. Stumbling among the tenderness, regrets, bitterness of recollections, they slipped into a strange silence. People from the hill who had come with words of solace sat in the veranda for a long time, then left when it grew dark, their silence saying things unsaid.

The family knew they would not be able to sleep that night. That was the fate of those who were preparing to leave the land. And of those who went in search of new lands.

When as usual he spread a mat in the veranda and lay down, Salamon heard Eshimuthimma's loud snores from inside. Finally she was asleep.

New moon was not far. Salamon's eyes searched for a new light among the dimly glimmering stars in the dark sky. Some sign. A sign just for him…

There was a faint breeze. Unable to sleep, he once again searched for something among the twinkling stars. The guardian star that had shown the way to their ancestors centuries ago, would it not still be there among them?

Some message. A sign for sailors who had lost their way.
A sign just for him.

Far away somewhere, he heard cocks crow the midnight
hour. A slight drizzle accompanied the breeze that followed.

He closed his eyes tight to preserve the remaining sights.
A wave of sleep caressed him. As he strained to dive into its
depths, he forgot that day, and that night.

Somewhere, with a light unseen till then, a sun was
preparing to dawn for him.

The Last Jew

The day was just breaking. A slight mist and early-morning chill.

Salamon sat on the granite platform near Karippayi landing, staring into the river.

A desperate search and great commotion must be on in Jew Street; shouts and laments, he thought. For the lone male of the family who had vanished from his spread-out mat. The one destined to take the famous Ephraim family forward to the future.

Evron's son, Solomon called Salamon.

It was growing late. The boat would leave. The train would leave. The plane would leave.

Thus finally the Ephraim family too was preparing to leave the land, leaving behind the last drop of their blood. It must be the will of God ... atonement for the elders, perhaps.

That day, for the first time, Salamon felt totally empty, drained. Nothing remained, as sights, as voices, as feelings.

Like the mind of the one who had placed his foot on this land for the first time, centuries ago. They were starting from scratch, weren't they, the people who came from somewhere? Now that was his fate as well.

The last Jew in this land.

No one knew the name of the first one to come. But perhaps someday someone might engrave on the wall of the synagogue the name of the last one.

Evron's son Solomon called Salamon. He was born here and he was buried here.

To merge, melt into the soil of one's birth – could there be a greater blessing than that?

By this time the sun was up. The ones who had to cross the river were calling out to the ferry that was on the other shore.

He did not hear anything. Neither did he see anything. For he had nowhere to go.

....

I Want the World to Know of
Kerala's Jewish Connection

Catherine Thankamma

⤙❦ ❦⤚

Translator's Note

⤙❦ ❦⤚

'*Bashana haba'ah*' *Yerushalayim*' ('the next year in Jerusalem') was the heartfelt prayer that kept the Jewish diaspora alive through centuries and generations of oppression, humiliation and suffering that they experienced in whichever part of the world they inhabited. The formation of Israel in 1948 was the realization of a dream, a chance to return to their roots, to be where they belong. The Jews who came to the south-western tip of the Indian peninsula as traders or as refugees experienced no alienation. They were welcomed by the local people and assimilated into the community with absolute freedom to follow their religious and cultural practises. However, when the state of Israel was founded they left for the unseen land, selling their precious belongings and breaking the generations-old ties they had formed in this land. Sixty-odd years later, Sethu writes about the emotional/psychological compulsions that forced the decision on them. In the process he has created a memorable novel that explores our ingrained notions of identity and belonging.

Catherine Thankamma

CT: You are a well-known and respected writer in the Indian literary scene. You won the Kerala Sahitya Akademi award twice, for *Pandavapuram* and *Pediswapnangal. Adayalangal* won you the Vayalar award and later the Kendra Sahitya Akademi award ... and these are just some of the awards that have come your way.

Sethu: I'm grateful.

CT: Your writing has played a major role in bringing about a change in the Malayalee reader's literary sensibility. What motivated you to write and to write the way you do?

Sethu: Well, I always wanted to write. For a long time, I went about carrying vague half-formed stories in my mind. But it was in Delhi in 1967 that I actually wrote down my thoughts on paper. There were many Malayalam writers living in Delhi at that time. Meeting them, talking to them, sort of urged me into writing a short story. It was published in *Mathrubhumi*. M.T. Vasudevan Nair was the editor at that time. That was the beginning.

CT: Coming to *Aliyah*, the novel occupies a unique place in your literary oeuvre. When did you first conceive the idea of writing the novel?

Sethu: Yes, *Aliyah* is different from my other works. Although I am neither a historian nor even a student of history, I ventured into this history-based theme with a definite aim. I have often felt sad that very little has been written about the Jews who inhabited our land for so many centuries. They enjoyed the patronage of successive rulers who conferred various privileges on them. However, with their return to the Promised Land of Israel in the fifties, their past was forgotten. As a person who grew up in a region that had a substantial Jewish presence – the Jews in Kerala were called Malabari Jews, those in our region were Cochin

Jews – I felt it was my responsibility to them and to my land to write about that bit of history. My village, Chendamangalam, was in fact one of the earliest Jewish settlements on the western coast. During my school days, there were about 200 Jews in our village, living around a synagogue in a valley near a hillock. They were an integral part of the community. So when they all started leaving in batches to the newly created Israel, it hurt. We just couldn't understand why they suddenly sold off everything they had and left for an unknown land across the seas. I must say their departure triggered a series of questions in my mind – who were these people? If they did not belong to this land, where they had lived for generations, why did they come here and where did they come from? What prompted them to desert this land en masse? Since fiction is the only format I am comfortable with, I did extensive research on the subject and decided to design a framework based on history, myth, legend and imagination. Once I started writing it, I found it very exciting and rewarding.

CT: I can understand. The novel has a dramatic beginning, not unlike *Pandavapuram*. Here Salamon has a nightmare. Why did you conceive such a beginning? Is it because our deepest unsaid desires/fears/anxieties surface during sleep?

Sethu: I would say the dream is Salamon's unconscious response to his personal misgivings regarding the return to the Promised Land. The 'return' is something that has been ingrained into him from childhood by his grandmother and other elders. At the same time he is unsure of his own feelings about it. I wanted the novel to begin with a dream sequence as it reflects the fears and doubts that Salamon himself might not be aware of.

CT: Structurally the first chapter is a masterpiece as it not only gives the reader an inkling of the dynamics that underlie the Salomon-Eshimuthimma-Evron relationship, but also highlights the emotive factors that underlie the concept of *Aliyah*. Would you care to comment on it?

Sethu: I did want to open the novel with a dream sequence which would give the reader a glimpse of Salamon's confused state of mind regarding what is in store for him and then bring him back to grapple with the harsh realities of life. Salamon is highly imaginative. He lives in his own world, a world of myriad shapes and colours, a world that is in stark contrast to the mundane background of trade, into which he is born. Eshimuthimma and Evron together represent everyday reality. They are his bridge to the real world. Each in her/his own way tries to prod him into engaging with life.

CT: The fact that you devoted two paragraphs in *Marupiravi* and again almost a page in the second chapter of *Aliyah* to the topography of Kottayil Kovilakam palace and its surroundings highlights something more than the obvious communal harmony; the fact that the tiny village in Kerala is perhaps the only place in the world where the Jews were welcome. Am I right?

Sethu: No, it was not the only village. There were several villages in the same belt where Jews were invited to set up their settlements. Significantly, the tribal inhabitants of the western coast accepted the Jews as 'friendly outsiders' long before the rajas entered the scene. Of course, the integration strengthened further during the reign of the rajas as they allowed the Jews to set up not just commercial establishments but also construct their synagogues with their own exclusive streets and areas of domicile. I, of course, have dealt with customs and rituals practised by the Jews who lived in my area.

CT: Something that struck me while reading the novel was the open-endedness with which you approach the theme of belonging

– for example the feeling of us and them in the case of Devassy mapla and Adrumman, and Paradesi Jews and Malabari Jews, or the insider-outsider feeling in the case of Ramanandan and Daveed chettan. What was your aim in creating such a perspective?

Sethu: I do not hesitate to admitting that many of my works are incomplete or 'open-ended' as you say. I have always felt that if the writer leaves the contours of his work open, it will provide space for the readers to approach the text the way they want. In other words, this will mark the beginning of an effective creative partnership between the writer and the reader.

CT: Varuthutty master refers to the tiny bundle of ash that was tied to the end of the tunics of brides departing from Methala. It is one of the many symbols that occur in the novel. How do you see it?

Sethu: It is an ancient tradition that many communities of the area practised during that period, a symbol of the bride's connection with the land where she was born and where she grew up, the 'unsnappable umbilical cord' with the place of birth. The women wanted the soil from the land of their birth to be sprinkled on their faces when they died. You must remember that, finally, that is all Eshumma wants to take with her. But it often became a 'loaded' symbol. For instance, the Jews and a sect of Christians of Methala considered themselves to be of superior lineage and obviously wanted to carry their 'high-born' label wherever they went. Therefore, when they were married into a family in a different region it became a means to show off their higher status.

CT: 'bashana haba'ah' Yerushalayim' ('the next year in Jerusalem ...') comes from the heart and it is what enabled the Jews all over the world to endure humiliation and oppression for

401

centuries. A dream that has become a matter of faith. However, you have very insightfully dealt with the different ways in which the various characters see it – Moses master, Elias, Evron, Salamon. Would you care to elaborate on it?

Sethu: Yes, I did want to underline the fact that there was more than one way of looking at it. As you can see, all these characters look at the prospect of returning to the Promised Land from different perspectives. For ardent believers like Moses master and Evron, it is the eternal dream of every Jew, wherever they may be. Elias sees it as a need. Salamon is unsure. So you see it is life and one's own experiences that shape one's perspective.

CT: Very true. I feel your depiction of the two diametrically opposite characters, Varuthutty master and comrade Pavithran, tells something about your political standpoint. Am I correct?

Sethu: To an extent, yes. Varuthutty master is a staunch humanist and not a political dogmatist like Comrade Pavithran. A former communist who was born a Catholic, Varuthutty Master is not held down by any kind of blind belief. He is open to all kinds of new ideas and debates and often ends up taking an uncompromising stand against established theories and beliefs. He does not mind taking on the religious and political dogmatists and prefers to stick to his own views and ideologies.

CT: After reading the novel I almost felt that *desham* is the real protagonist in the novel for it is that which allows the seamless incorporation of events – not just the coming of the newspaper to the village but electricity, the postal system and the weaving industry; as well as the inclusion of important milestones in regional politics like the fight against segregation led by Sahodaran Ayyappan, Vimochana samaram, the fall of the first ever elected communist government etc. Do you agree?

Sethu: Yes, to a certain extent. The evolution of the tiny village with a great historical past provides an effective backdrop to the overall narrative. The arrival of the first newspaper and the first post is always a historical event for any such village. For old timers like me, these events have been quite nostalgic and emotional. Indeed, the first postman was seen as a privileged guest. He seemed to come from another world bringing all kinds of interesting news.

CT: Your novels are known for their strong female protagonists. Eshimuthimma definitely belongs to that category. Could you say something about the other characters like Rebecca and Esther?

Sethu: They are my favourite female characters in the novel and so very different. Rebecca is strong-willed and practical but her life is a tragedy. The painful shadow falls across the lives of everyone, not just Evron and Salamon. Esther, on the hand, represents a different milieu. She is an earthy, passionate woman who makes the mistake of choosing to marry the wrong man.

CT: Elsie again is a strong character with definite views and goals. Yet she stumbles…

Sethu: Yes, Elsie is a strong-willed girl with definite values and goals. Her love for Salamon is an instance of attraction of opposites.

CT: How do you visualize Salamon?

Sethu: Salamon is quiet, an introvert and a daydreamer. He is not sure about what he wants from life or about the people around him. He is intensely conscious of colours and shapes but cannot figure out his feelings for the girl he loves. He is indecisive, the wavering type, unsure about everything, waiting for others to lead, like he waits for a signal from the heavens to guide his decision. When he acts it is on an impulse.

CT: The novel does not provide a clue as to why Salamon decides to stay back. Is it because of Elsie or would you rather leave that question unanswered?

Sethu: I would rather leave it to the readers. In any work of fiction there will be a number of unanswered questions, which are better left to the imagination of readers.

CT: You have created some powerful symbols and images in the novel – Ittaman's ferry, the locked room, the dimly lit corner under the stairs ... How do you see them?

Sethu: Imagery is an integral part of creativity. The ferry was the village's only means of communication with the outside world. That very practical and basic function can be extended to represent many things. The locked room, dimly lit corner under the stairs, etc., indicate the state of mind of the concerned characters.

CT: What, according to you, is the larger significance of the novel both for a pan-Indian and global audience?

Sethu: As I had indicated earlier, I want the world to know of Kerala's Jewish connection, about the unique relationship that existed between the Jews and the native people, how our land welcomed a people on the run with open arms. I am very proud of it and wanted to make known to the world the harmony that existed here. I also wanted to explore the emotive aspects of the idea of one's own land.

CT: I want you to know that translating the novel was both challenging and invigorating. I feel privileged that I got the opportunity to do it.

Sethu: Thank you.

In Hebrew *Aliyah* means 'ascent'. It is a word loaded with ethnic, religious, ideological and cultural significance as it refers to the return of the Jewish diaspora to *Eretz Israel* or the Land of Israel. Interestingly the word diaspora, which crops up so often in modern day discourse, originally referred to the scattering of the Jews all over the world following the Babylonian exile. The end of World War Two witnessed the declaration of Israeli independence and the formation of the nation in 1948; an epochal event, the reverberations of which continue into contemporary world history. Sethu's *Aliyah* is set against this historic event. It narrates the story of a Jewish community that settled down and grew roots in a small village in Kerala centuries ago. More specifically it deals with three generations of one family. Responding to the Zionist call, they, like the rest of their community, sell all their belongings, break off all ties binding them to the land, pull out their roots and leave for the unknown, unseen land. Sethu adopts a multipronged approach, combining history, myth, legend and imagination. In the process he weaves a rich and complex tapestry of familial and social dynamics, creating a path-breaking novel with some strong and memorable characters.

When Sethu asked me to translate the novel and I agreed, I had no inkling what I was in for. I was still grappling with the reality of my husband's unexpected death. He had had great regard for Sethu, both as a senior colleague and a writer. I accepted the offer more as a labour of love than anything else. But when I finished reading the novel I was overwhelmed by its depth and magnitude. Sethu delves into the psychological and philosophical underpinning of notions about one's land, belonging, notions of self and autonomy, of conformity and being different, familial ties, the relationship between individual and society; providing multiple perspectives, and creating a text the implications of which are mindboggling. It is truly a compelling read.

I wondered whether I could do justice to the novel. Integrity to the source text, to the style and intent of the author are the prescribed norms of fiction/literary translation. A defining feature of Sethu's style is its orality. This, combined with unexpected interventions of the narrative voice and certain defining structural features of the source language like the extensive use of the present continuous tense, the often bewildering flow from one tense to another, and the 'implicit' subject, made translation tricky. Fortunately I had Sethu's unconditional support. I was very comfortable working with him. I was equally fortunate t o h a v e Minakshi Thakur, Senior Editor, Harper Collins to help me with the final version before it went for print. She proved to be a sensitive and understanding editor, and was generous enough to accept some of my last minute changes to the text. I thank Keerti Ramachandran, my editor, who made sure that fidelity to the source text did not end up creating too literal a translation. Adopting idiomatic constructions that would make for easy transmission, including words and phrases from the source text to provide a flavour of the original, and transposition of sentence structures were valuable editorial interventions. More importantly she respected certain intentional choices that I made. I am happy that HarperCollins decided to publish the translation. *Aliyah* has great relevance in the post-globalized world of fading geographical boundaries, immigrations and multiple identities, identities that we create and those that are created for us through circumstances.

I dedicate my translation to that elusive being that I cannot see or touch but whose presence I feel and believe in, a belief that helps me go on.

Note on Names and Their Vocative Expressions

The single definitive divergence between English and Malayalam lies in their intrinsic syntactic patterns. English in the course of its evolution lost almost all its inflectional endings, save two, and therefore it became necessary to have a rigid word order. In English prepositions, conjunctions, etc., act as connectives to create meaningful sentences. Malayalam, which belongs to the Dravidian language family, is on the other hand an inflected language. Nouns, adjectives, verbs, adverbs and indeclinable words are the major word classes. Unlike English the basic sentence structure in Malayalam is subject-object-verb but inflectional endings make it possible to have a flexible structure. A sentence can run on for an entire paragraph with phrases/clauses following one another without punctuation marks. There is only one finite verb (where endings suggest tense/mood/causality), which occurs at the end. However, it is often preceded by gerunds. Again, it is common for the subject to remain implicit and unmentioned. The native or trained reader is able to decipher the meaning without any confusion. This aspect of the Malayalam language had to be taken into account while translating this novel into English.

Another peculiarity of Malayalam lies in the use of the vocative case. Apart from its obvious grammatical function the vocative facilitates ease of utterance. For instance, in names ending in consonants either the name is tagged with a vowel (Eliase for Elias) or the final consonant is dropped in the vocative (Ramananda for Ramanandan). At times even names ending with a vowel are uttered differently in the vocative as in the case of an 'e' replacing 'a'. Interestingly, such a use serves a psychological function as well. For instance, the use of 'Evrone' (Evron), which crops when the person is addressed, suggests intimacy. Here we need to remember that there are occasions in the text where Evron is addressed without the vocative ending when the matter discussed is solemn and does not warrant familiarity. Thus, it is only natural that Varuthutty master, an advocate of nativism and a believer of cultural syncretisation, who prefers the indigenized form Salamon to the commonly accepted Solomon, addresses Salamon with and without the vocative 'e' depending on his mood. However, characters like Daveedchettan, Elsie, Veroni, Menahem and Esther address Solomon as Soloma. The vocative use has been retained in the text to get across to the reader the flavour of the original. Manoolle like Salamonis an instance of indigenization as well.

The use of 'Eda' and 'Edo', which are vocative forms of 'You' again suggests subtleties of relationship as well as mood and attitude. For instance Manuel addresses Evron as eda suggesting friendship. But if an older man uses the word to address one younger to him it becomes a sign of authority/power. Therefore you have Menahem addressing Salamon as 'Edo' where authority is tempered with affection. Two other usages the reader needs to pay attention to are mone, vocative of mon (boy/son) and mole, vocative of mol (girl/daughter).

Apart from these there are some interesting and piquant sentences that are unique to Sethu's imaginative and stylistic processes. These are highly elusive and I could manage to achieve only a rough approximation. Here again the aim is to provide a flavour of the original.